Praise for the novels of Robyn Carr

Also by Robyn Carr

Sullivan's Crossing

THE COUNTRY GUESTHOUSE
THE BEST OF US
THE FAMILY GATHERING
ANY DAY NOW
WHAT WE FIND

Thunder Point

WILDEST DREAMS
A NEW HOPE
ONE WISH
THE HOMECOMING
THE PROMISE
THE CHANCE
THE HERO
THE NEWCOMER
THE WANDERER

Virgin River

RETURN TO VIRGIN RIVER
MY KIND OF CHRISTMAS
SUNRISE POINT
REDWOOD BEND
HIDDEN SUMMIT
BRING ME HOME
  FOR CHRISTMAS
HARVEST MOON
WILD MAN CREEK
PROMISE CANYON
MOONLIGHT ROAD
ANGEL'S PEAK

FORBIDDEN FALLS
PARADISE VALLEY
TEMPTATION RIDGE
SECOND CHANCE PASS
A VIRGIN RIVER CHRISTMAS
WHISPERING ROCK
SHELTER MOUNTAIN
VIRGIN RIVER

Grace Valley

DEEP IN THE VALLEY
JUST OVER THE MOUNTAIN
DOWN BY THE RIVER

Novels

A FAMILY AFFAIR
SUNRISE ON HALF MOON BAY
THE VIEW FROM
  ALAMEDA ISLAND
THE SUMMER
  THAT MADE US
THE LIFE SHE WANTS
FOUR FRIENDS
A SUMMER IN SONOMA
NEVER TOO LATE
SWEPT AWAY
  (formerly titled
  RUNAWAY MISTRESS)
BLUE SKIES
THE WEDDING PARTY
THE HOUSE ON OLIVE STREET

Look for Robyn Carr's next novel
available soon from MIRA.

ROBYN CARR

PARADISE VALLEY

mira

ISBN-13: 978-0-7783-8663-6

Paradise Valley

First published in 2009. This edition published in 2022.

Mira
22 Adelaide St. West, 41st Floor
Toronto, Ontario M5H 4E3, Canada
www.Harlequin.com

Printed in Lithuania

This book is dedicated to my son,
Dr. Brian Carr, US Army Medical Corps.
And to our armed forces, to all the men and women
who stand the watch. I am very proud and personally grateful.

VIRGIN RIVER

PARADISE VALLEY

One

Walt Booth was feeling lonely. He'd been widowed over five years ago when his kids were twenty-six and fourteen. Now that he was sixty-two, the kids were on their own. Vanessa was married to Paul and they lived on the property on the other side of the stable, and Tom had nearly completed his first year at West Point. Walt's niece, Shelby, had been staying with him, but during the February freeze she had left to vacation in Maui before pursuing her education in San Francisco.

But that only scratched the surface. He'd recently begun a relationship with his neighbor, a beautiful, vivacious, mischievous movie star just a few years younger than he was. Muriel St. Claire. Their liaison was just getting interesting, just heating up, when she was lured back to Hollywood to make another film. He was left with her two Labrador retrievers and her two horses. He'd had one phone call since she'd departed for L.A. via private jet, a call in which he had heard the background noise of a party. There was music, chatter, laughter, the clinking of glasses, and Muriel sounded on top of the world.

The truth of the matter was, he'd gone and fallen in love

with her. She had trapped him by being nothing like his perception of a movie star. She'd come to Virgin River almost a year ago, moved into an old farmhouse with her animals and restored it, almost entirely by herself. He'd never seen her in anything but slacks, usually jeans and boots, often painter's overalls. She was a crackerjack horsewoman, an expert shot and was training her own bird dogs for hunting waterfowl. Earthy. Basic. Yet her wit was sophisticated and her beauty natural and unforgettable. And right now, while he sat by the window in his great room, scratching her dog behind the ear, she was making a movie with Jack Nicholson. The truth? He wondered if she'd come back.

His doorbell rang and he hefted himself up to answer it. Two weeks ago he'd felt like a sixteen-year-old boy, looking forward to seeing Muriel every day. Today he felt old and short on time.

He opened the door to Luke Riordan and frowned. This was just about the last person he'd like to see right now. Luke and Shelby had had a romance that didn't work out, which Walt suspected was her reason for leaving.

"Morning, General," Luke said with a slight nod. "Got a minute?"

"I guess," he said, standing back from the door. "Coffee?"

"No thanks, sir," Luke said, stepping into the house. "It's just that— Well, I owe you an apology."

"That so?" Walt asked. He turned and walked back into the great room. The dogs spied Luke and immediately put the rush on him. Luce, the chocolate Lab, sat in front of him politely, but her tail wagged so violently it sent her whole body into a quiver, while Buff, less than a year old, lost all control and just barreled into him, jumping up and head butting for attention. "Buff! Down!" Walt admonished. It didn't do much good. The yellow Lab was pretty much out of control where visitors were concerned.

"Whoa," Luke laughed, grabbing the Lab behind the ears and sitting him down. "Got yourself some company here?"

"These are Muriel's dogs. She's out of town and I'm taking care of them."

"Out of town?" Luke asked, straightening.

Walt sat in his chair and clicked the dogs back to his side by snapping his fingers. He didn't volunteer any more information about Muriel's whereabouts. With a Lab on each side of him, he indicated the chair facing his. "Take a seat, Riordan. I'm anxious to hear about this apology."

Luke took his seat uneasily. "General Booth, sir, I'm the reason Shelby left a little over two weeks ago. I apologize, sir. She had every reason to think her future wasn't secure with me and she left."

Walt settled back. Shelby was twenty-five to Luke's thirty-eight and Walt had been concerned that his niece's involvement with this tough-edged Blackhawk pilot might end with her being hurt. "How does that not surprise me?" Walt said churlishly.

"I let her go, sir. I thought she might be better off. I hated to think she'd bet everything on someone like me."

Walt smirked. He couldn't have put it better himself. "I should've just shot you," he said. "I gave it serious thought."

Luke couldn't suppress a huff of silent laughter. "I figured you did. Sir." Luke hadn't been out of the army quite long enough to relax about that rank thing. The general was a general till he died and was accorded appropriate respect, even when he acted like a son of a bitch and threatened Luke's life.

"You should be apologizing to her, not me," Walt said.

"I've taken care of that, sir. Unbelievably, I'm forgiven."

"You talked to her?"

"Yes, sir. She came back. She was pissed as hell, but I threw myself on her mercy and she's given me another chance. I plan to do better this time."

Walt's eyes had grown wide and his bushy black eyebrows shot up high. "She's back?"

"Yes, sir. She said to tell you she'd be right over. She had something to take care of and I wanted a word with you first."

"To apologize," Walt groused. "I'd like to see my niece, if you don't mind."

"She'll be here pretty soon. But there's another thing. I'd like your permission to ask Shelby to be my wife."

Walt ground his teeth. "You're really pressing your luck."

"Oh, you don't know the half." Luke chuckled before he could stop himself. "Almost thirty-nine years old and I'm buying into the whole program. It's not even one of her conditions—it's one of mine. General Booth, she's everything to me. I can't live without her. I thought I could and I tried, but it's too late for me. I'm in love with Shelby. I'm going to be in love with her for the rest of my life."

Walt was sitting straighter. He moved to the edge of his chair. "What about her education? What about a family? I think my niece wants a family and I heard you say that wasn't—"

"You probably heard me say a lot of things I thought I meant and didn't, sir. Shelby can have anything she wants, do anything she wants—I'll support her. I'm not going to waste her time, sir. If she'll marry me, I'll give her everything I have, go anywhere she needs me to go. She won't ever again leave my house thinking I don't care about her. That could have been the biggest mistake of my lifetime."

Walt smiled in spite of himself. "Learned your lesson, did you, boy?"

Luke didn't mind so much being called a boy by this military icon, but the truth hit him pretty hard. "Oh, man," he said, shaking his head. "You have no idea."

Walt leaned back. "I like seeing you humbled a little bit, Riordan. What if I withhold my permission?"

"Oh, I'll ask her anyway. I'll tell her you disapprove and ask her to overlook that. But I'd like to do this right, sir. I've made enough mistakes—I don't want to make one more."

"Hmm," Walt hummed. "I guess I can still be surprised...."

"Sir?"

"I didn't figure you for intelligence."

Luke just shook his head. Well, this was no less than he deserved. He'd taken the general's niece into his bed, telling her he just wasn't the kind of man who could settle down. He used every rationalization he could think of to make that all right, but he knew all along that was going to be real tough for the general to swallow. He also knew if Shelby were *his* niece, he wouldn't have stood for it. Now Walt was obviously going to torture him for a while. Luke supposed it was his just due.

The front door opened and Shelby breezed in. Both men shot to their feet, but Luke got to her first, slipping an arm around her waist. "Take care of everything?" he asked quietly.

"Uh-huh," she said, smiling up at him. "I got off easy." Shelby had left Virgin River without saying goodbye to Luke's helper, Art. That in itself wasn't such a crime, but

Art was a thirty-year-old man with Down syndrome and things like disappearing without an explanation or good-bye could seem like abandonment to him. "He wasn't angry with me—just worried."

Then she went to her uncle. "I'm sorry I didn't call and let you know I was coming back, Uncle Walt. I had business to take care of with Luke first."

Walt looked at her beautiful, shining face. Her hazel eyes glowed, her cheeks were flush with love. But looking at Shelby wasn't the startling part. One look at Luke told the rest of the story. Luke had always had that bad-boy edge, an aura of danger and a short fuse. No more. All the rough edges had been ground down and his expression was docile as a puppy.

Walt just laughed as he pulled Shelby into his arms. He hugged her fiercely. "Shelby, Shelby," he said. He held her away from him and, grinning, he said, "Looks like you've tamed him. He doesn't have any fight left in him."

"Thank God," she said. "I don't think I could take much more. He's been a real handful. But Luke still needs a little work, so I'm going to be staying with him now. I'll be over to help you with the horses every day, just like always."

"That would be nice, honey," he said. "There are a lot of horses. Muriel's out of town and I've got the dogs and horses."

Shelby reached down and gave each Lab a little scratch. "Where is she?"

"She's gone back to Hollywood for a while. Going to make a movie."

"Really?" Shelby asked, grinning hugely, her eyes lighting up. "Wow. How awesome."

She would find that exciting news, Walt thought. He

had told Muriel she had his devoted support in achieving everything her heart desired, but in fact he wasn't feeling real supportive. He was feeling jealous and lonely and out of sorts. And this news about Shelby and Luke just added to his misery.

He shook it off. "Luke?" he asked, looking at the man. When he had Luke's attention, Walt gave his chin a firm nod. And that was all it took to make Luke Riordan's eyes light up as though beacons shone from within.

At 1:00 a.m. the phone rang next to Walt's bed. He thought first of Shelby; she'd thrown her lot in with Luke and Walt hoped nothing had gone wrong. He thought next of Vanessa, Paul and little Matt, his grandson. Young Tom crossed his mind—but a middle-of-the-night phone call from West Point was highly unlikely.

"Walt?" came Muriel's voice before he could gather his wits and say hello. "Darling, I'm sorry—I know what time it is."

Darling? Did she call him darling? Oh, those Hollywood types probably called everyone darling. "It's all right," he said sleepily. "Are you okay?"

"Oh, I'm okay. This is honestly the first chance I've had to call in days. But it's not going to stay this crazy. I hope."

"What's going on?"

"Well, everything. The production company has been staging small parties in key places all over town, trying to create some preproduction buzz about the movie by having cast members show up. I've been researching the character, spending some time with the writer, rehearsing lines they'll only rewrite the second I have them down, looking at wardrobe and set sketches with the production designer, and generally going out to lunch, drinks, dinner, drinks, and talking till midnight. Then I fall into bed and sleep like a dead woman till 5:00 a.m. when I get up and jump on the treadmill."

He just shook his head in confusion. "What's the treadmill got to do with anything?"

She laughed. "I have to be in good shape. And I don't have the dogs or horses to help me do that. I hired my old trainer back to firm things up a bit. I know it doesn't sound like it, but I'm working my ass off."

"Well, stop going out for all those drinks and you'll feel better."

"I stick to club soda when I'm meeting with actors, producers, promoters, et cetera. They're not catching me with my pants down."

He smiled and felt instant shame for having baited her like that. And pride; she was a consummate professional—he should have known that. "That's my girl."

"Tell me what's going on there."

"Shelby came back," he said.

Silence answered him. "She *did*?" Muriel finally asked in a shocked breath.

"Yes, ma'am. And apparently Luke did enough groveling to satisfy her, because she's moved in with him. And this morning he paid me a visit, asked my permission to propose."

"Get out of town! Did you grant it?"

"No. I told him to go to hell. I should have just shot him. I told him that."

"Oh, you'd like me to believe you're that kind of bully, wouldn't you?"

"The silly girl seems to love him. And you should see

him. Whipped into shape that fast. I bet if we pulled up his shirt, there would be lash marks all over his back. He's limp as a noodle."

"I bet he's not," she said with a laugh. "Well, good for Shelby. That maneuver never worked for me. When I stomped off into the night, they just said, 'Okay, bah-bye.'"

"What's Jack Whatshisname like?"

"Are you ever going to say his last name?" she asked with a deep sigh.

"No."

"He's a nice man. Professional, punctual, talented, and very much enjoys the way people fall at his feet. And they should. He's got the gift. I like him. I think working with him again will be a good experience."

"Muriel," he said softly, "when are you coming home?"

Equally soft, she answered, "I don't know, Walt. And yes, I miss you."

Jack's bar was the place in Virgin River where the locals gathered. Not that everyone was there every night, but you could always count on seeing a friend there. There was a military backbone to this community since Jack Sheridan, a Marine who'd done his twenty, had opened the bar. Following him to the town was one of his best friends, John Middleton, known as Preacher, who was his partner and the cook at the bar. Next to arrive was Mike Valenzuela who'd served with Jack in Iraq twice and was now the town constable. Walt's son-in-law, Paul, was one of Jack's boys from way back and had also served with him twice. Even Luke Riordan, being ex-army, was welcomed into this brotherhood. It was the kind of place Walt felt he belonged.

Since Muriel had left, he'd been going low profile, generally fixing himself a little dinner at home by himself. Since talking with her for a while last night, he was feeling a little more secure about things and decided on Jack's for dinner. In fact, he got there a bit early, before the dinner crowd. The TV perched high in the corner was on so Jack and anyone who cared could keep up with the news, with the action in Iraq.

Jack was toting his son David in the backpack while he served. "General," he greeted. "Good to see you, sir. Been a while."

"I guess it has," Walt said, hopping up on a stool. "What do you hear from Iraq?"

"Rick writes at least every couple of weeks. He doesn't scare me, but CNN and Fox News make me shiver. There were just a couple of big bombings over there. Casualties on our side."

Jack had a young protégé who'd entered the Marine Corps at eighteen and after a year of special training, had deployed to Iraq. The boy was like a son to Jack.

"You'll get a kick out of this, sir. I'm getting computer literate. E-mail is sometimes quick and easy for Rick when he's near a computer and I don't want to miss out on anything. Preacher's been after me for years—he has the books on the computer. And of course Mel needs one at home. So... I've finally had a conversion."

"Welcome aboard," Walt laughed.

"I suppose you've been spending time with the neighbor lady." Jack put the general's preferred brew in front of him without being asked.

"As a matter of fact, Muriel has left town for a while and I'm taking care of the dogs and horses." Walt said this with a touch of pride. The studio contract had provided for help with her dogs on location and someone to stay at the farmhouse and take care of the horses, but Walt didn't want these valuable extensions of Muriel in the hands of strangers and had asked her to trust him to do the job. "She's gone back to Hollywood to make a movie. I imagine she'll have long weekends here and there, but it'll probably be close to six months before they're done."

"No kidding?" Jack said. "I had no idea."

"It was pretty sudden."

"Must've been sudden."

"Oh-ho," Walt said, sipping his beer. "One minute she was considering a script she described as having possibilities for her if the right people were involved. The next minute I was driving her to the airport."

"Whoa."

"My exact reaction," Walt said. "I've spoken with her a couple of times. She's hard at work. And the animals are fine."

Jack smiled. "Gives you some time on your hands, then."

Walt just nodded. It was hard after all these years to regress. He'd forced himself to get used to living a single man's life after his wife died. In fact, he had never expected to find another woman to fill that space. But once Muriel had, it astonished him how quickly he got used to female companionship. And not just any companion, but a woman who seemed perfect for him. While she was here, riding, shooting, hunting, refurbishing her house, he realized they were made for each other. But the minute the call came from Hollywood he began to think he'd been ridiculous to imagine they had anything in common. It was so easy for her to pack up her cosmetics and dainties, board a fancy Lear and take off for another kind of life.

"I saw Shelby and Luke the other night. They came by for a beer and a take-out dinner. Looks like things are back on track there," Jack said.

"I guess so," Walt said. "Do they look content?"

Jack leaned toward him. "In every sense of the word," he said. Then he laughed. "Took Luke lots longer to bite the dust than I gave him credit for."

"I just want Shelby to be in good hands," Walt said.

"Oh, General, there's no question about that. Luke gave up the fight." And he grinned. "He's all hers."

"Better be," Walt growled. "I wouldn't mind shooting him."

Jack laughed at him. Walt put the fear of God in a lot of men, but there was no evidence he'd actually done any physical harm. However, he had enough hot air in him to float a balloon.

Only a moment later, Mike V came in the back door and sat up next to Walt. Then came Paul, whose approach was always signaled by the banging of his muddy boots on the porch before coming inside. Walt remembered why this place soothed him; a few men enjoying a beer at the end of the day, Jack with his coffee cup—male camaraderie. And then Mel came in, the baby tucked under her coat.

After she said hello to everyone, she asked Mike, "Brie coming out to dinner?"

"Not tonight. She's going to get the baby settled early, if possible. Little Ness likes to burn the midnight oil."

Mel looked at Paul. "Vanni?"

He shook his head. "Vanni's cooking tonight."

"And Abby?" Mel asked, speaking of their houseguest.

Paul shook his head. "Cameron's taking her over to Grace Valley for an ultrasound, and he offered to take her to Fortuna for something to eat afterward, just to get her out of the house."

"Ah," Mel said. "I knew he had an errand and I'm on call till he gets back. That's nice of him to do for Abby."

Paul nodded. Then with a semitortured look he tried to conceal, he turned to Walt. "Vanni mentioned Muriel's out of town, sir. Would you like some dinner?"

Walt looked him up and down shrewdly. Paul had his wife all to himself for a change and was going to begrudgingly invite her father to join them? "I don't think so, son. Though the deep sincerity of your offer touches me."

Everyone laughed but for an indignant Paul. "Aw, come on, I was really nice about that! Sir."

"You were a peach," Walt said, knowing he was getting a little grumpy. "I'll just sit here and have dinner with Jack."

"Where's Muriel, Walt?" Mel asked.

He was tired of explaining about this, and it hadn't been all that long. "Making a movie," he said unhappily.

"Really? How exciting! Since she was looking forward to a long break from that, it must be quite an important film."

"Yeah, so she says. Jack Whatshisname is the star."

"Jack What's… Jack who?"

"You know. Big star. *Cuckoo's Nest* guy…"

"Nicholson? Holy shit," Mel said.

"Melinda, we were going to stop saying shit in front of the kids," Jack patiently reminded her, glancing over his shoulder toward David in the backpack.

"Oh shit, I forgot. But, Walt, that's really something, isn't it? I mean, he's huge. This must be a thrill for her."

Walt got a fairly dangerous gleam in his eye. "I suppose she's thrilled to the heart of her bottom."

"Well, no wonder you're so pissy," Mel said with a laugh.

"Jack, since everyone's clearing out, I'm going to get some dinner from Preacher to take home. I'll get the kids fed and settled. Can you sneak away quickly if I get a call? Since Cameron's headed for Grace Valley, I need to be on call for medical emergencies."

"Don't worry about it, Mel," Mike said. "I'm going home, I'll back you up. If you get a call before Jack locks up, just holler. I'll walk over and sit with the kids."

"Thanks, Mike. Jack? Want to help me get loaded up?"

"Sure, babe. Let me get this little guy into his jacket and I'll give you a hand. Walt, I'll have your dinner in a minute."

"Take your time," he said. "I have a beer to finish." And wounds to lick, he thought.

Cameron Michaels found himself in a very unique position—trying to court a woman who was pregnant with his twins. They met a few months ago in Grants Pass when a series of strange circumstances brought them together. It was a night of unforgettable bliss. Neither of them thought they'd ever see the other again.

He'd been at the Davenport Hotel Steak House because that's where he and the partners in his former pediatric practice liked to have dinner together every other month or so and she was there for one of her best friends' wedding. Nikki Jorgensen had married Joe Benson and the reception was at that hotel; Vanni was the matron of honor and Abby an attendant. One thing led to another and Abby fled to the hotel bar to escape all that true love and mush at the reception. Cameron had no idea some of his friends from Virgin River were in the banquet room when he met Abby in the bar. It was a fling—the kind of fling Cameron thought he'd outgrown and Abby had never before in her life considered. And of course it had to lead to pregnancy, something they were both carefully trying to prevent.

When she came to Virgin River to sit out her pregnancy, Cameron was the last person she expected to run into. But Cameron had ties to Virgin River and loved the place. He had known old Doc Mullins, deceased a few months ago, Mel and Jack Sheridan, Vanni and Paul. He saw a chance for a change of lifestyle and decided to give Virgin River a year. No small part of that decision was the fact that he couldn't find the woman he'd had a wonderful night of love with. How strange that he ended up in the same town she'd chosen to hide out in. Cameron was certified in family practice and pediatrics and his service to Virgin River was invaluable.

Right now the complications in his relationship with Abby were extreme. Abby was in hiding because she'd been legally married when she met Cameron, though she hadn't seen her husband in almost a year. The husband was a semi-famous rock star who'd had her sign a prenup promising fidelity or there would be no alimony. When the divorce was final, he'd also left her with a hefty pile of credit-card bills and she needed *his* money to pay off *his* debts. If anyone found out she'd conceived the twins before the divorce was final, she'd be in a deep financial mess.

Cameron was trying to take it nice and slow. Abby had lots of reasons to fear rushing into a serious relationship. The first time she did that, she ended up married to an unfaithful jerk who tied her up with a binding prenuptial agreement. The second time she'd thrown caution to the wind, she'd gotten pregnant. With *twins*.

So Cameron had called her and said, "Mel would like you to have an ultrasound and meet Dr. Stone, the OB in

Grace Valley. I thought maybe I could take you and then, if you'd like, we could have dinner in Fortuna. Something simple and quiet. Just a chance for you to get out. And for us to spend an hour or two together."

And she had said, "That's a very nice offer, but why don't I just take myself to Grace Valley, meet the doctor, have the ultrasound and come back home?"

"Because, Abby, I'd like to *see* the ultrasound." When that statement was answered with silence, he said, "It's typical for Mel to take an OB consult to meet John Stone—he won't think there's anything unusual about me taking you. This can be our secret as long as that's what you need, but really—we have to spend a little time together at some point. Talk, like we did before all this happened. Get to know each other. Again."

He could hear the reluctance in her voice when she finally accepted. What the hell? He'd backed her into a corner. He knew the babies were his and he wasn't going to give them up. He couldn't force her into a romantic relationship, he *wouldn't* force her to acknowledge the relationship that produced the babies, but he wasn't going away quietly. They were his children. It meant a lot to him.

She meant a lot to him. But he couldn't make her fall in love with him.

Cameron arranged for the ultrasound to be scheduled for the end of the day, when John was done with his appointments. It would be logical to go have dinner after that. He picked her up at 4:00 p.m. and conversation was a little lumpy and strained on the way over. He'd prepared a script: *Tell me about growing up. I'd like to hear about your flight-attendant years. What are your plans for after the babies are born?*

But none of that worked out because she took the conversation in another direction right off the bat. "I need to tell you something, Cameron. Vanessa has guessed about our secret. She remembered that I slipped away from the reception and of course she knew you lived in Grants Pass. It must have been something in the way you looked at me or spoke to me, but she knew. She was very direct. She told me you were a good man and deserved a chance."

He was speechless. "God bless Vanessa," he finally said in a breath.

"Yes, well, I trust her and I know she has good judgment, but that doesn't eliminate certain difficult facts. One, even though I slept with you, I don't really know you. We're probably highly incompatible. And two, I'm still hung out to dry by a nasty little prenup. An unfair, diabolical prenup that was the closest thing to a swindle I know. And three, Vanessa is sworn to secrecy because I don't want anyone to know about us. I'm pretty embarrassed about what I did. I can't afford to risk word leaking back to my rotten ex."

"Well," he said. "That certainly spells it out for me."

"I intend to protect these children to the best of my ability."

He reached across the front seat and gave her hand a pat. "I really appreciate that, Abby. That's courageous of you." She looked at him and saw that his eyes had grown very dark, almost navy blue. And dead serious. "So do I."

And from there all the way to Grace Valley they traveled in silence.

John Stone was as cordial as he could possibly be, happy to see Cam and delighted to meet Abby. They talked for a while about how he'd like to follow the pregnancy closely, along with Mel, because he assumed the babies would come early. It was important to be sure the babies were in position for a vaginal birth, and ultrasounds would be required. John didn't want her to be too far from a neonatal intensive care unit if they came too early or if a C-section was required. He asked her to step up her appointments for caution's sake.

And then he set her up for the ultrasound. "Little early to determine the sex of the babies. Do you want to know if it's obvious?"

"Yes. Sure," she answered.

He'd barely gotten started when he laughed. "Whoa," he chortled. "Right out in front, we got ourselves one boy. He's blocking the other one, but in a couple of months they'll be bigger, move around a little more and we'll get a better view."

And Cameron, who had seen and done so much medically, especially where children were concerned, began to lose the edge of control he'd always managed to maintain. His eyes clouded; his heart pounded. *A son! Oh God, a son!* He tried to blink back the emotion, but couldn't seem to stop it. He grabbed Abby's hand and squeezed it. "Look, Abby," he said in a whisper. "That one in front, the bossy one taking over, it's a boy."

Thank God she was emotional, too. It might take the focus off him. "My God," she whispered.

"They look perfect," John said. "And you're on target for July second, but if we make thirty-six weeks, we're in good shape. They look good, Abby." He was poking her belly, trying to get them to move around, directing the wand to check their internal organs, their limbs, their skulls. "I'm going to have Mel draw some blood, check for things like Down syndrome, spina bifida, a few other genetic abnormalities. But there's no reason for you to be less than completely optimistic."

She looked up into Cam's eyes, he looked down into hers. Both of them had tears on their cheeks. Cameron gently wiped hers away.

"Oh boy," John said.

Cameron looked up. "Listen, John, whatever it is you think you might know, you don't know anything. Am I clear?"

"Everything in this clinic is confidential," John said. "Is there anything I can do to help?"

"No," Abby and Cam said in unison.

"Well then," John said. "You have at least one boy on the way. And my lips are sealed. But damn—those are some good-looking babies." He grinned. "I can't wait. How about you?"

The first ten minutes of the car ride from Grace Valley to Fortuna for dinner were silent but for the sound of Abby's completely irritated, shallow breathing. Finally, through clenched teeth, she said, "I can't believe you did that!"

He knew exactly what he'd done. "I was overwhelmed." No apology, no further explanation.

"And now Dr. Stone knows!"

"So what? I'm the *father!*"

"You gave me your word that you wouldn't divulge! You said it could be my secret as long as I wanted it to be!"

"Vanessa knows!"

"That's because she guessed!"

"And John guessed when I got tears in my eyes at the sight of *my son!*"

"It's *my* son! You're just a sperm donor who wanted a quick roll in the hay with some chick you met in a bar!"

Cameron drove a few hundred yards and then slowly pulled off to the side of the road. He turned the car around and headed back in the direction they'd come.

"What are you doing?" she asked.

"I'm taking you home," he said.

"Fine!" she retorted. "That's fine with me!" She crossed her arms over her chest and glared out the window into the deepening dusk. And it was a long, long ride back to Virgin River in silence.

When Cameron got to Walt's property, he didn't go immediately down the road toward Vanni and Paul's. He stopped the car as the road veered around the back of the stable. He turned off the ignition and pivoted in the driver's seat, facing her. "Do you remember the night we met, Abby? And the conversation we had before going to the room? It was about that list you had—the one about what you were looking for in a man?"

She glowered at him and nodded, grudgingly.

"An important item was manners. You might want to remember that."

"Listen, Cameron—you got me into this mess and—"

"I had help," he said firmly. "Lots of help."

"Just take me home. Please," she said just as firmly.

"In a minute. You need to listen to me now. Pay attention, Abby. If being considerate and accommodating isn't going to work with you, I can change my approach. Regardless what nasty twist you put on things, I never intended to be a sperm donor. Nor was it my idea that we never see each other again after that night we spent together. I *looked* for you. I wanted more time with you. I never saw it as a quick roll in the hay. That was your doing when you disappeared on me, refused to contact me, even though you promised you would.

"It's very important that you understand something," he went on. "I'll try to work with you as much as you allow me to, but if you try to separate me from my children, I'll fight. I'll come after you. I'll launch a search that will make Columbus look like a novice. So don't even think about pulling something sneaky. Whether you like it or not, we're in this together."

"Take me home. Please."

"Did you hear me?"

"I heard," she said. "Now I'd really like to go home."

He turned back toward the road and pulled around the stable to the front of Vanni and Paul's house, Abby's current residence. When she went to jump out of the car to flee, he grabbed her wrist and held her back. She turned and looked at him with a little panic in her eyes. "Abby, I can't make you like me, but I can make you allow me to be a father to my children. I know a hundred ways. Please remember that."

Without reply, she pulled her wrist from his grasp and exited the car. Cam watched her walk up the porch and into the house. He sat for a moment, took a deep breath and turned on the dome light to look at his watch. Just after six-thirty. Mel was on call tonight until he checked in, and there were seldom any calls. Doc Mullins had managed a forty-year practice on one whiskey at the end of the day and Cam needed one. Bad.

He turned around and headed for Jack's.

Abby walked into Vanni's house and leaned her back against the closed front door. Vanni and Paul were in the great room, both of them on the floor with the baby. She looked at the scene of domestic tranquility and burst into tears.

Paul and Vanni were both instantly on their feet.

"Oh my God," Vanni said, rushing to her, Paul on her heels. "Was the ultrasound all right?"

"Beautiful. Dr. Stone said they're perfect."

"Why in the world are you crying?"

"I had a fight with Cam," she said, tears running down her cheeks, her words caught on a sob.

"Cam?" Paul asked, confused.

"I was upset. He got all teary when he saw the ultrasound—one of them is for sure a boy. I hated that he got emotional in front of John Stone and I lost my temper."

"Oh, Abby…"

"He got emotional?" Paul repeated, more confused. "Cameron?"

"Vanni—I called him a sperm donor! I was so *mean*."

"Oh, *Abby!*"

"Sperm donor?" Paul said, totally lost.

"He laid it out for me, very seriously. Angrily. He's not getting out of my way on this. He's going to be a problem—as if I don't have enough problems." She leaned toward Vanni and wept on her shoulder. "He said he can't make me like him, but he won't let me take the babies away from him!"

"Like him?" Paul said. "Babies? What the hell's going on here?"

Vanni looked over her shoulder at Paul. "Cameron's the father—don't tell anyone."

"Please don't tell anyone," Abby stressed tearfully.

Paul was quiet for a long moment while Vanni just held

Abby, comforting her. Finally he found his voice. "Are you fucking kidding me?"

"I didn't mean to be so hostile," Abby wept. "Maybe it's pregnancy."

"Sure it is, honey," Vanni comforted.

"Wait a minute," Paul attempted. "Wait a minute here."

"Long story, Paul," Vanni said. "Just don't tell anyone. I'll explain later, okay?"

"But I thought they just met!" Paul said.

"Obviously they didn't just meet. Don't be a dimwit. I'll tell you about it later, after Abby gets calmed down."

Paul turned away from them and went to pick little Matt up from the floor where he played. "Must be a long story," he muttered. "Very, very long. Say, about five months long?"

"Abby, you're going to have to apologize," Vanni was saying. "You can't be like that to him. I mean, you don't have to be in love with him or anything, but you have to be civil. He has his rights. And he's not a bad guy. In fact, he's a very good guy."

"I know, I know. It just got under my skin that I'm in charge of carrying these babies and giving birth to them and I still have no control! None! I just lost it."

"Well, when you tell him that, everything will be—"

"Um, ladies?" Paul said from behind them. "You're going to be at this a while, aren't you?"

"Yes, Paul," Vanni said. "Sorry."

"Oh God," Abby erupted. "You were going to have sex! You were alone for the first time in forever and were going to have sex, and I came home early and ruined everything."

"It's all right, baby," Vanni said. "We can have sex anytime."

Paul ran a hand around the back of his neck. "Well, actually…" Having sex at all around here was a lucky shot, with a baby, a houseguest and the general popping in, something that would be happening more now, with Muriel out of town. Anytime was pure fiction.

Paul pushed little Matt at Vanni. "Know what? I'm going to step out for a while. Go have a cup of coffee with Jack or something. You two get yourselves settled down. Hmm?"

"Sure," Vanni said, taking charge of the baby. "Probably a good idea."

As Paul was going out the door, Vanni was asking Abby, "Have you eaten, honey? Let me get you a little something to eat and we can talk about this."

Two

Cameron walked into Jack's and found at least a dozen people at different tables finishing up dinner. He sat up at the bar.

"Hey, Doc," Jack greeted, slapping a napkin down. "How's it going?"

"Great," Cameron said unenthusiastically. "Can I have a scotch? Neat. Something good. Good and powerful."

"Sure. Long day?" Jack asked as he turned to select a label that might do the trick.

"It got long. Don't worry—I'll have some dinner and coffee and take your wife off the hook for on-call."

"We have that all worked out, Doc. But I thought you had dinner out with Abby tonight."

"That didn't exactly work out."

Jack laughed. "That should thrill Paul. He had the idea he was going to be alone with his wife."

"Yeah, well, it was beyond my control," Cameron said. "Believe me."

"Everything all right?"

"Dandy," he said. He lifted his drink. "Swell."

Cameron hadn't even sipped his drink when Paul walked

in. He sat next to Cam and put his elbows on the bar. "What you got there?" he asked Cameron.

"Scotch."

"Gimme a Crown. Same recipe," Paul said to Jack.

Jack got down a glass and poured. "I could've sworn you had plans for the evening," he said to Paul.

"I thought so," he said. He lifted his glass and took a drink. "But then Abby came home, having some kind of emotional crisis, and Vanni got all hooked up in that." Paul glared briefly at Cameron. "Lots of crying. Carrying on."

Cameron turned toward him. "I did not do anything to bring that on," he said rather harshly. "I was completely courteous. Thoughtful. I was *wonderful*."

"I know that," Paul said. "I gather she brought it on herself. She said she lost her temper. Said some rude things. Mean things." He sipped. "You're gonna have to let it go, man. Cut her some slack. For being pregnant and out of her mind. You know?"

Jack was leaning on the bar, listening closely to this conversation that was, thankfully, not overheard by other dinner customers. Only Paul and Cameron were at the bar.

"I handled it the best way I could," Cameron said.

"She said she feels like she has to do everything—having the babies and everything—and feels like she has no control."

"*She* has no control?" Cameron asked hotly. Then he laughed bitterly.

"Yeah, well, she's feeling real bad about it now."

"Is that so?" Cameron said. "Well, guess what? I feel real bad about what she said, too." Then he looked back into his drink and sulked.

"Come on," Jack said. "What the hell could she have said?"

Cameron looked up from his drink. "She called me an unkind name."

Jack laughed at him. "Well, you're a big boy. What could a little pregnant girl call you that would get you so riled up?"

"Never mind. It's over."

"How about—sperm donor," Paul supplied.

Cameron shot Paul an angry look. "Way to go, dipshit. Anybody ever tell you you have a big mouth?"

"When Vanni said not to tell, I didn't think she meant you. I mean, *you* know. Right?"

Cameron glanced at Jack.

"Don't worry about Jack," Paul said. "He doesn't talk. Well, he does, but when he has specific orders not to, he can manage to keep his mouth shut."

Then Jack, caution drawing every word, said, "Now, why in the world would she say something like that to you?"

"I can't imagine," Cameron said, pouting.

"Well, if it makes you feel any better about things, Vanessa called me a dimwit for asking just about the same question." He took a drink. "Apparently we have ourselves a situation. Dad."

"Whoa," Jack said, straightening up. He reached for another glass and tipped the bottle over it. Jack usually waited until closing to partake, but it seemed appropriate to commiserate with these two. "Was everything all right with the ultrasound?" he asked warily.

"Fine," Cameron said, sipping. "Babies look great."

"And at least one's a boy," Paul said, picking up his

drink. After a swallow he found Cameron glaring at him again. "What? I wasn't told not to tell that."

"You are a dimwit," Cameron patiently pointed out.

"Yeah? Well, I'm a dimwit who was going to get lucky once the baby was tucked in, until you got Abby all upset and crying and—" He stopped suddenly. He shook his head dismally.

"Gentlemen, I propose a toast," Jack said, lifting his glass. "Let's drink to silence. If this conversation ever leaves this bar, we're all going to die. Skinless."

"Silence," the other men agreed.

"All right," Jack said, "since there's a pact of silence, I just want to know when this could have happened. How this could have happened."

Cameron put down his glass. "The weekend of Joe Benson's wedding in Grants Pass. And, in the usual way."

"You weren't at that wedding," Paul pointed out.

"I had dinner at the hotel restaurant that night. I met her in the bar. Now, that's all I'm saying about it. And if you let on to Abby that I said that much, my situation is only going to get more impossible. You follow me here, Paul?"

"Well, what are you going to do about it?"

"Do about it?"

"Well," he said, looking over each shoulder to make sure they weren't being overheard, then leaning close to whisper. Jack, of course, leaned down to not miss a word. "She's pregnant. You're the father. Anything come to mind there, bud? Like maybe marriage?"

Cameron put down his drink impatiently. "Pay attention, Paul. I couldn't even get her to go to Fortuna to eat at a restaurant with me. She hates me. I was a perfect gentleman, back then and tonight, but she hates me. She called me a *sperm donor*."

"Whew," Paul said.

"Whew," said Jack.

All three men lifted their glasses in misery.

Vanessa put water for tea on the stove for Abby and while it heated she put little Matt down in his bed with his bottle. When she got back to the kitchen, Abby was blowing her nose, wiping her eyes. While Vanni let the tea steep, she put some leftover roast beef, potatoes and carrots on a plate and warmed it in the microwave. She put the tea in front of her friend and left the dinner in the microwave. Vanni pulled herself a beer out of the refrigerator and sat down opposite Abby. "Done crying yet?" she asked.

Abby nodded. "I'm sorry. I don't know what's wrong with me."

"Well, I do. My emotions were so crazy when I was pregnant, I don't know how anyone could stand to be around me. I was a complete wreck."

"I should be so ashamed," Abby said with a sniff. "You had it so much worse."

"That has nothing to do with it," Vanni said. "You've got a good bit of stress right now. Between being unmarried and having all those bills and that horrible prenup, it's small wonder you're a bit…reactive."

Abby blew her nose. "I complain about having no control, then I lose control. It makes no sense."

"Abby, I'm not known for wisdom, I'm best known for having the worst goddamn temper. Direct quote from my husband who has no temper at all. I want you to know, I'll stand by you and support you, no matter what your next move is. But, here's what I think you should do. I think you should go to the clinic first thing in the morning and apologize to Cameron. I think you should have a frank talk with him about how you two are going to manage parenting these children. You two only have to make one commitment—that's to them. This can't go on. You're not going to let them go, and neither is he. You have to find a way to work together, whether you're friends or not. But so much better if you're friends. For them. Huh?"

"It just makes me so furious!" Abby got out, another tear rolling down her cheek.

"What makes you so furious?"

"That he ended up here! That he found me out! That now, in addition to everything else, I have to find a way to deal with him! I just wanted to have my babies, take them to my mother's and get on with my life."

"Yeah? Well, Abby, you have no right."

Abby looked up, eyes wide and glassy, a tissue scrunched in her hand.

"Listen, I told you I knew Cameron before Paul finally stepped up to the plate and told me how he felt about me. Well, I can't say I knew him all that well back then—we had two very platonic dates. But we did a lot of talking and I learned that he really expected he'd be married with a family by now. He wanted a wife, children. He loves kids so much that he did a second residency in pediatrics. He—"

"Yeah, I know all that...."

"Abby, just listen to me. We've been good friends for a long time, you and me. We flew together, partied together, cried over the miserable losers we'd hooked our hearts on together. When I think of some of the jackasses we thought we could turn into husbands... God, it makes me shudder.

"As your friend, I can be honest with you. And as my friend, you owe it to me to hear me out. Abby, you have no right. You have as much responsibility as he does for this situation you're in. And he has as much right as you to be a parent here. I think it would have been a tragedy for Cameron if you'd succeeded in disappearing with his children. He deserves to be able to tell his family he's going to be a father. His mother deserves to know she's going to be a grandmother. It might be complicated and imperfect, but I bet it's one of the best things in his life right now. I think that if a problem arises in working this out so you can parent your children together, the problem will be you. Not him."

Abby was speechless for a moment. "Wow," she finally said.

"That's harsh, I know. But, Abby, that's the truth as I see it. You don't have to marry him, you don't have to love him, but you do have to let him be a father to his children. He hasn't done anything wrong. He doesn't deserve your rage. Kid Crawford, your sleazy ex-husband, you go ahead and hate him if you want. But I can't sit quiet while you punish Cameron. He's a good soul. And if he hadn't turned up here, running into you by the sheerest accident, I would consider it your responsibility to find him and tell him the truth."

Abby leaned across the table toward Vanessa. "Listen," she said pleadingly, "are you sure you'd be so sane and logical if you were in this mess?"

"Eventually," Vanni said easily. "It might be hard to get to sane and logical, but I'm not worried—you'll eventually get there, yourself. Because Cameron won't ever do anything to hurt you. You'll at least share parenting, and he's so great with children, he'll be a wonderful father. Do you have any idea how many women wish they had parenting partners that wonderful? Get it together, Abby. You're stuck with this and it's not a bad deal to be stuck with. What if they were Kid Crawford's babies?" She stood up and went to the microwave, giving it another forty-five seconds to rewarm the dinner. "Let's get some decent food in your stomach, a good night's sleep, and tomorrow you can start mending your fences."

When Abby went to bed, she lay awake for a very long time, just thinking. She knew Vanessa was right about almost everything. Of course Abby had to be more cooperative with Cameron, and she had no real concern about Cameron's ability to be a decent parent. If she hadn't guessed that much when she met him a few months ago, she certainly knew it now. He took her crap and still honored her needs, protecting her privacy, trying to keep her from panic and fear. His attention was a hundred percent aimed at the welfare of the children.

And there was the rub. Despite what she said, Abby still had memories of their night together in Grants Pass that made her skin turn hot. Cameron was a dream lover. His every word and action made her feel adored. In his hands satisfaction had been complete, shatteringly perfect. He was just the kind of man every woman hoped for.

He was probably exactly that way with every woman he coaxed into bed. The charm, the sensitivity, the power, even the humor. After all, once he realized he was face-to-face with her and she carried his babies, he hadn't said he thought himself to be in love with her. He'd demanded his paternal rights but hadn't suggested marriage.

He had said he'd looked for her. Wanted more time with her...

She flopped over in bed. She had to let him off the hook for that love-and-marriage thing—she'd have laughed off any declarations of love anyway and she'd never have agreed to marry him, a virtual stranger. That would be crazy.

But he was right, and Vanni was right. He'd been considerate of her feelings and she had been a shrew. Her children would be better off with a good father they could be proud of, than they would be with no father at all. These ideas cost her quite a lot of sleep that night.

She was up very early, but she didn't beat Paul to the kitchen. He was having a cup of coffee as dawn was just barely peeking over the horizon. He looked over the rim of the cup with round eyes. "I apologize," she said before even saying good-morning. "I was a little crazy last night, but I'm going to the clinic first thing this morning to apologize to Cameron and try to work with him on our...project."

He smiled slightly. "I guess that's a good idea. Considering."

"Got any better ideas?" she asked.

"Abby, I don't know anything about having babies," Paul said. "I just know that when little Matt was coming I worried so much about him. Vanni was so upset and sad, I worried that might hurt the baby in some way. I think Mel was worried, too, but she told me that if being worried and scared caused serious problems, there wouldn't have been a single healthy birth in the history of the world. I just wish you could be happy." He cleared his throat. "I bet Cameron's on your side. Bet he wishes that, too."

She tilted her head and just smiled at him. "You're right. I have to work on that. After all, I have some problems, but they're under control at the moment. And I'm going to move forward with Cameron. If he doesn't hate me too much…"

"Oh, he doesn't." She shot him a questioning look. "I'm sure he doesn't," he amended. He smiled lamely.

"I wish I could have a good strong cup of coffee," Abby said, looking jealously at Paul's big mug.

He laughed at her. "See, that by itself could make you cranky. All the things you give up to be a good mother."

Vanessa was barely up with the baby when Abby was shrugging into her coat to leave the house. She thought if she got to the clinic before they opened, she could have a word with Cameron in private. She wasn't sure what that word was going to be besides, "Sorry."

She had to bang on the door more than once and finally, she saw a shadow approaching. She glanced at her watch; it was only seven-thirty and they weren't due to open for business till nine. When he opened the door, her first word was right on. "Oh, sorry."

He was wearing sweatpants, his chest and feet bare, a towel slung around his neck and his hair wet from the shower. She flushed a little, remembering that wide, hard chest as it had been pressed against her breasts. And those muscular arms that had held him up over her to keep from crushing her with his weight.

"I wanted to get here early, but I think I got here too early," she said.

"Don't worry about it," he said, opening the door for her. "You all right?"

"Well, I guess so."

"What's wrong, Abby?" he asked, looking instantly concerned. "Are you sick? In pain? Anything physically wrong?"

"I was a bitch. I came to apologize."

"Oh," he said, letting out a slow breath. "Forget it. You were upset. We were both upset. Having twins isn't stress free. Let's let it go."

"I thought maybe we could talk a minute, if you have time."

He gave her a small smile. "How about a cup of herbal tea?"

"I'd rather have a strong cup of coffee with a little Irish Mist and lots of cream, but I suppose that's out of the question...."

He laughed lightly. "Bad idea. But there's tea in the kitchen. Mel has it on hand for the pregnant girls."

"That's me," she said. "Mel's not a tea drinker?"

"Oh, no. Mel's a hard-core caffeine junkie. She'd take it in the vein if she could."

"I relate. I might be in withdrawal. That could be half the problem."

"The tea is herbal, so it's also decaf."

"Beautiful," she said sarcastically. "One blow after another."

And this time his laugh was a little stronger. "Come to the kitchen. Have you had breakfast?"

"If it's all the same to you, I'll save that for after we've talked a bit."

He filled the kettle and glanced over his shoulder. "Something about this little mission of yours upsetting your stomach?"

"Something about two babies is upsetting my stomach.

Double morning sickness. It'll pass." She sat down. "I've already thrown up this morning, so we're safe for a while."

Cameron stared down at the kettle on the stove. She wouldn't understand this, but he wished he could have been there for that. He'd like to be around for even the worst parts of the pregnancy; he'd like to be the one she complained to, blamed, criticized and harangued. Even though he was already getting plenty of that, he hated that she suffered her upset without his arms around her, comforting her as she calmed down. Crazy as it was, he wanted to watch her turn pea green, shoot for the bathroom, come out white as a sheet and fall into his arms. He'd like to be the partner, not the silent partner. He'd like to feel her big belly pressed up against him at night, waking him with the romping inside. He turned around and looked at her. "Would you like some soda crackers?"

"No, thank you."

"You're still having morning sickness at five months?"

"'Fraid so. Mel said it happens. Some of us are lucky. And I'm double lucky. My hormones have obviously gone wild."

He got a cup and tea bag ready, poured himself a cup of high-test coffee, strong the way Mel liked it, and sat at the table with her.

"I don't know where to start," she said. "Cameron, I was mean and horrible last night and I'm sorry. I think I felt out of control. I'm not really angry with you. I'm not afraid you'd be a terrible father. It's just this mess of mine. I'd like to keep you out of it. I'd like to keep the babies out of it."

"I understand."

"That night... The night this happened..." She took a breath. "I was upset, depressed, didn't know which way to turn.... I never meant for something like that to happen. I shouldn't have let it happen. It's all my fault."

"Abby, there's no fault," he said. He reached for her hand, but the teakettle whistled and he pulled back. He stood and fixed up her tea, bringing it to her. He got a spoon, cream and sugar. Then he sat down again while she dunked the tea bag. "Listen, it wasn't about fault. We're adults. We were adults that night, and it wasn't a bad night. It was nice."

"It was a mistake," she said. "That isn't the way I get to know men."

"I know that. It isn't the way I get to know women either," he said. "We deserve a second chance."

She sighed. "Which is the point. Vanni sat me down last night. She gave me a stern talking-to. If we're both going to be parents, we have to at least get along. I can't treat you like the enemy—you've been nothing but nice to me. I guess I just don't know how to go about that—the getting along part. The part where you get to be the father without anyone knowing you're the father."

"We should have just talked about it. Because I have some ideas about that."

Her eyes shot open wide. "You do?"

"I do," he said.

She leaned her chin on her hand. "I can't wait to hear this."

"First of all, we don't have to explain anything to anyone, ever. There's the starting point. We can be friendly now without any suspicion. We can see each other casually, become friends. Abby, you're a beautiful, sexy, funny woman. You're carrying twins and I'm a pediatrician. I love babies and beautiful women. The fact that you're a single pregnant woman wouldn't scare me off—why would it? For someone like me to be attracted to someone like you, even if we hadn't had our history, isn't so strange. People are likely to think it's a Lifetime movie. Nothing but happy endings."

"I don't know about that," she said.

"Well, I'm not embarrassed by what happened. If we wanted to, we could just say we met in Grants Pass while you were visiting your good friend, we got to know each other, we got along. We didn't date long, but there was an attraction and…well…these things happen. The details aren't important and none of anyone's business but ours."

"These things happen," she repeated, shaking her head.

"It's not mysterious. In fact, it's not a crime. The few people who know aren't going to tip off Kid Crawford, if that's what has you panicked."

"Few people?" she asked.

"It's up to a few. There was Mel, Vanni and Dr. Stone. Now there's Paul, and thanks to a little time we had at the bar together last night, Jack. Jack's the only wild card, I think, and he won't say anything because he doesn't want to have to deal with Mel on that issue. Paul doesn't want Vanni to kill him, so he's airtight."

"Shew," she said.

"Thing is, it might get out eventually. It's kind of funny in a way—"

"Funny?"

"Think about it—two strangers are sitting alone in a bar, feeling sorry for themselves, and not only do they get together and find a lot of comfort in each other, they start a family. And not just a baby, but twins. Then they end up in the same small town. No one would believe it. I know it wasn't planned, but I'm not sorry about the outcome."

She looked angry. At least indignant. "Well, *I'm* sorry!"

"No, you're not. You hate the complications, but there are twins coming and I'm going to be around to help you with that. One's a boy. I hope the other one's a girl. These might be the only kids I get, and I hope I get one of each." He grinned stupidly and knew it.

"You know, if you had all these legal and financial things hanging on you, you wouldn't be so cavalier."

"I think we should see a lawyer," he said.

"I *have* a lawyer!"

"I'm not sure you have a good one. You got screwed."

"Listen, Cameron, I can't afford another lawyer. The last one almost wiped me out. I pulled all my retirement funds, cashed in my stock, which wasn't much, sold my condo..."

"I'll take care of it."

She was struck dumb. "Why would you do that?"

"Because, Abby, it's in my best interest to help you get this monkey off your back. If we have a clean slate, maybe we can work as a team." He sat back. "That's my hope."

"I don't want you to do that," she said sternly. "I don't want to owe you that much."

He just shrugged. "You're stuck with me either way. They're mine as much as they're yours."

"What a godawful, stinking mess," she said, pouting and lifting the cup to her lips.

Cameron was silent. Frowning. When she put the cup down, she looked at him and said, "What now?"

He shook his head and said, "You wouldn't want to hear about some of the sad things I've seen in my practice. Abby, you're worried about all the wrong things—about who's going to pay for the lawyer, about being embarrassed that we didn't have a long relationship before this happened.

Give thanks. The babies are healthy and strong and, so far as we can tell, perfect."

Her hand went to her tummy. "Are you the calm and reasonable one because you're not the pregnant one?" she asked.

"No, sweetheart. Because I'm the desperate one. You're holding the prize."

By the time Jack got home at the end of a long day, the children were asleep and Mel was on the computer. He kissed her, then went to the kitchen and looked through the mail. He found a letter from Rick.

Since the boy was thirteen, Jack had looked out for him, tried to help him into manhood with strength and courage, with goodness. It was with a combination of pride and trepidation that he had sent him off to the Marine Corps at the age of eighteen. It was Rick's decision, one hundred percent. Jack never fought him on it, though he had wanted to send Rick to college and had put aside money for that.

Now Rick was in Iraq where Jack had served two tours in his own Marine career. Rick sent a letter home to Jack sometimes as often as every two weeks, at least once a month, and he usually sent it to the bar so that everyone could hear the latest news. He also wrote to his grandmother, who was his only family, and his girl, Liz, who lived in Eureka.

But this letter hadn't gone to the bar. Jack ripped it open at once.

Dear Jack,
God, I'm sorry to do this to you. I gotta get this out—
and I don't want my grandma or Liz upset. But you

know about this stuff. You know how it is, and I have to lay it on someone who won't freak out. You would've gotten some of this on the news, but you wouldn't have known it had anything to do with me. We moved on Haditha Dam, doing house-to-house searches, trying to root out al Qaeda insurgents, and one of the squads right in front of us was obliterated by a bomb. A truck bomb. There was only one survivor in that squad, and they were a tight squad. Tighter than ours. One survivor, Jack. Holy Jesus, I think I'd rather be dead than watch eleven of my best friends blow up. I knew some of them. Sonny was waiting for a baby, Gravis was engaged, and Dom was this little Italian kid who was just scared shitless all the time. He wanted to go home so bad, he cried. Cried. But his whole squad was holding him up, taking care of him, trying to bolster him and prop him up all the time. They never cut anyone out of their fold—no matter what kind of problem they had. The guy that made it, the one guy, he has a girlfriend back home, and he'll get back to her, but he's going to be messed up. But he doesn't even get to leave yet—they're moving him to another squad. Holy God, I hope they move him out of the worst of this shit—it's horrible.

They were right in front of us, Jack. Another two minutes, it would've been us. I can't hardly sleep since that happened. A couple of my boys puked and one fainted, I think. He got back on his feet real fast and denied it, but I think he really passed out. There was so much screaming I couldn't tell if it was me or the rest of them. It was all black and cloudy and then it was all blood. I wanted to die on the spot. I hit the ground because there was so much shooting I didn't know for sure I wouldn't take one from my own platoon.

Right after the bomb and all the shooting, an Army Cobra came in and bombed the shit out of one of the buildings. Debris everywhere, really heavy stuff. Big hunks of cement and wood, flying like missiles through the air.

This place is like hell sometimes. I'm sorry to write you this stuff. Don't tell anyone—don't get anyone scared or upset. My grandma and Liz can't know this shit. We just have to keep them thinking positive.

And then—if all that crap isn't bad enough, I think I killed a guy. We couldn't recover a body, but I saw a sniper and I nailed him. If he managed to crawl away, he didn't get far because he left behind too much blood to make it out alive. I didn't believe this could happen, because I was so far away, but I saw the look on his face. And for just one second I thought, why'd I get him before he got me? War can't be luck. Not with the amount of training we put ourselves through.

My squad's all shook up. Hell, the battalion's all torn up. Since I've been over here, I haven't seen an American die—and then eleven of them went up in one giant explosion. Jack, it was the worst thing I've ever seen. And then I killed a guy.

I'm sorry. I had to tell you. Don't get anyone upset with this. Burn this.

Jack, I'm not scared. Sometimes I get nervous, my adrenaline gets pumping real hard, it works on my brain a lot, but I'm okay. I don't want you to worry that I'm scared and will do something stupid—I use

the fear to keep me sharp. Some of the boys are terrified, but it's real easy to see it isn't going to do them
any good to give in to that.

I'm still okay. But I had to write this to someone
who could take it, someone who'd understand, because it's so freaking awful and if I keep it in my gut,
it's going to eat me alive.

Rick

Jack's hands shook as he read. And reread. He had fallen
into a kitchen chair. He felt his wife's small hand on his
shoulder and turned his eyes up to her.

"What is it?" she asked him.

"It's from Rick. It's not good. It can't be shared with
anyone, he says."

She held out her hand. "That doesn't include me," she
said.

"Mel, it's very ugly."

"I need to know what makes your hands shake, Jack.
We get through things together."

"Yeah," he said wearily. He handed her the letter, let her
read. Before she got to the end, tears were running down
her cheeks. "Dear God in heaven," she whispered. "Our
poor boy. God, all the poor boys."

Jack was up until three in the morning, writing to Rick,
telling him he could send any kind of letter he wanted,
Jack would always be there to read it. He wrote anything
he could think of to pump him up, tell him how proud he
was, how completely sure he was going to make all the
right decisions. He praised him for his ability to empathize
with his boys—the ones who survived, the ones who were

having a hard time. And he wrote, "Yeah, buddy, we've all seen some bad, bad stuff. When you're home, you'll better appreciate all the good stuff. I swear to God."

And then Jack went back to his previous practice of writing a letter a day to Rick. Anything to keep him going, keep him positive.

A few days later, at about four in the afternoon, before the dinner crowd showed up and the bar was quiet, she came in. Liz. Rick's girl. She stood just inside the door and smiled at Jack. Jack smiled back. What irony that she should turn up just a few days after Jack had received that letter, the one that threatened to rob him of any hope for a good night's sleep till he had his boy home.

The first time he'd seen Liz she had been a fourteen-year-old hottie. She wore tight tops, skirts the size of napkins, high-heeled boots and heavy, dramatic makeup. His boy Rick went right over the edge. Despite all Jack's counseling, Rick ended up in trouble with the girl; he just didn't get that condom out of his pocket in time.

The next time Jack saw Liz, she had been so different. She actually looked younger than the first time. A pregnant child; a little girl of fifteen with no makeup, dressed in jeans and a sweatshirt pulled over her pregnant tummy, her hair pulled back in a childish ponytail. And that was the real Liz, the girl Ricky loved and stood by. That was the girl who got him in so much trouble at school while he made himself late to every class making sure he got her past the sniggering girls in the hallway and into her classroom. Rick never once complained. He wanted nothing so much as to do right by her.

Jack had been so proud of the way the boy stuck with her,

protected her, was there for her through everything. Then their baby had been stillborn—a tragedy, a horrible way for these kids to grow up. But they'd been so strong, so brave.

And this was what Liz had become—a beautiful young woman, almost eighteen. She was so lovely it almost took his breath away. Her hair was long, light brown with blond highlights, her eyes sparkling. She still wore daringly tight clothes, but she'd started adding tasteful elements, like today's tan suede jacket. She wasn't the showy, seductive nymphet anymore. And her makeup was light, only enhancing her natural beauty, rather than making her look like a too-young hooker, thank God.

She walked up to the bar, jumped up on a stool and leaned toward him to give him a friendly peck on the cheek. "How are you?" she asked.

"Never mind me. How about you?"

"Good. I graduate in June. I have straight As. Rick will be happy about that."

"Are *you* happy about that?" he asked with a laugh.

"I'm very proud of it. I didn't think I could do it."

"But…are you doing it for Rick?"

"Well, I *was,*" she said with a nod. "But I have to admit, I like the feeling. School was so easy for Ricky—he always got straight As without hardly trying. I'd like to think I'm almost as smart as he is, even if I do have to work at it real hard." She smiled at Jack. "But, I signed up for community college in the fall."

"Good for you. Nothing wrong with hard work. If it's any comfort, it never came easy to me, either. Any idea what you'd like to be when you grow up?"

"None whatsoever. Well, I know some things—I know I

want to be with Rick. When he's ready." She sighed. "Jack, sometimes I miss him so much."

"Me, too, kiddo. What do you hear from him these days?" he asked, praying she wouldn't ask him the same question.

"I got a letter last week. I think he's having a hard time. He won't tell me anything bad, but there's a certain…something. I can't describe it. It's like he's having trouble writing things down, and he keeps repeating the same things over and over. I just hope he's all right."

"Lizzie, men who serve, even when they're not real close to the action, tend to bring home some issues with them. Know what I mean, honey?"

"I know." She dropped her gaze briefly. "I'm trying to read about it, but it's scary."

"There are groups, Liz. Military spouses who get together to support each other. You could check it out."

"Oh, I couldn't, Jack. I'm not a wife. They wouldn't—"

He smiled. "Bet they would. You're not the only girlfriend waiting for her guy to come home. If you think it could help you understand some things, you should give it a shot."

"Do you think that would make it easier for Rick?" she asked.

Nothing is going to make this easier, Jack thought. But he didn't say it. He smiled. "Maybe. The point is, if it helps you, it might end up helping him. Why not at least ask? If you can find a group in your area?"

"I guess I could check. Does it cost anything?"

He frowned. "I doubt it. Why? Is that a problem?"

"I'm saving every penny Aunt Connie pays me for helping in the store. When Rick gets his R & R, I want to meet him. I'll go anywhere. I got a passport."

Jack was momentarily stunned. That had never occurred to him—that Rick would spend his leave anywhere but Virgin River, and that Liz would travel to see him. The shock must have shown on his face, because she smiled.

"I've never been anywhere," she said quietly. "Anywhere at all."

"This is kind of a big step."

"Bigger than spending nights with him at his grandma's house? Bigger than having a baby with him? Than promising I'll love him forever? Come on, Jack." She laughed. "By now you should be used to this. We're not giving each other up."

Jack smiled at her, but he was thinking, *All I want in this world is for everything to work out for you two now. You've earned it. Burying a baby, going to war, being left behind. You've gone through things some couples married twenty years haven't gone through—and held it together. God, no one deserves it more.* But he said, "Liz, things usually work out the way they're supposed to. You need to have faith and think positive."

Three

Since moving part of his family's construction company to Virgin River, business had been good for Paul Haggerty. He was working on a new construction, a forty-five-hundred-square-foot house for a couple from Arizona. It would be their second home; the people were obviously stinking rich. He'd snagged the job out from under the local contractors by promising to deliver the finished home ahead of schedule. With the reputation of his family's company in Grants Pass plus a little tour of a couple of his completed properties, it was a quick contract. In addition to getting the job, he'd convinced them to talk to Joe Benson, his best friend and architect from Grants Pass, about a design.

Now he had to deliver.

He had a couple of houses and three renovations in production. But business was only as good as his crews. He'd hired some solid, skilled people, and when someone messed up, didn't show for work or couldn't follow orders, he didn't screw around—they were gone. Which meant the hiring and firing was a continual process.

He kept his office in a construction trailer at the big homesite. That was the project that was taking the most time. The weather was warming up a little, but it was still brisk in the mountains in March. He looked up from the schedule on his clipboard to see a man walking toward him holding a folded newspaper. Another job applicant. Well, good. With any luck he'd be hireable.

The man was good-sized and appeared strong. He wore an odd-looking cowboy hat, jeans, denim jacket and boots, looking so much like everyone else up here in the mountains. He was clean shaven and his clothes appeared to be fresh; Paul took that as a positive sign.

When he got up in front of Paul he stopped and said, "Hi. I'm looking for the boss at Haggerty Construction."

Paul put out his hand. "Paul Haggerty. How you doin'?"

The man accepted the shake. "Dan Brady. Good. You?"

"Excellent. What can I do for you?"

"You advertised for a drywall man and painter. That spot filled yet?"

"I can always use help with that, if you have what I need. Let me get you an application." Paul turned away to go into the trailer.

"Mr. Haggerty," Dan said, stopping him.

Paul turned. He was used to being in charge, but he didn't think he'd ever get used to being called mister by a man his age or older.

"I don't want to waste your time or mine. I served some felony time. If that's going to stop you cold, let's not go through the routine."

"For what?" Paul asked.

"Farming the wrong produce, you might say."

"Anything else on your sheet?" Paul asked.

"Yeah. I turned myself in."

"Any other arrests? Of any kind? Even misdemeanor?"

"That's it. Isn't that about enough?"

Paul didn't respond or react. He'd keep secret the fact that he'd feel better hiring a pot grower than someone who'd had a bunch of DUIs. One thing that could really mess up the works and get people hurt was drinking on the job. "Do you have a parole or probation officer you report to?" Paul asked.

"I do," he said. "Parole. I was released early, if that matters."

"How long have you been out?"

"Not long. Six weeks. I checked in with the family and relocated."

"Why here?" Paul wondered aloud.

"Because Virgin River is known for discouraging marijuana growing."

"Well, Dan, my business isn't limited to Virgin River. There's lots of work around these mountains and I'm willing to take any good bid if I have the crews to cover it. There could be a job in a place that caters to illegal growing, like Clear River. That going to be a problem for you? Or for me?"

Dan grinned. "Old acquaintances of mine aren't likely to be doing honest work. I think it'll be all right." Then he shook his head. "One of 'em might order up a big house, however. I just hope not."

Paul laughed in spite of himself. He wasn't going to be doing business in cash. If that ever came up, they'd have to use a bank, and growers didn't like banks. "Then the next step is your application. I'd like to see what you've done in construction, then we'll talk."

"Thank you, Mr. Haggerty. Thank you very much."

Paul got him an application, gave him a pen and clipboard. Dan sat on the steps to the trailer and filled it out. A half hour later he handed it to Paul who scanned it.

"You've had a lot of construction experience," he said, surprised. He looked up. "Marine Corps?"

"Yes, sir. I started working construction at eighteen, Marine Corps at twenty-five."

"The Corps came kind of late for you. A lot of us went in younger…"

"I thought about it for a long time first. And the military benefits seemed worth the time. Not a lot of benefits in the construction trade."

"I offer medical benefits for full-time crew," Paul said.

"That's no longer a priority," he said.

"You have an address in Sebastapol."

"That's my folks' place—my permanent address. I haven't found anything around here yet, but I have the camper shell, so I'm good while I look."

"You're a framer, too. I need framers."

"I could probably do it, but I have an unsteady leg. Since Iraq. I do a lot of other things that don't go fifteen feet off the ground and that would probably keep your workman's comp manageable."

Paul pondered the application for a good two minutes. The guy looked real good on paper. He'd been a felon, but then again, Paul had fought wildfire as a volunteer beside incarcerated felons recruited for that purpose. "What are the chances of getting a letter of recommendation?"

"Slim. But the sheriff's department might be willing to confirm that I was a cooperative suspect. I guess my parole officer might step up. I could ask, but you know that won't guarantee I'd be a good employee."

"How bad you want a job?" Paul asked without look-ing up.

"Bad."

"Bad enough to take a urine test every now and then?"

Dan Brady laughed. "Sure. But I can make that easy on you. I can sign a release to give you access to the parole officer's random urine test, then you don't have to pay for a lab. I don't do drugs. Never did."

"Then why?" Paul asked, mystified.

"Money," he said with a shrug. "It was for the money."

"Do you regret it?" Paul asked.

Dan Brady paused a long moment before he said, "I have a list of regrets about a hundred miles long. That would fall in there somewhere. At the time, I needed the money. Times were hard."

"Are times still hard?" Paul asked.

"Those times are past. Oh, I still need money, but it's all different now. Prison changed a lot of things, believe me."

"Says here you do just about everything—drywall, tex-turing, painting, plumbing, wiring, counters, roofing—"

"Roofing—there's that high-up thing again. Sorry, you have to know the truth, my unsteady leg can take me by sur-prise. I'll do anything, but you should have the truth about that for both our sakes. One, I don't want a broken back, and two, you don't want an injured jobber on your insurance."

"When was the last time you took a fall from that leg?"

"Well," Dan said, scratching his chin, "a couple of years ago, I fell in my mother's upstairs bathroom, and that wasn't even high beams. I didn't hurt myself much, but one minute I was standing up, the next I was on my ass. Like I said, I could get up there on the roof, if that's the price of getting the job, but I've made it a policy to stay close to the ground if at all possible. In case."

Paul laughed. "How'd you like the Marines?"

"The truth? I think I was a decent Marine, but I didn't love it. I got mostly shit assignments. I went to Iraq right off the bat, when things were as bad as they could get. When I was discharged, it was one of the happiest days of my life."

"I did my four and joined the reserves and went back to Iraq a second time. One of us was smarter. I vote for you. But that felony thing—"

"I understand...."

"What if I give you a shot? Think I'll regret it?"

"Nope. I'm good in construction. Before I started doing it for a living, I helped my dad build our house. And I'll pee in a cup for you. I don't steal or get in fights. But if I were you, I'd keep me close to the ground. I'll get a lot more done."

Paul smiled and put out his hand. "Well, what the hell, Dan. You paid your debt. But I am going to check in with the parole officer, just to get another read on you."

Dan put out a hand. "Knock yourself out there, sir. He thinks I have potential."

"Then we're off to an excellent start. If you have any talent, you're coming on at a good time. This company is young and growing."

"Yes, sir. Thank you, sir. I'll do my best."

Dan Brady worked the rest of the week for Haggerty Construction. He was moved around so Paul could see his work. He did some drywall and texturing, hung a couple of big, carved front doors with leaded-glass windows, spackled, fitted countertop, even helped with some wiring. "Do you do everything in construction?" Paul finally asked.

"Just about," Dan answered with a shrug. "I started when I was fifteen, trained by the toughest boss in construction. The man was a tyrant." Then he grinned proudly.

"Your dad," Paul said.

"You work for him, too?" Dan asked facetiously.

"Tell you what, you stay out of trouble, you might work out." Then Paul slapped him on the back.

Dan worked on Saturday as well; they were pressed for time on the big house. But the crew supervisor told everyone to knock off at two in the afternoon and be back Monday morning bright and early.

Dan had less than forty-eight hours to get a few things done. He had to do some laundry, buy some nonperishable food he could keep in his camper shell, and he should see what he could find out about renting a room, apartment or small house. But first, he was due a beer. He might be able to accomplish more than one chore by stopping in that little bar in Virgin River. The guy who owned the place might know if there was anything to lease in the area. Just on principle, Dan didn't want to ask his new boss.

He walked into the bar and a couple of seconds later Jack came out from the back.

"Aw, Jesus Christ," Jack said. "You again."

Dan took off his hat and ran a hand through his hair. "Nice to see you, too."

"Aw, man—you're the one. Paul hired *you!*" Jack stepped up behind the bar, hands on his hips. "He said he hired a big guy who wore a funny-looking cowboy hat. Guess he doesn't know a Shady Brady when he sees one."

Dan just shook his head and gave a half smile. "You

hold some kind of grudge or something? What'd I ever do to you?"

"Just seems like when you're around, there's some kind of trouble."

"Yeah, and sometimes when I'm around, someone needs a lift. Didn't I pick you up off a dirt road in the middle of a wildfire? Jesus, some people have no gratitude. Can I get a beer or are you going to glare at me all day?"

"You got clean money this time? I don't take money that smells like fresh-cut cannabis."

"Didn't you get the word? I'm rehabilitated. I work construction, and that's all."

Jack lifted one eyebrow. "You went to jail?"

"For a while, yeah. Paul didn't tell you?" Jack shook his head. "How about that," Dan said. "He's a gentleman, too."

Jack pulled a cold Heineken out of the cooler, remembering the man's preferred brew, popped the cap and put a chilled glass on the bar. "Listen, he's a good man. He works hard, he's honest, he treats people right. He's a family man and has good friends around here. *Real* good friends. You better not screw with him." Jack nodded at the beer. "You need a Beam to go with that?" It was usually a boilermaker—Heineken and Jim Beam.

Dan smiled. "No thanks, this is fine. Look, buddy, all I want to do for your friend is construction. He gave me a job. I need a job." He put out his hand. "Dan Brady."

"Brady?" Jack asked with a laugh. "Had to be Brady."

"Interesting, huh?" He put the hat on the bar. "My signature."

Jack hesitated a moment before he put his hand out and shook Dan's. "Jack Sheridan."

"Yeah, I know. Now, can we move on? No reason we

have to go head to head every time we see each other. I'm
hoping to live here. At least for a while."

"Why here?" Jack asked suspiciously.

"I'm not likely to run into any old business associates in
here." He grinned. "The bartender won't take stinky money."

"You saying we understand each other?" Jack asked.

"I never had a problem understanding you, pal. Fact is,
if this were my bar, I wouldn't have taken my money either. But that's all in the past. And I need some information, if you have it."

"We'll see," Jack said.

"First of all, I'm bedding down in a camper shell and
it's fine, but I thought you might know of something to
rent around here."

Jack knew of a number of possibilities. Luke Riordan
had six cabins on the river, recently updated. There was a
couple in town who let out a room over their garage from
time to time. And Jack had his cabin in the woods. But
there was a vast difference between giving the man a job
and watching him work and inviting him to spend the night.
"Sorry," Jack said. "That's the thing about these mountain towns. Rentals and property sales come up so seldom,
Paul's company is doing well. People have to build from
scratch or remodel."

Dan watched Jack's eyes as he said this and he knew he
wasn't getting the whole truth. He didn't blame the guy.
It was going to take a while to prove he wasn't a low-life
criminal. He knew there'd be a price when he made the
decision to enter the marijuana trade. Right now he could
probably get assistance from someone still growing, but
Dan didn't want to go that route. He meant it when he said
that was in the past.

"Okay," Dan said, "I get that. And like I said, I'm not uncomfortable. I park at a rest stop at night. There's hot water and facilities. What are your hours of operation? I'm looking for an occasional hot meal and a packed lunch to take on the job."

"We can handle that for you. I'm usually here by six-thirty and Preacher lives on the property. He has the coffee on by six. We stay open till about nine at night, later if someone asks us to stay open. If you let Preacher know in advance, he can have a packed lunch ready for you in the early morning. If you need any—" The phone rang in the kitchen. "Give me a second. I'll be right back."

"Take your time," Dan said.

While Jack was gone, Dan wondered, just curiously, if the till was locked. Would Jack Sheridan leave him alone in the bar with a money drawer open? Did he trust him a little bit, or not at all? He wouldn't blame Jack if it took him some time to warm up to Dan—after all, this was the first hour of the first day they had a legitimate relationship. But Dan and Jack had history. Lots of history. And it wasn't all so good.

The first time they'd crossed paths, Dan had to get the local midwife to help him with a birth gone bad at an illegal grow site. That midwife was Jack's woman, and that whole episode went over like a turd in a punch bowl. The next time they came into contact, Dan had actually rear-ended that same midwife, and she was nine months pregnant. Again, not an auspicious beginning for their friendship.

But then he'd redeemed himself. Dan was in the area when some local men were searching for Preacher's wife, who'd been abducted by her homicidal ex-husband. It hadn't been Dan's plan to save the day, but the rest of these louts couldn't hack it and someone had to act. So Dan whopped the ex-husband on the head with his flashlight, knocked him cold and facilitated rescue.

Then there was the forest fire last summer. By the sheerest coincidence, Jack was sitting by the side of the road, hurt and dehydrated, as Dan was making his escape from a couple of lunatic growers. He picked Jack up and got him to safety.

Jack had apparently forgotten the good parts. Or decided they weren't good enough.

Shortly after that fire, there had been a warrant for Dan's arrest and that's when he'd turned himself in. By virtue of being highly cooperative, he'd only served six months of a three-year sentence. But still, he was now and forever an ex-con.

His beer was long gone. Whoever was on the phone must be important or Jack Sheridan wouldn't leave someone he didn't trust alone in his bar. Hell, he wouldn't even take his money if it smelled like—

His thought was cut off as Jack wandered back into the bar, his face white and his eyes unfocused. He clutched a piece of paper in his hand and he didn't look at Dan. He didn't go behind the bar, but stood just outside the kitchen door and stared blankly at nothing.

"Hey, man," Dan said. "Hey, Sheridan."

Jack didn't respond. He was a million miles away.

Dan got up and approached him warily. He looked weird, and weird could sometimes mean unstable. Unstable could mean anything.

"Sheridan? What's up, man?"

Jack's unfocused eyes slowly pivoted toward Dan. He

licked his dry lips, blinked a couple of times. "My boy, Rick," he said in a hoarse whisper.

"What?" Dan asked a little frantically. He'd had a boy of his own once. He'd probably worn those same eyes at the time. "What about your boy Rick?"

"Rick," he said, and lifted the piece of paper on which he'd scrawled notes. *Haditha, Al Anbar, hostile, critical, grenade, Landstuhl Medical Center, Germany.*

"Shit," Dan said. "Hey! Snap out of it! What happened?" He gave Jack a couple of pats on the cheeks, carefully. He didn't slap him; Jack might be reactive enough to coldcock him. "Whoa, buddy." He grabbed a bottle off the glass shelf behind the bar and tipped a shot over a glass. "Hey," he said, lifting the glass to Jack's lips. "Come on, burn it down, buddy. Get a grip."

Jack's shaking hand came up to grab the glass. He closed his eyes, threw back the shot and kept his eyes closed for a long moment. When he opened them, they were burning with a feral gleam.

"Something happen to your son, Jack?" Dan asked.

He shook his head. "Rick is *like* a son. He's in the Corps in Iraq."

"Yeah, I got that," Dan said, looking down at the paper. "Haditha, in Iraq. Landstuhl Medical. Been there."

"He's wounded. He might not make it." He shook his head. "I gotta think straight," he said to himself.

"Jesus," Dan said. He shot into the kitchen. "Anybody back here? Hey! Anybody back here?"

In a second a woman came through a door into the kitchen. He recognized her. She was the woman who'd been abducted—Paige. The last time he'd seen her, she was pregnant. "What is it?" she asked, confused.

"Gimme a hand out here, huh?"

She followed him into the bar. Jack was leaning against the cupboard behind the bar and a little sanity had crept back into his eyes.

"Somebody named Rick is hurt in Iraq," Dan said. "Can you find Jack's wife? Call her or something?"

"I'm all right," Jack said. But Paige bolted to the kitchen. "I just have to think. I was in his file as next of kin, probably because his grandmother is old and sick. Lance Corporal Sudder, they said. Took a grenade in Haditha. They got him out of surgery in Iraq and transported him to Germany, but he's not in good shape. They had to resuscitate twice and there will be more surgery," he said. "I have to think."

"Whew, have another one. Slow down the brain a little," Dan said, pouring a half a shot of something, he wasn't even sure what.

He handed it to Jack, and Jack threw it back. He shut his eyes hard. A single tear escaped and ran down his cheek. He opened his eyes again and looked at Dan through slits. "Black Label," he said hoarsely. "You act like you own the place."

Dan laughed out loud. "There you are. You on my planet now? What happened?"

"Gimme some water. I'm getting there."

Dan poured a water and Jack took a big drink. By the time he lowered the glass, Paige was standing in the kitchen doorway. Dan glanced at her.

"My husband has gone for some supplies," she said almost apologetically. "The kids are napping. I called Mel at home and told her to come right now. It's Saturday, the clinic isn't open."

"I'm okay now," Jack said. "Rick was wounded in Haditha. He's hurt real bad. Legs, head, torso, miscellaneous injuries. They airlifted him to Germany. I have to tell Lydie Sudder and Liz." He looked at Dan. "Liz is his girlfriend. Then I have to go."

"Go?" Dan asked.

"I'll have to get to Germany. This is my fault. Kid never would've gone into the Corps if it hadn't been for me and all my boys, here all the time, making him think it's just one big goddamn party. Shit." He swiveled his eyes to Dan's. "They said he's bad. He might not make it. That I should be prepared for that."

"You got phone numbers on this paper, buddy. Once your brain is engaged again, call back and get some more numbers so you can check in at Landstuhl, find out how he's doing. You had a big shock. You need to get stable."

"I need a cup of coffee," Jack said. "I had to think a second who Lance Corporal Sudder was. God, my worst nightmare."

"Sit down on a stool," Dan said. "I'll fix you a cup of coffee."

Jack looked at Paige. "Try to get Mel before she makes the drive. Tell her I'm just coming home in a little while."

Without a word, Paige went back into the kitchen to use the phone.

Jack sat up at the bar, a place he was never seen. In his usual place behind the bar stood Dan, serving up coffee in a big mug. He didn't ask any more questions and didn't need to.

"Ricky turned up when he was thirteen and I'd just started working on the bar. It was a shithole then. I slept in the rubble while I tried to get it straight. He was small back then—his face was covered with freckles and he couldn't shut his mouth for five minutes." Jack laughed and shook his head, remembering. "I let him hang around because his mom and dad were dead and he just had his grandma. And the goofy kid sucked me in. He's twenty now. No more freckles. Six-two. Strong…"

"Gotta remember he's strong, Jack," Dan said. "Don't give up on him."

"He shouldn't have done it, joined the Marines, but he was first in every training program, he was good…."

"Is," Dan corrected. "Get it together, man."

"*Is* good," Jack repeated. He took a deep drink of hot coffee. "I don't know what I can tell Lydie and Liz…."

"You tell them he's hurt bad, in the hospital, and you're going there. That's what you tell them. You don't give anyone permission to give up. If the worst happens, then you'll tell them the worst. You don't tell them the worst before it happens."

"You should've seen him, man," Jack said, drinking more coffee, smiling. "I taught him to hold a hammer, fish, shoot. He was such a little nerd at first, all gangly and pimples and that damn giggling, I thought he might stay that way forever. But he grew up fast—turned out to be a little faster in the saddle than was good. Whew. I felt like a father to that kid—"

"Feel," Dan corrected. "Feel like a father…"

"I do, that's a fact."

Paige popped her head back into the bar. "She's already on her way, Jack."

"Aw, we shouldn't have bothered her."

"She needs to be here," Dan said. Paige withdrew again, leaving them alone. "She'll go with you to see the grandmother, the girlfriend. Then you'll go see Rick. You think you're together enough to do that? To go to Germany? Because if you're nuts or in some flashback, you can't chance it. It wouldn't be a good idea."

Jack took a drink from his coffee cup, then slowly raised his eyes. "I won't let him down. I think I was in shock for a minute."

"Yeah," Dan said.

Dan stood behind the bar while Jack sat as a customer. Dan refilled his coffee mug, then pulled another Heineken out of the cooler, but this time he drank it from the bottle. For a few minutes they talked quietly about Rick and what he meant to Jack. About the letter not so long ago that described how dangerous it had been in Haditha lately.

The sound of boots on the bar's porch brought Jack off the stool and toward the door. He pulled it open and there stood Mel, her eyes wide and her mouth open slightly. "Ricky?" she asked in a breath.

"Wounded in Iraq. He's had surgery to stabilize him, but I'm not even sure on what. He had leg, torso and head injuries and has been airlifted to Germany, to a military hospital there. Mel—"

"Are you all right?" she asked him.

"I'm coming around. It knocked the wind out of me. Where are the kids?"

"Mike came over from next door—they're sleeping."

"I have to tell Lydie and Liz."

"First Lydie," Mel said. "Then we'll go home and while you pack, I'll get on the computer and find you plane tickets. Then we'll go to Eureka to see Liz. We'll go in two cars, I'll take the kids with me. When you head for the airport, I'll bring the kids home. Unless you need me with you in Germany. Thing is, I don't have the kids on my passport.

Shit, how dumb was that, with Rick in Iraq! Why didn't I take care of that? Well, maybe I should come. I can fly to L.A., get the passport handled in a day, and—"

"Mel, stop. You're not dragging the kids to Germany," Jack said. "Come on, let's get going." He held the door for her.

As she was leaving, she looked over her shoulder at the man behind the bar.

"I'll—ah—leave a few bucks on the bar," Dan said. "And help the lady in the kitchen till her husband gets back, if she needs me."

"Don't worry about the few bucks, unless you want to pitch in for that Black Label you threw down my throat," Jack said with a weak smile.

"Thank you," Mel said.

"Hey—" Dan shrugged "—glad I was here."

Jack started to leave, but then he stopped again and looked at Dan. "The thing that did it, the thing that knocked me out for a while… When I told the sergeant who called that I'd get right over to Germany, he asked me if I didn't want to wait until Rick was out of surgery, until they knew his condition, in case he didn't make it. And I said no, I wasn't waiting. I was either going to see him or bring him home. Just thinking that? It put me in shock."

"Well, stop thinking it now," Dan said. "Get going. Remember, he's strong."

"Yeah," Jack said. "Yeah."

"Jack. Remember, you're strong, too."

Lydie reacted exactly as Mel expected. She gasped, got teary and twisted her hands, asking questions for which Jack had no answers. But then she straightened her neck and stiffened her spine and began to pray. "I'll be all right," she said bravely. "When you get there, tell Ricky his grandma is fine and praying for him. He worries about me too much. I don't want him to worry when he should be working on getting better."

"I'll come by and check on you later today," Mel said. "Don't get upset and forget to test your blood, take your insulin and eat. Promise me."

"I promise. Now go. Don't waste your time here. He needs you."

Liz was another story. After booking a flight and packing a duffel, Mel and Jack drove to Eureka in separate vehicles. Liz met them at the door before they were halfway down the walk. "Is he alive?" she asked before they even told her why they were there. Her eyes were as big as hubcaps and frightened. "Is he *alive*?"

They couldn't even get in the door. "He was wounded, Liz," Jack said. "He's seriously hurt, but he's in the hospital. They airlifted him out of Iraq and he should be in Germany soon. I'm going to see him, and when I get there, I'll call you immediately and tell you his condition. I'll—"

"Take me," she said, whirling around and fleeing back into the house. Over her shoulder she said, "I knew all day. I knew. I couldn't get him off my mind and I was worried all day. I worry a lot, but not like lately. I have a passport and—"

"Liz! No!" Mel said. "Now stop, honey. Let Jack—"

"No, if Jack won't let me go with him, I'll go by myself. I've never been on a plane, but I'll figure it out. I have to go, I have to be there for him, I have to—"

"Maybe she should," Jack said quietly.

Mel tugged on his sleeve to bring his ear to her lips.

"Jack, what if you get there and it's the worst case? You shouldn't have to deal with all this."

"It's not going to be worst case," Jack said. "And if it helps Rick... Maybe it'll help Rick." He looked at Liz. "You have a computer?"

"Of course."

"You pack. Mel will get you a ticket. You have to hurry. We have to drive to Redding."

"I knew all day long," she whispered. "I have almost a thousand dollars saved."

"Where's the computer?"

"In here. In my bedroom. Will it cost more than a thousand dollars? Because I could borrow some from my aunt Connie."

Jack took the baby out of Mel's arms, hanging on to both children, freeing her. "Put it on the card, Mel. Get her a ticket on my flight if you can." Mel just looked up at him with a large question in her eyes. "It's his girl. He loves her. And she knew all day. There's a bond. He'd probably rather have her there than me. Besides, we have to get it straight, how you act around someone who's been critically wounded. Liz is up to it."

"Liz, will your mom be okay with this? You'll miss a bunch of school."

"I'll call her. She's got her cell phone. It doesn't matter—I'll make up school. This is Rick. I have to be there with him."

"Liz," Mel said. "What if it's terrible? What if he's not okay?"

She threw a soft suitcase on the bed and looked at Mel with clear, determined eyes. "Then I have to be there even more."

Mel sighed and sat down at the computer.

* * *

By the time Mel left Jack and Liz to begin their long journey to Frankfurt, her kids were just about psychotic from waking too early from naps, being hungry, having been transported all over the place. It would make sense to just go home and try to settle them, but she couldn't. She had to speak to Connie, Liz's aunt. She should tell Preacher and Paul, Marines who felt close to Rick. She should tell Cameron to look out for Lydie, since he was living at the clinic and Lydie was just down the street.

And after that she would go home to a lonely house and two fussy kids. It wasn't typical for Mel to feel totally frazzled, but she did. She loved Rick as much as Jack did.

She went first to Connie, but didn't stay long. Then to the bar where Preacher already had the news from his wife. He wondered if he should close the bar. "The word is going to travel," Mel said. "And we're not going to hear anything for twenty-four hours or so. Stay busy. Everyone loves Ricky. If it's not your fanciest dinner tonight, no one will complain."

"My dinners tend to get fancier when there's trouble...."

Next, Mel checked on Lydie, who was doing remarkably well under the circumstances, but by the time she got to the clinic to talk to Cameron, her kids were screaming and tears were running down her cheeks.

"Hey, hey, hey," he said, coming down the stairs in his jeans and T-shirt. "What's going on here?" he asked. He immediately took David off her hands so they could each comfort one child.

"God," she said, trying to sniff back emotion. "You've heard us talk about Rick, right?"

"Sure. Is he all right?"

"He is not all right. He was critically wounded in Iraq.

Jack and Rick's girlfriend, Liz, have rushed off to Germany, where he's been airlifted for surgery. My kids have been slung around all afternoon so we could get the two of them on their way, and I just realized I haven't let myself feel it yet. He's like Jack's boy. He's like *my* boy. And these two are absolutely insane. I need to rock and feed and tell more people who are close to Ricky and I—" She started to cry. "I'm so worried and scared I could just die."

Cameron put an arm around her shoulders. "Come on, Mel. Let's rock and feed and cry if you need to. I'll make you tea or hot milk or—"

"Tea or hot milk?" she asked through her tears. "Great."

"I have a beer in the refrigerator," he offered, wiping her cheeks with his thumb.

"Better," she sniffed. "I came for a reason, not just to cry. I didn't plan that part. Lydie Sudder, down the street, that's Rick's grandma. His only living family. And she's—"

"I know all about Lydie. Diabetic, failing vision, high blood pressure, and her heart—"

"I just want you to be alert to her. It's not as though pounding on her door at two in the morning to see if she's all right is going to help. But I checked on her and told her to call one of us if she had any problems related to this scary news. I told her to call a pager. I can't go home yet. I still have to call on Vanni and Paul."

He led her into the clinic's kitchen and deftly pulled a couple of the prepared bottles she kept there out of the refrigerator. Emma was almost a year old, David two, and both of them were happy with the cold milk. Then he handed Mel a beer with a smile.

"How about dinner for these two?"

"Right now they're just tired to the bone and need some calm. But I can't sit around here too long."

Cam had David in his arms while Mel held Emma. Both children settled down quickly with their bottles and some warm, calm arms holding them. Mel sniffled a couple of times, but having her children under control and a quiet place to sit calmed even her.

"You should have seen Liz," she said softly. "She's never been on a plane before, much less to Europe. She packed in ten minutes. She kept asking me questions while I was trying to get her a ticket on the computer. She'd ask, 'Hair dryer?' and I'd answer yes. 'Cold or warm there?' and I said cold. Ten minutes and she was ready to go. She's loved him since she was fourteen."

"Do you know anything about his injuries?" Cam quietly asked.

"Not a lot, no." She repeated what Jack had told her. "I wanted to go with him, but I have a passport problem and two small children. I still wanted to go. In the end, Liz went. Seventeen-year-old Liz. And I was jealous."

He laughed at her. "It was probably good that she went, if it'll help the boy."

"That's what Jack said. But suddenly I feel abandoned. I know it's stupid, but I still felt it."

"It's not stupid, Mel. It's the real deal. Thing is, there's just no help for it. Why don't you leave the kids with me while you make your calls to deliver the news."

She shook her head and laughed hollowly. "That makes perfect sense, but because of this I just can't be separated from my kids. I have to have them near."

"I see," Cameron said. "Tell you what—I'll follow you out to Haggerty's, then to your place. I'll help you with the kids, get them fed and settled. We'll make a sandwich. And when all is calm and quiet, I'll take off." He grinned. "I didn't have plans for tonight anyway. And I'm wearing the pager."

"I have baby food," she said. "I don't know what grown-up food I have."

He laughed again. "You're hopeless. Fine. I'll make us a couple of sandwiches here, pack them, and we'll go get the job done. Do you have chips?"

"I don't know," she answered.

"Is Jack completely in charge of the food at your house?"

"Pretty much," she admitted, taking a drink of her beer. She snuggled Emma, calmed down, sniffed back her tears, and thanks to Cameron's offer of help, felt a lot better about the rest of her mission.

"I have chips," he said.

She smiled at him. She'd spent so much time being grateful to Cameron, the doctor, for practicing medicine in her town, she hadn't realized how great Cameron, the person, really was. "You've turned into my good friend," she said. "Like Doc."

"That's very nice," he replied. "Thank you."

It was a very long night and day before the phone rang at the Sheridan house and Mel lunged for it. She said hello and heard Jack's gravelly voice. "Baby."

"Jack! What do you know?"

"He's going to be all right. He cracked his head, lost a spleen, is scraped up all to hell, but the injuries are apparently not life threatening at this point."

"Was he burned?" Mel asked, thinking about a grenade and the heat.

"No. Pitched through the air, though. But not burned."

"Oh, thank God!"

"Mel, he lost his leg."

"Was the damage too severe? Was it inoperable?" she asked.

"He lost it in the explosion. There wasn't a chance. Losing the leg was what almost killed him. He lost a lot of blood."

"Oh, poor Rick. Where'd they amputate? Above or below the knee?"

"Above. But they saved a lot of thigh and femur. He's still in recovery. We haven't seen him yet, but he's going to be all right, Mel. Mel," he said, then paused. "This is rough. We're not family. Liz isn't a spouse and I'm not his father. We're not getting a lot of help, if you know what I mean."

"I'm not sure I do."

"I don't know if they're going to let us bring him home. He might be transferred to some military medical facility for rehab. If I was his father, I could probably bring him home and take him to the nearest hospital for rehab. If I'd just worked with Lydie to adopt him legally before all this—"

She heard the regret in his voice. Jack felt as if he'd let Rick down. "Jack, just see Rick, let him know you're there, find out how he's doing medically, with pain and trauma. Decisions about where he's going next will come when they come."

"I know."

"And Jack? You might want to sleep. I hear the exhaustion in your voice. You have to be strong for Rick. Very strong. You can't cave in to things like pity, worry…"

"I'll be strong."

"How's Liz holding up?"

"Better than me. She was so relieved to hear he's going to be all right, she started to cry and laugh at the same time. She doesn't quite get it, that she's not getting him back right away. And when she does, he won't be the same."

"You both just need to see him. He's not going to be himself for a while." She paused. "I wish I was there with you, Jack. I could help. And I miss you so much."

"Are the kids okay?" he asked.

"They're fine, Jack. We're all fine. Just missing you, that's all. But you're where you have to be."

"Really, if I could just get him home, with our family, I'd feel so much better."

"That will come." She took a deep breath. "He needs to finish this journey. He needs the rehab, a prosthetic leg. Some counseling."

"Yeah," Jack said. "Yeah, I know."

"Would you like me to tell people? Or would you like to make calls yourself?"

"Will you do it, Mel? Lydie, Connie and the boys? If you can call Preach, Mike and Paul, they can call the squad. Are you up to it?"

"Of course, darling. I'll make the calls right now. Everyone is waiting. Will you do something for me?"

"Anything I can."

"When you see Rick, please tell him I love him. And I'm proud of him. Tell him I'll do anything in my power to help him. And tell him... No, it's too soon for that...."

"For what?"

She took a breath. "When I lived in Los Angeles, I worked with a doctor in emergency for almost a year before I learned he wore a prosthetic leg. He was quick, confident, strong and very talented. It's not only possible, it's probable. It's just that… I'm sure getting there's a real bitch."

Blessedly, Mel had a very slow Monday morning in the clinic. Cameron had a couple of walk-ins, but Mel busied herself with paperwork and the children. It was lunchtime when a familiar guy walked in. He pulled off his Shady Brady inside the door. "Hi," he said.

She rose from the desk behind the reception counter. "Hi. How are you?"

"Fine. Good. Um, I was just wondering if you'd heard anything from your husband. About the kid. Rick."

"Yes," she said, walking toward him. "He's going to be all right. He has multiple injuries, all treatable. He's got head injuries that aren't a threat, he lost a spleen, is scraped up real bad but not burned, and he lost a leg in the explosion."

The man's eyes grew wide and shocked at that last. Then, when he collected himself, he asked, "Above or below?"

She knew exactly what he meant and wondered about his association with amputees. "Above the knee. Sounds like you know something about that."

"In fact, I was sent to Landstuhl after an injury and got cozy with a lot of guys who lost limbs. Below the knee was easy compared to— Well, you know."

"He's got a lot of rehab ahead, but the outlook is potentially positive. He's safe for now."

"Hmm," he said, dropping his gaze, shaking his head. "Good. He made it through. Poor kid. What did your husband say—that he's twenty years old?"

"Just barely. And the sweetest kid you'll ever meet. Nice of you to inquire."

"I've been thinking about that whole scene. Shook old Jack up pretty good. I haven't seen him very often over the past few years, but I've never seen him shook up like that."

"Rick's pretty special. Listen, speaking of the past few years—I think about that woman and baby a lot."

"Listen," he said. "I'm sorry I had to lie to you, but that baby had nothing to do with me. I knew about the woman— I knew her man left her out there, ready to pop. I checked on her a couple of times and knew she had a sketchy past, like a lot of us, and she refused to go to a clinic. She said it would be all right, but I found her in a mess."

"Why didn't you tell me the truth? Why'd you let me think it was yours?"

He shrugged. "I didn't know if you'd help otherwise. And I did get her on a bus. If she didn't run out on that sister, they were willing to take her in, help her. Sorry, that was about all I could do."

"You could have done nothing," Mel said. She smiled. "If you'd done nothing, it would've been a disaster. She and the baby—"

"Yeah, well, I gave it a shot. Glad it worked out. Hope things work out for Rick, too."

"So how come you're around here twice in the same week?" she asked him.

It brought a grin out of him and she remembered, way back to that scary night, when he'd said, *Tough little broad, arentcha*? He had grinned just like that. "I got a job with the construction company. Haggerty's."

"A real job?" she asked, eyes wide. "Where they take taxes out of your check and everything?"

"And everything," he said, smiling.

"You live around here?" she asked.

He chuckled. "Exactly. I'm staying in a camper until something comes up for rent. If you hear of anything…"

"Sure," she said. "If I hear of something, I'll let Paul know."

"Thanks. You take care." He turned to go.

"I never did get a name."

He turned back. "Dan," he said. "Dan Brady."

Four

Rick was just about twenty-four hours post surgical when he was allowed a visitor. Jack and Liz had to negotiate. "Let me go," Jack said firmly. "Let me see what we're dealing with. He's hurting, he's drugged, the prognosis is good from our perspective, but he lost a limb and that's gonna be hard."

"I just want to see him, touch him, that's all," she said. "I don't care about anything but that he's alive."

"Please," Jack said. "I know how you're feeling right now, but I've been down this road before and wounded Marines are unpredictable. Sometimes they're just grateful to be alive, sometimes they can be real loose canons. If he's unstable and angry, let him unload that on me first."

"Will you tell him I love him?"

"Sure, honey. I've only got ten minutes with him. Let me get the lay of the land. If he's mentally stable, you'll go in next."

She bit her lip and nodded reluctantly; he could just imagine how crappy that made her feel, but Jack couldn't be sure how Rick was going to take to either one of them being here. Logically, he should want his closest people near him. But getting blown up and waking up in a hospital ward could skew someone's sense of logic something fierce.

It was a small ward, only six beds. But six where there should only be four. Hospitals catering to the war-wounded were crowded, even with the number of wounded decreased. He spotted Rick right off—a white bandage wrapped around his head, his face cut and scraped, a bandaged stump where there had been a right leg. He wore green scrub pants, the right leg cut off, no shirt and his sheet was kicked away. There was a surgical bandage on his side; the spleenectomy, Jack assumed. An IV dangled above him; Jack hoped there was plenty of morphine in it.

He looked around; green walls, white linoleum floors, that hospital smell of disinfectant and medicine. There was a guy in a circular bed with pins in his skull, a guy with a thigh-high cast on one leg, another sitting up in bed who looked for all the world to be uninjured, though there was a wheelchair beside his bed, a young man with his arm in an elevated cast level with his shoulder and a man flat on his back, in traction. And Rick. It was clearly an orthopedics ward. Jack nodded at the other patients as he entered and they returned the nod, grim-faced. Right away he knew, they weren't angry—it was that Rick was the newest patient and they were waiting to see what happened next.

He stared down at the boy and saw the tears on his cheeks and his mouth parted in a dark slit as he took breaths slowly and deeply.

"Rick?" he said softly.

Rick's eyes opened. "Jack," he said in a whisper.

"You have a lot of pain, son?"

He winced and nodded, squeezing out another tear.

"Did they tell you about your condition?" Jack asked him.

He nodded. "When did it happen?" he asked in a hoarse whisper.

"'Bout a day ago. They got you right up here. You're out of Iraq, you're in Germany. You know where you are, son?"

Rick gritted his teeth and nodded.

"Remember anything?" Jack asked.

"I... Ah... I remember someone screaming at me. He kept saying don't you give up, don't you quit. Fucker. I ever see him again, I'm going to kill him."

Jack felt himself almost laugh; at least he had fight in him.

"I brought Liz."

Rick's eyes came open instantly. "No," he said in a breath. "No."

"If I hadn't brought her, she was going to try to make it on her own. She needs to see you're okay, Rick."

"I don't want her here! Just get her out of here!"

"Listen," Jack said, leaning over the bed. "I could no more leave her behind than—"

As Jack put a hand down on the mattress beside Rick, Rick let go a howl of pain that nearly shook the walls. Jack jumped back in shock and fear, but Rick just kept screaming and flailing around. The nurse was beside the bed instantly. "I didn't touch anything," Jack said apologetically.

The nurse ignored him and just talked to Rick. "Deep breaths, I'm upping the drip a little. Deep breaths, hang on, it'll kick in right away. Come on now, just breathe." Still, it took a moment for Rick to calm down. The howling ended with some soft whimpering that finally gave way to a couple of moans.

The nurse turned toward Jack. "Did you sit on the bed?" she asked.

"No," he said. "I leaned a hand on the bed, but I wasn't anywhere near him."

"Phantom pain," she said. "You probably leaned your hand where the leg used to be. It's spooky, but it's the real deal. He felt it and it hurt."

"Jesus."

"Better if you just don't touch anything. The first forty-eight hours are real rocky, but it's going to get better. Is this your first experience with an amputee?"

"Yeah," Jack said weakly.

"I have some pamphlets. Why don't you take a couple of hours to look through the literature. I think he's going to rest for a while now. I just gave him a nice boost."

Jack followed her to the nurses' station, glad to see someone was willing to be helpful to him there. When Liz saw them leave the ward together, she was immediately tailing them. Jack turned and asked her to give him just a minute with the nurse and continued on, leaving her behind. The nurse handed him some pamphlets and he asked, "You take care of a lot of these guys?"

"Full-time," she said with a little nod of her head.

"Help me out with something here," Jack said. "I just told him I brought his girl and he freaked out. Told me to get her out of here. Right up to the injury, there was no problem between him and the girl."

She frowned. "Reactions like that usually come later, after the reality settles in. This soon after the injury, patients are just being stabilized, they're struggling with the pain and trying to get a fix on what their condition is. His response might be connected to pain and drugs. But later... Not too unusual, I'm sorry to say. Some men and women adjust so well, it's astonishing. Sometimes the new amputee is very needy, desperate for confirmation that he's still worth loving. Sometimes he doesn't even want to chance it, pushing loved ones away. There are a lot of psychological and emotional adjustments to go along with the physical. Everything from the pain and fear to self-esteem issues. You're going to have to learn about all this, and be patient."

"How long does that go on?" Jack asked. "The adjustment?"

"Purely individual. But you should see what you can learn about this for now. And maybe you can help get the young lady through it?"

"Aw crap, what am I going to tell her?"

"I always recommend you start with the truth. This isn't an easy time for anyone. Try to watch those expectations. But you could tell her most of what the corporal is feeling is beyond his control. He'll need help getting through it. And yet, he might resist help. It's a contradictory process for some."

"When are you going to get him up, out of bed?"

"We had him up, briefly. He didn't like it. He's still in a lot of pain."

"God, I need my wife here." In fact, he couldn't remember a time he needed her quite this bad. "Thank you," he said. "I'll look through this stuff right away."

He turned to go back to Liz. The second he noticed she didn't seem to be where he'd left her, he heard the screaming. *"Get out! Just get out of here! I don't want you here! Go away! Get out!"*

"Oh, Jesus," he muttered, running for the ward. He stopped in the doorway and what he saw emptied him out inside. Liz stood beside Rick's bed, her hands over her face, her beautiful long hair hanging down like a curtain, her shoulders quaking with her sobs while Rick nearly came off the bed, screaming at her. Jack moved quickly, put his arms around her and pulled her away. When they were back in the hall he held her against him protectively while she cried. He'd never felt so helpless in his life. It almost felt as though if he crouched down, he could scoop up the pieces of her broken heart off the floor.

The same nurse was beside them again. "I'm going to give him something to calm him down a little bit. And I'm going to tell him you've left the hospital for now. Let's give him some space. Like I said, the first forty-eight hours are real rocky."

"No shit," Jack muttered. "Come on, honey," he said, pulling Liz down the hall and away.

Jack took Liz as far as the main floor of the hospital where he found a quiet corner in the waiting room. He just held her hand while she cried. She whispered *why why why* breathlessly, sobbing almost uncontrollably. It was a long time before she could stop long enough to ask, "Why did he tell me to go away? Why?"

Jack squeezed her hand. "We're not going to talk about what just happened until you calm down and we're out of here. We need quiet. Privacy. Take your time."

"I just don't understand," she whimpered.

"Lots of things are going to be hard to understand," he said, giving her hair a stroke. "And if you think I have any inside track on this, you're going to be disappointed." He showed her the pamphlets the nurse had given him. "We have some reading to do, and some talking to do. Then we need food and sleep. Can't stay on top of this emotional roller coaster without those two things."

An hour later they were seated in a restaurant eating bratwurst, potatoes and kraut. Jack was having a very tall beer, and Liz, a glass of water with her meal. She picked at her food, her stomach upset. She seemed to be barely holding it together and every so often a tear would escape and roll pathetically down her cheek. Her fingers continually wandered to that diamond pendant necklace Rick had given her, the promise diamond.

"I'm not sure the best way to handle this," Jack said. "Here's my idea. See if you agree with it. I'll go back tomorrow and spend some time with him. I won't mention what happened until he turns the corner on the pain a little more. We can't take too much personally while he's on such heavy drugs. Might be he comes out of that drug haze and feels a little more in control."

"And if he doesn't? What if he won't see me?" she asked, and as she spoke, her eyes filled up with tears again.

"Like I said, we'll get through the influence of anesthesia and pain drugs before we revisit the issue. We can't really judge his feelings while he's on that morphine planet. But he'll get used to the morphine pretty quick and it won't make him insane anymore. Then he'll see you. He will. The nurse said this sort of thing happens a lot, but usually later on. Some patients get real clingy, need a lot of reassurance that they're still lovable, some actually have such an inferiority complex about their body image, they push loved ones away. Like they don't deserve love even when it's offered."

"Why couldn't he be a clingy one?" she said softly.

Jack actually laughed. "Rick? We both know why. Because he's too damn proud for his own good, that's why. Liz, honey, there's no reason Rick can't have a completely full, productive life. There's almost nothing a guy with a prosthetic limb can't do. I've seen news stories on guys with fake legs running marathons. And Rick will learn, he will. He'll do whatever he wants…eventually. But if I know my boy, he's going to be a giant pain in the ass getting there."

She laughed through some tears.

"Mel told me this story. She said it was too soon to tell Rick, and she didn't know the half of that. She said she worked with a doctor in the emergency room back in L.A. for a year before she realized he had a prosthetic leg. She never did say how she found out. I don't know what you know about big-city trauma centers, but those docs have to be fast and strong and steady. And I don't know how well you know Mel, but she's demanding as all hell. If she worked with a doc who didn't pull his weight in any way, she'd be all over him." He took a drink of his beer. "Yeah, she didn't know about the guy's leg for a year. What does that tell you?"

"There's hope?"

"You bet. But, Liz, it isn't going to be easy on Rick. He's dealing with way more than just the leg—he's been to war. And if it's not easy on Rick, it's not going to be easy on us. What do you think of my idea? We give him a little time to settle down? Get through the drug haze before we push on him? We don't need another crazy outburst."

"I guess that's okay," she said. "I'm sorry, Jack. I'm so disappointed."

"Aw, honey, I know. Believe me, I never saw that coming."

"I'm sorry I couldn't help by being here. I thought he'd be glad to know how much I love him."

"I bet when we're through the worst of this, he will be."

She was shaking her head. "I don't know."

"My idea?" Jack pushed. "You'll have some time on your hands. I don't think you should try to see him until the timing is better. Not just for him, honey. For you, too."

"But I want to go with you. I won't go in his room until he says it's okay, but I want to be there. In case."

"You sure the temptation won't be too strong?" he asked her. "Because I think until we get a little stability here, you shouldn't even peek in the room."

"I'll stay in the waiting room downstairs. I brought my backpack with school stuff. And they have a TV—I saw an English news program on it. I'll try to be patient. I promise."

"Good for you. You done eating? We can share this reading material. And I want you to get some rest so you can deal with these ups and downs."

"Okay," she said with a small smile.

Two hours later, Jack stepped outside the hotel and used his cell phone to call Mel. It was nine hours earlier in California and she was at the clinic. When she answered, he just said, "Baby."

"Jack! Did you see him?"

He took a breath. "Mel, he's going to recover. But it was the worst experience of my life. I shouldn't have brought Liz. He took her apart. Ripped her heart out."

Over his thirty-five-year military career, Walt Booth had seen hundreds of injured soldiers. He'd made dozens and dozens of goodwill visits to hospitals; he'd attended many wheelchair-basketball games and races. He had nothing but respect and admiration for the men and women who turned their physical disabilities into productive lives.

But something about Rick Sudder's injuries got to him.

He didn't even know Rick that well. It was probably all about the timing. Walt's son was army now. Rick and Tom were only a year apart in age and had become friends. Sometimes when Walt thought about Rick coming home with one leg, he got confused in his mind and pictured Tom. He hated that. It cost him sleep. There was no logical reason for it. Tom was tucked away at West Point, working his butt off, studying day and night, not in a war zone.

He knew he was affected, that it showed on him. Vanni had asked him if he was all right and he admitted the truth—thinking about that strong and vital young man dealing with an injury like this was working on him, grieving him. Muriel had asked him what was wrong in one of their phone calls and he laid it out for her—Jack and Liz had gone to Germany to be there for Rick when he was waking up after surgery and he worried about all of them. "This war is a hellish business," he had said. "And, Muriel, there's always a war somewhere. That was my life's work, staying on top of the wars. And Rick, he's such a nice young man. So proud and dedicated. I hate to think of his suffering."

She'd been so lovely in her response, consoling him, praising his sensitivity. But what he really wanted was to wrap his arms around her and hold her close. He had no idea how long it would be until he could do that again.

They didn't even talk every day. When he called her, he almost always got her voice mail; when she called him, it was usually very early or very late. Sometimes she called him while she was on the treadmill, killing two birds with one stone, and the huffing and puffing was too annoying for him to listen to.

He soldiered on. It was what he was trained to do. The bar in Virgin River was a little sparse and quiet these days, but he dropped by to see if there was any news from Jack. Sometimes he had dinner with Vanni, Paul and Abby at their house. And he tended Muriel's horses twice a day, letting them into the corral after feeding them, mucking their stalls, brushing them down, checking their hooves.

On this particular night, he ate a sandwich and headed for Muriel's with the dogs in tow. They seemed to love going home. He drove up at dusk and noticed there was an old car parked in front of the porch and all the lights were on inside the big house. The dogs immediately started barking at the front door. He thought about calling Mike V to tell him Muriel's had been broken into, but instead he fetched a pitchfork from the barn and used his key to let himself in. He knew the dogs would let him know where the intruder was.

They ran right up the stairs. He followed at a distance and then heard a squeal he definitely recognized.

He appeared in the bedroom doorway, pitchfork in hand, clad in jeans and a plaid flannel shirt, and looked at the woman in the bed. She was struggling to keep the sheet over her naked breasts, laughing, petting her dogs. "Well!" she said. "About time! Maybe I should get a better caretaker. I thought you'd never get here."

"What in the world are you doing here?" he asked, leaning the pitchfork up against the wall.

She grinned at him and pushed her dogs off the bed. "Bringing comfort and joy."

"How long have you been here?"

"A couple of hours. Completely naked and getting cold. Did you close the front door?"

"I don't think so," he said, a state of shock overwhelming him.

"Then, Walt, what say you close it. So these dogs don't have free run of the property."

"Muriel," he said. "Holy damn, are you a sight for sore eyes."

"So are you," she said softly. "Now, get that door closed for me. Hmm?"

He grinned largely. "You got it."

"Thank God. I'm in no condition to take care of that. But I am in a condition."

He was downstairs and back upstairs in short order. He closed the Labs out of the bedroom and stood at the side of the bed. He looked down at her and his eyes glowed. "You look a little different," he said.

"I've had my hair colored several times. They don't think I have it right yet." She held out her hands. "Nails. I have nails again. And I'm wearing makeup for a change. But I have the same body. I don't know if that'll come as good news or bad."

He grinned at her. Then he pulled off his boots and clothes, dropped everything on the floor and crawled in beside her, taking her into his arms. "Good news," he said. "God, Muriel. I've missed you."

"I've missed you more, I think."

"We can't even have a goddamn conversation."

"Insane, isn't it? I hate the schedule. But I tried to tell you—it's not about being a star, it's about working your tail off. There's never a break."

"And yet you're here."

"I had a small fit. I'm entitled once in a while. I know all about when and how to do that, you know. A couple of our wannabe stars were missing all sorts of fittings and readings and I finally said, Hey, I have property, animals and a *boyfriend* up north and I'm not feeling happy about wasting time here, waiting around for people to get it together. I need a day off! So one of the producers rounded up an airplane and gave me a little time off."

"Is there a Lear at that little airport?"

"There is."

"Whose car do you have parked outside?"

"Something left in long-term parking by an airport-tower guy who's out of town. I have permission."

"And how much time do you have?"

"A night and long morning. I'm sorry. I'm not that good at tantrums. But I wanted to see you." She ran her fingers through his silver hair. "How are you, Walt? I've been a little worried."

"I'm better now." He lifted the sheets. "I'm getting better by the second." He ran a big hand down over her shoulder, her breast, all the way to her hip. "You're the same here. Your skin may be softer." And then he covered her mouth with his. He kissed her deeply and thoroughly. "I haven't fed the horses yet."

"I fed them. I didn't want us to be interrupted," she said. "Ohhhh. I'm really glad I showed up. Do you have any idea how wonderful your hands feel on me?"

"Tell me," he said, kissing her cheeks, neck, shoulder, breast.

"Mmm. Well, almost as good as your lips…."

He chuckled. "Muriel, did you just come back for sex?"

"Certainly not," she whispered, her eyes closed, her body straining toward his. "I'd like to talk." She sighed deeply. "After."

He laughed at her again. "If I'd said that to you, you

would have been highly insulted. But a man is almost never offended to learn he's needed for sex."

"Oh, good," she said, smiling. "You don't mind, then."

"Mind? I'm flattered." He positioned himself over her. "I hope you're not in a big hurry. I'm planning to take my sweet old time."

"Jesus," she whispered. "Thank you, Jesus."

"Muriel," he laughed. "Thank *me*."

"Let's see what you've got first. Then we'll see if thanks are in order."

He didn't laugh, though he thought she was funny. Instead, he worked her body. He stroked her, kissed her, licked her, entered her and rode her, remembering those wonderful sounds she made when she was getting close. When she came apart on him, boiling over in a fantastic climax, he gave her a moment to thoroughly enjoy herself, and when she was no longer preoccupied with her own pleasure, he took his. He wanted her to feel it deep inside her. And she moaned deliciously, holding on to him, kissing and sucking his shoulder.

With his hands on her soft bottom, her lips on his neck and shoulder, he struggled to catch his breath. She probably wouldn't understand how much he had needed a connection like this with her. He'd been lonely in general, but specifically for Muriel, the woman he'd begun to think of as his other half. Talking to her, touching her, got him past the edge of despair, but it was like this, deep inside her, loving her man to woman, that fed the part of him that was so hungry.

"Thank you, Walt," she whispered. And he laughed.

"I think I can squeak in a couple more of those before the landing gear goes up on that Lear."

"Oh, my heavens...."

He rolled onto his side and took her with him, holding her against his body. "Is this normal?" he asked her. "Are we supposed to be having wild, insanely satisfying sex at our age?"

"Yes," she said.

"Someone should have told me," he said. "I'd have taken better care of myself."

"You're very well cared for. I have no brain left. You drove it out of me. I can just see the tabloid headlines. The famous Muriel St. Claire found with her brains screwed out in her old farmhouse. Only one suspect comes to mind...."

"I thought people, especially men, petered out as they got older...."

"Didn't you have regular checkups in the army? Didn't your doctor ever ask you how things were working?"

"Yeah," he said. "My heart, my ears, my eyes—"

"What about that god-awful prostate exam I've heard tales about?" she asked.

"Yup. That was part of the drill. No pun intended. But the closest he ever got to my sex life was asking me if I could still pee over a jeep." He heard her giggle. He ran his hand along the hair at her temple, brushing it back. "I needed to be with you like this, Muriel. For a while after you left I was afraid I'd imagined the whole thing—our relationship. Thank you for coming back to me. I was starved for your body, your laugh."

She locked her fingers together behind his neck. "I know," she said. "I wanted to be there for you. But I have to be honest, darling. I needed you. Just as damn much."

"What's it like? What you're doing now?"

"The movie?"

"The movie."

"It's barely begun. We haven't started filming, but for me it's well under way. It's like giving birth—it's a creation for me. I become another woman. I feel her, channel her, give her the space to grow. And when we're finished and if the editing is good, I'll see something I made as surely as if I gave it life. She won't be me, though the character is about as close to my own as I could get. She'll be a completely new being that I shaped. It does something for me that's really close to my heart. My soul. To you it will be just a seven-dollar ticket and two hours of your life you'll never get back, but to me it's conception, gestation and delivery."

He was quiet for a moment. "Then you can't ever stop doing it," he said.

"I don't know about that. I was a full-time actress for forty years and I worked whenever I could get work, which, fortunately for me, was very often. Now if I work, it will be for something I consider very important, very much worth my personal investment. I put a lot of myself into these roles, it's not just showing up on the set. I'm lucky—I like this life I have here and I no longer have to work full-time to make ends meet. For someone in my business, it's a huge luxury."

"I hope the way I say this doesn't come out wrong," Walt said. "I hope you have lots of chances to do something that fills you up like that. And I hope you don't."

She smiled. "We're going to work this out, Walt. There are lots of options for us. You can always travel, too. Come to me."

He stiffened in shock. "Muriel, can you honestly see me on a movie set? With two dogs following me and a pitch-fork in my hand?"

It made her giggle. "I can see you almost anywhere."

* * *

In only a couple of days, Rick's pain management was greatly improved. As long as he didn't get behind on the drugs, he'd be relatively comfortable. And while he wouldn't get his final prosthetic leg for two to three months, he'd begin rehab immediately and have a temporary limb he could work with in a few weeks. They were going to ship him out to the Naval Medical Center in San Diego to at least start his rehab until they could find a facility closer to home. But he didn't necessarily want to be closer to home.

"If it can be worked out," Jack said, "I'd like to bring you home to Virgin River to stay with me and Mel. We can get you to rehab several times a week—"

Rick looked down into his lap. Every time he did that, the stump shocked him. "Listen," he said quietly. "I appreciate it, I do, but I already told the caseworker I didn't care where they sent me for rehab. Because I don't want to go home with a walker or crutches. Without a leg."

Jack was mute for a second, staring at him. This was the first he'd heard of this. He grabbed a chair from across the room and pulled it right up to Rick's bed and spoke quietly so as not to be overheard by the other patients. "That's not necessary, Rick. It's not as if you can keep this a secret. I called Mel, told her your condition so she could tell all those people waiting to hear. It had to be done."

"I know. I'm not trying to keep it a secret. I'm alive, that's enough. But if there's going to be a struggle, I don't need everyone watching."

"You sure you want to take that route?" Jack asked. "Because I don't see a lot of watching, but maybe a lot of supporting. We're on your team. You can't be as happy to be alive as we all are to have you alive."

"Listen, can I just do this my way? This isn't going to be simple. Do you know how much is involved in getting a leg? Learning to use it? I just heard a little about it this morning and it sounds like— It takes a long time, it hurts, it's hard to manage, do you realize that?"

"I absolutely do," Jack said. "Me and Liz, we've been reading up. Talking to people. Learning the ropes. So we can do whatever you need us to do."

Rick looked away. "I need you to leave me alone."

Jack was speechless for a second. Then he gathered himself up and spoke. "Okay, I'm done screwing with this. You have to see Liz now. Today. A couple of days ago you—"

"I know," he said, not making eye contact. "It was the pain. I know I overreacted. I'll see her. I'll tell her I'm sorry about how I acted."

"Look at me," Jack said sternly. When Rick met his eyes, Jack said, "I know you're not in a good place right now, but this will pass. I'm going to send Liz in. At the least, tell her you didn't realize you were being mean and that you appreciate her coming all this way and sitting in a hospital lobby all alone, scared to death to show her face around you."

"Listen, Jack," he said, meeting his eyes. "Don't you get it? I'm bad luck. I'm not good for people."

Jack's head jerked to attention. "What?"

"Bad things happen to me, around me. Things don't go right when I'm around. It started when I was two."

Jack was astonished. "What the hell are you talking about?"

Rick shook his head. "My parents died. My grandma got real sick. One strike and I got my girl pregnant. Her baby died. I went into the Marines and the squad clearing the street for us died. I got blown up. Come *on*. I'm a walking disaster." He laughed unkindly. "No, I'm a disaster who can't even walk."

Jack leaned toward him. "You'll get a new leg that will work almost as good as the one you lost and you can get on with your life. It's the stuff of life, we have some shit to deal with and we move ahead. You'll move ahead, too."

"Did your parents die when you were barely two? Did your first baby die? Did you get blown up in the war?"

Jack had a tempting moment. He never focused on the things that had gone terribly wrong—it was hard enough to put them away when you didn't think about them all the time. It was a horrible trap, letting yourself list the stuff in the negative column. He'd always stayed away from that. But Rick's questions were like a challenge and he wanted to stand up, bear down on him with a glare and shout, *Yeah, I held more than one Marine while he was fucking dying and there was no way to save him—it gets me screwed up sometimes. I couldn't find a woman to bond with till I was forty! My mother died too young! My baby sister was raped and beaten! My wife, my heart, almost died of a hemorrhage! My boy Rick got blown up in the war. It wasn't the same stuff, but it was nasty stuff that made me weep.* Instead, Jack calmly looked at Rick and said, "A lot of what happened to you—it happened to me, too. Because I was there with you. Someday you're going to find out that when someone you care about suffers, you suffer right along with him."

"That's why," Rick said. "That's why I want to be left alone. So you don't have to suffer."

Jack stood up. "Not that simple. Sending me away isn't going to make me feel a lot better, but I'm not getting into that with you till you have some time to adjust. I'm going to tell Liz to come in now. Be nice to her. I'm going to take her back to California and I don't want her crying all the way home."

Rick made a face that was most definitely a grimace. As he looked up and saw the determined set to Jack's jaw and his narrowing eyes, he knew there was no way out of this. It terrified him. If he couldn't hang on to the anger, he was going to break down and cry like a girl. He would *not* cry in front of Liz; he would *not* cry in front of these wounded soldiers. "Fine," he said to Jack. "Tell her to come in."

Rick took a lot of deep, fortifying breaths while he waited. Then he looked over his shoulder and saw her standing uncertainly in the doorway to the ward. God, she looked more beautiful than he'd remembered, than the vision of her in his dreams, of which he had far too many. He scowled. He wasn't sure he could do this. He stared at her and crooked a finger, bidding her to come closer. She walked slowly across the room until she stood in front of him.

For a second he almost hated her; at least he hated the look of pain in her eyes. He wanted to shout, *You think it hurts to get yelled at? Try this!*

He attempted a small smile and said, "Be careful, Lizzie. Don't get too close. If you rub up against the wrong place, I'll go through the roof."

"Can I kiss you? If I don't touch any other part of you?"

Bad idea, he thought. But he was stuck—everyone in the room was watching. Without even looking he knew Jack was standing in the doorway, making sure Liz was safe from him. "Lean over toward me. Real careful."

"I know about the phantom pain," she said. "I read all about it. I'm staying far away from where the leg was."

He tilted his head and studied her for a minute. This was going to be harder than ever because she wasn't put off by the sight of the bandaged stump. There was no question about it—nothing in her feelings had been changed by this. And that was such a big mistake on her part.

He put out his hand, on his left side away from the amputation, and pulled her closer to that side. She leaned toward him and he met her lips for a short, unsatisfying peck of a kiss. Behind eyes he briefly closed he remembered making love to her, before and after the baby they'd lost. Wonderful, beautiful, fantastic love that could sustain him for a lifetime. It all came back to him in a colorful, sensual flash; he could smell her skin, taste her sweet body. And then in an equally quick flash, he tried to picture making love to her without his leg.

He opened his eyes and pulled back. "I'm sorry I was mean to you, Liz. I was kind of out of it."

"It's all right. I'm sorry that my being here didn't help you as much as I thought it would. But when I heard you were hurt, I just had to—"

"Did anyone tell you what's going to happen next?" he asked her unemotionally.

"Sort of. You'll have rehab."

"I'll be transferred to Balboa, the Naval Medical Center. Some people go to other places once they're healed up a little, but some stay there, live in barracks. Two to three months. Then I'll be medically discharged or medically retired. After I learn to walk on a fake leg."

"Prosthesis," she corrected, pushing her long hair over her ear.

"Yes. Fine. While I'm doing that, you get ready to graduate. Right?"

"I'm ready now, except for a couple of papers and finals," she said. "I've been getting all As."

He almost smiled but caught himself. "Listen, I know you want to help me, but the best thing you can do for me right now is understand—rehab is going to be a big job. Full-time. I'm not coming home until I'm through that."

"But we'll be in touch," she said, nodding, smiling tremulously. "We can finally have phone calls again."

"Yeah. Sure."

"Rick?" she asked, tilting her head, tears gathering in her eyes. "Will we have phone calls?"

"Sure," he said, squeezing her hand. "Don't start crying, Liz. I can't take care of you right now, you have to get that. You have to be strong because I can't take care of you. Taking care of this is enough work." He waved at the stump with his free hand. "I can't be worrying that something I did or said made you cry. Cut it out."

She sniffed back the threat of tears and held her mouth in a rigid line so her pinkened lips wouldn't tremble. "I'll be fine. It won't take that long. And at least it's not Iraq." She sniffed again. "It's just hard to say goodbye to you again, that's all."

"It probably wasn't a good idea for you to come all this way. If I hadn't given up a spleen, I'd have been out of here in forty-eight hours. On a medical transport to the States. Kind of hard to catch up with." He saw the stricken look in her eyes and quickly said, "But hey, it was real nice of you to come and I appreciate it. I'm sorry I was so mean— I had no idea what I was doing, saying."

"I know. It's okay. I love you, Ricky."

Say it back, he told himself. You can't not say it back, that would be cruel. But he didn't want her to know he still loved her, it wasn't good for her to be bound by that. And then he reminded himself, he wasn't going to break it off with her here, like this. That would come later. So he took too long but he finally said, "I love you, too, baby." Maybe adding baby would lessen the blow of his hesitation. "Sorry, my brain is like mud. All these drugs, you know."

"Jack said in another few days you'll get used to the pain drugs and be more lucid."

He almost smiled. His Lizzie didn't use words like lucid and understand the meaning. "Right," he said. He pulled on her hand. "Now, come on, give me a nice little kiss goodbye, be strong for me, and we'll catch up later, when I'm settled in rehab. Huh?"

She leaned toward him and gave him another kiss, another kiss like she might've given her brother if she had one.

"At least I know you're safe now," she whispered. "I'll still miss you, while you're in rehab."

"I miss you already," he whispered back, not wanting to, not meaning to. "Now go on. Don't drag this out. It's too hard."

He turned and watched her go, seeing Jack standing in the doorway, glowering. Oh, he'd pissed off the big man. Too fucking bad, he thought. Maybe everyone would have been better off if he hadn't made it. He brought bad karma.

He turned back to the wall and struggled with self-pity. Just thinking about those phone calls he used to have with Liz, back when they were younger and talked every night, was enough to make him cry like a baby. He couldn't believe the level of self-loathing he felt, that he brought so much pain on people. And if that wasn't bad enough, he couldn't see the end of his own pain. The empty space where there was supposed to be a leg and foot hurt like hell. He couldn't imagine how that was possible, but the doctor explained something about neurons still delivering the message to his brain that his missing limb hurt. The stupid neurons didn't know his leg ended above the knee.

He heard the sound of one of his roommates, a thirty-five-year-old guy he knew only as Stu, using the trapeze over his bed to heft himself out and transfer to his wheelchair. Then he heard the squeaking of the wheels and hoped Stu was going for a ride down the hall.

But no. Stu wheeled himself in front of Rick. Stu wasn't sent out of Landstuhl because he'd been stationed here when he had an accident that caused a spinal cord injury. Stu had his legs, but he wasn't going to be using them.

"Interesting," Stu said, looking up at him. "Beautiful girl, adores you, and you shut her down. You have a brain tumor?"

"Maybe," Rick said, looking away. "That's one thing I haven't had yet."

"I know the leg hurts, but your lips don't."

"Why don't you mind your own business?"

"This is a little town here, this ward. It's impossible to mind your own business. And you're FUBAR, man."

"Well, we knew that," Rick said, smiling meanly. "No reason for me to fuck her up, too."

"From what I heard, just minding my own business in this little town of ours, you already fucked her up, and now you're cutting her loose. We need to get you a new MRI on your head—you definitely have a brain tumor."

"Leave it alone."

"Maybe you don't get this yet, but people care about you. They come running all the way from the States when you're hurt. And you're going to walk back into that homeplace of yours, looking just like you looked before you left until you take your pants off. Everything's going to work just fine.

But you're too lame to see that right now. You working on pissing everyone off till they hate you? You could just be happy you have this much going for you. How about that?"

Rick glared at him. "No, Stu. I can't just be happy."

Five

Jack thought about sending Liz home and staying around Frankfurt until he could see that Rick was on his way to San Diego, but in the end he decided to go with Liz and let Rick have the space he was asking for. He didn't think Rick was being logical or smart, but stubborn went a long way. Rick verged on irrational, and yet, as Jack was beginning to understand, this behavior was not out of the ordinary for a young man in his situation. After all, he was hurting all over, physically.

So he said to Rick, "You're leaving in the morning and I'm going back tonight. I'll get in touch by phone and once you've had a decent start on your PT, I'll come down and visit. Just a real quick visit—you don't have to put out the china or anything. I just want to check in."

"You don't have to," Rick said. "I can just let you know how I'm getting along."

"This might be more for me than you," Jack said. "And if you need anything, even just someone to talk to, call. If you need me, I can come. Got that?"

"Sure," he said. "Thanks."

Jack put a hand around the kid's neck and pulled him

briefly against his chest, holding him close for a second. Even like that, Rick was so far away. He didn't hug back. He put one hand on Jack's arm and that was it. For a brief and terrible moment, Jack wished Rick would fall apart, take his comfort.

When Rick and Liz's baby was born dead a couple of years ago, Rick had needed Jack's and Preacher's strength to keep him on his feet, to keep him from crumbling. He'd needed the men he'd grown to think of as fathers to bolster him so he could keep Liz from losing it. They'd spent hours talking, supporting, soothing, lending the strength of their experiences.

Right now Rick didn't want anything from anyone, and for Jack this was horrible. It was like being rejected as a father figure.

"Hey, Jack," Rick said. "It was nice of you to come all this way. Sorry I'm not good company."

Jack smiled at him, a completely indulgent smile. "Rick, there wasn't anything else I could do. Like it or not, that's the way it is with best friends. If it was me in the bed, you'd be right here."

A flicker of emotion crossed Rick's features, but it didn't last long. "Thanks. Have a good trip home."

Normally Rick would have told him to give Mel his love, but on this visit he hadn't even asked about her or the kids. In fact, he asked if his grandmother was holding up and that was all. He didn't want to talk to anyone, see anyone, think about anyone. The way he was isolating himself from feeling not only worried Jack, it was completely familiar to him. Jack had been in a few bad situations in the Marines and he'd been too goddamn stoic for his own good. But, he reminded himself, he had somehow grown out of most of that. He had survived the traumas of combat.

The one who surprised him more was Liz. Jack was afraid he'd be dragging a weeping, sniveling seventeen-year-old basket case back across the Atlantic, but Liz, although troubled and sad, seemed to be in control of her emotions. "I'm afraid, you know," she said to Jack while they sat together on the airplane. "I'm afraid he doesn't love me anymore. But I understand I can't know that for sure until he gets better. And he will get better. I was terrified that we'd get to Germany to find out he was—" She couldn't finish.

Jack squeezed her hand. "I know, kiddo," he said. "Listen, he's hurting and he's screwed up right now, but he has no idea what he's getting himself into. I offered to bring him home to my house and drive him to PT as many times a week as he needed to go and he rejected that. He said he didn't want anyone watching his struggle. Well, I talked to the social worker right before we packed up and left. When he gets to the hospital in San Diego, *everyone* will be watching him. They have a new care unit they call C-5—Comprehensive Combat and Complex Casualty Care. There's a large amputee unit that combines everything from orthopedics and psych to drug treatment. He might be kicking and screaming the whole time, but as long as he's there, there will be treatment for whatever is going on with him. And that missing leg isn't all that's going on with him."

"What *is* going on with him?" she asked. "Because I'm not sure I get it."

"Any guess." He shrugged. "Could be what they used to call battle fatigue, but it's really just the shock of seeing terrible things, doing things you wish you hadn't had to do, denial, rage, fear. Add on top of that, he got hurt real bad and is minus a leg. He can get a good prosthesis, but he can't ever get that leg back. He's wounded, worried about the future and, for that matter, worried about the past. His war past. He's going to the best possible place to get help with that. You and me? We can't help him as much as they can. Bad as it hurts that he doesn't want our help, it's probably the best thing that could happen."

"I hope he gets himself back," she said. "Because no matter what, I'm probably going to love him forever."

She leaned her head against Jack's shoulder in the narrow, confining airplane seats. Without looking at Jack, she said, "Remember back when I was pregnant?" Then she laughed hollowly. "Fifteen and pregnant. God. Talk about hurt, scared and pissed off...."

"Rick was only seventeen," Jack inserted.

"And he did everything he could for me. You can't believe the things he did. He protected me from the popular girls who made fun of me, pointed at me, tortured me. He got in a fight because some guy said something mean about me and Rick defended me. He didn't want to get married, but I wanted to so bad because I was scared of being alone, of my mom and aunt taking the baby away from me...." She looked up at Jack and smiled. "So he ran away with me. Trying to give me anything I needed to feel safe."

Jack smiled back, stroking her hair. "You didn't get too far," he said, remembering. He'd gone after them, brought them back.

Her fingers were on that small diamond again, running it back and forth along the chain around her neck. "You know what I want to do? I want to hitchhike to San Diego and stand outside his hospital room and yell and cry and beg."

"Ew," Jack said.

"I want to, but I won't. I can see he doesn't want me right now and that would only make things worse. I just can't think what I should do."

"Did you ever check out those support groups?"

She sighed heavily. "Jack, if you're not married to the Marine, no one has any time for you. And that's that."

"I thought the people in the group would…"

"Would bend the rules?" she asked. "No. Jack, I think I'm on my own this time."

He smiled and brushed her hair across her pretty brow. He couldn't relate to this. There was no special girl from years back that, if he saw her again, he'd regret letting get away. And he wasn't even sure Rick and Liz were meant to be, despite all they'd been through together. But they were, individually, such incredible kids. So strong. They shouldn't have to be that strong at their tender ages.

Could fate throw any more at them?

"Nah, you're not on your own. Not while I'm around. Not while Mel's around. I'll mention to Mel that you're not getting any support. If anyone has ideas, it's Mel." He didn't feel it was his job to get them together. But if there was anything he could do to get them through this dark patch so each of them could carry on without terrible damage, he'd damn sure try.

Jack and Liz flew from Frankfurt to Kennedy International to Denver to Redding. Before heading out of Redding to Eureka, they visited a cell-phone store where Jack bought a phone. There was no reception in the mountains; they relied on pagers and landlines. But there was plenty of reception in San Diego. He FedExed the phone to Rick, to Lance Corporal Richard Sudder. He scrawled a note:

Just so I can reach you. So you can reach me. And anyone else you want to talk to. Jack.

Then he took Liz home to Eureka. He carried her suitcase up to the porch for her and it was there that she wrapped her arms around him, laid her head on his chest and cried. "Thank you for everything you did for me. For Rick. I'll pay you back somehow."

He lifted her chin. "Liz, I did it because I thought it was an important thing to do. It wasn't a loan. Forget it."

"But I think you wasted your money."

"Hey. We needed to see him alive. Think about it—alive and pissed off is so much better than what it could've been. Let's stick with that. And move ahead the best we can." He paused. "He needs time."

Then he drove the rest of the way to Virgin River.

Normally, when he had dealt with something confusing or emotional, the one person he wanted to talk to, be with, would be Mel. She had this uncanny knack for zeroing in on a problem, cutting through the flab and attacking the situation with reality, honesty, wisdom.

This time he went to his bar and looked for Preacher. They'd been to Iraq together twice and had been through some ugly stuff. Preacher had been wounded pretty bad the first time and Jack had carried him about a mile to get him to medical transport, but Preacher had come away with all his parts.

The bar was quiet; a couple of guys were sharing a pitcher

and playing cribbage, so Jack went back to the kitchen where Preach was slicing and dicing. "Hey," he said.

"Jack! Whoa, man. When did you get back?"

"Seconds ago. I need to go over to the clinic, see Mel and the kids."

"How is he?"

Jack shook his head. "He's a goddamn mess. Hurt, pissed, so angry, isolating, doesn't want a friend, doesn't want help, barely acknowledged that Liz and I flew across the fucking Atlantic to carry his body home."

Unbelievably, Preacher smiled. "Good. He's getting stage one covered."

"Stage one?"

"Yeah, maybe one and two. Anger and denial. He's gonna have to grieve the leg, the war wounds, the time he lost from his young life. There's probably going to be five stages."

Jack leaned on the worktable, his brow wrinkled. "How do you know this shit?"

"I looked it up on the computer. You know, after you figure out e-mail, there are other things you can do on that computer."

"So what's next for him?" Jack asked.

"I'll have to get my cheat sheet, but it could be bargaining—I'll never commit another sin if you just let me live. That kind of thing. We've all done that. All that's really important is—it ends in acceptance."

Jack straightened. "How long does it take?"

"Well, there's the thing," Preacher said. "It depends on the person. Rick? He's pretty tough. It could stretch out. He doesn't let go easy."

"Christ," Jack said, running a hand along the back of his neck. "Why do I always think I know you?"

"I dunno, Jack," he answered with a shrug. "But Rick—we're just at angry? And his body, his health—that's under control?"

"He's still in a lot of pain, on drugs for it, shipping to San Diego as we speak. Balboa. NMCSD. He'll heal up the stump and start physical therapy. They could keep him until he gets his leg or farm him out to some smaller facility."

"It has to heal and shrink. They can't fit him until it's ready—no swelling, no redness, no tenderness. They'll get that stump in a shrinker, looks like a skull cap kind of. It's real important, before they fit the prosthesis, that it's not swollen or anything. They'll work with him in PT to avoid muscle contractures and desensitize that stump to get beyond the phantom pain. A lot of physical therapists will put a healthy, healed stump in a bowl of crunchy dry cornflakes and grind it around to kind of teach the nerves that the leg ends there."

Jack's eyes grew wide. "How do you *know* this shit?" Preacher just tilted his head and smirked. "You looked it up, I know."

"Well, I wanted to understand the news you brought home."

"And how is the news?" Jack asked.

Preacher shrugged. "Pretty much on target."

Rick began his stay in San Diego in the Naval Medical Center orthopedics ward, which he shared with other young men recovering from recent injuries. While there, he was evaluated for his pain management and physical therapy program. Before the end of the week, he was having PT every day and had been issued both a walker and wheelchair, but he had little interest in leaving the ward.

He assessed the condition of the other patients and came to the conclusion there was no predicting how people got through trauma like this. Some were downright cheerful in spite of terrible pain, some were horribly depressed. He judged himself to be right about in the middle—neither cheerful nor catatonic with gloom. Once they started slacking off on the narcotics, it was harder to sleep. It was like trying to catch a nap in an amphitheater—there was always noise, light, movement. There were cries in the night, sometimes from a breakout of pain, sometimes from nightmares. One guy cried for his mother in his sleep. Moans, groans and, unbelievably, even laughter punctuated the darkness. Rick was afraid to succumb to sleep lest he scream and expose the depth of his vulnerability.

Once the cell phone had arrived, there was already a message waiting—Jack. "Rick, give me a call when you get the phone so I know we're operational. Call anyone you like—there's no limit on the minutes." Rick didn't call him. He kept thinking he would pretty soon, but after a few days the phone twittered and the caller ID signaled Jack. This time the message was more commanding. "Rick, if you don't call me back, I'm going to drive down there to be sure you're getting by all right."

Trapped, he returned the call. "Sorry," he said. "I just haven't felt like talking."

"Understandable," Jack said. "We don't have to talk long. How are they treating you? Tell me what's going on."

Rick sighed. This wasn't what he had in mind. But, it was better to have Jack on a phone than in his face, so he'd have to play along. "I'm still in the hospital, moving to barracks with other PT patients tomorrow. I get around in a chair or walker. Mostly the chair because it's easier. Another week or two and I'll get a preparatory prosthesis and start walking."

"Preparatory?"

"The first step before the real fake leg."

"Ah. How are the other guys there doing? Meeting anyone you can, you know, talk to?"

Rick was silent for a long moment. Then he said, "Not a lot of laughs around here, Jack."

"Maybe that'll get better when you're in barracks."

"Yeah, maybe. Listen, I'm pretty tired...."

"Really? Haven't had enough rest yet?" When Rick didn't respond, Jack said, "Okay, buddy, I'll let you get some rest. I'll call tomorrow."

One thing about the barracks, the men were in various stages of recovery. They weren't all newly injured like Rick. One guy was practicing tying his shoes with two prosthetic arms while another was strapping on his preparatory prosthesis in the morning and using only a cane to assist him with balance. But the routine was different here—no more food on a tray or bath out of a basin at the bedside. Here it was a mess hall and showers. Rick had to admit, a real shower felt damn good, even if he did have to have his stump wrapped because the wound wasn't completely healed. And he sat on a stool in the shower to be safe. But getting himself to the cafeteria for a gang meal wasn't his idea of a good time.

There were guys here who played poker, passed around pictures of their wives/girls/kids as well as magazines— mostly porn. "Gotta keep the pipes clear," one guy laughed as he tossed a nudie magazine on Rick's bed. There were men in barracks with no hope of ever clearing the pipes, paraplegics who'd lost movement and feeling from the waist down. Rick knew that if his brain and emotions were engaged right, he'd see they had it worse and experience some gratitude. But his head was tangled around powerful feelings of doom and an overwhelming sense of loss that he couldn't talk about. Hell, he couldn't even understand it. He just felt it so deep, as if everything had slipped away from him and couldn't be rescued—the life he'd had before war, the body he'd had, the dreams and goals.

He'd like to talk about it but just couldn't bring himself to. Liz called a couple of times and even though he didn't pick up, he listened to her messages over and over. She loved him, she was praying every day that he was doing okay in rehab, that he was feeling more positive.

He'd always been able to talk to Liz. Even though they'd started out as lovers, right out of the chute, they had always been best friends. They'd been thrown into the deep end of the pool, with pregnancy, fetal death, war. They'd never have stayed together so long if they hadn't been able to talk and write about their issues. They held on to each other through so much confusion and fear, got each other through not just by talking, but by listening. Jack had taught him that: *Don't worry about saying the right thing, Rick. Let Liz tell you what scares her and tell her you won't abandon her—that's all she really wants from you.* Had Jack talked to Liz? Advised her? Because it seemed as if she'd always done that for him, too.

He wasn't sure how she got on the naval base, but he opened his eyes one night and she was there, sitting on the edge of his bed. He could hear the sounds around him, so he knew he was awake—there was snuffling in beds, moaning, humming, snoring.

"What are you *doing* here?" he asked her, panicked, immediately afraid she was going to be in deep trouble. Maybe arrested.

She reached out a hand and ran her pretty fingers over his temple, down his cheek, softly over his lips. "I thought maybe you needed me, Ricky. And I knew I needed you." Then she leaned over him and touched his lips with hers. He inhaled sharply, smelling her scent, tasting her special taste. His girl. Not a girl, a woman, and she never let him forget she belonged to him and he belonged to her. He'd had some dates, some making out with girls before Lizzie, but she was the whole deal for him. They might have started out a couple of clumsy, stupid kids, but by now they knew each other's bodies and needs and their sex was rich and powerful and satisfying.

She fed him sweet kisses and he swallowed her little moans. "Shh," he said to her. "We're going to get in so much trouble."

"It's okay," she whispered. "I pulled the curtain."

He glanced and saw that they were as alone as they could be in a barracks, the privacy panels separating his bed from his neighbors. And the sounds of sleep and dreams were all around him. He went after her mouth again. Her perfect, soft, round mouth, her full lips. He ran a hand down her side to her hip and over. She was wearing that tiny denim skirt. Ohhh, that little skirt. He slid his hand under and she was bare. He let his fingers explore while she kissed him; his baby, she was wet and ready. This wasn't a good idea, he thought. Not here. But he was ready, too.

"Come here, baby," he said, lying her down next to him.

And she answered with that soft little moan he knew so well. "Come here, I need you. I need you so bad right now." It was crowded in his little bed, but he rose onto his side, looking down at her. His Liz, his beautiful, sweet, loyal Liz. He slipped one hand under her shirt to capture a breast, the other went under her skirt to probe her a little. He had to cover her mouth with his to silence her moans. But then he pushed up her shirt and pulled her pretty nipple into his mouth and he didn't care if she moaned. He was in heaven.

Sometimes this was all it took; Liz had always been so hot. He'd run his tongue around her nipple, suck a little, stroke her between her legs and she'd plunge right into an orgasm. "Don't wait for me," he whispered into her mouth. He licked, sucked, stroked and she came apart, hot and wet, gasping. He heard himself laugh softly. Then he positioned himself over her, mounted her, rising above her, finding and entering her. God, she felt so good he thought he was going to die.

He pumped and drove into her and heard her hum. "Don't forget," she whispered. And his hand snaked down between their tight bodies to find that clitoris again, rubbing it. He knew his woman; this was what she wanted.

"If we don't get caught, I'm going to put my face in you and stay there an hour," he promised her. "I just can't get enough of you."

"Please," she said softly. "Please please please please…"

And he erupted. Went off like a rocket, pulsing and coming until there was nothing left inside him. His eyes were pinched tight, he was bathed in sweat, and for a second he wondered how she'd gotten him on his back. And then he opened his eyes and realized he was alone.

She'd only been there in his mind, in his dream. But

God, what a dream. It was so real, so perfect, exactly as he remembered.

He panted for a while, catching his breath. He looked and there had been no privacy screen. But it seemed everyone was asleep; no one was sitting up looking at him. He had a momentary hope he hadn't been talking in his sleep, but a glance around told him it had all happened in his head, under his sheet.

And then he realized that in his dream, he'd held himself over her with two complete, undamaged legs, kneeling between her legs. He gasped at the memory, so vivid. Soundless, hot tears rolled from his eyes across his temples. Oh, Liz... Oh, baby....

Mel and Jack struggled to get their family back to normal. Jack had been home for two weeks. He had talked with Rick, but he wasn't getting very far with him. Rick would take his calls if he was near the cell phone, but he neither initiated nor returned them. "This might require more patience than you have," Mel said. "He isn't headed for a quick fix. It's going to take months. Maybe years."

"Months," Jack mimicked, disappointment drawing out the word. And then, *"Years?"*

"Jack, even if he weren't wounded, catastrophically wounded at that, his return from a war zone would be a serious adjustment. Every family of every soldier goes through this. And you know that."

But while Jack knew it, he didn't really know it from experience. He'd always been active duty and had only visited his family. He moved on to the next challenge and if anyone thought he'd gotten depressed or crazy, they didn't mention it. Certainly Jack knew he was adjusting after a combat assignment, he just didn't think anyone else knew. And of course he'd never sustained an injury that would retire or discharge him.

Although Rick was on Mel's mind every bit as much, she had other people to care for. She had called Liz regularly and talked with her in person when Liz came to town to help her aunt Connie in the corner store. She convinced her to visit that counselor who helped her after her baby had been stillborn, a definite step forward. A couple of women from town were prenatals and she did all she could to assist Cameron in the clinic with other patients.

At the end of March spring teased the mountains—one day pleasantly warm and a few days later, an icy rain, a threat of snow. Mel was seeing a prenatal patient one afternoon when she heard a commotion in the front of the clinic. Fortunately she wasn't doing internal exams; she stepped out of the room to see a breathless, skinny man who looked to be in his sixties in a panic as he yelled at Cameron, waving his arms excitedly.

"She's dyin', I know it! You gotta come! She's dyin'!"

Cameron looked over his shoulder. "Mel?"

She stepped forward. "Where are we going, sir?" she asked calmly.

"A couple blocks. Hurry!"

"Let me excuse my patient, Cam. Fire up the Hummer, get the gentleman in it and I'll be right there."

So while Cameron and the man got into the Hummer, she told her patient she had an emergency and would call her to complete the exam another time. They didn't bother locking up for something like this; the drug cabinet and patient records were already locked. Because Mel had appointments, the children were with their aunt Brie for the afternoon, otherwise she wouldn't be able to hurry along with Cameron until Jack or someone could come for them.

Cameron followed the man's directions two blocks to a house that Mel recognized at once. She'd been here before, months and months ago, when she fetched thirty-two-year-old Cheryl Creighton from her alcoholic stupor and carted her off to a county-funded treatment facility. She had never seen Cheryl's father, who this must be. But she would never forget Cheryl's mother—she was a morbidly obese chain-smoker who wheezed with every laboring step she took. One look at her and Mel had worried about the woman's heart. If it hadn't been for the fact that since she first laid eyes on Mrs. Creighton they'd had a major forest fire and lost their town doctor, Mel would have had a pang of guilt for not checking on her, even though she was not a patient.

"What's your wife's name, Mr. Creighton?" Mel asked as they pulled up to the house.

"Dahlia," he answered. "Dahlia Marie. She can't breathe and she's grippin' at her chest."

Cameron threw the Hummer into park and, grabbing his bag, ran up the steps, across the broken-down porch and through the front door, Mel close on his heels with her own bag. "She'll be in the kitchen," Mel said.

The familiar squalor greeted them; the little house hadn't been cleaned in forever and smelled like an ashtray. As Mr. Creighton hurried behind them, she was aware of *his* wheezing.

As Mel had predicted, Dahlia was slumped back in her favorite kitchen chair, the mess of paperbacks, magazines, newspapers, Coke cans, ashtrays and miscellaneous food items like cookies and chips all within reaching distance. Her eyes were round and fearful, her lips turning blue while her pallid skin glistened with sweat. She had trouble breathing. "Let's see if we can help, Dahlia," she said.

Cameron had the stethoscope in his ears and pressed against her chest. He listened for only a second before reaching in his bag and giving her an aspirin. "Can you swallow this for me, Dahlia?" he asked. While she did so, he reached for the new blood-pressure cuff that fit around her wrist, tightened it and took an electronic reading. He lifted that hand against her breast, nearer her heart, for accuracy.

Mel was locating the emergency drugs she kept ready in her bag—atropine, epinephrine.

"Mel, can you manage the oxygen canister?"

"Of course," she said, darting out of the house. By the time she got back, Cameron was slipping a nitro tablet under Dahlia's tongue. She pulled out the tubing and fit the cannulas into the woman's nose. "This will help," she said.

"We need a transport," Cameron said.

"We can do that," Mel said. "Give me one second." She saw the old-fashioned wall phone beside the refrigerator and picked it up, dialing with the rotary dial. "Preacher, hey. Cameron and I are at the Creighton house and have to take Mrs. Creighton to the hospital right now. Yes, that's exactly what I need—both of you. Thanks." She hung up and told Cameron, "Jack and Preacher will be right here to help."

Cameron looked at her, smiled slightly and lifted an eyebrow.

"I'll go get the gurney and bring it in."

"Let me—"

"No. You handle this and start an IV. I won't be a minute."

By the time Mel had the gurney out of the back of the Hummer, Jack and Preacher were jogging up the block toward the house. She didn't wait for them, but began to push the gurney toward the house, over the cracked and broken walk. When she reached the porch, the men were beside her, lifting the gurney up onto the slanted porch, avoiding the missing boards. "What is it?" Jack asked softly.

"Possible coronary," she said just as quietly. "She needs to go to the hospital."

"Want me to drive so you can ride in the back with Cameron?"

She grinned at him suddenly. "You boys come in so handy. Thanks."

Jack and Preacher got the gurney as far as the kitchen doorway and lowered it like professional paramedics. Then they went into the kitchen and stood one on each side of her. "Afternoon, Dahlia," Jack said. "Let's take a ride. How about that?"

Cameron lifted the portable oxygen canister and IV bag, hanging on to them.

Dahlia Creighton got a very frightened look on her face and Jack said, "Dahlia, this will be easier if you just let me and Preacher do the work, okay? We're going to lift you onto the gurney and wheel you out, easy as pie. But if you struggle or wiggle around, we could drop you, so be still and trust us. We'll be rolling you into the Hummer in seconds. How about that, huh?"

She nodded, but she hadn't said a word yet.

Jack and Preacher slipped arms under her thighs and behind her back, counted to three and hefted close to four hundred pounds of woman into their arms and carried her the short distance to the gurney, lowering her onto it. They pulled it up, which took enormous effort given her weight, and got her to the back of the Hummer to slide that gurney inside.

"You have gas in that truck, Mr. Creighton?" Mel asked. When he nodded, she asked, "You all right to drive? It would be better for you to follow us to the hospital so you have transportation." He nodded again and started fishing in his pocket for his keys.

And something happened during this whole operation that Mel would never comment to anyone about but that filled her with a warm pride. Dahlia had had a little accident, possibly from stark fear that she was dying, or maybe fear that the men would drop her. She'd wet herself and, in the process of moving her, Jack's sleeve had been soaked.

Cam and Mel jumped in the back of the Hummer. Mel asked Preacher to call the hospital and tell them they were en route. The door slammed behind them and, without a word, Jack and Preacher unbuttoned their shirts and exchanged them. Jack was swimming in Preacher's dry shirt; Preacher was walking back to the bar in a sleeveless T-shirt in the cold late-March afternoon, carrying Jack's soiled shirt. And within ten seconds, Jack was behind the wheel of the Hummer, driving out of town.

Oh God, she thought. Where do you find men like these? Men who will do absolutely whatever it takes to help people, no matter what? She'd chosen this profession; she'd chosen to be up to her shoulders in whatever medical problem or mess came her way. She'd been bled on, crapped on, peed on, puked on, and it never discouraged her from providing whatever was needed medically. But Jack was just Jack. Preacher, a cook! They weren't nurses, doctors or medics, and yet she couldn't count the times they jumped in and helped, even if it left them covered with blood or amniotic fluid or—this time—the wet accident of a woman he barely knew who was in a traumatic, life-threatening situation.

They were made of gold.

Dahlia Creighton made it all the way to Valley Hospital before she arrested. She was resuscitated in the emergency room and the staff cardiologist was conferring over the phone with a doctor at a larger hospital about transporting her for an angiogram and possible bypass surgery.

Cameron, Jack and Mel didn't hang around—there was nothing more they could do for her now. The drive back to Virgin River was long and quiet in the Hummer. When they got to town, there wasn't enough day left to open the clinic. Jack pulled up in front of the clinic and Mel said, "I'll get a bucket of soapy water to clean out the back."

"I'll help," Cam said. "We'll get it done quickly."

"Need another hand?" Jack asked.

"Nah," Mel said. "Your dinner crowd will be showing up pretty soon. I'll stop by the bar before I head out to Brie's to pick up the kids."

Donned in latex gloves with twin buckets, Cam and Mel scrubbed things down. Mel took the gurney out and was working on it while Cam crawled inside the back of the Hummer, washing it down, standard procedure between uses. When everything was shining, supplies in the Humvee and medical bags refreshed, buckets of water tossed in the flower beds around the porch, Cam said, "I've been meaning to talk to you. I'm going to have to make a few adjustments in my schedule. I'm going to have to find another job in a few months."

She smiled at him and dried off her hands. "I figured something would have to change."

"I invited Abby to come here for dinner tonight. I want to talk to her about things. I'm going to try to convince her we should be roommates."

"Roommates? How romantic," Mel said.

"Yeah, well, she doesn't have romantic feelings, but I want to take better care of my family. Whether she likes it or not, she's my family. At least, she's giving birth to my family. In another month, she's going to realize how much she needs me nearby. After they're born..." He shook his head. "After they're born, she's going to need me even more."

"So. You have a plan?"

"I don't want to let the town down. But if I can find a hospital or practice nearby that could use a doctor, at least part-time, I'll live in Virgin River and keep appointments here as often as possible. I'd like to be on hand either in the mornings or afternoons, and evenings and weekends for house calls. The problem is the emergency care."

"Cam, we have an emergency that needs medical intervention and transport about three or four times a year. There's a fair chance you'd be taking a day off or out of town visiting your family when those emergencies occur. On the other hand, there's an equal chance you could keep a job in Fortuna or Eureka and be right here when we have an emergency. What I really need is a physician who keeps appointments and makes a few house calls, not an E.R. doctor. We call the sheriff's department or paramedics—it might take them a little longer, but that's how it is when you live in a rural area. Our people understand that. If you hadn't been here today for Dahlia, I could have called Mercy Air, medical transport." She smiled. "I might hang on to you a little longer if you have a way to take care of your family."

"Maybe," he said with a shrug. "In the end, where I live isn't going to be up to me. I'm not letting them get away. If Abby insists on living in some godforsaken place like London, I'll follow."

Mel couldn't help it, she burst out laughing. "Godforsaken London? I'd give my eyeteeth to spend a year in London."

"You know what I mean," he said.

"I understand—you got your head wrapped around being a small-town doctor, living in the mountains, a low-stress lifestyle, and then, whoops—you're going to be a father."

"As you would say, boy howdie."

"So—tell me your plan," she said. "I know you have one."

"The beginning of one. I'm solvent for a while yet. I won't be desperate for more income before the end of summer, but I should start looking. I want to hang close for now because those babies could come in a couple of months, hopefully not earlier, and then after they're born, I want to help Abby get a couple months under her belt before I start working two or three jobs. There's room for her in the clinic while I look around for something to rent that will hold all of us, something real close. I can give her my room and sleep in the patient room. If there's a God, I'll find a nice, comfortable three-bedroom not far from here."

"I can help you out there. The cabin's empty. Two bedrooms and a loft, ten minutes from town, no farther away than I am."

"Don't you need it for family and friends?"

"Now that Luke Riordan has those cabins on the river

all fixed up, we're in great shape. The Sheridans show up from time to time, but we have a guest room and guesthouse. We bought the cabin to have a handy alternative for emergencies. This qualifies."

He hung his head and shook it. "You must think I'm a complete idiot."

Her laughter brought his head up. "Me?" she asked. "Cameron, I never planned a pregnancy in my life, and I'm the expert! Just work it out if you can. I want the best for all of you."

He smiled. "I'll work out some rent agreement with you and Jack."

"Don't be absurd. You practically work for free. The longer I can keep you around, the better. Besides, that cabin has good fortune. I gave birth to David there." She laughed at the shudder she saw pass through him. He was no doubt imagining his twins coming out in that cabin. She put a hand on his arm. "Work things out any way you can, Cameron. You can have the cabin for as long as you need it."

"Should you check with Jack about that?"

"Please," she scoffed. "Jack will do anything I ask." Then she grinned. "Besides, Jack would approve of this idea. If it works for you."

Six

Abby was primping in front of the mirror, Vanessa standing in the bathroom doorway, arms crossed over her chest, watching. "My *face* is fat," Abby said.

"It's not," Vanessa argued. "You look beautiful. Amazing. And huge."

Cameron was cooking Abby dinner at the clinic tonight. He thought they should talk about a few things, which was totally reasonable. Abby plucked at the mother-to-be top Vanni had loaned her. "Are you sure you wore this the very last week of your pregnancy?"

"I was only having one, remember. Abby, you look wonderful. You do want to look wonderful, don't you?"

"I'll be content if I don't spoil his appetite with the way I look," she said, but she leaned closer to the mirror to carefully line her lips. Then she ran the comb through her shiny hair one more time. Then she licked a finger and smoothed it over one finely arched eyebrow, shaping it.

"Uh-huh," Vanni said doubtfully. "So, what's on the agenda tonight? What does he want to talk about?"

"Not sure," Abby said. Then she ran her hands over her belly. "It's not like we don't have plenty on the roster.

Vanni, I'm only six months pregnant and I look like I'm going to drop them tomorrow. I don't know if I can stretch anymore!"

"Bet you can." Vanni laughed. "I won't wait up."

"I'll be home early," Abby promised.

"Please, not on my account. Why don't you just throw caution to the wind and try to enjoy yourself." She glanced at Abby's big belly. "You enjoyed yourself once. I bet you can again. Cam's a great guy."

Abby knew this, and not just because Vanni wouldn't let her forget it. If she had to get knocked up by a virtual stranger, at least she picked a decent guy. And it was just too bad that their relationship was so rife with complications, with unknowns. The only things that were for sure—Abby was a nice person, Cameron was a great guy, and two babies were going to come barreling out of her in about two months, give or take. She could already tell she'd never make it to term.

Abby got to town promptly at six and found the clinic door unlocked. "Hello?" she called after stepping inside.

Cam looked down the hall from the kitchen, a plain white apron wrapped around his hips and a spoon in his hand. He smiled at her. "Hi. Go ahead and lock that door, Abby. They have to knock after clinic hours."

"Sure," she said, throwing the dead bolt. When she got to the kitchen, he had discarded the spoon and helped her out of her coat. He hung it on the peg by the back door and said, "You look pretty, Abby. Beautiful, in fact."

"Thanks. I look full-term and I'm not even close."

"You look perfect. Healthy and strong and very pregnant." He grinned at her. "You feel okay?"

"Sure," she said. "Fine." In fact, her back was aching,

her ankles were swelling and she was getting these mysterious pains in her lower abdomen that Mel and John Stone described as ligament-stretching pains that felt at least like a pulled muscle, sometimes every bit as powerful as a knife thrust. Sleeping was getting difficult and heartburn had settled in with a vengeance. "I get some heartburn" was all she admitted to. "It's a good excuse to eat ice cream at night. What did you cook?"

"Spaghetti with meatballs and sausage," he answered with a grimace. "I don't have ice cream, but I do have Tums. I never even thought of heartburn."

"I might go light on the sausage, but I so love it," she said, sitting down. He'd set the table in mismatched stoneware. She ran a finger around the plate in front of her.

"Doc's old stuff," he said. "If I'd known the kitchen wasn't very well stocked, I could have brought my own stuff. I don't mind cooking and I'm kind of good. All my kitchenware is in storage at the moment."

"So is mine," she said. "We're both like a couple of Gypsies right now, aren't we?" She leaned back in her chair and rubbed the small of her back.

"How about sparkling cider?" Cameron asked, glancing down at her feet. Her slacks rose up just enough for him to see her ankles.

"That would be great, thanks. And water?"

He got both for her and then sat in the chair beside hers. "Just a little heartburn?"

"Oh, you know…"

"Backache, edema, heartburn… What else?"

She took a sip of her cider. "Something they call ligament pains that feel remarkably like a wide-awake cesarean section."

He winced.

"I pee on the half hour."

He laughed.

"You think it's funny? A few more years, when your prostate is a bit larger, you won't think it's all that funny."

"I hope it's more than just a few more years, Ab," he said. But he smiled. He touched her hand, gave it a little squeeze. Then he stood and went to the stove. He gave the pasta a swirl, the sauce a stir, then grabbed a leafy salad from the refrigerator and put it on the table along with a small bowl of dressing. "How'd you like to toss that for me?"

"Sure," she said, digging a pair of large spoons into the salad. "So. What did you want to talk to me about?"

"Well, for starters, how about names? For the kids?"

"You want to be involved in names?" she asked, surprised.

"Sure. If I were having the babies, wouldn't you want input in that? Or—if I were having them, would you drop out of sight? Pretend you didn't know?"

Shock settled over her features. Jesus, did that ever cut deep. Would she? Would she shake it off, run for her life, refuse to be involved, just let him deal with it? Oh God, of course not! She swallowed. But isn't that just what she'd hoped he would do? Go away and leave her alone. "Um, have you thought of any?"

"My grandmothers are Alice and Eleanor. They're awesome and those are cool names...."

"Alice and Eleanor?" she said, making a face.

"Ally and Elly, that's what they go by. Wait till you meet them—you'll love them."

"But we don't know if we're getting a girl! We only know about—" She stopped talking.

He glanced at her over his shoulder as he lifted the steaming pot off the stove and tossed the cooked pasta into the colander in the sink. He glanced over his shoulder again and grinned at her. She realized what she'd done— she'd coupled them in parenthood.

"I hope we get a boy and a girl, but I'm good with two boys. I love all those little-guy things—T-ball, soccer, catching bugs."

"I played T-ball," she said softly. "And soccer. And I used to go to the lake with my family and catch a jarful of fireflies to put on the nightstand for when I went to bed." She swallowed. "If I'd known I was killing them, I would never have done it."

"See, you'll be good with either boys or girls. We're all set—but they don't have names." He picked up her plate and put some pasta and sauce on it for her. He included a couple of meatballs and a sausage and put it in front of her. "Don't eat anything you think will give you heartburn." Then he served himself and sat down with her. "Try it, Ab. See how I cook. It's an old family recipe."

She took a tentative taste, rolled the food around in her mouth and tilted her head with lifted eyebrows. "Mmm."

"I wasn't smart enough to leave out the sausage—but I didn't make it as garlicky and spicy as usual. I toned it down for you."

"Normally I like spicy. But it's out to get me lately. So," she said, lifting some salad into his bowl, then hers. "What else is on your mind?"

He chuckled. "In a hurry to get this over with?"

"No," she said, surprised and maybe a little embarrassed. "I'm just— I mean, we talk all the time and this sounded kind of serious."

He stabbed some lettuce and brought it to his mouth, chewed, swallowed. "We have a few minutes on the phone, see each other at Jack's for a couple of minutes here and there, and there's no yelling or shooting—which is a big improvement—but we don't get down to business. Abby, we're having two babies in a couple of months, three months at the outside. Nah," he said, shaking his head. "We'll never make it three months. Do you have any of the details worked out?"

"Well," she said. "Sure. Some."

He leaned toward her and smiled pleasantly. "Care to share?"

"What would you like to know?"

"Well, there's nothing to suggest we have a high-risk pregnancy, but it's pretty common for the mothers of twins to go on bed rest for a while to delay labor while they grow and get stronger. And when babies come, it's often early and fast. And taking care of them as newborns is pretty demanding. Also, you have a financial situation that's giving you some stress. And—"

"Okay, okay," she said. "Sheesh. I'm not too worried about bed rest, I'm in good health and I have Vanni and Mel. John Stone is watching real close for early and fast. My mom will come as soon as they arrive and—"

"So will mine," he said, and she actually grabbed her belly.

"What?"

"Oh yeah. We can hold her off for a week, maybe, but these are her grandchildren and she's never missed a grandchild's debut."

"Have you *told* her?" she asked, aghast.

"Not yet," he said, twirling a little spaghetti around his

fork. "But I have to do that. It's going to be hard enough to explain not telling her sooner and making sure she had a chance to meet you. They're not just our children, Ab. They have grandparents, great-grandparents, aunts, uncles, cousins…et cetera…on my side of this family as well as yours."

"Oh God," she said, dropping her fork. "I don't feel so good."

He just laughed lightly. "Relax. Nothing to worry about. They're fantastic people and you'll be real happy to have them in your life, I guarantee it."

"But won't they think… I mean, we're not married and—"

He shrugged, got up and fetched himself a beer from the old refrigerator, using the underside of his heavy class ring to pop the top. "I'm sure they've heard of things like this before. A man and woman, not married, having children. But telling my family is just one item on this list. Abby, the list is long. We have so many things to work through before you go into labor. And not all that much time to do it."

She rested her forehead in her hand, her elbow on the table. "Hit me with another one. What else do we have to work out?"

"Do you have cribs? Clothes? Gear—car seats, diaper bags, et cetera?"

"I should make a run to the mall," she said absently. "You're right. I have to get moving on this. But, I talked to my mom about all this stuff and we decided, since I didn't want anyone to know I'm pregnant, we're not saying anything to friends and family. Then when they come, after they've gotten a couple of months old, we'll send announcements. I'm even thinking of fudging the birthday. I hate to do that, but… So, no showers or early gifts or any of that. I'll take care of the newborn items. It's the only way—"

"Where are you on that debt from your ex you're working through?"

"Close," she said, sitting straighter and smiling, very proud of herself. "Very close. I've put almost all the money he sent me toward the credit-card bills, just using a tiny smidgen of that money for incidentals. I have just six thousand left to pay." She beamed. She tasted a little more spaghetti, a little more salad. "I wouldn't have used any of his money, or any of the money my folks insisted on sending, but I'm tapped out and had to. I had to have maternity clothes—Lord, did I need maternity clothes! Do you see this? I'm growing out of Vanni's largest hand-me-downs!"

Cameron's expression darkened. He shook his head, took a swig of his beer and muttered, "He has millions! What a nasty thing to do to an innocent woman! I hope that son of a bitch burns in hell."

"Cameron! What a thing to say!" Then she smiled. "And I couldn't have said it better."

"Okay, let's start with that, then we'll get to our mothers. I'd like you to stop endorsing his checks and I'll clear that debt. Then—"

She was shaking her head. "No, I've got it all worked out. It won't be much longer—just another month or two and then—"

"Abby, I talked to Brie Valenzuela. She said to tell you to drop in and see her anytime. I'd be happy to go with you. Here's the way she sees it. He probably just stuck you with those bills on his lawyer's advice. In any case, the debt was a part of the dissolution of the marriage, which means it's court-ordered and you're stuck with it. But if he wants to chase down that prenup and try to prove you had sex with someone before the divorce was final, he'll have to take you to a civil court to sue you. It's not a felony, it couldn't make criminal court—no one would prosecute you for it. It would cost him more to sue you than he'd get if he won. And if he does take you back to court, he's going to look like the devil himself—he walks out on you after six weeks of marriage, never pays a penny of support for nine months of separation while he openly lives with another woman, and he wants over forty thousand dollars in credit-card debt on cards you never had and never used? When he's a millionaire? Never going to happen. He could make his situation worse."

"That's not what my lawyer said," she inserted.

"Which is why I talked to another one. Brie's a very experienced former state prosecutor and has been through a divorce of her own."

Abby groaned. "And so there's another person in town who knows."

"Take it easy. It's all lawyer-client privilege. Confidential. While she didn't deal with divorce in her practice, she knows everyone in the state and made some phone calls. As long as you clear the debt and don't take his money like some gold digger, that's going to be the end of it. You'll walk away from it. Unless he hates you for some purely personal…"

His voice trailed off at the unexpected sound of her laughter. "Personal hatred? I don't think he remembers my name. Cameron, he's on woman number ninety-two at least. He's been married three times and he's probably not smart enough to stop. Plus, I'm relatively sure he's using drugs, drinking himself stupid…" She wound some spaghetti around her fork and put it in her mouth. "This is very good," she said. "Does Brie really think if I obey my court instructions, I could get beyond this?"

"She does. And she's willing to help if there's a problem. Remember, he's a rock star on tour. How much energy do you think he has?"

"What about his lawyers?"

"Well, that's an issue. They could recommend more motions—if they want to make more money for themselves. Brie recommended a polite, legal letter bringing this whole business to a close. Let him get screwed by his lawyers and not by you."

"Hmm. That actually sounds very sensible. What else is on your mind?"

"Then," he said, leaning back a little, "after the debt is gone and you're finished with that business, or so we hope, I'll support you."

"Oh no, I don't want that...."

"Okay, I'll carry the babies and you support me," he suggested, winding his own spaghetti around his fork and grinning.

"Deal," she said, rubbing her lower back.

He continued to eat his spaghetti and salad and while he did so, he talked to her, friend to friend. "Here's the deal—we have stuff to handle. We have mothers—enough said. We have your prenup, which can be handled, but it's making you tense and you don't exactly need tension. That needs to go away. You can't live on air—you'll have to eat and cover your head, so you'll need some kind of income. There's furniture and supplies to buy. We have twins coming and I know you didn't hand-pick me for the job, but I'm the dad. Bad break for you, maybe, but I could turn out to be a good dad for them—I know a lot about kids. And this pregnancy is not the usual thing. I'd like to be close to the situation, to keep an eye on you and the babies. I *am* a doctor—that can come in handy, y'know?" He lifted a brow. "We should be in close contact, daily, on these issues and others—like names. They should get names before they come. Don't you think?"

She swallowed. "Well, I guess that's a good idea. You have my number."

"Why don't we consider moving in together? While we head for this event?"

She gulped. "What?" she asked weakly.

"Let's clear the debt, get Kid Crawford out of the picture, I'll take on your upkeep rather than Vanni and Paul shouldering your food and board, and we'll evolve into..." He cleared his throat. "We don't have to explain anything. People will just say, 'Dr. Michaels likes that nice pregnant girl.' We'll share a house. I'll be your roommate. You'll have your own room. But there will be late nights you're worried about some belly pain or later, night crying from the babies. You don't want to do that to Vanni and Paul and—"

"I was just going to go home to Seattle. To my mom and dad's."

"They have room for me?" he asked, lifting his fork and arching that brow.

"Oh, for God's sake," she said, slamming down her fork. "You can't mean to say you plan to just follow me and demand to live with the babies!"

"Well, no," he said. "That would be obsessive. But Jesus, Ab, I don't want to miss out on anything. Do you know how much babies change from two to six weeks? It just kills me to think you'd take them that far away from me. I mean, they are—"

"I know," she said, frustrated. *"Yours."*

"Yeah, sweetheart. And they're also yours. And I swear to God, I will never try to take them away from you. That would be cruel."

He had just aimed an arrow at her sense of justice. The shock of realization must have shown on her face, but he took another bite, had another drink of his beer, smiled.

"Live together?"

"Here's how it'll go if you stay with Vanni and Paul. Toward the end, when you're sleepless, you'll be up at night. You'll be tired during the day, but there will be a toddler around, making noise and crying. And you'll have all those late pregnancy complaints, worries. Then you'll have a small guest room stuffed to the ceiling with paraphernalia. Then babies—and grandmothers as additional guests? Newborns, sometimes, cry for hours. They could have Vanni and Paul up all night, walking the floor with you. Nah, that wouldn't be good. And besides, it's not Paul's job to help, it's mine."

"Where do you suggest we live? *Here?*"

"Here isn't bad," he said with a shrug. "But Mel and Jack offered us their cabin. It's a nice cabin—two bedrooms and a loft, ten minutes from town. Ideally, we should hurry and look around for a place that can accommodate a man, a woman, two newborns, two grandmothers and… We don't have to make room for the lawyers, do we?"

"Very funny," she said, crossing her arms over her chest.

"Abby, we have things to work out every single day. We have to buy cribs, car seats, swings, layette items, lots of stuff—it's going to take more than one trip to the mall.

We have to let the families know there will be babies coming—it's only fair. We should have dinner together every day, just so we can communicate, catch up. If there's anything you need or anything you're worried about, I want to be close so I can help. If you think I'm going to molest you while you're huge with my babies—"

"You know, I'm getting sick of that word, huge." She blinked at him. "Are you independently wealthy or something?"

"Nope," he said, shaking his head. "Just barely got all the bills paid from med school and residency. I have a little set aside. Not too much. In fact, after the babies are a couple of months old, I'm going to try to find a second job in one of the bigger towns to supplement my income. Then I can live in or close to Virgin River so I don't let these people down. I promised Virgin River a year. I'd hate to renege on that. They need a doctor here. But if you need me more…"

"You expect me to stay here while you give them that year?" she asked.

"Abby, I just hope I can take care of you and the kids well enough, help and make you happy enough, so you'll give me some time before you spring some major change on me. Because I care a lot about all of you. I do. I'm trying everything I can think of. And, Abby—I wouldn't run out on you." He swallowed. "But," he said with a shrug, "if you can't stay here, for whatever reason, I'll look for work wherever you and the babies go."

Oh goddamn, she thought. She was getting teary. Why would she get teary? He was trying so hard. But, he asked her to be his roommate.

He'd also offered to help her with everything in her life,

from her finances to her medical condition. And didn't he
suggest he'd walk the floor at night with screaming babies?

"The idea," she said, "is totally nuts."

"Not a first for us," he agreed, grinning handsomely.
"We're not exactly running with the pack, you and me.
Think about this. It could work. We could take care of each
other and our kids real easy. Eat more of that spaghetti. I
have a little cheesecake in the refrigerator."

"When do you want an answer?" she asked.

Cameron hoped it didn't show on his face that he was
elated to have gotten this far. Realistically, he had expected
to be wearing the spaghetti dinner just for the suggestion.
But she was actually considering it? Amazing. "Take your
time, Ab. There's no emergency." He glanced at her belly.
"For a good week or two."

"I think I've lost my appetite," she said.

"Nah," he laughed. "I didn't do anything scary. I didn't
threaten or beg. I offered help. We've had a few rough spots,
but we have good rapport. Abby, I really want to be part
of this. You're awful special to me. Keep eating and tell
me about those fireflies you caught as a kid. Tell me about
going to the lake with your family."

She did. It took a couple of minutes before she loosened
up, started talking about her childhood with laughter. She
never expected it, but this was so much like their first night
together, their *one* night together. They began as strangers and before an hour had passed they were telling their
stories, their secrets, laughing, touching hands, like old
friends. Like lovers.

She asked him about his childhood, about his family.
He told her anything she wanted to know and she realized
how much she had missed him since that fateful night. The

only reason they'd spent the night together in the first place was because they clicked so well, had so many common feelings and experiences.

Then they picked up the dishes and began scraping and rinsing them. She pulled out the trash can from under the sink and before dumping her leftover sausage and meatball into the bin, she started to laugh so much she bent over her tummy. She stuck her fork into the opening of a discarded jar and lifted it out of the trash. She presented an empty jar of Ragú spaghetti sauce.

He grimaced.

"Old family recipe?" she asked, laughing.

"Well, they're an old family," he said. "Or so I heard."

"Cameron," she laughed. "You're such a liar!"

First thing in the morning, Abby drove into town and went to the clinic. She had primped and tried to look her best, then she'd had a stern talk with herself about this situation.

Cameron not only made sense, he was being both reasonable and honorable. Whether they'd hand-picked each other or not, they were having a set of twins. Children who needed parents. Parents who would have to rely on each other and should not only get along, but be familiar with each other. There was no better way to accomplish that than by being roommates. She looked down at her stomach. There was certainly no chance of them being lovers.

But there was more to it. As gracious as Vanni and Paul had been about her extended stay, they deserved a life of their own. After all, she hadn't intended to impose for the duration—she had planned to rent something and go it alone. It took about five minutes to realize, going it alone was really not an option. She had to have a support system. She could live somewhere else and see Vanni every day if she wanted to. Not only did Vanni and Paul need their space, so did Abby. She wasn't used to living with people. She'd had a roommate years back, but they had been very independent of each other. And there was that brief time with her husband—very brief. Other than that, she was used to solitude.

At Vanni's house there was always someone around: a baby crying or squealing happily; Walt popping in regularly; Shelby and Luke dropping by, often bringing Luke's helper, Art, along, sometimes for dinner. Most evenings the house was full and noisy or they were all going to Jack's and got a little funky and worried if she tried to beg off and stay home. In the end, she always went along. She had almost no time to herself.

At least with Cam, he'd be at the clinic every day and wouldn't pester her to death in the evenings. And she would have her own room to flee to if Cameron made her feel the least bit crowded.

Really, it made sense. It would just be so awkward.

And boy, was there going to be a lot of talk!

When she walked into the clinic, she found Mel in the reception area going over some paperwork at the counter. She turned and smiled at Abby. "Well, hey there. How are you?"

"Good, thanks. I'm here to meet Cameron. He wants to show me your cabin...."

Mel got an unmistakably wistful look on her face. "I hope you like it," she said softly.

"If you're absolutely sure it's okay," Abby said.

"Oh, I'm thrilled for you to use it. That little cabin changed my life. I lived there until I married Jack, then we lived there together until our house was finished. When the weather gets a little warmer, you'll wake up to deer in the yard. New fawns with freckles on their backs. David was born there. Jack delivered him."

Abby got a wild look in her eyes. "I'm not planning to get that far back to nature," she said nervously.

Mel laughed. "I wasn't either. I didn't plan it," she said. "And Jack certainly didn't. But I wouldn't worry—with Cameron hovering over you to make sure everything is all right, that won't happen. I think you're in good hands."

"Mel," she said tentatively. "I'm a little worried about…"

"What?"

She took a breath. "Gossip. Everyone talking about us."

Mel's eyes twinkled and she smiled. "Abby, you're an unmarried woman pregnant with twins and you've been spending time with our pediatrician. He never misses a chance to sit by you at Jack's. Surrender. The gossip is way ahead of you."

Abby gasped. She leaned forward and whispered conspiratorially. "Do they think there's something to us? Like a relationship?"

One of Mel's light brows lifted in amusement. "They *hope*."

"Oh God!"

"Yeah, I've been there," Mel said. "The whole town had me married to Jack before I had my first really good kiss with him." She waved a hand. "Ah, hell, go with it. At least they're not malicious. Just very nosey. I got through it. You can, too."

Heavy footsteps started down the stairs. "Hey," Cam said cheerily. "You made it bright and early—thanks. I have some patients this morning. Ready to take a look at that cabin?"

"Sure," she said uneasily. And she thought, *What the hell am I doing?*

Ten minutes later they pulled into a clearing in the forest and she looked at a charming little cabin surrounded by huge trees. It had a peaked roof and a wide porch with Adirondack chairs. She could imagine the deer, colorful flowers bordering the porch. There was a beam of light that glanced through the trees and shone on the porch. And she said aloud, "What the hell am I doing?"

Cameron laughed at her. "Nesting," he said. "Come on." He got out of the car and went around to her side, giving his hand to pull her out.

He opened the door for her to walk into the house and what she saw was—a little cabin. One big room included living room, kitchen, breakfast nook and breakfast bar. There was only room for a sofa and overstuffed chair, ottoman and rocker surrounding a big stone hearth. A polished old chest served as a small coffee table in front of the sofa and there was one small side table and lamp. Back through the kitchen was a washer and dryer, water heater, pantry and stairs to the loft. It was shiny clean and quaint. Cute. *Small.*

The bedrooms weren't large, but big enough, with a bathroom separating them. And the loft wasn't enclosed by any more than a rail. There was a queen-size bed in one bedroom, a double bed in the loft. "This will be your bedroom and I'll take the loft," Cameron said. "I'll take a day off so we can go into Eureka and get some baby furniture for this room." He pulled her into what had been Mel and Jack's nursery, bare and ready for a couple of infants.

"Here's an idea, if it works for you," he said. "The first thing we do is get rid of that credit-card debt, get Brie to draft a letter saying you've paid your bill and don't want any more alimony, or any more contact with the ex. I'll set you up a bank account and get you a credit card." He chuckled. "Try to remember I'm not a filthy-rich rock star, I'm a relatively poor pediatrician and family-practice doctor who gets paid in beans a lot. Then we finish furnishing this place with cribs, et cetera. Now—it's out here a little ways, so if we find ourselves in a situation where you need bed rest or something, we'll just stay in town. You can have the bedroom I use at the clinic and I'll stay in the other room, so you're not alone. Other than picking out names, we're covering all the bases. If you think you can stand this little cabin, that is." He looked around. "I actually like it. It's cozy. Sweet."

But when he looked back at her, tears were running down her cheeks.

"Oh, Jesus, Abby," he said, pulling her toward him. "Do you hate it?"

"No," she sniffed, shaking her head. "I kind of like it."

"It could be temporary while we look for something better. I just want to keep us in close quarters, so I can help."

She shook her head and found words with difficulty. "What have you gotten yourself into?"

He wiped away a tear. "I know this is so hard for you. If you'd rather be at Vanni's, I'm sure she wouldn't mind. But, Abby, I— Honey, I want to help, be a part of it."

"I never thought I'd end up doing something like this. It's so…so…*calculated*. Such a practical arrangement."

"Abby, give me a chance here. I want to take care of you. I know you don't like hearing that—you're used to taking care of yourself." He slipped a hand over her belly. "Right now that's *not* practical. We have to think about your health. This isn't an ordinary pregnancy." He smiled sweetly. "It's an extraordinary pregnancy." She sniffed again and he pulled her close. "If there's a better way, better for you, just tell me. I'll do anything I can."

She shook her head against his shoulder. She inhaled his scent, remembered the lusty night that had gotten them here. She closed her eyes. Such a sweet memory....

And he felt one of them kick him in her belly. He pulled her closer, tighter, wanting more of that. "There are a few problems with this cabin," he said. "No TV, for one thing. Mel and Jack never installed a satellite dish. I hardly ever bother with TV. I catch the news at Jack's, listen to music and read a lot."

She pulled back from him just a bit and looked up into his blue eyes. "I have a portable DVD player. Vanni has lots of DVDs to loan. Maybe I'll watch a movie sometimes, but I like to read. I go through a couple of books a week— lately most of them are about pregnancy and childbirth. I guess you already know all about that."

"I'm pretty much up to speed. But I wouldn't mind looking at what you're reading."

"Maybe, if you're very nice, I'll let you watch a movie with me."

He smiled at her. "I bet they're all girl movies that make you cry." He used his thumb to wipe a tear away from her cheek.

"Cameron, everything makes me cry. Haven't you noticed?"

"It's pretty normal. Pregnant women cry a lot, whether they need to or not. When would you like to move? I don't want you alone out here, so I'll come at the same time. After I help you get your things transferred."

"In a day or two? All I have is clothes. Are we going to have some kind of routine or something?" she asked.

"Yes," he chuckled. "I'll go to work, but my schedule isn't demanding. I have a lot of free time when there aren't patients, but I won't hang around here and drive you crazy. You can do what you want—either stay here and relax, listen to music and read, or go hang out with Vanni. We'll have dinner together when you feel like it. We'll talk sometimes, like friends do. Pick names for the babies. When you give me permission, I'll call my mother, who is going to freak out."

"Oh God!"

He hugged her close. "It's going to be fine. She might be a little put out that we're not married, but the twins will mollify her. When you think I've earned the right, we'll share a DVD." He smiled at her.

"And after they're born? When it's time for me to get on with my life?"

"We'll talk about what you'd like to do, where you'd like to be, and what you want will be a priority. I'll see how I can fit in that plan as a dad. But, Abby, can we get to that later? One thing at a time? As long as I promise I don't have any plan to screw up your life?"

"Sure," she said. "One thing at a time. Aren't you worried what people will think?"

"Hell no," he said, shaking his head. "I've only been here a few months, but there are a million interesting little stories that verge on scandals in this town. People love 'em. If I had the slightest worry anyone would treat you meanly, I'd never have suggested this."

"What kind of little scandals?"

"We have lots of time for me to catch you up on the local stuff, like Mel and Jack, Preacher and Paige, and I guess you probably already know about Vanni and Paul."

Very suddenly, Abby felt relief flood through her. She knew that whole story—that Paul had been in love with Vanni for years, but she'd married his best friend. And then, after Vanni's husband Matt was killed in Iraq and the way to her was clear, Paul had such guilt and shame about his obsession, he couldn't act. If that wasn't bad enough, he thought he had gotten a woman back in Oregon pregnant. "Does everyone know about that?" she asked in a stunned whisper.

"I doubt we could find anyone around here who doesn't know at least a version of the story." Then he shrugged. "Abby, you have to remember—the important thing is that you're healthy, we're working together to bring healthy twins into the world and we're going to do the best we can to be good parents. Who's gonna throw rocks at that idea? Only a petty fool. And I say, screw the petty fools."

She grinned at him. There *was* a reason she'd gone to that hotel room.

Seven

It was ten days after Mel and Cameron's emergency run to Valley Hospital with Dahlia Creighton when Cheryl came to Virgin River. Mel had heard that Dahlia hadn't survived long enough for bypass surgery. She'd had far too many medical problems to get through what might have otherwise been an uncomplicated surgery.

This was only the second time Mel had seen Cheryl since she'd entered an alcohol-treatment program over six months ago and the change in her still startled Mel and brought a bright smile to her lips. When Cheryl walked into the clinic, despite the fact that she had just lost her mother, Mel nearly beamed at her. She had to quickly reel in the reaction. This was not a time to grin stupidly. But Cheryl looked so good—fresh, healthy, pretty. It was hard to imagine her the way she'd been when Mel first met her, slouched and dirty, wearing men's clothes, looking bruised both physically and emotionally.

"Hi, Mrs. Sheridan," she said. "Did you hear the news about my mother?"

"I did, Cheryl. I'm so sorry for your loss. We did all we could."

"Of course you did, as did the other doctors. My mother was very sick. Really, she didn't stand a chance. And she wouldn't even consider medical treatment before. Truthfully, I don't think she thought she needed any. And between my father and I, we weren't alert or smart enough to know, either."

"This must be a very difficult time for you," Mel said.

"It is. And challenging, but I have it worked out, sort of. My dad has gone to live with his brother in Yuba City, on the other side of the mountains. I have to deal with the house. It's mine now. I can't support my dad, so he's better off with his brother and Medicare. That's the best we can do. He has a ton of health problems, too. He has serious emphysema, among other things."

"Will you move home?"

She shook her head. "I'm never living in that house again. I'm done with that part of my life. I have a decent job in Eureka and someday I might even have my own place."

"Are you still living in your group home?" Mel asked.

"Well, I have roommates. We're all in the same program, so it's like a group home, but not official. I'd sell the house, but it's just not salable. It's falling down. I'm going to clean it out of trash. I brought some friends to help," she said, jerking her chin over her shoulder toward the street in front of the clinic. "I'm going to stop by Jack's and ask him if he has a problem with us filling up that Dumpster. Most of the junk left behind by my dad will be tossed and we'll take the bigger stuff to the dump in the back of the pickup."

"I'm sure Jack will be happy to let you use the Dumpster if it'll help."

"As long as we can close the lid when we're done. Have

to close the lid around here or wildlife will get in there and make a mess, disturb the town."

"And then?" Mel asked.

She shrugged. "I might just let it go, the house. If I can't keep up the taxes, I'll lose it eventually, anyway. In the meantime, if anyone you know needs shelter, I can let them use it. As long as they're not alcoholics or drug addicts. I can't go along with that."

Mel smiled. "Still heavy into your program, are you?"

"Amazing and hard to believe, isn't it?"

"Not really. You were ready."

She laughed, and her face was so pretty. Her hair so shiny. "More than ready. I just wanted to stop by, say hello and thank-you."

Mel tilted her head, and her smile was a little sad. "I'll be sorry not to see you again."

"I'll probably be back a couple more times before I'm all done here. Let me give you a phone number, just in case someone desperately needs a roof. That's about all it is. And if you do run into someone like that, please tell them I didn't clean the place, just emptied it of trash. It wasn't really my house. I'm embarrassed by the condition it's in, but not embarrassed enough to spend days scrubbing it. Being there...it just takes me back to a bad place."

"I understand," Mel said, lifting a small notepad off the counter.

Cheryl scratched out her number in Eureka. "Jesus, I wish I could do something for you. I owe you my life. I really do."

Mel put a hand on her shoulder. "Listen to me now. I made some phone calls. That's all. You did all the heavy lifting."

"There's the thing," she said. "No one ever made phone calls for me before. I was the town drunk and no one ever thought I had a chance of being anything else. Till you came here. And that's the God's truth."

"Well," Mel said, sniffing back emotion. "Weren't they short-sighted? You're clearly headed for wonderful things."

Later the same day, Mel hauled both her kids to the bar at five o'clock. Since he'd moved into the cabin with Abby, Cameron was anxious to get home at the end of the day, even though his dinner at Jack's was on the house. This was not at all mysterious to Mel.

Jack came around the bar and took David off her hands. "Hey, my man," he said to his son. "Wanna ride on Da's back for a while?"

Mel jumped up on a stool and said, "Just hang on to him for a second, Jack. Let me have a diet cola and I'll get these maniacs home. Bring us something of Preacher's later?"

"Sure, babe." He deftly drew her a cola, one-handed, his son on his hip. But David wasn't in the mood to be confined. He was two now and well into the terribles. He was bowing his back, kicking his feet, whining. "Settle down, bud," Jack said, hanging on to him. It wasn't a good idea to give him his freedom in the bar and grill. Nothing but trouble and breakage awaited.

"Got any chips or popcorn?" said a voice just a couple of stools down from Mel.

"Yeah, I can rustle some up," Jack said. "Gimme a minute, huh? I have my hands full of madness."

Mel turned and saw it was Dan Brady, having himself a beer.

"I thought if you could hand me the progeny, bring us

something to snack on, you and your wife could have a minute." He held out his hands toward David. "I'm checked out. I know how to hang on to a kid wild with the devil."

Jack's eyebrow lifted. "Do you now? Aren't you just full of surprises. I honestly didn't know you could do anything but grow weed." He shifted and handed David across the bar.

At first David squealed in annoyance, but Dan grabbed him and brought him onto his lap. "Hey now," he said, holding him with a firm arm around his waist, bouncing him on his thigh. "Take it easy. Only in a town of six hundred would it be considered normal to have a kid your age right up at the bar. Count your blessings."

Jack shook out some Goldfish crackers into a bowl. "His favorite," he explained.

"Perfect," Dan said. He turned his attention on David. "So, little man, you want one?" He maneuvered the small cracker into David's mouth. "Now. Give one to me? Please?"

David thought about it a second, then slowly pushed one toward Dan's open mouth. "Mmm," Dan said. "Your turn." And he plucked one out of the bowl and directed it toward David's mouth, but pulled it back, making the kid laugh. "Oh, you want that? Can you say please?"

David shook his head obstinately, stiffening his back, grinding his fists into his eyes, pushing out his lower lip. Dan took the Goldfish for himself and laughed. "Let's try that again," he said, picking up another. "Please?" he coached.

"Pease," David said in a pout.

"Wonderful," Dan approved, popping a Goldfish into his mouth.

"You're gifted," Jack observed. "He's been a real asshole lately."

"Jack! We were going to try to stop swearing!"

"Yeah, I know. I think I'm doing better at that than you are, by the way. But hasn't he been?"

"He can't help it—he's at the asshole age. He'll come around."

"See?" Jack said, grinning at her. "You have a rotten mouth and you can't help yourself."

She grinned back at him. "I never uttered a single curse until I met you."

Dan focused on David. "Your parents are flirting with each other. You better have another fish. You could be on my lap a long time."

Jack studied him for a moment. "You got some experience there, pal," he finally said.

"Some," Dan answered. Then he looked at David and said, "My turn. Please." And he opened his mouth for a fish.

"Like with kids," Jack said. "Nephews and nieces or something like that."

"Something like that," he said. And then, to David. "Your turn. Say please."

"Pease," he said, smiling and opening his dripping, goopy mouth.

Dan looked at Jack. "How's the boy? Rick?"

"Aw, I don't know. Mel and Preacher both say he's working through the whole thing, but he's different. He doesn't reach out, you know? He doesn't call me, doesn't call the girlfriend. He was so into that girl, I can't even explain how much. Nowadays, he avoids her."

"Having a hard time, I guess," Dan said, right before he looked at David and said, "Your turn. Say please."

"Pease!"

"How's the girl handling that?" Dan asked Jack.

"You know, I didn't have a real conversation with you for three years and now you're like a neighbor. No, you sound like a goddamn shrink."

Dan smiled at him and opened his mouth for a fish. But David shouted, "Pease!"

"She's trying to understand," Mel said, answering for Jack. "I think it's hurting her a lot, but she's amazingly patient and understanding for a young girl. There's a counselor she talked to once before who's trying to help her out. At least there's that." She shook her head and kissed Emma's fat cheek. "She's only a senior in high school. Just turned eighteen. They fell in love too young."

Dan looked back at David and said, "Please." Then it was David's turn again, but Dan turned to Mel. "Eighteen and... What did you say he was? Twenty? They have a lot of time to get beyond this. It could take a while, but they have a while. They're just kids."

"They hurt," Mel said. "I just hate to see them hurt like that."

"Nobody gets through the years without a ton of pain, you know?" And then David yelled at him. "Oh. Please," he said, opening his mouth for a fish. He chewed and smiled. "You're going to get so sick of the good manners here. It gets old."

The door to the bar opened and Cheryl Creighton stuck her head in. "Jack, we're all done over at the house and I'm afraid we filled up your Dumpster. The house isn't how it should be, but it's cleaned up some. Let me leave you a key. If anyone needs to use it, just let me know, huh? Mel's got my number. I don't know what I'm going to do with it yet. But really—"

"House?" Dan said. "Trailer? Condo? Room? Shed? Lean-to?"

"Cheryl's house is empty," Mel said. "She says it's not in good shape."

"Would you let me see it?" Dan asked.

She frowned. "Listen, it's falling apart. It's—"

"Does it have hot water? A toilet that flushes? Lights that turn on and off?"

"And that's about all."

"Would you let me see it? Is it for rent?"

Cheryl frowned slightly. "Listen, first of all, you're not going to need much of a look to see you'd be better off sleeping in your truck. And second, I'll only let someone stay there on a recommendation from the Sheridans. I don't really care if the thing burns down, but I don't want anything bad to happen in that neighborhood because I let some riffraff in."

Dan smiled slightly. "First of all, I *am* sleeping in my truck. And second, I could maybe get a reference from my boss. He seems to like me."

"I'll vouch for him, Cheryl. If he thinks he wants to rent it," Jack said.

This caused a look of surprise to take over Dan's face, but it disappeared as David was shoving a Goldfish into his mouth.

Cheryl thought about it for a second. Then she shrugged. "Well, at least it'll go cheap if you're interested. But you won't be interested. Come on, let's get this over with. I want to get home." And she turned and left.

Dan stood and hefted David toward Jack. "Well, gee. Maybe my luck is turning around."

"If I vouch for you," Jack said, "I'll be watching you."

Dan laughed. "Oh golly, Jack. I just wouldn't have it any other way."

Dan got in his truck and followed Cheryl the short couple of blocks to the neighborhood. She had three other people besides herself in an extended cab truck—one guy, two women. The truck bed was loaded with what appeared to be broken-down furniture, covered with a tarp and tied down. He supposed if they were cleaning out the house, she had needed some help.

He looked first at the neighborhood in general—it wasn't upper middle class, that was for sure. The houses were small, most in poor repair. But there were a few that stood out and looked as if they were maintained with care, kept immaculate with tidy flower beds and healthy yards. When Cheryl pulled up in front of an old house, some of the flaws were instantly apparent—the porch was missing boards and was about to fall down altogether, one window was covered with plastic kept in place by duct tape and the roof was about half-rotten shingles. Well, he wouldn't be getting up there. But he worked for a builder who had roofers— maybe he could get a discount to keep the rain off his head.

Inside was actually better than he expected. It didn't smell great, but all that would take was soap and water. He stepped right into a living room/dining room—the walls needed plaster and paint, the floors needed resurfacing, that window needed glass, the lighting fixtures were ancient and therefore so was much of the wiring. But there was a large stone fireplace on one wall, large windows on the other. A door off the dining area probably led to the bedroom.

The kitchen was small, barely room for a little table and four chairs, about 1950s vinyl decor. The linoleum on the floor was scarred, cracked, peeling and permanently stained. A couple of cupboard doors were missing and the stove and refrigerator were at least as old as he was. There seemed to be a room behind the kitchen, but the add-on was sloppy—it wasn't level with the rest of the house. Dan stepped carefully across that uneven chasm and pushed the door open.

"There's a larger bedroom off the dining room," Cheryl said. "Bathroom's right there." She pointed to the right of the kitchen.

He peeked first into the bathroom—nice size with a newly installed, as of about fifteen years ago, perfectly hideous shower. It was more like a large pan on the floor with a drain in it, a disgusting-looking shower curtain on a circular rod attached to the wall. He tilted his head and frowned as he studied the contraption.

As if she could read his mind, she said, "My mother was a very large woman and couldn't handle the tub, so my dad, who is obviously not very handy with things like this, put in a shower for her. It's a terrible-looking thing, I know. And it needs a new curtain, but honestly, I never expected anyone to want to look at it. And when you get down to it, I don't have the money to make things nicer around here. It's as is."

"Is there a washer and dryer, by any chance?" he asked.

"Uh-huh. They still work, too. Out back on the porch. It's not heated out there, but it's enclosed. And the water heater is only a few years old, so that should make it a while."

He took a quick look at what one would call the master bedroom. It was really an awful-looking little house that had the potential to look nice—barely big enough for a couple and one child. He could spend some time checking the structure later, but for now it appeared all its ugliness was merely cosmetic. Some elbow grease would make it civilized, but some remodeling talent could make it quaint.

"How much?" he asked her.

She was stunned. "You're kidding me."

"I thought maybe I could do a few things around here to make the place presentable if you give me a break on the rent. I'm a builder by trade. You thinking you might sell it someday?"

"I don't know. I know I'm not interested in living in it—I work in Eureka. But I just found out the house was my responsibility, so... I guess I'll either rent it, sell it, or let the state take it for nonpayment of taxes."

"Shew," he said. "You really do have some thinking to do. Listen, here's the deal. I'll pay you some rent and take care of the utilities. If you give me a break on the rent, I'll see if I can fix it up a little bit. If you decide to sell it and I make you an offer, you'll deduct my materials and labor from the price. Think about that."

Her eyes just grew wider. "You can have it for two-fifty a month. Do whatever you want. You can't make it any worse, even if you're the worst builder in America."

"Two hundred," he said. "That should pay your taxes. Give you time to think. But you have to let me have it for a year, to make it worth my while to do some things to it. And I'm not the worst builder in America." He grinned at her.

She put out her hand. "Deal."

"You have some kind of contract?" he asked.

"Nope. Try to be a nice guy about this and if you decide to abandon the place, lock up and let Jack know. Mrs. Sheridan has my number in Eureka."

"Well, Jesus," he said, taking off his hat and running his hand over his short hair. "Don't you want to know my name?"

"Sure," she said. "What is it?"

"Dan Brady."

"I'm Cheryl Creighton. Be a good neighbor, will you? I think the last people who lived here were a lot of trouble."

"And who would that be?"

"Me. Us. My parents and I."

He chuckled. "Would you like to seal this deal over a drink?"

"No, thanks. I don't care for a drink. Do you drink a lot?"

"Me? I've been known to have a beer or two."

"Get drunk a lot?" she asked.

He frowned, having no idea what her issue was. Maybe she came from a hard-drinking family and it put her off in a big way. "I get drunk not at all," he said. "It's not convenient. But I like a beer sometimes. That going to be a problem?"

"Gee," she said. "That must be nice."

"Huh?"

"Get the utilities taken care of right away. Get them in your name. I'll come back out in a couple of weeks or a month and if you still want to live here, I'll pick up your rent check and give you an address to mail it to me." She wiggled a key off her key chain, handed it to him. "If you change your mind, give the key to Jack."

No first and last months' rent? No security deposit? he

wondered. Then he realized a security deposit on this dump was ridiculous, but you'd think she'd want to get a month's rent out of him. He pulled out his wallet and peeled off five twenties. "Here," he said. "That'll take care of the rest of the month. Don't worry, I won't do anything bad to your house. And I work for a guy from town, so I'm not going to steal from you or anything."

She actually gave a huff of laughter. What could he possibly steal? The forty-year-old stove and refrigerator? "Yeah, good," she said. "Well, at least you'll get the ugliest hot shower of your life."

"Hey, that will be a good thing," he said.

She gave a curt nod, turned and left. He just stood there a minute, totally perplexed. She was a little messed up from cleaning out this dump of a house, but there was no concealing her basic good looks, trim figure. But there was also no concealing the unhappy person inside.

And then he heard her truck depart from the front of the house. Her business was done here.

Since her one-night visit to Virgin River, Muriel had tried to talk to Walt every day, but occasionally she'd miss one. By mid-April she'd been working on her movie two months. They had started some sound-stage filming in a fake farmhouse built on a studio lot, and there was a lot more of that to do. But now came the real deal. The cast and crew were moving to Montana to film on location. This was her perfect opportunity for another escape. While most of the company moved on to set up, she could take some time and arrive when they were ready for her. Given her experience, trusted professionalism and—oh, yes—she was the *other* big star, she could take a break. No production company Lear this time, so she got a ticket on a private commuter and flew into the little Garberville airport. One of the ground crew gave her a lift out to her house.

Lately, whenever she'd talked to Walt, Muriel had been hearing something distant in his voice. Maybe it was just his loneliness with her being away. Or maybe he was unwilling to compete with her career. Maybe, regardless of what he said, he'd expected her to say no to a fantastic acting opportunity to stay home with him, proving her love. Given the number of men she'd been through in her life and her independence, she could just say *Phhhhttt*—get over it. Everyone gets a life, bub, not just the boys.

And that's what she would say, if she became convinced he was just another difficult man who had to be sure he was always on top, that he was first ahead of her work, her sense of self, her need to be productive. She just hadn't seen that in him. There was something different about Walt, and she'd known it since the first moment she'd met him. He had all the ingredients of the superior male beast—big, tough, heroic, masterful, dominant. But then she'd see him with his daughter or grandchild and realize that he was more than that. He had a tenderness so deep, a loyalty so strong, and a reliability so constant she wanted to embrace it and never let go.

So she was taking her brief ten-day hiatus in Virgin River to find out if Walt was just another man, or maybe a little lonely, in need of reassurance. She'd earned the break. And Walt, she thought, had earned the benefit of the doubt.

The pilot of her plane had asked around and found her a ride. Once home, she called Walt's house, but there was no answer. Jeez. Hollywood might be all superficial fluff, but at least they could exist on cell phones!

She rustled up her extra set of keys and took her truck into town. Ah, there he was—his Tahoe was parked in front of Jack's with quite a few other vehicles. A glance at her watch told her it was probably dinnertime. She walked into the quiet hum of conversation; Jack's was rarely real noisy. She pulled off her hat, ruffled her hair with her fingers and scanned the room. Then she saw his broad back. He sat up at the bar talking with his niece, Shelby, while Luke stood behind Shelby with a hand on her shoulder. On Walt's other side was Paul, lifting a beer.

"Hey, now," she heard Jack say, causing them all to turn.

Muriel had taught herself to read people a long time ago. It was necessary in her line of work to get a message from the body language and the eyes. Walt smiled a little bit, but his posture opened to her and his eyes grew instantly warm. Yet it was Shelby who jumped off her stool. "Muriel! What are you doing here?"

She gave Shelby a hug. "Taking a little break from filming while I can. How are you?"

"Perfect! But what about you? Is it incredibly exciting?"

Muriel chuckled. "No, sweetheart. It's mundane. It just happens to fill up about sixteen hours a day and is usually exhausting." She walked toward the men, arm in arm with Shelby. "Walt, I tried to call. You weren't home so I came here."

"Good bet," he said, leaning toward her. He slipped an arm around her waist and gave her a peck on the cheek.

Ah, there it was. She could feel the vibration under his skin. He was glad to see her. Maybe relieved. She didn't want to make a scene by throwing herself into his arms, so she turned to Luke. "How are you? I see he didn't shoot you."

Luke laughed and shook his head. "Not yet. But I'm still listening for that rifle cock."

"Hell, *I'm* still listening for that," Paul said, sipping his beer.

Jack chuckled and said, "What's your pleasure, Muriel?"

"How about a beer? Whatever you think I'll like."

"Done," he said, slapping a napkin on the bar.

"How's the family, Jack?"

"Exceptional. Mel's exceptionally gorgeous and demanding, Emma's exceptionally beautiful and David is an exceptionally bad terrible two. We may not survive him."

"Oh, weaker men than you have made it through that stage," she said. She picked up her beer and raised it. "I hope you have some good gossip. I've missed the hell out of this place."

"I think we can keep you entertained for a little while," Shelby said. And for the next half hour or so, she laughed and hummed at the local tales, both funny and serious. Shelby had decided to make Luke's life and marry him, date to be announced, the local pediatrician was living with Vanni's pregnant girlfriend, Jack was having trouble getting Rick to open up on the phone about how he was doing in rehab, but within a couple of weeks he could go down to Naval Medical Center in San Diego to pick him up, bring him home. And little David had a big, round, purple lump on his forehead from throwing himself on the floor in a temper and banging his head.

Walt didn't let it go on very long. Jack handed him a sack of some of Preacher's takeout and he stood from the bar. "You must be starving," he said to Muriel. He lifted one dark brow and tilted his head toward the door.

Now, Muriel was too aware that if anyone else in this bar had pulled that trick, the laughter and jeering would have been relentless. No one got by with anything around here, and certainly nothing that obvious. But this was the general and even Shelby, who had him wrapped around her little finger, was cautious. Respectful.

"Starving," she said with a smile. Then she turned to Jack. "I'll be around for ten days. I'll see plenty of everyone. Tell Mel I said hello and I'll catch up with her."

"You bet."

Outside, on the bar's porch, Walt slipped an arm around her waist. He put his rough cheek against hers and said, "Your horses are fed. Come to my place. The usual suspects now know better than to step foot near it."

A few minutes later she was laughing hysterically as her Labs assaulted her while Walt tried to pin her against the wall just inside the door. And, oh God, had she needed to come home!

"Ten days?" he asked, his voice coarse.

"Ten."

"What do you want to do while you're here?"

"I want to ride, run the dogs and sit on my porch with you and a glass of wine, watching the sun go down. Then I'd like to sit on my porch with you in the morning with coffee and watch it come up. And this," she said, running her hands over his shoulders and down his arms. "I want to stay real close to the feeling of your arms around me."

"Sounds doable," he said. "How about we start with a nice, slow, relaxing orgasm? Then we can make plans while we have dinner."

"I can do that," she said, kissing him.

Rick Sudder had been at the San Diego Naval Medical Center for a little over a month. He'd transferred from the ward into the barracks weeks ago and had his new preparatory prosthesis. It was a hard plastic socket for his stump attached to a mechanical knee and then a titanium pylon attached to a plastic foot. It would probably be a couple more months before he'd get the real deal, a fake leg that at least looked like a fake leg instead of a rod stuck into a running shoe. And that was another thing—the running shoe. He didn't *wear* running shoes unless he was playing basketball. He wore *boots*. But this was safer, sturdier, and the height of the sole was significant in measuring the length of the pylon so he'd be level. From what he heard from other amputees around the barracks, he should feel lucky to be level.

He was still learning the ropes. A below-the-knee amputation was a piece of cake compared to his—he had to learn to balance and operate a mechanical knee. Frankly, he preferred the wheelchair or crutches. The wheelchair had to be weighted on the front side bars so he wouldn't tip over backward because he no longer had the counterweight that his leg would have provided, but he still would rather that than a walker. And crutches were a little unstable, not that it mattered to him. But they insisted on the walker, which made him feel like an old man. Plus, he was still hurting. His foot where there was no foot itched till he wanted to lose his mind.

The pain was so much more manageable, but leaning his weight on the prosthesis was tough and the phantom pain still drove him crazy, especially at night. That, he was told, wasn't exactly easily remedied. It was a process of retraining the nerves, a tedious, frustrating exercise. He was walking now, inside the parallel bars and with the walker.

In rehab he'd been focusing on straightening the leg to prevent contractures—the shortening of the muscles in the thigh of his amputated leg. He'd been forced to lie on his belly, something they called proning, and lift that stump to extend his hip. Then he'd stand at the bars while a therapist pulled back on it. And he was instructed to repeat these exercises while on his own, but he didn't. Getting better didn't interest him enough, and he knew that. He also knew he'd probably be sorry, but motivation was hard to embrace.

Then there was group. Group was almost unbearable. Let's all get together and talk about what it feels like to lose your limbs or not be able to move your body from the waist down, what *fun!* Let's have a little chat about how scrambled your brain is after you've been shot/blown up/ crushed. Or, how about we have a good cry followed by a group hug? And then, the frosting on the cake, accept praise from the group moderator—who, by the way, has arms and legs and doesn't have to get around in a chair—because you let it all out and cried in front of the boys.

Rick wasn't sure he could stand much more of this. The only thought worse was going home like this, with a brain like so much spaghetti and one leg even worse than Captain Ahab's.

He had to admit to himself, being in the barracks as opposed to the ward was better, especially the freedom of movement. All the men had some form of disability, and they traveled back and forth to the hospital physical therapy department, but also to the exchange to buy anything from snacks to paperbacks, to the base movie theater, or on outings with friends or family members. His roommates were more relaxed, more honest. He was actually forming some relationships. They were like members of a squad, almost. But at least they could bitch about the physical terrorists, the counselors, their families or girlfriends or buddies back home who just didn't seem to get it, and they didn't have to bare their souls or cry to be doing it right.

He couldn't complain about the food or the weather. He couldn't remember the Marine Corps or navy ever feeding him decent food before this. And San Diego in April was like a piece of heaven. The sun was bright and warm, the breeze was clean and smelt vaguely of the sea, at night the sky was usually clear or the storms gathered off the coast and put on a light show over the ocean. He spent as much time outside as he could, finding a bench or chair in either the courtyard or in front of the barracks and just parked there, soaking up the sun. The southern California sun was so much sweeter than that mean, harsh desert sun in Iraq.

There hadn't ever been this much sun in Virgin River; if the height of the trees didn't block it, then the clouds did. In Virgin River you wore your sealskin eleven months of the year; mountain life was chilly to cold almost year-round.

His cell phone chimed in his pocket and he pulled it out to see who was calling. Unknown. That was a trick only Liz tried, hoping he'd pick up. Jack never bothered with that because Jack wasn't a crafty teenage girl. He let it go to voice mail. Liz had been sending him things at least twice a week. Stupid things. Cookies she made that weren't all that good, magazines that looked used, cheap cologne, as if he'd be going out on some date or something, Soap-On-A-Rope and razors, like the Naval Medical Center wouldn't keep him clean. A Saint Christopher medal. For what? To keep him safe from now on? Stupid, stupid things. Things that made his eyes water at her sweet caring, her simple but beautiful attempts to bring him any level of pleasure. He treated her like such shit she should just cut him loose and spend all those efforts on someone else, someone who deserved it.

A car pulled up in front of the barracks, a woman jumped out of the driver's side and ran around to the passenger door. Her skirt was short and flouncy, her knit top snug, legs long and shapely. And man, what an ass—round and tight and pretty. Aaron's woman. Aaron was one of his roommates, about a week ahead of him in this rehab program.

She held out her hand to Aaron and helped him stay steady while he stepped out on his prosthetic leg, the preparatory kind. And once he had himself balanced in the open car door, he pulled his woman against him and she molded there, planting her lips on his, her firm breasts pressed up against him, his arms around her waist with one hand slipping down to that fabulous butt to pull her even closer.

Aaron was about thirty and this was his fiancée. He was one happy-go-lucky son of a bitch, like nothing much was wrong. He had also been wounded in Iraq, but he hadn't been blown up. He took a bullet and it shattered his knee so catastrophically they had to amputate, yet to listen to him, talk to him, you'd think this was some minor fucking inconvenience. Rick vacillated between admiring him and hating him.

While Aaron kissed his girl, Rick's voice-mail message alert bleeped. But Rick watched Aaron. He wondered what it would feel like to believe he had the right to do that to a woman, with a woman.

Aaron had said he was going to run some wedding-planning errands with his girl and if he was real lucky, he'd be able to talk her into some afternoon delight at a hotel that was accessible, haw haw haw. He looked pretty delighted, pretty relaxed. Apparently that had worked out for him.

"Want me to walk you in, baby?" the fiancée asked.

He grabbed for his cane out of the front seat. "Nah, sweetheart, I got it. I'll talk to you tonight." Then he grinned. "Glad we got everything taken care of."

"Yeah, me too," she said, giving him another quick kiss. "Practice up now so you can come home."

"You bet I will," he said, smiling.

Aw, Jesus, Rick thought. Can we get any sweeter? You're a goddamn cripple! Have you noticed, crip, you haven't got a real leg there? And the one they gave you—it's not working that good.

She held his hand, backing away from him so slowly like they couldn't bear to be apart. Rick felt it squeeze his chest. Vaguely, in the back of his mind, it reminded him of the way he'd pulled away from Liz when he said goodbye to her before leaving for Iraq.

He squashed the memory.

Aaron walked slowly toward Rick, who sat on the bench outside the front door of the barracks, his walker beside him.

"How you doing, Rick?" Aaron asked.

"Great," Rick said, because he knew how the game was played. You stay up! You stay positive! You act like getting this fake piece-of-shit leg was your fucking dream come true! "How was your afternoon? Or do I even need to ask?"

"Good," Aaron said, not taking the bait. "We got some things done. Sandy has this whole wedding business nailed. All I do is say, looks good to me." He smiled a bit wistfully. "She's so great."

"Maybe you had a little afternoon delight, too," Rick suggested.

"Any time I get to spend with Sandy is perfect," he said.

"Just out of curiosity, isn't it kind of difficult?"

Aaron stood right in front of him, forcing him to look up. "What, exactly?"

"You know what."

"Sex?"

Rick was speechless for a second. He'd rather speak in code, but Aaron was pretty upfront. Especially with these issues. "Uh, yeah. That."

Aaron laughed. "It was a lot harder to learn how to take a shower."

"Where's the leg go?" Rick heard himself ask.

"Right up against the wall, pal. It's not real soft and cuddly. But I get some very fine traction without it." Then he chuckled. "You worried about that, my brother?"

"Just curious."

"Then let me make this easy for you. I take it off. That seems to be the popular solution for most men. And I'm going to get this thing broken in as quick as I can. I want to walk Sandy down the aisle and dance with her at the reception. It might not be Fred Astaire style, but if I don't fall on my ass, I'll be damn happy."

Rick grinned, but he thought, you simple fool. You screw with a stump and limp around the dance floor like an idiot and you're damn happy? Fool. "Good for you," Rick said, because that's what he was expected to say.

"You have a girl, don't you, Rick?"

"Nah," he said, shaking his head. "No girl."

"I thought I heard there was a girl back home."

"Nah. I dated some, that's all. No girl."

"Well, then," Aaron said, grinning. "You have something to look forward to. I didn't find my Sandy till I was twenty-six."

And didn't you have a couple of legs then? Rick wanted to ask. But he said, "Sure. Yeah."

When Aaron had gone inside, Rick checked his message.

"Hi, Rick, it's me. You never pick up and I guess I stopped expecting you to call back, but I just wanted to call you anyway, tell you I think about you every second. I'm graduating in less than two months, can you believe that? This girl you had to beg to stay in school? And guess what? I have all As. But I think I told you that already. Maybe a hundred times. That is, if you listen to the messages. I don't know—maybe you just delete them. But anyway, I know you're going to be out of there before too much longer, and it would just be so...awesome...if you came to graduation. I'd be so proud to have you come. I guess I won't know anything about that until you call me back. Hey!" she said, changing her tone. *"I sent you a little something. I hope you like it."*

Rick clicked off the phone. Then he turned it back on and replayed the message. Then replayed it again. Then listened to an older one, her voice making his eyes sting and then cloud. He missed her so much. But he couldn't... couldn't...couldn't...

Yeah, sure. Like I'm going to watch you graduate, your boyfriend, with a peg leg in a pair of dorky running shoes. Get real, he thought. Then he turned off the phone and put it in his pocket.

Eight

Abby called Cameron at about three in the afternoon to say, "Don't eat at Jack's tonight—I'm cooking us a special dinner."

"You got it. Can I bring anything home from the corner store?"

"Nope. I already shopped at the grocery in Fortuna. I've been shopping all day, buying little things for the babies. Just the essential newborn things in neutral colors until we find out the sex of the second baby. I can't wait to show you everything."

She was so happy, so excited, it left Cameron grinning like a schoolboy, hardly able to abide two more hours with nothing to do at the clinic. But he didn't want to rush home and spoil Abby's special dinner.

Still, Cameron left the clinic early and drove all the way to Grace Valley to buy her a bouquet of flowers. He made a mental note to tell Connie she might want to stock a few bouquets from time to time—he couldn't be the only husband who wanted to surprise his wife with some flowers. Oh, that's right! he thought with a laugh. I'm not a husband, she's not a wife. They were just playing house. But they were playing it very well. The first thing they'd done after she moved her clothes into the closet at the cabin was drive over to Eureka and buy two cribs, a changing table and small chest of drawers. They spent some time looking at baby products online at Babies 'R' Us so Abby could pick out what she liked and they could start a steady stream of purchasing right up to the births.

What had Abby said, that they'd probably be completely incompatible? Far from it. They moved through that tiny cabin so smoothly and with such ease, it was as if they'd lived together for years. In barely two weeks, they were becoming good friends, almost a couple. This was what he'd expected since the moment he met her, that they'd bond this way. And there was affection as well. They found plenty to talk about that had nothing to do with her pregnancy or the twins and had become comfortable enough in each other's company for the casual touching of hands, arms, shoulders; there was even an occasional kiss on the brow or cheek. At first it was Cameron, giving her that avuncular peck, but soon it was Abby, also, standing on her toes to kiss his cheek.

The only thing that could make him happier would be if they could become a real family—husband, wife and kids. This was still in its infancy and Abby needed time. But she liked him, he knew she did. She couldn't keep it secret. She liked him, depended on him, respected him. It was going in the right direction.

He walked into the cabin to see pots on the stove, the makings of a salad in progress scattered around the counter, and Abby's feet hoisted up on the arm of the sofa. He leaned over the back of the sofa and looked down at her. "You all right?"

"I don't know. I don't think so."

"What's the matter?"

"Well, my ankles got bigger and bigger all day, and while I was making dinner my back started to kill me. Then I had a contraction! I *felt* it! It was big and long. So I stopped what I was doing and just laid down. And I've had a few more since."

"Good call, getting off your feet," he said. He tossed the flowers on the counter and went around to the front of the couch and sat on the trunk. "You probably overdid it today, got a little dehydrated—that can bring on the Braxton Hicks. You're carrying a big load for a full day of shopping."

"I feel like an elephant. And I could hardly stand up anymore."

"How's your back now?"

"It's okay, lying down. But, Cameron, I have to make it at least six more weeks and I'm not sure I can expand any more without exploding."

"You'd be surprised," he said, opening his bag on the floor beside the sofa. "I'm going to take your blood pressure, just to see where you are, but I bet you were just on your feet too long today. You're probably going to have to watch that. And roll onto your left side for me—try not to lie flat on your back like that. It distresses the babies sometimes." He fit the digital cuff around her wrist and held her wrist across her heart for a more accurate reading. When it beeped, he looked at the little screen. "It's just up a little. But your heart is racing. Calm down, everything is all right."

She got tears in her eyes. "What if I go into labor too early? What if something goes wrong?"

"Okay, honey, listen. If you're earlier than thirty-five weeks, we'll airlift you to Redding to have a neonatal ICU available in case we need it, but there's no indication that's going to happen. You're in perfect health, but you're very pregnant and your body is going to let you know when you need more rest and relaxation. And you have to keep up the fluids. You should start lying down on your left side for twenty minutes or so every couple of hours to keep the swelling under control and give your body a chance to rejuvenate. That's not going to be too hard to do."

"It sounds dreadful," she said. "Highly inconvenient."

He lifted one dark brow. "How does complete bed rest sound? Because it's not unusual for women carrying twins to be put to bed at the end to hang on and grow them a little more. You can avoid that for a long time by taking it easy while you can."

Her eyes clouded over. "I think I want my mother."

He brushed the hair back from her temple and over her ear. "You're past traveling, Ab. But we can call your mother if you'd like, ask her if she can come. I could give her my bed and sleep at the clinic. Maybe a visit from your mother would help. Think about it—but remember, she'll want to be here when the babies come. That's not far away, Abby. Even if you go as far as Dr. Stone and Mel would like."

"It's just that…she always calms me down when I get all upset."

"Well, I'd like to apply for that job—see if I have any talent in that department."

"Oh! Cameron! There's another one," she said, her hand on her belly and her eyes wide as doughnuts.

He carefully lifted her top and put his hand, firm and warm, on her belly. "Doesn't hurt at all, does it?"

"No. But it's for real."

"Braxton Hicks. Bet it doesn't last thirty seconds. Having a lot of those can soften the cervix, which is probably why there are some OBs who think the more of those practice contractions you have, the smoother and quicker the labor will be, but I can't recall if there's any research to that effect. Ah." He grinned. "Over in less than thirty seconds. It's all right, honey. Nothing to worry about."

"You're sure?"

"I could check you, see if you're dilated or effaced at all, but really, I don't think it's necessary. Not yet."

"God, don't do that. It's so…intimate."

He laughed at her. "Abby, we didn't get this way sharing a glass."

"I know, but— That was such a long time ago."

"Thirty weeks," he said. Then he smiled warmly. "Stay calm. I had some training in this." He leaned over and gave her belly a kiss. "Sweet," he murmured, pulling her top down.

She smiled a small smile. "Have you told your mother yet?"

"Not yet. I better do that, huh?"

"Probably. What will you tell her?"

"That's the part I'm having some trouble with…."

"What if you were blatantly honest?"

He laughed. "The unvarnished truth would be—I met this knockout woman, had a wonderful but too short relationship with her, and found out later we're expecting twins. So of course we're having them. Together." Then he added, "Congratulations, Gram."

"And if she says, 'Cameron Michaels, you get married at once, or else!'"

"I'm thirty-six, Abby. My mother can't tell me what to do anymore. What we do is our business, not hers."

"Right," she said quietly. "You'd better tell her soon."

"I have some good news for you," he said, deftly changing the subject. "Your credit cards are paid off. You don't owe anything more to your ex-husband. Brie is drafting a letter to him to explain you won't be accepting any more alimony and want to consider the matter closed. You might want to talk to her about that so you understand exactly what she can do, what she can't do. But it looks like it's just about over."

"That *is* good news. I can't wait until all that's behind me. Do you think there's any chance I can still get into trouble for—you know—breaking my prenup with you?"

"I think that's so unlikely. He has bigger fish to fry. But just so you don't let that possibility get you all worked up, if there's a problem, we'll have Brie negotiate it down and pay it off, fifty dollars a month if we have to. Abby, even the worst case isn't going to be a big deal. Let's move on from that. It's given us enough trouble."

"I like that idea," she said.

"Why don't I finish the dinner you started," he asked.

"You don't mind?"

"What do you have going out there?" he asked, pointing his chin toward the kitchen.

"Chicken cacciatore."

"Hmm. You couldn't have been whipping up an omelet or hamburgers, huh?"

She laughed. "It's almost done. Simmer what's in the skillet, make the pasta, finish the salad."

He stood up. "You must have been hungry when you started this meal. What about your heartburn?"

"Well, it's chicken cacciatore without onions and peppers and only a small amount of garlic. It could be awful."

He touched her nose. "Go get into something comfortable. Your flannel nightgown or some sweats. Grab your DVD player and some movies. We'll eat on the sofa and put on a DVD."

"Good idea," she said. "Sorry about the dinner."

He grinned. "Sorry about the backache and the—"

"Cankles," she supplied.

"Cankles?"

"That's when there's no definition between your calves and ankles." She held up a foot. "Cankles." And she pushed herself up from the couch, falling back. He put out a hand to pull her up and she said, "Thank you."

When the dinner was ready, Cam fixed a nice-looking tray and brought it to her. She took it and held it out in front of her for a moment. Her lap was gone; there was no place to put it. With a chuckle, he took it from her, placed it on the trunk and handed her the salad bowl. On instinct, she was soon balancing it on her big belly, making him laugh. "We should get some pictures one of these days," he said.

"I don't think I could bear it...."

"But later, when you're in your old body, you're going to wish you had some. Mel's great with the digital camera. We'll get her to shoot a few." He lifted her tray and with it balanced on his knees, he cut up her chicken. "Just something to remember this by. We're long past that craziness of wishing it wasn't so, aren't we? I mean," he said, cutting and slicing, "I hope you are. I don't think I felt that way for one second."

"What are you doing there?" she asked.

"Abby, you can't do this, sitting on the couch. I thought I'd make it easier."

"I'm starting to feel like an invalid," she said.

"Just concentrate on feeling like someone who deserves to be spoiled." Finished, he put the plate back on her tray and went to fetch his own. "How's the food taste? Did I do anything to screw it up?"

"It's good," she said. "Bland, but good."

"It's fine, Abby. And there's ice cream if it's not bland enough. What movie did you decide on?"

"*What Women Want*. Mel Gibson."

"I better pay attention to that one," he laughed. "I seem to be deficient in that department." When they'd finished, he picked up their trays. "You can start it or wait for me to do dishes, your choice."

"I'll wait," she said. And once the water was running in the little kitchen, she murmured, "And you're not deficient in *anything*."

It was dark in the little cabin but for the light from the portable DVD player. She had set it to play repeatedly, so had no idea when they might have fallen asleep, but the romping of babies woke her. Cam had slipped under her legs, resting them on his thighs to keep them elevated, so she was too cozy to stay awake. She looked over at him and had to stifle a laugh. His feet were up on the trunk, his head tilted back, his mouth open, and his hand snaked under her sweatshirt to feel her belly. But the movement of the babies hadn't roused him. Yet.

She pressed her hand over his and watched him. He slowly came awake, closing his mouth, sitting up, meeting her eyes.

"Oh. Sorry. I must have done that in my sleep."

"It's all right," she laughed. "Do you have any idea what time it is?"

"No," he said through a yawn. "Was it a good movie?"

"I don't know," she said. "We both bit the dust. Me, from tension probably. And you, from working yourself to death to stay ahead of my tension." Then she sighed. "My children are up."

"That's not a good sign. It would be better if they slept when we slept."

"We have to go to bed," she said. "It could be three in the morning. I'm afraid to look."

He stood up and put out his hand. "Come on, sleepyhead."

When she stood from the couch and faced him, she looked into his beautiful blue eyes and said, "Would you like to sleep next to your children?"

His eyes were startled, his mouth agape.

"It won't be like the last time," she hastened to promise.

He smiled slowly. "It will be even better," he said, slipping his hand over her belly. "Whoa," he laughed.

"It's up to you."

"I wouldn't pass up an invitation like that. I'd like to feel all of you up against me, cozy and safe."

"Then come on."

Abby had her turn in the bathroom first and when Cam came out, she had changed into a huge T-shirt that came almost to her knees and, he assumed, panties. So he stripped down to his boxers and crawled in, curling around her back. "Nice," he whispered against the back of her neck.

"Mmm," she hummed, snuggling in.

His hands found her belly and rested there and sleep

found him, content and confident for the first time in so long. He was going to make this work. Yes, he was.

In the early morning he woke and he was facing her, her head on his arm, her breath on his cheek, her belly against his belly. And one hand under her shirt, cupping her bare breast. And a huge, throbbing, early-morning erection in his boxers. He pulled his hips away from her first, then slowly removed his hand. Whoa, shit, he thought. That would probably ensure this was his last visit to her bed. But what was he supposed to do? He couldn't control what he didn't know he was doing. But still, there must be a way to assure her that he'd never... That he knew she was as big and ripe as a full-term mother.... That it wasn't necessarily that he wanted... But of course he wanted her, but he didn't have to... Oh God, he couldn't figure out how to get out of this embarrassing situation without offending her, insulting her. Or scaring her to death.

He gently pulled his arm out from under her and headed for the shower.

Cameron beat Mel to the clinic in the morning. While she was bright and cheerful, he was awful quiet. He busied himself at the computer. When she asked him what he was doing, he said, "Car seats. We need two car seats and Abby just about wore herself out shopping in Eureka yesterday, so I told her I'd look online."

"Oh," Mel said. "Good idea. I guess a pediatrician knows what to look for."

Two hours and two patients later, he was still acting as if something was wrong. So she went head-on, as she was known to do. "What's eating at you? You're all funky and weird, like you and Abby have a problem or something."

He ducked his head. "Oh, you and Abby have a problem. What's the matter? Can I help? Is the pregnancy all right?"

"I don't think you can help," he said, turning away from her and heading for the kitchen.

She followed him. "You don't really know, though, do you? Until you run it by me?"

"It's kind of embarrassing," he said, not facing her.

"For God's sake, I look at cracks and talk about sex for a living. You can't embarrass me."

He turned around. "I was thinking it would be embarrassing for *me*."

"Well, get over it. I'm your midwife."

He took a deep breath. "Abby and I are getting along very well. It's incredible. Better than I thought it could be. We're so compatible. And last night I slept beside her, holding her and the babies...." He dropped his chin.

"Aw," Mel said. "That's sweet. I'm so happy, Cam."

"And woke up with my hand up her shirt and with the biggest hard-on."

Mel looked momentarily perplexed. "I'm sorry. Did I need to know that?"

"I can't believe how much just being near her is getting to me. I can't let her think that— I mean, I let her think it would be completely safe for me to just lie beside her and... Aw, Christ. I have no control at all. What a damn mess."

"Cameron, take it easy. Most of that's just nature. Huh? It happens all night long. I'm sure Abby knows that."

"It's not just happening when I'm asleep. I really have a problem here. I've wanted that woman since the first second I saw her, but she's in no condition for me to want her like that. What kind of man wants to... I mean, I won't touch her, I swear I won't. But if she thinks she's not safe from my instincts, then I'll be sent back up to the loft. And I don't want to go back up to the loft!" He took a breath, shook his head dismally. "I should probably go back up to the loft."

Mel's face cracked into a huge grin. "My goodness. The Madonna syndrome? *You?*"

"What?"

"The mother of your children can't also be a sexual human being?"

"Not if she's ripe as a tomato! She's thirty weeks! With twins! It would be irresponsible to— You know we don't want a lot of action down there."

"Cameron, surely you have a better imagination than you're letting on. I mean, there are a few alternative methods of sharing affection that don't involve intercourse. But of course I agree—intercourse now is probably not the best idea, even though we're not necessarily concerned about early labor. Yet."

"We don't have that kind of relationship. At least, not now. We agreed to share this space so I could be there for her. So we could have them together and rely on each other. Not so we could explore alternative methods of affection, by which I'm sure you mean manual or oral." He ran a hand over his chest as if wiping it dry. "She probably shouldn't play around with orgasms anyway. That's all we need is a little early labor now."

"Hey, this is something for you to talk to her about," Mel said. "You afraid you'll shock her? Didn't you get her pregnant? Isn't she aware you have a healthy libido?"

"I'm pretty sure she has no idea how healthy. Really, I wasn't prepared to find her sexier than ever. She can't even get up off the couch without a hand and I'm ready to spring into action and—" He stopped himself. "Jesus."

Mel just chuckled. "Listen, while she's feeling big as a cow, I doubt she'd be insulted to learn she actually turns you on. Know what I mean? It might lead to some meaningful communication, which it sounds like the two of you could use." But she couldn't help herself. She chuckled again and put a hand over her mouth.

"You don't have to laugh at me," he groused.

"Aw, I think you're cute. Talk to her. You said you're getting close. Tell her how you've been feeling, et cetera. And you can also explain why it's not an excellent idea to have a wild romp in the hay just now. But you don't have to be embarrassed by your feelings and frankly, I don't think a little orgasm or two would hurt. You're not tempting fate for at least a couple more weeks. Desiring her when she's in this phase of motherhood—that's sweet." She shook her head. "Jack sure didn't have this problem. He wasn't embarrassed by his feelings. Frustrated by them, yes. Embarrassed? Pah."

"Maybe Jack is the guy I should be talking to...."

Mel lost every trace of humor. "Okay, I have to draw the line there. You can't do that. Jack might say too much— he's been known to do that once or twice. And I can't have you conjuring up pictures of me in—" She straightened her spine. "I'm your boss, I think. I am, yes I am. You're the doctor, but it's my clinic. I can't have you picturing me in compromising positions, even if they might help your pathetic sex life, because I'm your boss."

He just grinned largely, happily. As of her last words, he didn't need Jack's input to drum up an image or two. Her turn to squirm. She'd certainly enjoyed his discomfort, but all he said with regards to hers was, "Why, Melinda. Hmm."

* * *

As the April afternoons became warmer and perfect for riding, Muriel rode along the river with Vanessa and Shelby while Walt watched the baby. It was Muriel's last day in Virgin River and spending time with the girls had become almost as important as spending it with Walt. And spring in the mountains was exhilarating; bright green with a smattering of colorful wildflowers along the riverbank. They rode along at a leisurely pace, enjoying the fresh air and conversation.

"Is there a date set for the wedding yet?" Muriel asked Shelby.

"No, not exactly. We can't figure out when to do it, where to do it. Luke still has two brothers in the Middle East. I think we should wait for them to get home and he thinks we'd better hurry."

"What's the hurry?" Muriel asked.

"We want to have a baby," she said, smiling.

Muriel just frowned. "Shelby, you're so young—you have lots of time. It's not like your clock is ticking."

"I know," she laughed. "Luke's clock is ticking. He'll be thirty-nine next month. He's afraid he's going to be going to high-school football games with a walker."

"Oh," she said. "Don't you want to have a little time with him first? Alone time? Before you add a baby to the mix?"

"I wouldn't mind that, but I get his point. I'm just so pleased he's going along with the family idea, I'm being cooperative."

"And school?" Muriel asked.

"The nursing program officially starts in September, but I'm going to take classes this summer to get a head start. There will be an orientation day in June and I can take Luke with me, but I had a tour already. The students in that program are men and women, all ages, and I mean *all* ages—from eighteen to fifty. The only thing I had to work out with Luke is that he's going to be a totally involved father and not leave it to me to manage all the child-care issues alone so I can go to school."

"And?" Muriel asked.

Shelby laughed. "For someone who insisted marriage and family would never be in his future, he can't wait. If it was up to Luke, we'd take off for the justice of the peace. But his mother would absolutely kill him if he did that."

"You'd better plan enough in advance so I can make it," Muriel warned.

"Really?" Shelby asked. "You'd come?"

"Of course I'd come. It'll take some planning, and maybe some conniving, if I'm still on this movie when you do it."

"Muriel, are you anxious to get back to the movie?" Vanessa asked her.

"In a way," she said with a shrug. "Sometimes the chemistry is so good on a set, with all the people involved, that it's like forming a family. That's not typical. It's like all the planets lined up—the script, the cast, the crew, the direction. And I think the fact that we're going to Montana gives everyone a real positive attitude. Montana in the summer—a great idea. A lot of people are bringing families." She was quiet for a moment. "They could have filmed here," she said as she moved her mare down the river path, right between Vanni and Shelby on their mounts. "The setting is just as good, the weather just as wonderful in summer."

"You're going to miss the general," Vanessa said.

"Oh, yes," she admitted. "I wish he'd come to Montana. At least for a visit. They rented me a small house up there."

"Have you asked him?"

"Uh-huh. Something about that idea bothers him. He keeps saying we'll see. Maybe it's because I'll be putting in long hours—I had to tell the truth about that. But really, I suspect Walt doesn't think he can fit into my world."

"Are you two serious?" Vanni asked. Muriel shot her a look and Vanni actually blushed. "I mean, are you… I mean, you don't have to say anything.… I mean, I was just wondering if— Oh, hell, mind your own business, Vanessa!" she self-admonished.

"What's serious?" Muriel asked. "Do I think he's just about the greatest man I've ever met? I do. If I started to list all the things that make him wonderful, we wouldn't have time. Are we going to get married or anything like that? No. But could this fantastic relationship we have go on for a long time? Why not?"

"I hate to put my foot in my mouth all over again, but why are you so sure you won't get married?" Vanni asked.

"Darling, I've had five husbands and a number of steady guys. Why would I attempt that again? I'd like to think it was their fault, but what if I'm the one who's not so good at it? And why would Walt take a chance on a woman who's had five husbands and a number of steady guys? Especially when this friendship we have feels… Well, it feels perfect. I wouldn't want to screw it up. Besides, there's no panic—my clock isn't ticking. Hell, I threw it against the wall years ago."

"But aren't you afraid of—" Vanni shut her mouth before she did it again.

"Afraid of what, darling?"

She took a deep breath. "Afraid of growing old alone?"

Muriel laughed lightly. "Oh, you're so young. No, I'm

not afraid of growing old alone. I'm afraid of growing old *trapped.*"

They were quiet for a few long seconds. Then Shelby said, "Wow. I never even thought of that."

"Why would you? Either of you? You're young, in love, have long, steady lives ahead. And I certainly don't feel that ending up with a man like Walt would trap me in any way, it's not that." She looked steadily at Vanni, then Shelby, then ahead at the gloriously rising mountains covered with towering trees. "I don't think I could live with myself if I trapped him. What if there was another role that intrigued me, that I wanted to try? I thought I was ready for retirement, to leave the movie business behind, but then a great role for a fifty-six-year-old woman came to me and I found it irresistible. And here I am, not wanting to pass it up, yet not wanting to leave Walt and this wonderful life behind." She laughed. "It's been years since I've faced a dilemma like this. Really, I had sworn off men."

"I'm just guessing here," Vanessa said. "But somehow I don't think Daddy would feel trapped by you or your career."

Muriel was quiet for a long time. Then she said, "I don't know about that. He keeps asking me when the filming will be done, but he won't even commit to a long weekend visit in Montana." Then after another few minutes of silence, Muriel said, "I probably should have given up acting to breed horses years ago."

There was a time, before Jack had two children, Preacher had his two, Mike and Paul one each, before the living quarters at the bar were enlarged for Preacher's family and before everyone had their own homes on the outskirts of town, that it was standard for the same gang to meet for dinner several times a week. Now they had to make an effort to all be there on the same night.

It's not as though this bothered Jack much—he saw everyone every day. Sometimes a day or two went by without his seeing one or two of the women, but the guys would always stop by for lunch or a beer or something. He was missing the old squad, though. Time for a Semper Fi reunion. He wanted the brotherhood around to bolster him. All this came to mind because he was leaving in the morning for San Diego; he was going to pick up Rick and bring him home.

Rick didn't want the escort. He told Jack to stay home and if it wasn't too much trouble, catch him at the bus when he got in. Like Jack was some neighbor guy he didn't want to impose on or something. The kid was coming home after being blown up in Iraq, and Jack, who loved him as much or more than anyone, shouldn't go to any trouble? That wasn't how it worked. Not in his experience.

Mike walked in the back door and right behind the bar. He liked to get his own beer. He also liked to stand back there with Jack. Then, not a minute later, the sound of Paul kicking the mud off his boots on the porch could be heard, and he walked in. He sat up at the bar and tapped it twice, his signal that he was ready for a beer.

Another minute passed. Then Paul said, "Ready to go?"

Jack should have known they were there to give him a little moral support. The whole ordeal with Rick had been a load for everyone, but clearly hardest on Jack. "Yup," Jack said. "I'll leave at about 5:00 a.m. if I sleep in, then drive down, spend the night, scoop him up and bring him home."

"Be good to have him home," Mike said.

"He's not like he was," Jack said. "He's got a peg leg and a giant bug up his ass."

"None of us were like we were. For a while," Paul said. "He's a kid. He'll get through it. Or we'll get him through it."

"Mel's working on finding someone for him to talk to. A professional," Jack said. "I have PT all worked out, but he needs other stuff, too."

"Liz know he's on the way home?" Mike asked.

"Yeah. Because I told her. Rick couldn't be bothered to pick up the phone when she called him, or call her back. Almost two months and he didn't take even one of her calls." He grimaced and shook his head. "Really, I want to choke him, but I know what's going on. And I know he can't help it."

"He's screwed up," Paul said.

"He just doesn't know how tough it's going to be when he's ready to start unscrewing himself, if he keeps burning all his bridges," Jack said. "Ask me how much I look forward to ten hours in the truck with him?"

"Maybe he'll sleep."

"Go easy on him, Jack. You said it yourself—it's not like he wants to be messed up."

"Yeah, yeah. It's just tough. I've always been amazed at how strong he is. Right now—his glass is *not* half-full. Know what I mean?"

"Well, everyone's entitled to be imperfect sometimes," Mike said.

"Yeah. It's just that…"

"What?" Paul asked.

"It's just that I can take about anything but self-pity.

Anything. But feeling sorry for yourself is the most candy-assed thing you can cave into."

Mike chuckled. "Because you never indulged? Oh my brother, I did some self-pity that would've put your head on fire. Man, I was in a hole so deep…"

"But you got out," Jack said. "You climbed out."

"Not when you were ready, Jack. When *I* was," Mike said. "Go easy."

"Yeah, yeah."

"Maybe I should go," Mike suggested. "Jack, you never really got shot up. Or blown up. Maybe I should go."

"I'm going," Jack said. "I'll go easy."

The next morning, Jack pocketed the cell phone he only took when he would be out of the mountains and had reception. He threw his duffel in the back of the truck and Mel said, "Jack, try to be patient. Your expectations of him have always been high. You miss him, you want him to bounce back, be his old self because you care about him, because you miss him."

"I know," Jack said. "And because I don't want him to feel any pain. Everyone is so ready to help him with any pain or fear or worry he has, and he's got this wall. It's awful."

"Let him talk. Try not to tell him how he should feel."

"I know," Jack said. "And if he doesn't talk?"

"Remember that you want him to talk because you miss him. If he doesn't want to talk yet, let him be quiet."

"I just want to know why he couldn't at least call Liz and tell her what's—"

"Jack, that's between them. When he gets home he's going to have to work it out because she'll be around and he can't send her to voice mail when she's standing right in front of him. Jesus, this is your weakness. You, who didn't fall in love till you were forty, think you can fix up everyone's relationships." She shook her head. She got up on her toes and kissed him. "Well, your heart's in the right place, that's for sure. Make sure your mouth is in the right place, too. Closed."

"Yes, ma'am."

"And for God's sake, drive carefully. I need you back."

Nine

When Cameron got to the clinic in the morning, he had a patient waiting. Mel had arrived early, opened up the office, and checked in a young mother and her eighteen-month-old son who suffered with an obvious ear infection. He had a fever, was batting his ears and crying. Mel could have handled it, but knowing Cameron was due, she waited for the pediatrician.

In no time, he had sent them on their way with Tylenol, antibiotic and decongestant. Then he found Mel in the kitchen. "I usually beat you here," he said.

"Aw, Jack left this morning for San Diego. He's gone to pick up Rick. And he's not handling the situation all that well. He didn't sleep much, was up by four, anxious to get on the road, troubled about the whole ordeal. There was such a ruckus around the house, the kids woke up too early and they're all cranky, so I left them having morning naps at their aunt Brie's. We're all out of sorts." She took a breath. "Jack's so worried about Rick. And sometimes when Jack gets worried, he acts out." She shook her head. "He has so much love in his heart. He just wants his people—the people he loves—to be all right."

"God," Cameron said. "You have no idea how nice that sounded."

"It did?"

"You can't imagine what it would mean to me if the right woman said that about me."

She lifted her coffee mug to her lips, taking a sip. "Well, maybe she has, Cam. If she hasn't, she just doesn't know you well enough. You and Abby doing okay?"

He smiled. "I haven't been banished to the loft yet."

"Good for you, Cameron," she said. "That's something."

"I probably should be. I also haven't talked to her about it yet."

"Well, why not?"

"Because I'm afraid when I tell her the truth about how I feel about her, she's going to run for her life, that's why not." The wall phone in the kitchen rang. "I got it," Cameron said. He lifted the old-fashioned receiver. "Clinic," he said.

"Cameron," Abby said in a whisper. "There are deer in the yard!"

"Really?" he asked. "Why are you whispering? Can they hear you?"

"I don't want to scare them off. Oh, I wish you were here. There's a baby. And a couple of deer look ready to pop. Not as ready as I look, but wild animals probably don't get this big."

He laughed into the phone. "I told you, you're perfect."

"If you'd been home another half hour, you'd have seen them. Cameron, there are six of them."

"Any bucks?"

"Just the mamas. And one baby."

"That's a fawn," he said.

"It looks like it's barely born. He's wobbling on his legs. Oh, I wish you could see him."

He turned the phone away from his mouth. "Mel? Can you spare me for a little while? Abby has deer in the yard."

"Sure, there aren't any appointments. I can call you if someone wanders in and needs you," she said, smiling, cradling her coffee cup in two hands. "Go on."

"I'll come," he told Abby. "I'll park down the road and walk up. I might scare them off anyway if they smell a human. But I'll give it a shot."

He drove a little faster than necessary out to the cabin because he couldn't wait to see the look on her face, all lit up and excited about the deer. He parked before he got to the clearing and crept up the long driveway as quietly as he could. By the time he got to the clearing, the deer had moved to the tree line. He gave them a wide berth by going around the far side of the cabin to the door. He had to tip-toe across the porch. One doe lifted her head; they could no doubt smell his human scent, but they didn't bolt. That surprised him. There were too many hunters up this way for them to feel safe.

Abby held the door open for him. Her face was bright; she was all stirred up. So happy. "You saw them?"

"They're half hidden in the trees, but I saw."

"Mel said this was an enchanted cabin. I guess she's right." She went to the kitchen window, leaning across the sink the best she could to look out. She could feel him move up behind her and put his arms around her. His hands instinctively rested on her belly. The kids were still now. Of course. Their parents were awake.

He leaned forward and inhaled the scent of her hair, breathing deeply. She let her eyes drift closed.

"I have to tell you something," he said. She started to turn around and he said, "No, just stay like this." He gently massaged her belly. "There's something I should have told you from the beginning, Abby. I didn't mean to mislead you, but I was afraid if I was completely honest, you'd never agree to move into the same house with me."

She closed her eyes tight. He'd been lying beside her in bed at night; she'd felt him draw her closer, fondle her in his sleep. She knew he didn't realize what he was doing, but she was more than aware. That had never been part of their plan. He was going to tell her now that's not how it was supposed to be between them. "Okay," she said softly.

"At night, when I'm beside you, holding you…"

Oh, here it comes, she thought. *Don't cry, don't cry. It'll be worse if you cry.*

"I've been a little carried away in my sleep," he said. "I apologize. I didn't intend to do that, but you have to know the truth. It's not just when I'm asleep that I have that urge. That reaction." He took a deep breath. "The truth is, I have that impulse all the time. I respond to you." He took a breath. "Boy, do I."

"Huh?"

"God, I hope this doesn't make you angry or really offend you. But you should know—I get turned on by you all the time. All I have to do is see your eyes, smell your skin, touch you, even innocently. And I just about go out of my mind. My feelings haven't changed one bit since that first night I met you. The second I touched you, it was like an explosion under my skin. I told you I wanted us to be friends, but the truth is, I've always wanted so much more than that. Abby, the truth is, I had ulterior motives. I thought if I got you under the same roof with me, I could get you to fall in love with me."

She was quiet for a moment. Finally she said, "You're just overwhelmed by the thought of parenthood. You said, even before we kissed, you wanted a family."

"I do. I have for years. But I've met a lot of women who could have been mothers to my children, who would have volunteered for the job. And I've just never felt like this. When morning came in that Grants Pass hotel, I didn't want to let you go. Ever. You just plain turn me on. Every bit of you—your laugh, your scent, your eyes, your hands, your soft hair...your mouth. When I look at your mouth, I almost lose my mind with lust."

A small huff of laughter escaped her. "Are you crazy?"

"A little bit, yeah. I guess I thought that big belly with my babies inside would cool me down, but it didn't. But you don't have to worry. I'll live with my feelings and not expect you to reciprocate them. And I will help you and keep you safe, just as I promised. I give you my word, Abby, I'll never lose control." He took his hands off her belly and grasped her upper arms, squeezing them. "I should probably go back to sleeping in the loft. I don't want to make you uncomfortable. Or worried."

"Oh?"

"Listen, I'm damn grateful that you're willing to try to cohabit so we can get to know each other better, so we can be on the best of terms to be the best of parents. That means a lot. You probably didn't realize it, but my hand has wandered while we slept and—"

"I realized it."

"You did?"

She smiled to herself. "Can I turn around now?"

"Are you going to slug me?" he asked.

She laughed. "Do you think I should?"

"Maybe. Probably. I molested you in your sleep. Well, in my sleep."

She slowly turned around and took in his vulnerable expression. "You don't have to sleep in the loft."

It took him a moment to absorb that. He swallowed, cleared his throat, gave his head a little shake. Then he focused on her eyes. "Listen, I know your emotions are all over the place—bad divorce, ugly legal problems, major pregnancy… Abby, I love you. I'm not just a guy under the same blanket with a girl. If it wasn't you, this wouldn't be happening. God, I hope that doesn't scare you away."

"Is that even possible?" she asked him. "Love?"

He shrugged. "I didn't ask myself if it was possible. I couldn't seem to help it. When you didn't get in touch after we met in Grants Pass, when I couldn't find you, I was miserable. I told you back then, I liked our chances. I don't think I've ever met anyone in my life I felt so much for, so quickly."

"I can't say it was that way for me, Cameron," she said.

"I know. I guess I hoped that over time…"

"But I liked you," she said. "You were very sweet to me."

"That didn't take any effort at all," he said, giving her hair a soft stroke. "You were like heaven. I couldn't believe I was that lucky."

"I thought about you afterward. All the time."

"You did?" he asked, surprised.

"But I was scared to death to find myself hooked up to another guy I thought was everything I wanted, only to find out I was just delusional. To let myself believe in you, count on you and have you run out on me?" She shook her head. "I wasn't up to that. I thought it would be a lot safer if I never saw you again."

"I understand, Abby. It doesn't matter what place I have in your life—I'll never run out on you. I'll support you and the kids, I'll be a good father, I'll—"

"You were even kind and supportive after I called you a sperm donor...."

He chuckled. "You were in high temper that night. Remind me not to get into fights with you."

"Cameron, when you asked me to move in with you, I thought it was all about the babies. That it had nothing to do with me."

"Ohhh, it had everything to do with you."

"The past couple of weeks..." she said. "I don't know when I've been happier."

"Really? If I could just elevate myself above sperm donor—"

"Why? They don't get any better. Talk about packing a punch," she laughed. "That night, I remember thinking, if I had a little more time, if my life weren't so screwed up, I could fall in love with this guy."

His breathing got a little heavier. "I have nothing but time," he said, and his voice had grown raspy.

"Then we don't really have a problem here, do we?" she said with a smile. "We could—"

She was cut off by his hands on her face, his lips on her lips, kissing her with a passion she hadn't even dared hope for in so long. He groaned and moved over her lips with heat, urging her mouth open and kissing deeper, hotter. Long and wet and hungry. It was quite a while before he could even break from her lips a tiny bit.

"That's what I remember," she whispered, breathless.

And that fast he was on her lips again, devouring her, feeding her deep kisses and tasting the inside of her mouth. Her arms went around his neck, his went around to the small of her back and they were locked in a passionate kiss that didn't end until he felt a strong kick against his belly. She laughed against his lips.

"I have a feeling that's going to be an issue from now on," he said. "More so after they're born."

"No question in my mind. I have to start on the parenting books right away."

"Abby," he said, running his fingers through her dark blond hair. "I'm a pediatrician. I can help with that."

"Cameron, I love you, too. I want this to work for us. I can't imagine being away from you ever again. You've made me so happy."

He groaned. "God, why couldn't you have told me that when you were less than thirty weeks…."

"I guess it's too risky now," she said in disappointment. "I'm sorry, Cameron. Although really, it baffles me that you can even think of sex when you look at me."

"I think about touching every single curve of your body. I think about kissing and tasting every part of you. I think about things I'm not allowed to do until after you deliver and mend. I can't stop thinking about all of that."

"But you're allowed to hold me, right?"

"I'm allowed to never let you go," he said.

Their one night together had been filled with fire, explosive in its power. This lazy morning was not—it was sweet and gentle, as though Abby were fragile and precious. They started out embracing in the kitchen, then moved to the bedroom to lie down on the bed, clinging to each other, kissing. Then, inevitably, clothing was pushed out of the way then removed. Cameron was determined to keep his pants on, a safe barrier, but that idea crashed when her hands on his zipper slowly glided it down.

Cameron undressed her slowly, shed his own clothes quickly, then stretched out beside her, bringing her gently into his arms. Holding her, kissing her, caressing her, he made a study of her body with slow hands and soft lips. Just skin on skin, lips on lips, nothing but a breath separating them, brought such relief and contentment to both of them. "I'm going to have to go back to sleeping in the loft," he whispered against her mouth.

"I would hate that," she said. "You can't imagine what it feels like, to finally have your hands on me again. It's so wonderful."

"We can't do it. And we can't even do this too much longer. We'll just get carried away."

"Mmm. Carry me away, Cam."

"You shouldn't fool around with orgasms. They could get you contracting."

"Can I fool around with one?" she asked in a breathy whisper.

He chuckled low in his throat. "One long, slow, gentle one?" he asked. He slipped his fingers into her wet folds, stroking her, bringing a delicious moan from her. "Just lie back and relax, baby. Nothing wild. We're going to have to save the wild part for later."

"Oh God," she whispered. "Oh, Cameron..." And then her hand was on him, tight and hot, stroking him aggressively, pulling on him.

"Uh, Abby, maybe you shouldn't do that."

"Or maybe I should," she sighed.

"Honey, I can't take that. It's been too long, I've wanted you too much…. I'm going to explode all over you."

Her eyes closed, lips parted slightly, she whispered, "Does it seem as though I don't know what's going to happen? To both of us?"

"God," he groaned. He pampered her clitoris, slipping one finger just barely inside her, just enough so he could feel the spasms when she reached climax. It was only seconds before he felt exactly that. "Oh, honey," he said, capturing her mouth in a deep, long kiss that hung on while she enjoyed every last bit of it. Imagining himself inside her, he came and came and came until a loud groan escaped him and his eyes rolled back in his head.

And then they lay there, their hands still intimately touching each other. He tried to imagine whether that could have felt better if he'd been buried deep inside her, but this intimacy with her brought such emotional and physical satisfaction, he couldn't imagine anything better. He gently kissed her cheek, her neck. "Pregnant sex," he laughed. "If this wasn't a multiple pregnancy, we'd be doing it like bunnies right now. I'm not sure exactly how, but we'd find a way."

She giggled then sighed and snuggled close.

After a while, he stirred. "Stay put," he said. "I want you to stay down, resting. I'll get a washcloth and towel." He was back a moment later wearing his boxers. With a warm, wet cloth and soft towel, he cleaned her up. Then he crawled in beside her, taking her again in his arms, pulling just the sheet over them. She drowsed in his embrace and he listened to her soft, steady breathing. Abby might have drifted off, but he didn't. He watched her, felt her belly against his, alert for any start up of Braxton Hicks contractions. In an hour, nothing was amiss. They hadn't disturbed the uterus.

It was tempting to spend the day in bed with her, pleasing her as often as she'd like, but he knew that wasn't a good idea. For another week or so, they might enjoy a little discretionary satisfaction if she felt inclined, but then to be safe, they should wait. This didn't matter to him—his happiness was complete. She loved him, wanted him. And he would do anything for her.

By the age of thirty-six, Cameron had had plenty of sex, and by far much more interesting than what had just occurred with Abby. Definitely more energetic and creative sex than that. But he couldn't remember ever feeling more whole, more fulfilled.

He hated to disturb her, but he had to get back to town eventually. He'd been gone all morning. "Abby," he whispered. "Sweetheart." She moaned softly and stretched. Her eyes opened and she smiled. "Feel better?" he asked.

"Much. You?"

He nodded. "I want you to know something—I want to marry you. Whenever you're ready. But that's not the most important thing. I'm committed, totally. No matter what you decide you want to do, I'm in this with you all the way. I'll never leave you. I love you, and I don't just toss out the L word. You can count on me, Abby."

She ran a hand along his cheek. "Thank you, Cam," she whispered. "I love you. You can count on me, too."

He smiled. "Thank God those deer came into the yard. This could be the best day of my life."

When he got to the clinic at around lunchtime, Mel was in the kitchen. He knew he had a special smile on his face and that there was far less tension in his posture. He couldn't hide the feeling that his entire life had suddenly fallen into place. He tried to appear nonchalant, but he suspected he had the faraway look of a man in love. He didn't say anything, but she looked him over and grinned. "Must have been quite a herd," she said.

"Big herd," he said. "Abby was very excited to see them."

She chuckled. Then she stood and gave his shoulder a pat. "Cam, there are times Jack rounds up a poker game with some of the guys…."

"Oh?"

She shook her head and as she passed him she said, "Don't ever play."

When Jack was finally able to pick Rick up at his barracks, more than twenty-four hours after he'd started his trip, he was a little disappointed by what he found. Rick was waiting outside, alone, with his packed duffel and a walker beside him. Jack didn't think he'd still be relying on the walker. And he had hoped there'd be some guys around, seeing him off. "You're still using this, huh?" Jack asked.

"Better than falling on my ass," Rick said. "You have no idea how hard it is to get up."

"I can imagine."

"Grab that duffel, would you, Jack?"

Jack hesitated before picking it up. "Good thing I didn't leave you to catch the bus, huh?"

"No time to be the smartest one, okay?" Rick said, making his way to the truck. And of course, Jack's truck was jacked up. Rick opened the door and just looked up at the climb.

Jack threw the duffel in the back and stood beside him. "Well, let's figure this out right off. You can put weight on the prosthesis, right? Left hand up here, right hand on the door, left foot on the runner, and pull. I'll get the walker."

"Gimme a hand, huh?"

"I'll spot you," Jack said. "You have any trouble, I'll catch you. Give it a go."

"What if I don't *want* to?"

"What if you try?" Jack replied, very proud of himself for not saying *fucking try.* Mel would be proud, too.

Rick made a face and a noise of displeasure, placed his hands and foot, gave a tug and hoisted himself up into the cab. He did it, first time. But while it made Jack so happy, it obviously gave Rick no pleasure at all. "Well, there you go." Jack grabbed the walker and put it in the truck bed. Really, he wanted to throw it as far as it would go. He wanted his boy back; he wanted the dependence on the excuse of this disability to stop, probably long before it was reasonable.

Jack was too impatient. He knew that. He wished he could be another way. But he felt so desperate to have his Rick back, no matter how many pieces he was in. Even if it took a while, that was okay, as long as Rick wanted to get back as much as he should. It was this attitude of defeat that was killing Jack.

He should have gone down to San Diego a few times while Rick was in rehab, if only to run through fast food and feed him. He'd gotten thin. All that upper body strength he'd had before Iraq had wilted. Rick was going to need the muscle to compensate for the missing leg. A little time on Preacher's food would help, but he had to work those muscles, and that took motivation.

"Let's get some breakfast," Jack said.

"I had breakfast," Rick said.

"How about more breakfast? Looks like you could use it."

"Get some for yourself if you want. I'm not hungry. I'll wait in the truck."

Jack just kept driving. It was going to be a long trip home.

Every couple of hours Jack stopped, someplace there was food if he could help it, and forced Rick out of the truck to move around. "Come on, the PT guy in Eureka said you need to move around to avoid something—I can't remember exactly what it was...."

"Contractures," Rick supplied. "I'm fine. But this leg has got to come off for a while."

"Right after this stop. Let's do it, Rick. Look around—you have your choice. Big Mac, Subway, fish 'n' chips, whatever you see."

"I'm not hungry."

"Christ," Jack muttered. He hauled the walker out of the back and put it down beside Rick. "Walk around the truck at least twice. Then we'll get the leg off." Then he took off across the street and walked into a sandwich shop, coming back out with two big submarine sandwiches. He almost smiled to note the walker was back in the truck bed and Rick back in the cab. Not so disabled when he wanted to be done with his exercise. And Jack wasn't sure how he'd accomplished it, but the prosthesis was in the backseat of the extended cab.

Jack tossed one of the sandwiches in Rick's lap, put two giant colas in the cup holders and started up the truck.

Rick just stared at the food in his lap.

"Eat what you can. It's been hours since you've eaten and I've eaten three times. When we get back, I'm going to get some of Preacher's weights out of the storage shed for you. You should probably bulk up those arms, shoulders, chest. Give you back your advantage."

"For?"

Jack was stupefied. He shook his head. "For getting through life?" he said by way of a question.

"For?" Rick said again.

And Jack thought, you can't slug him. You have to keep your mouth shut and be patient, that's what Mike said, what Mel said. So Jack talked to himself. *Okay, I'm not the best person to deal with this. I never had it this bad, and sure not when I was this young. Mike, he's been through a terrifying, life-threatening injury. Mike might be able to step in.* Mel had done as she promised and lined up a counselor through the VA. He couldn't make Rick help himself, but he could throw him in the truck, drive him there and sit outside till the hour was up.

Eventually Jack said, in his sensitive and mellow voice, "Eat the goddamn fucking sandwich. And I mean it."

A few seconds later, Rick peeled off the wrapping paper and took a bite, then another bite.

But Jack had lost his appetite. He was glad Rick was eating something, but this didn't feel victorious at all. The drive had to come from inside Rick, not from the bully in the seat next to him.

Jack forced down about half his sandwich, wrapped up what was left and managed to keep heading north. After Rick had eaten what was presumably his fill, he leaned back in the seat and dozed, his own wrapped half sandwich on his lap. Jack lifted it carefully; he put it in the sack for later. Rick's nap gave him a little time to think.

He remembered what Mel had said, that Jack needed his boy back so bad, he was pushing on him. He remembered when Mike Valenzuela picked Virgin River as a place to recover when he'd been critically wounded on the job at

LAPD—because his family and friends needed him well again so badly they were suffocating him. And he remembered that he'd never loved a kid as powerfully as he loved this one, except maybe David and Emma, and his love was strong. Sometimes it caused him to act in desperate ways. He could end up doing more harm than good.

It was a good couple of hours before Rick woke with a painful cramp in his thigh, his stump. He groaned in pain and started rubbing.

"We'll come up on a rest stop real soon here. Hang in there," Jack said.

Rick just kept rubbing, gritting his teeth. He pushed back in the seat, lifted his butt and fished a pill bottle out of his pocket. He swallowed a pill with a gulp of old, watered-down cola.

"Whatcha got there, pal?" Jack asked.

"Not the good stuff," he answered. "Just some anti-inflammatory laced with a little codeine. It gets me by."

"Ready for a pit stop?" Jack asked, driving into a good-looking rest stop.

"Yeah," Rick said, a little breathless from discomfort.

"Want the leg?" Jack asked, pulling up to an accessible spot right in front of the men's room.

"Nah," Rick said, drawing up the leg of his jeans and tucking it in the waistband. "Just the walker."

"Sit tight." Jack got out, grabbed the walker, and instead of insisting Rick do some wild gymnastics getting himself out of the truck without the help of a prosthetic limb, he just slipped a strong arm around his waist and pulled him out, lowering him gently to the ground. Then he followed Rick as he made his way slowly into the bathroom.

Rick turned around once. Over his shoulder he said, "I'm good."

"I'm right behind you," Jack said.

Head down, hands braced on the walker, he moved slowly into the john, took his place up against a urinal, braced himself, balancing precariously on one leg, hand against the wall, and got the job done. He was wobbly, especially getting his zipper back up. He moved slowly to the sink and washed his hands. Seeing the potential for disaster if Rick put his wet hands on the metal walker, Jack handed him some paper towels while he was still braced up against the sink. When Rick moved away from the sink, his jeans were wet in front from the dripping sink. "Fuck," he said.

"Learning curve is kinda high," Jack remarked. "Yet another reason to work on the leg, huh?"

Rick moved slowly out of the bathroom. Without looking at Jack he muttered, "One of the guys said it was easier to figure out how to have sex than how to take a shower."

Jack laughed. "Good to know."

"I doubt it'll come up."

When they got to the truck, Jack braced him under the arms and said, "Swing on up there, buddy." When they were again under way, Jack just gave it some time. They were another half hour on the road after a long day, and now well into Mendocino County, when he asked, "How's the pain now, Rick?"

"Okay. Pill kicked in, mostly."

"We'll be home in less than a couple of hours," Jack said. "I'm sorry about back there, about the sandwich. The way I acted. We aren't going to get too far if I try the bully approach. I apologize."

"Forget it," he said.

"You understand, I just want to find the best way to help you get on your feet."

"Foot," Rick said, not looking at him. "You want me to get on my *foot*."

Jack ground his teeth and told himself, *Let it go. Rick won't be angry forever. Will he?* "Listen, there are a couple of things we should talk about."

"Like?"

"Rehab, for one. You're set up at a clinic in Eureka. It's supposed to be a good little shop and I'll take you. Vets from around this county use it a lot. And there's some counseling..."

"No counseling."

"Gimme a break, huh? You hear yourself? You wanna feel like this the rest of your life?"

"Listen, we did that whole group-hug thing at Balboa. It was a waste of time. I felt worse, not better."

"This will be one-on-one and you don't have to hug anyone."

"This one have two legs?" Rick asked sarcastically. "Because I just love it when some joker with all his parts tries to help me cope with what's left of mine."

"He could have two fucking heads for all I know," Jack said. "Sorry. That was frustration. I'm just frustrated."

Rick laughed humorlessly. "Is that a fact?"

"Moving on. I'd like you to stay with me and Mel. Once you get up the porch, the house is flat. The shower is a flat walk-in. You don't have to negotiate a tub. I can get you around till you're driving again, which will be as soon as you're ready. You can spend as much time with your grandma as you like and I'll even drive her out to our place, but her house is a challenge and she shouldn't be taking care of you."

"We'll be fine," he said. "She won't have to take care of me."

"Rick, try to be reasonable. Mel and I can help, but Lydie has enough challenge taking care of herself."

"She won't be taking care of me. We'll manage."

"Are you totally opposed to making this as simple as possible? Are you going to let me help at all?"

"I let you drive me home, didn't I? And aren't you glad for the good company?"

"Yeah. It was a slice of heaven...."

"Next item? Or is that it?"

"Liz," Jack said.

"Nothing to talk about there."

Now it was Jack's turn to laugh without humor. "Buddy, on this we're gonna talk. I know you didn't take her calls, didn't return them. I don't know what's up with that, but we're going to be back in town and she works for her aunt Connie every week. You can't avoid her. She's scared to death of how you're going to act toward her."

"She doesn't have to be scared," Rick said quietly.

Jack sighed. At least that last lacked the edge of hostility. "I'm sure she can't help it. You've been ignoring her. I gotta say, I don't get that."

"I know you don't. Don't worry. I'll talk to her. I'll be nice as I can."

"Rick, what the hell's going on with that?"

He took a deep breath. "Jack, it's going to be all right. Lizzie's young. Young and beautiful. She's sweet. And strong. She'll be fine."

"Something about what you just said sounds real bad."

"Nah, it'll be okay. Might take a little getting used to, that's all. She doesn't need a guy like me weighing her down."

Jack had to concentrate to keep from driving off the road. "What the hell? Is this about the leg?"

"It's not about the leg, but face it, that's not a great asset. It's about everything. Ever since Liz ran into me, her life has been messed up. I'm not good for her. She can do a lot better and deserves to."

"She's not going to agree with that. She's going to fight that idea."

"Well, not too hard, because that's how it is. Jesus, don't you think the girl's been through enough?"

"I don't know what to say," Jack said, but what he really meant was he didn't know what to say that wouldn't include a lot of frustrated swearing. He just wanted to shake Rick until all the marbles in his head fell back into place.

"What a break," Rick said. "Don't worry. I'll be nice."

"You'll be nice while you're dumping her? After all she's gone through for you? Don't you think if she felt she'd been through enough, *she'd* cut *you* loose?"

"Next item?" Rick said. "Or have we covered everything?"

"Listen, I'm going to try to be reasonable here…."

"I thought we were moving on?" Rick answered.

Oh, he's going to make me choke him! Jack thought. He shook his head a little violently, trying to let Mel's voice rise to the surface, because his instinct was to stop the car and say something like, *Listen, asshole, that little girl stuck by you while you were sticking by her and if you don't love her anymore, okay, stuff happens. But you don't just decide*

*you're not good enough and shit can her like that. And you
have enough fucking parts!*

"You've been through a lot," Jack chose to say. "Physically, emotionally, psychologically. Maybe you shouldn't make any fast moves. If you get through some of this stuff, get your problems sorted out and get good on the leg, get the high-tech leg, and then if you still feel this way… All I'm saying is, do you have to be so sure about major changes like that before you're fully recovered? You and Liz have been together a long time. You're just planning to push her away right off because you're still all messed up in your head. Which, by the way, is in the goddamn pamphlet."

He could see Rick's jaw tighten. "Next item?" he said.

"Aw, Christ," Jack said.

"Look, I'm trying hard as I can! I want to do what's right! In my messed-up head, it isn't right to hold on to Liz or let Liz hold on to me when she can do so much better! That's it! I've had months to think about it! Now—next fucking *item!*"

Jack took a defeated breath. "Okay. Preacher made barbecue."

Oh God. His worst nightmare. A town gathering, welcoming him home. He'd crumble. Cry like a girl. He wasn't up to it. "Tell him thanks. Tell him I'm in pain. We'll catch up."

"You're not in pain," Jack said.

"I am now. It's not happening, Jack. I can't. Do. It."

An hour from home, Jack thought. Maybe he'd change his mind. But if he'd learned anything in the last ten hours, Rick had enough determination to get him through almost anything. Except complete recovery. "Okay, pal. Whatever you say."

* * *

When Rick got to his grandmother's house, Lydie was overwhelmed by his homecoming. Rick could feel Jack standing behind him, just inside the front door, holding his duffel and the prosthesis, watching as Rick embraced his weeping grandmother with one arm while he balanced the walker between them. She was so small in his big arm and he had no instinct to shut her out. She was old, frail, and had suffered too many losses in her life. For a few moments, while he held her against his chest, Rick was grateful that he could come home to her in any condition. "Hey hey," he said. "Come on, Gram. You're gonna drown me with those tears. No crying, sweetheart."

"Ricky, I can't remember when I prayed so hard. Thank God you're home."

"I'm home, Gram. Everything is all right," he said, thinking about how wrong it all was. But he wouldn't put his gram through that. He comforted her until she wiped her old eyes and just stood there in front of him, studying his face with her trembling fingers. And behind him, he could hear Jack breathe.

"I bet there's doings at Jack's tonight," Lydie said.

"There is," Rick said. "I'm just not up to it, though. It was a long ride and my leg aches. I'm going to skip it."

"Are you sure?" she asked him, frowning.

Be welcomed home like a one-legged hero to this little town? *Ha, not on your life,* he thought. "I'm sure," he said. "But if you want to go see the neighbors, I'm sure Jack will take you."

"No, no," she said. "We'll stay home. Thing is, I didn't cook anything, Ricky. Thinking we'd be at Jack's…"

"No problem," he said. "We'll pull something together."

He gave her crepey, soft cheek a stroke, wiping away a tear. "We have to get up our strength, huh? And you need your insulin and food."

Jack brushed past them, taking Rick's duffel to his old room, the one he grew up in, the one he had briefly shared with Liz when their baby was almost due. "I'll bring you something from the bar. Can't have you trying to cook your first night home," he said as he passed.

"That's okay, Jack—" Rick began.

"Not a problem, Rick," Jack said. He was back quickly; the house was small—just five rooms and a bath. He met Rick's eyes and said, "I'll pass on your regrets and get a batch of barbecue, bring it down. You rest."

In a brief attack of humility for being such a giant asshole all day while Jack tried his best, Rick said, "Thanks, Jack. I appreciate that. A lot."

"Sure," Jack said, clearly still miffed at him, disappointed in him.

Rick got over the guilt right away. Jack, maybe most of all, would be better off if Rick just wasn't around to bring disaster after disaster into his life.

He got the prosthesis back on. He had a quiet meal with his grandma, she took her insulin and he popped a pain pill, and it was barely eight o'clock when she was nodding off in the chair and he sent her to bed. Then he dimmed all the lights so if anyone passed the house they would think he was asleep.

Rick was aware that there were lots of people at Jack's bar, just down the street. In fact, he could hear engines and voices even though the front door was closed. It brought back memories of all the good times there, the times he'd come home on leave, the visits from Jack's boys who all treated him like a little brother. He went back further in his mind to when he worked there, all through high school. It was like a second home—hanging out with Preacher and Jack, bussing tables, loading stock, going to Eureka for supply runs.

That job was his life for a while. Jack always made sure Rick's school sports and homework came first, fit his work at the bar around those things, like a dad would do. And when Lizzie got pregnant, Jack and Preach did everything they could to give him work while freeing him up to take good care of his girl, the mother of his baby. Here he'd gotten himself in this giant mess and they were totally there for him, holding him up, keeping him sane.

It brought tears to his eyes, thinking about those days. Some of them, like when the baby was stillborn, were the worst days of his life. But remembering that day—Jack and Preach, Mel delivering the baby when she herself was pregnant and due any minute, Lizzie somehow getting through it and still loving him.... How was it possible he could remember such a terrible day with such fondness?

His grandmother almost always left the front porch light on at night, but Rick turned it off. He just sat on the couch in the darkened living room and thought back to all those times, sorry but simultaneously relieved he wasn't down at the bar being welcomed home by the town.

In spite of himself, he felt bad about it. He knew Preacher would have put out his favorites and women from town would have brought their own special dishes to add to the party. He knew they meant well. He just didn't think he could stand the scrutiny.

At ten o'clock, Rick knew the party was long since over; farmers and ranchers didn't stay out late. Livestock and crops got them up real early. When he heard a light tapping at the front door, he thought it would be Jack, mother-henning again, checking on him. Maybe the guy wanted to tuck him in.

He opened the door and found himself face-to-face with Liz.

Ten

Rick's very first thought was, how can she be even more beautiful? Her eyes bluer and hair thicker, silkier, making his hands ache to run through the strands. She didn't look like a girl anymore; Liz could pass for twenty-one, easy. She was a knockout with a body that cost him sleep. His very next thought came right out of his mouth. "What are you doing here?"

"Well, I got the message, Rick. You're not going to take my calls, not going to call me back, not going to get in touch even when you're right across the street from my aunt Connie's store, where I work every single weekend." She shrugged. "So, I'm here to see you. To talk to you. To find out exactly what your problem is."

He laughed a little cruelly. "Well... Let's see," he said, scratching his chin. "What could it be?"

"Stop it, Rick. Eventually you're going to be honest with me. The leg doesn't have anything to do with *us*. I don't care about a goddamn leg and you know it."

He just stared into her eyes. This was a whole new Liz from the one he'd left. Well, that wasn't entirely true— she'd been on her way to becoming this Liz for a couple of years at least. He'd put her through an awful lot and instead of crumbling into a mushy pile of little-girl tears, she'd gotten tough. Confident. Her back was straight and her eyes glittered. "Let's put this off a while, all right?" he said. "Not tonight."

"No," she replied. "We've put it off long enough." She touched her diamond pendant. "I'm the girl you promised to *marry*. You've been mean and horrible and I understand you're going through terrible stuff, but that doesn't give you the right to turn your back on me. I'm not going to let you do that to me. I've been through stuff, too. The way it was with us, we helped each other."

"No one's gonna be able to help me with this," he said, and he started to close the door on her.

But her hand was against the door, keeping it from closing. "Let's go for a short ride."

"I can't do that," he said. "My grandma's in bed."

"Yeah? Leave a note. Write, 'Went for a ride with Liz.' She isn't going to ground you."

He actually chuckled. He remembered his Liz as a soft, sweet, vulnerable girl. The one he made cry at the hospital in Germany; the girl he had to be strong for. "I don't want to have this conversation tonight," was all he said.

"You're going to," she said. "We can do it right here, right now, maybe wake up your gram, or we can sit in my car and do it in private."

"Look, Liz, I'm real tired and I'm in some pain here. And I don't want to—"

"Okay then," she said, walking into the house. She sat down on his grandmother's sofa. "Here, then."

He took a breath and shook his head. He limped over to the kitchen counter, pulled a piece of paper off the notepad and scribbled a note to his grandmother. Then he limped toward the door, grabbing his coat off the rack.

"You want crutches or something?" she asked him.

"No. This isn't going to take too long." And he limped out the front door. Once he looked down at the three porch steps, he stopped. He grabbed the railing and hoped he wouldn't end up facedown on the walk—working that knee was still a crapshoot. Liz stayed behind him, giving him time. If she'd grabbed his arm to help him, he would have brushed her away, but she was smart and just waited till he made it.

And then, to his surprise, she left him to open his own car door. When she was settled behind the wheel, he was surprised when she started the car and put it in gear. "I thought we were just going to sit in your car," he said.

"We are," she said as she pulled away from the curb, "but we're going somewhere you can't chase me off or walk away from me."

"Well, just pull down the block. I'm not real fast, in case you hadn't noticed."

"What I've noticed is that what's wrong has nothing to do with your leg," she said. "You have definite problems, all right." She glanced over at him. "Okay, lay it on me, Ricky. Go ahead. Get it off your chest."

"I think you better stop the car first. Really, let's not go too far from home, okay? I meant it—I'm tired and my leg hurts."

"We're not going far," she said. "While I'm driving, do me a favor, Ricky. Try to remember me. I'm the girl who's always on your side no matter what. Huh? I'm the girl who would do anything for you. I'm the one who stuck by you a hundred percent when you said the Marine Corps was what you needed to get your head straight."

"You probably shouldn't have," he said quietly.

"Whatever," she said, waving a hand. "I did. I still am, even though you act like I'm dead or something."

He just stared straight ahead, not commenting, wondering how he was going to do this. One thing he had accepted—no matter how he handled it, he was going to hurt her bad. But in the end, she'd get over it and be better off. Problem was, she smelled so good and even though she was acting real tough, he knew that underneath all that strength was a softness so lush and deep, he could lose himself for a while, and it was getting to him. Maybe if she hadn't had the starring role in so many of his dreams, he could have forgotten.

He leaned his head back on the seat and closed his eyes. If he did this right, it would be over tonight. Then they could move on from what had been one disaster after another since the day they met.

Liz turned off the road and drove right down to the river. She parked, killed the lights and the car engine, and turned in her seat to face him. And waited.

"Liz, I don't think we should be together anymore." He gazed into his lap rather than at her. He waited for her reaction and when there was none, he looked at her.

"Why?" she asked.

"Because, Liz, us together is one bad break after another and I'm pretty sure every one of them was my fault. It's not fair to you."

"Oh," she said, "so you're doing this for *me*?"

"I know you don't want that. I know you don't. Don't you think that makes it even worse? That no matter how much

I screw up your life, you'll hang in there with me? I want you to stay away from me, Liz. Get on with your life, find a guy who won't mess you up every time you turn around. All right? Let me off the hook here, Liz! Let me go so I don't have one more thing to feel guilty about! You hear me?"

She just looked at him. There wasn't even a big moon and yet he could see her blue eyes sparkling like stars. She gave her head a gentle shake. "You're going to get past this," she said. "I know you're hurt and mad, but it's going to pass, Rick. And when it does, you won't want me to be gone."

"I'm telling you—"

She put her small hand against his cheek and just gently shook her head. "No," she whispered. "No, you won't."

He glazed over. His hand covered hers while he looked into her eyes, took in that small, soft, pink mouth, inhaled her scent, imagined… And then before he knew what was happening, he grabbed fistfuls of her thick, long hair and pulled her mouth onto his, eating her mouth, devouring her, moaning in the back of his throat while he invaded her with his tongue and allowed hers into his mouth. That taste—it was the taste he remembered, dreamt of. And he couldn't stop. He snapped. His hands went from her hair to her back, to her breasts, down to her butt, around to the front, grabbing her in that vee that joined her legs. "Jesus, this can't happen," he whispered against her mouth even as he was pulling apart her jacket and lifting her sweater. "Can't," he said, unhooking her bra and filling his hand and then his mouth with her breast.

Liz shifted her weight, making it easier for him to touch her, kiss her. While he roughly suckled, she kissed his temple, his ear, ran her fingers through his hair, buried her lips in his neck, inhaling him, tasting him, murmuring to him that she needed him, loved him, wanted him. This wasn't the way it usually was between them—he was desperate and fast now, not sweet and slow. She didn't care—he was touching her again and what that meant to her was that he didn't really want them apart. Maybe he thought it would be smart or wise for them to break up, but it wasn't right.

His hands grabbed the snap on her jeans, ripped it open, ran down the zipper and then slid down down down. A deep growl rumbled in his throat and he was back on her mouth. "Oh God, that's good," he muttered. "Good, so good…."

"Oh, Rick," she said in a breath.

"Take them off," he said against her lips. "Take them *off!*"

"Ricky, in the car? Like this?"

"Not the first time, Liz. Off," he commanded. "You have to. Come on!"

And he was tugging at her jeans, his thumbs hooked into the waistband. She put her hands over his and stopped him. She looked into his wild eyes for a moment and then slowly helped him draw down her jeans. She kicked off her shoes, lifted her legs and slid them off. She still had her panties on, but as panties go, they weren't much—just a tiny thong that barely covered her and wouldn't keep him out. And they didn't—his hand was instantly inside her panties, then inside her. She sucked in a breath, trying not to dissolve against his touch, but it caused him to moan.

And then his hands were fumbling with his own pants, undoing the belt, unsnapping, struggling with the zipper while he was in a sitting position.

"Here," she said gently. "Let me." She drew the zipper down easily and set him free.

He grabbed her hips and pulled her over him and then he stopped. "I'm sorry," he whispered. "Oh God, Liz…"

"It's okay," she whispered back, kissing him softly. "Okay, I know…"

And then he pulled aside that small, silk thong and lowered her down on him.

"Your leg—" she said.

"Nah, it's okay. Like this, it's okay. Ahhh," he said. And then he started to pump his hips with rising ferocity. He grabbed the back of her head, pulled her mouth down to his, kissed her deep and hard and exploded inside her with a muted growl. He thought he'd never stop, he was caught in such a long, desperate orgasm. And she just held him, let him ride it out, kissing him. And finally he began to relax beneath her, though he was panting as if he'd run a mile.

"God," he whispered. "No condom. *Great.*"

She smoothed her hand along the hair at his temple. "I've been on the pill for a couple of years, Rick. Since the baby…. We'll be all right."

"I think I just lost my mind." He looked up into her eyes, saw her soft smile. "I didn't even make you come."

"You seemed in kind of a hurry."

"Was I rough on you?"

"It's okay," she said, which was the same as yes. "You don't know which end is up right now."

"But did I hurt you?"

She shook her head.

He squeezed her bare behind in his hands. "See, this just can't happen…."

She laughed softly. "It's happened plenty of times. Not exactly like that. If that had been our first time, I might not have loved it. But it wasn't our first time."

His hand caressed her hair. "Liz, I'm no good for you, baby. You have to listen to me."

She shook her head. "We'll get through this."

He sighed. He'd certainly screwed that up. Came with her to tell her she had to give up this idea of *them* and then ripped her clothes off. "Come on, let's get you dressed. And home. I should get home myself, before I do any more crazy, stupid, painful things to you."

"Rick…"

"Please, Liz," he said, fastening his pants, helping her into her jeans. Then he held her face in his hands. "I don't want to hurt you anymore. You have to hear this—what I need right now is a time-out from us…. Can't you see, Liz? I can't be part of a couple."

"Give yourself time to—"

"No! I don't want this anymore! It's not going to work!"

For the first time since she showed up at his grandmother's door, he saw tears collect in her crystal-blue eyes, but they didn't spill over. "Worked pretty good for you a few minutes ago, Ricky."

He was quiet a long moment. "Let's get out of here, okay? I think I hurt my leg."

A few minutes later, she pulled up in front of his grandmother's house. She stared straight ahead and said, "You could let me be your friend. After all we've been to each other."

He looked at her profile. "No. I can't. I'd just use you and hurt you. I'm sorry, but that's it."

She turned toward him. "You've gone nuts. This isn't you at all—and it's not just the leg. You'd better get some help with it, Rick, before you throw away everything good in your life." When he didn't say anything for a moment, she said, "Get out then. You know how to get in touch with me."

Rick wasn't all the way up the porch stairs before Liz drove off, and not slowly. *Angrily.* She sped out of town. It was Friday night. Hadn't she said she worked for her aunt every weekend in the store? Maybe he got that wrong.... Anyway, she was gone, and that was good. Two months of ignoring her didn't send her packing, but this last deal would.

He got himself in the house and saw that the note he'd written his gram was still on the kitchen table. He dropped his jeans and unfastened the leg. He unlaced the running shoe and worked the prosthesis out of his jeans and leaned it against the sofa. He pulled up his jeans and sat down on the sofa. He grabbed the leg by the titanium pylon and threw it across the room. It clattered to the floor over by his gram's old piano. Then he put his head in his hands and felt the sting of tears in his eyes.

What the hell had he done? He had planned to tell her, calmly and sanely, they couldn't be a couple anymore. She should get on with her life, forget about him, find herself a guy who could take her the places in life she deserved to go. He even had a little speech about how she should go on with school, get herself real smart and snag an intelligent man who was going to earn a decent living and not bring mayhem into her life at every turn. And what had he done? Practically raped the girl! The fact that she hadn't tried to stop him didn't undo the fact that he'd been out-of-his-mind desperate, driven and rough. If she had told him to stop, could he have?

"Ricky?"

He lifted his head from his hands to see his gram standing under the living-room arch, clutching her old chenille robe together.

"I heard a loud noise...."

Thank God she couldn't see well enough to catch the tears in his eyes, on his cheeks, the leg across the room. "Sorry, Gram. I took off the leg and dropped it. It's really heavy. Sorry I woke you."

"You sound like you're getting a cold."

"Maybe, yeah," he said, sniffing. "I'm fine. Go back to bed."

"You need your walker?"

"I got it. It's right at the end of the couch."

"Can I get you anything, honey?"

"I'm fine, Gram. But thanks."

I'm not fine, he thought. *I'm a fucked-up mess. What the hell have I done to myself? To everyone else? Was I born under some kind of curse?*

All in one day, he'd beat up two of the most important people in his life—Jack and Liz. All day long he'd been an asshole to Jack and now look what he'd done to Liz—had sudden forceful, rough sex with her, and then told her she had to go away and leave him alone. He felt lower than a worm. And yet he couldn't for his life think of a better way to handle the situation. It was better for them if they didn't care about him so much.

There were going to be more people to deal with. People he didn't want pulling for him, being kind to him, befriending him when it could only come back on them in a bad way. Everything Ricky touched, as far as he was concerned, blew up. Just like that goddamn grenade in Iraq.

There was also Preach. Mel. The boys from Jack's squad. Connie and Ron. The whole frickin' town.

Then he realized with a shock—he was ashamed of having been blown up. Now, that made absolutely no sense, but there it was. He should have come back from Iraq with some head troubles, but not this kind. He'd listened to guys in that stupid support group talk about shame at having been wounded, shame at having to put their families through dealing with a disabled vet, and he thought it was beyond ridiculous.

But here he sat, on his grandmother's floral couch, knowing that everything in his head would be different if he had returned to Virgin River with two legs. And he didn't know what to do with that knowledge. There was no changing things.

He didn't sleep well, but when he got up, real early, the first thing he did was use his walker to get to his gram's front porch and look across the street at Connie's house, right next to the corner store. And there was Liz's car. It had a dewy coat over it—it had been there a long time. Where had she gone after dropping him off? Obviously she hadn't gone home to her mother's in Eureka. His head began to pound. Had she gone out to the woods or river to cry?

Rick felt like a monster.

He hid out the whole day. He could have walked down to Jack's and been friendly, but after ditching the welcome-home party, he thought he'd just play the wounded Marine for a while longer, let everyone think he wasn't up to public appearances. So Jack came to him.

"Just checking to see how you're doing today," he said. "And brought you and your grandma something of Preacher's for dinner."

"Thanks," he said, taking the bag. "Is Preacher pissed?"

"Preacher hardly ever gets pissed," Jack said. "But just for future reference, you don't want to be around when he is. So—today's better?"

"Yeah. I'm getting by. Trying to get a little rest."

"Good. I want you down at the bar at 9:00 a.m. Monday morning. We have PT in Eureka," Jack said.

"We?"

"I'm taking you. PT Monday, Wednesday and Friday. The counselor Tuesday and Thursday. Also morning."

"You don't have to do that...."

Jack lifted an eyebrow. "You going to call a cab? Or maybe you have another ride in mind so you don't have to talk to me?"

Rick just looked down, frustrated with himself for wanting to hurt people so much. "Okay, thanks," he said quietly. "I'm not real hot on that counselor idea. I told you that."

"I know. I heard that. Just so you know, Mel *is* hot on it—and she found the counselor. Go ahead, tough guy—call her and talk her out of it."

"What if I don't call her and just refuse to go?"

"I'm taking you—I happen to think it might help. I guess I could be a stubborn fool and refuse to talk." He shrugged. "If you decide to go that way, just listen. Maybe you'll pick up something. By the way, what happened with you and Liz?"

His eyes popped open. "What makes you think something happened?"

"She said she saw you last night, and she doesn't seem to be doing real well. I asked her. She said she can't talk about it."

Even if he wanted to, he couldn't tell Jack he'd treated

her the way he had. He just couldn't handle the look he'd
see in Jack's eyes. If he'd learned anything, Jack's opinion
of how men should treat women was firm—they were to
be handled with the greatest of respect and care. He could
tell Jack he'd practically raped her, then told her to go away
and leave him alone, and although Jack wouldn't give up
on him, he'd be completely ashamed of him. Rick decided
it wasn't worth it. He couldn't bear the added guilt. "I can't
talk about it either," he said.

Jack was silent for a moment. "Good thing we have that
appointment with the counselor. You can tell him."

Don't count on it, Rick thought.

On Tuesday morning, Jack dropped Rick at a modest
home in Grace Valley and said he'd wait out Rick's counseling session at the café in town. Rick stood at the curb
and stared at the house for a minute or so—but Jack just
drove off. Finally, he went to the door of a remodeled garage
that had a sign by it. Jerry Powell, followed by a bunch of
letters, including PhD. When he knocked, a man shouted,
"Come on in."

He found himself in a small waiting room that was,
thankfully, empty. There was a door to another room and
presently a tall, spindly man with a sharp nose and thin hair
that flopped onto his forehead appeared there. He smiled.
"You must be Rick."

"And you must be the counselor."

Jerry laughed. "Come on back."

Rick slowly followed while Jerry waited at the door. He
indicated a couple of chairs facing each other and then he
closed the door. "I'm not expecting clients right now, but

I close the door in case anyone wanders into the waiting room. This room is soundproofed for our privacy."

Rick sat. Between the chairs, a small table bore a box of tissues. That was for when he broke down and cried.

Before sitting, Jerry offered his hand. "Jerry Powell, Rick. It's nice to meet you. And even though you might be tired of hearing it, thank you for the service you perform on behalf of our country. Not only do I appreciate it, I'm deeply touched and personally indebted to you."

Rick was surprised. He tilted his head. Actually, he hadn't heard that. Maybe if he'd gone to his own welcome-home party at the bar, he might have. But instead of saying thank-you, he said, "Just so you know, I don't want to be here."

Jerry actually smiled. "Which puts you in the majority. I do some work for the county and from time to time a junior-high or high-school student, in trouble at school, comes my way as part of penance. A way of not getting expelled. If you think they want to be here…"

"What happened to me wasn't high-school stuff."

Jerry sobered. "I'm aware of that." He let that go a beat. "Well, I should explain—I've never counseled a disabled veteran before. I've had vets, I've had amputees, I've counseled lots of people with disabilities, but I've never counseled a person trying to adjust to civilian life after a war injury."

"Maybe you don't know what you're doing?"

"Or maybe we'll learn from each other," he said easily, not in the least intimidated by Rick's hostile nature. "I'll try to keep up. Anywhere in particular you'd like to start?"

"Maybe you didn't hear me—I'd rather not do this at all."

"Okay, I'll start. I've been in Grace Valley about ten

years now. There's a rumor going around that I claim to have gone on a ride in a spaceship with aliens." He shrugged. "It's the absolute truth—I really did. I swear. I don't even care that hardly anyone buys it—it happened to me. Screwed me up pretty good for a while. I'll make a deal—you tell me some of the stuff that's giving you trouble. I'll tell you about the spaceship."

Rick's mouth hung open. He stared at him in total astonishment. When he did finally shut his mouth, he opened it again to say, "You're fucking *kidding* me!"

Jerry smiled. "God's truth."

"You're a nutcase? And you think you're going to help *me*?"

"I'm a survivor of a traumatic experience. It took a lot of counseling and I was already a counselor. As for us, you and me, there's client privilege, which means I never talk about your issues. In fact, I don't tell anyone who my clients are. What you say about our sessions is up to you—but I won't mention I've met you under these circumstances. I don't even take notes, in case they're ever subpoenaed, but you don't have to think about that—your session with me isn't court ordered. So. Maybe you'd like to jump in, take a chance. Hear about the spaceship for dessert?"

Rick shook his head. Unbelievable. It was surreal. The guy who was going to help put his head back together thought he'd been abducted by aliens? "Holy Jesus," he muttered. Jerry just lifted his pale brown eyebrows, waiting.

"Okay, here's the deal," Rick said. "Bad stuff happens to me and the people who care about me. Started when I was two and my parents died in a car wreck. I bet if we could check back further, my mother probably almost died in childbirth...."

"That a fact? Like you're bad luck or something?"

"Not *like* I am. You get mixed up with me, care about me, you're in for it."

"And you believe that?"

"I can't help but believe it. There's a long history of it." And Rick explained the details, his voice cold and flat.

A half hour later, Jerry asked, "Tell me about your girl."

"She's not my girl anymore. I broke up with her, for her own good."

"But you still know about her. Tell me some things so I know who you broke up with and how you're feeling about it."

He took a breath. Now, this was where the tissues might actually come in handy, if he broke down. "She's amazing," he said softly. "We had some of that accidental teenage sex when I was sixteen and she was fourteen. Happened so fast, we didn't even see it coming. One time. I got her knocked up. She was scared to death, and she was just a kid. But she wanted to have the baby, and she wanted me. Her mother and aunt Connie wanted her to give the baby away, but in the end it was me who couldn't live with that."

"How'd you feel about the pregnancy?"

"Are you kidding? I wanted to disappear. Run for my life."

"Did you?"

"I couldn't do that to her. I stuck with her. I knew even way back then I loved that girl. It was totally nuts to love someone at that age, but I did. And we were going to find a way to keep that baby. My grandma and Jack, they were on board to help if they could. I was willing to do anything. Anything. Work ten jobs, whatever I had to do. I should have known I was no good for her when she got knocked up after one time. But then, just to drive the point home, her baby was born dead."

Jerry cleared his throat. "I don't think I missed anything there, Rick. It was also your baby. Correct?"

"I did it to her, though. I put it there, she loved him and took good care of him, and he was born dead." His voice cracked on the last word.

"Very tough for the two of you," Jerry said. "Very, very painful. You must have had a great deal of grief."

"Yeah," he said, his voice filled with both anguish and self-loathing. "And my way of dealing with it was to abandon her. I told her I had to get my head together. I enlisted in the Corps." He lifted his head, shook off the threat of tears. "She was scared to death of me doing that, plus I was going to be gone a long time, and she *needed* me. There was a war going on—I knew I'd end up going. And this girl, still just a girl in high school, she said if that's what I needed to do, she'd stick it out. She'd wait. She'd be faithful, write me every day, and wait. How many fifteen-year-old girls do you know who could get through that? Get knocked up, bury their baby, send their boyfriend off to the Marines, then to war, and *wait*? I told her I wouldn't hold her to that, but it was her decision."

Jerry was silent. And so was Rick, for a little while.

"She missed every high-school thing that came along. While I'm off turning myself into a big man, she's sitting home alone. She's so beautiful, you just can't imagine. And sweet. But she's not a little girl anymore—she's gotten so strong." He let go a laugh. "Because of me. Because I put her through so much, probably. She'd stay home from things like prom and homecoming because she didn't want any guys who would ask her out to think she was available.

She'd stay home and write me letters instead. When I got blown up, she came to Germany, where I was in the hospital. She'd never been on a plane before in her life, and she flew halfway around the frickin' world to see me, make sure I was alive. And I treated her like crap. Told her she shouldn't have come."

Quiet reigned a moment. "Sounds like a wonderful girl," Jerry finally said. "Devoted. You must have been in a bad place, emotionally, while you were in the hospital. Would that be correct?"

"She just didn't deserve all that. You know?"

"She made her own choices, Rick. As did you."

"Yeah," he said, laughing without humor. "The choices I made were all selfish. The ones she made were all unselfish. All for me."

"I bet if you asked her, she'd say her choices served her needs. She must have wanted to be a part of your life."

He shook his head. "No matter how bad it is for her?"

"You so sure it's bad for her? Sometimes being someone's partner is fulfilling."

"I doubt it, Jerry. Not anymore."

"Hmm?"

"I told her in Germany, she should get on with her life—that I was going to be busy trying to get through rehab. She called, sent me stuff, but I shut her out, hoping she'd just wander off and get a life. Find a guy who could give her stuff, like maybe a future that didn't hurt all the time. But damn, that girl's stubborn. She never quit. I wouldn't take her calls, wouldn't return her messages, but she just kept at it. When I got back to Virgin River the other night, she came over to my gram's and asked me to go for a ride with her, to talk. I went, and I tried to talk to her, but once we were parked at the river, I just grabbed her. Like a maniac. I couldn't stop myself. I tore off her clothes and just did her—just like that. No lovey-dovey stuff. After her jeans were off, I pulled her onto my lap and just plugged her. I practically raped the girl who's stuck by me through everything. And then I told her I couldn't be part of a couple anymore, that she had to let me go."

Now Jerry's silence lengthened, but Rick didn't fill it for quite a while.

"How impressed are you with me now?" Rick finally asked.

Jerry cleared his throat. "I'd like to ask a couple of questions, if it's all right with you."

"Knock yourself out. I'm all out of secrets now."

He cleared his throat again. "Did you hit her?"

Rick was startled. "Of course not! I wouldn't hit Liz!"

"Did you hold her down?"

"I told you—I pulled her on top of me. I can't do anything with this leg."

"Did she struggle? Try to pull away?"

"No. She let me."

"Did she ask you not to?"

He shook his head. "She'd do anything for me. But that's no excuse for what I did to her."

"Did she say anything like, no? Or, please don't? Or, stop?"

"I told you, she *let* me! That makes it *worse!*"

"Afterward, did she say you hurt her?"

"No," he said weakly. "She said I'd seemed to be in a hurry. And it was okay that it wasn't good for her."

"Did she cry or complain that she'd tried to get through to you or—"

"I *told* you. She went along with it. I was rough and only thinking about myself. I was getting *off!* I was out of my mind. Liz is not made for that! She's a good, sweet, giving person! I don't want her giving in to someone like that. Like *me*."

Jerry smiled patiently and watched as Rick wiped angrily at his eyes, refusing to let himself cry.

"I think," Jerry said, "that sex will be better for both of you if you're conscious of each other's needs and desires. People in the throes of passion sometimes get a little selfish. Take advantage. And in the end, if they're two people who care about each other, it's not entirely satisfying. It sounds like maybe it wasn't all that satisfying to you."

Rick narrowed his eyes meanly. "I got off. She didn't."

"And it also happens, with couples, that people give rather than take sometimes. If one partner is particularly needy and the other doesn't feel at risk—"

"You are the biggest dork," Rick snapped.

Jerry laughed. "You're going to have to do better than that. I've been called way worse than dork. And I concede to dork."

"Didn't you hear what I just told you about the other night?"

"You didn't rape her, Rick. You didn't even almost rape her. I've only known you for fifty minutes and yet I believe, if she'd tried to pull away or told you to stop, you would have."

"I'm not so sure about that."

"You're not sure because you weren't tested—it didn't come to that. What's interesting about this is that my bigger challenge is usually explaining what rape is to a young man who thinks he didn't when, in fact, he did. Not listening to no. Holding a girl down. If what you're telling me is accurate, that wasn't the case."

"What I'm telling you is *horrible*," he ground out.

"I think if you caused her pain, it probably came afterward, when you told her you didn't want her anymore. I'd like you to think more about that decision so you can outline your motivation on that for me, and we'll talk about it on Thursday. I'd also like you to try to make a list of the good things that have happened in your life. Don't strain yourself—give me five. Maybe you should think of them as 'lucky' things. But our time is up for today."

"Wait a goddamn minute!" Rick snapped. "You have to tell me about the fucking spaceship!"

"Will your ride be waiting?" Jerry asked.

"He'll wait!"

"Well, okay then. I was camping with a couple of friends. We were in Arizona, way out in the middle of nowhere. We'd been in Sedona, but we moved out into the desert. When my friends woke up in the morning, I was gone. I woke up—I don't know when—inside this spaceship. I had no memory of being snatched. It was like silver glass on the inside and the people—the aliens—had on suits that covered them from head to toe, breathing like Darth Vader, and I was stripped bare and lying out on a silver table. They were studying me and poking at me and talking in what sounded like high-pitched squeaks. Like dolphins.

"My friends got a search party going back in Arizona, but after two weeks of not being able to find me, they all gave up the search. They assumed I'd wandered off and died in the desert. But at some point, again in a total blackout, I found myself back in the desert of Arizona—alone. A park ranger found me and picked me up. The story goes that I wandered off from our camp and hallucinated due to dehydration, but that isn't what happened."

"Maybe it did," Rick said.

Jerry shook his head. "I wasn't dehydrated. And after weeks of being missing in the desert, my clothes weren't damaged. Not torn or dirty or anything." He looked at his watch. "I've researched—mine is not the lone account of such a thing. I'll be glad to give you what other details I can remember at the end of our next session, if you're interested."

Rick sat back in his chair and just stared at the guy. "How often does this spaceship trick work for you?"

Jerry grinned. "Every time."

Jack didn't ask about the counseling session. He didn't even bother with something as benign as, "Was it as bad as you thought it would be?" He just left it alone, so there was no talking. When they got back to the bar, Jack said, "Tomorrow morning is PT. See you at 9:00 a.m."

"You're going to get real tired of this," Rick said.

"Get? I'm already tired of it. 'Course I wouldn't be if you weren't so angry with me for God knows what."

"I'm not angry with you, Jack. It's the situation."

"Well, that's good to know," Jack said. "Tomorrow—9:00 a.m."

"Actually, I need to come in now. Talk to Preacher."

"By all means," Jack said. And he thought—why the hell can't you talk to me?

The big man was working in the kitchen. Paige was sitting at the workstation, holding Dana, now nine months old. "Well, hey," she said, grinning broadly when she saw Rick enter. With baby in her arms, she went to him, embracing him. "I wondered when I was going to see you. How are you feeling?"

Rick's hand automatically wandered to little Dana's head, smoothing over her thin cap of brown hair. "I'm okay, Paige. I wanted to apologize for the other night. To you and Preach."

Preacher lifted his shoulders in a shrug. "No problem, man. Jack said you were worn out and the leg was hurting."

"I have to double apologize," Rick said. "That wasn't it. I just couldn't take on the town, Preach. I'm sorry. Maybe I can run into them one at a time. But a big gang like that— I didn't feel like I could do it. I wasn't sure how I'd act."

"Oh?" Preacher asked.

"Ah, how can I explain? Nah, I can't explain. It's like I'm not always in charge of how I behave. Sometimes I say mean things, ungrateful things. Do things it isn't like me to do. And sometimes I break down and it's embarrassing. That's the best I can do for an explanation."

"Got it," Preacher said. "Still real rocky, getting on with things. Yeah, I been there."

"Huh?"

He lifted a bushy brow. "Jack ever tell you about how I got hurt in Iraq and cried like a baby, calling for my mother?" He shook his head. "Wasn't like me either, and my injury was minor."

"It was major enough that I had to carry you over my shoulder for a long damn stretch," Jack said.

"I wasn't even in the hospital after," Preacher said. "So, I know the best way to fix your situation. Marines back from war are always comped around here. 'Course, you'd be comped even if you hadn't gone to war, but since you did, you eat and drink on the house here, just like cops, doctors, firefighters. You know—like we've always done. You serve the town, Jack serves you. You must be getting some serious cabin fever sitting around your grandma's. Walk down here sometimes, just to say hello. That'll get you back in touch. One at a time, like you want."

"Maybe," he said. "I gotta warn you—I'm not great company. Ask Jack."

They all looked at Jack. "I'm hoping it gets better. After some adjustment. Maybe we should go out to the river...." He grinned yet his eyebrows frowned in a menacing way, as though he was thinking of drowning Rick rather than catching fish.

Rick almost smiled. Jack was a real good guy, but he wasn't good at taking shit, and Rick had given him a real load of it. "See?" he said, looking back at Preacher and Paige.

"Well, try this," Paige said, pushing the baby on him. "She puts everyone in a good mood."

"Is that a fact?" Rick asked, taking Dana into his arms. "Where's the little guy?"

"Chris is in school. He's in first grade now."

"Aw, jeez, was he in that bus accident?" Rick asked. "Jack told me about it."

Paige shook her head. "He was home that day. I kept him home because of the nasty weather. If it weren't just first grade, I probably would have sent him. Now, till I get my confidence back, I drive him."

"I rode that bus for years. Must have scared you to death," Rick said, and sniffed the baby's neck while she patted him on the cheek.

Preacher smiled and exchanged glances with his wife. "Scared everyone in town, Rick," Preacher said, not wanting to draw attention to the fact that Rick was caving in to the baby's softness, sweetness. "How about a sandwich? I'm just making up some for lunch. And I want you to see the new house Paul built on the bar for me and Paige—it's amazing. Turned that little apartment into a real house."

"That'd be great," Rick said, and then he actually laughed as Dana pressed her forehead against his and blubbered her lips in a spitty noise.

Jack just wandered into the bar. But he smiled to himself. It was true, he wasn't patient. But all he had to see was one ounce of recovery and it gave him some hope to hang on to.

Eleven

Friday afternoon came and Jerry Powell sat at his desk. He didn't take notes during sessions, but afterward he wrote out a summary for the client files. He heard the outside door open and quickly closed and put away the file. Then he smiled as Liz walked into the office. "Hey there," he said.

"Hi," she answered, taking one of the chairs in the room.

This sort of thing didn't happen in Jerry's practice as often as one might think it would, given the size of the towns. He'd been counseling Liz since right after her baby was stillborn. He had a nice contract with the county school district. There were school counselors in both Eureka and Fortuna who liked his work and made referrals to him. And after Rick had been wounded in Iraq, Liz came back to him. After all, he'd been able to help before and they had history, so he was a logical choice.

If Rick and Liz talked about it, they would find out that he was counselor to both of them, but they wouldn't learn it from him. And information he got from them about each other didn't factor in his therapeutic work, though it was pretty impossible not to be aware. Therefore enlightened, he hoped.

Even though he felt a lot closer to Liz, and knew her much better, it hadn't taken him long to feel a certain attachment to Rick. Here were a couple of kids who had been to hell and back. And while they loved each other, they were in a bad enough place that they might not get through it together. In fact, Jerry knew they were already apart. The one thing he couldn't do was fill in the blanks for them— it would be a breach of ethics. If he were in a place where more PhDs were available to counsel, it would probably be wise to push one of them off on another counselor. If they were a married couple seeking individual as opposed to marriage counseling, he would be forced to. Otherwise, it would be a conflict of interest.

They needed him. And he was confident he could counsel them without prejudice.

Jerry came around his desk and went to the chair facing Liz. She came by his office every Friday after school on her way to Virgin River to help her aunt in the store. She had been for a couple of months now. "How was your week?" he asked her.

She shrugged. "Not great," she said. "I'm worried I might be sliding backward."

"Go ahead and tell me about it, Liz," he said.

"Well, I had myself toughened up a little. Like I've told you before, I started concentrating on school more, so Rick would be proud. But then I liked it. Liked that I could get the grades when I tried. Liked that I already got an acceptance into community college. It was for me. And I hung in there pretty good, even though Rick wouldn't take my phone calls or anything. But then I finally saw him and talked to him. Last Friday night. I had to go to him, of course, even though he knows exactly how to find me. He made it real clear—he wants us to break up. He's through with me. All week I haven't been able to study at all. And I have finals coming up." She swallowed a couple of times, as if trying to keep her tears in check. "All of a sudden, I don't care anymore."

"What don't you care about?" Jerry asked.

She shrugged. "Not much of anything."

"Does that mean, it's not just schoolwork that's been affected?"

She scooted forward on her chair. "Here's the thing, Jerry. I knew this all along. I've known it since I read the pamphlets with Jack in Germany. He's breaking up with me for my own good. He said as much."

"Can you remember what he said?"

"That with him there was one bad thing after another, and they were always his fault. Which is the craziest thing I've ever heard. But I read in all the stuff they gave us and the stuff I found online, some wounded military guys go through this kind of thing. They feel as if it's their fault or something. As if they don't deserve to be loved. What the hell is that? Why doesn't he blame me for all the stuff that's gone wrong since we've been together? Why don't I blame me?"

Jerry smiled a little, tilting his head. "If you'll remember, we worked through some of that."

"We did, huh?" she said, suddenly reminded. She straightened. "Yeah, we did. I *did* blame myself before. I thought I'd done something wrong to make the baby die. Like I ate the wrong things or didn't eat the right things. Or slept on my back or something. Yeah." She actually smiled, though it was a weak and sad smile. "That's right. But I never broke up with Rick because I thought I wasn't good enough for him."

"We went over some of this, too," Jerry reminded her. "Everyone has an individual response to crisis, grief, et cetera. I don't say this to you to influence the direction you take in your situation, Liz, but you do have to keep that in mind. He has many adjustments to make that might not make sense to you. Just like if you'd told him you were guilty, as if you'd hurt the baby, it might not have made sense to him. The important thing is that you understand *yourself*."

She made a face, lowered her gaze. "Having a little trouble there," she said.

"Hmm?"

"My feelings are so hurt. And I drove out of town, parked and cried. But before I even got done crying, I was so mad. I'm still so mad. Instead of studying like I should be, I just go into these mental arguments with him, yelling at him in my head."

"Can you play some of those tapes for me?" he asked.

"What do you mean?"

"What are you yelling in your head?"

"Oh, things like, Who do you think you are? You think you're the only one who ever felt terrible and scared and alone? Who felt loss? Who felt you weren't good enough? Don't you think I'd have given up *both* legs if it could have saved the baby's life? Things like that. I mean, I went through a real bad time with the baby, you know."

"I do know. Did he help you with that at the time?" Jerry asked.

She was quiet a moment. Finally she said, "Totally. He did everything he could think of. Even though it hurt him just as much. I know it did. After the baby was born, when he was holding me and the baby together, he was touching his little-bitty hand and tears were falling on my hair and the baby's head. But he held me. He came to Eureka almost every day. He called to see how I was twice a day.... And now...he won't let me be there for him," she added quietly. "He wants to do this alone. And he can't."

"Can't?"

"When we went out to talk, we made love.... Well, not like we used to. He was a little nuts, grabbing me. I tried to slow him down a little, shushing him, kissing him softly, but he was just gone. That's what makes me confused—he doesn't want us to be together anymore, but he can't control himself when he's with me. Explain that to me."

Jerry deferred. Instead, he said, "Did he hurt you, Liz?"

"Physically? Of course not," she said, shaking her head. "He even said he was sorry while he was trying to get my jeans off. Like he was sorry he was so desperate or something. Because he didn't stop."

"And you didn't stop him?"

"No, I didn't care. He's been away a long time, he's been through so much, and I was missing him, too. I wanted him—that wasn't the problem. The problem came after when he said, 'See? We can't be together.' And I thought— what was that? That *was* together. I understand it—I read all the stuff. He's pushing me away. But at the same time, I *don't* understand it."

"Now what?" Jerry asked.

"Now? Now nothing. From me, anyway."

"Can you explain that, please?"

"I took him back to his grandmother's house and told him to get out of my car. I reminded him that he knew how to find me. I've spent months reaching out to him. I don't think it would be good for either one of us if I pushed on it anymore."

"Think you're going to be able to follow through on that?" Jerry asked.

Her lips pursed, her eyes watered, a trembling hand rose up to her chest and just as a giant tear rolled down her cheek, in a voice so soft Jerry had to strain to hear her, she whispered, "My heart hurts. Hurts so bad. I... I just don't want him to see me cry anymore...." She hiccuped and blinked until her cheeks were wet. Jerry didn't hand her a tissue; she knew where they were. She'd used up his supply several times. "If I didn't love him so much, I'd hate him." She swallowed and reached for a tissue. "My heart hurts so bad...."

By the time May was full on the land, the afternoons were almost always sunny and warm. The forest animals were out of hiding, often with new babies, along the meadows and river at dawn and again at dusk. Spring wildflowers were in full glory along roadsides, up the mountainsides and through the meadows. Virgin River was at its most beautiful in spring.

And Dan Brady was glad he'd made the decision to come here. He'd given it a lot of thought. Indeed, there'd been lots of time to think about where he'd settle while he cooled his heels in Folsom Prison. He was a low-profile prisoner— just a pot grower. He didn't even take a hit for dealing— he'd only been caught growing, but the assumption was, he grew it to sell it. It was the pedophiles and rapists who were in constant danger from other inmates. And there was fighting among the gangs. Dan just did his time quietly. And thought.

It was a logical decision for him. Virgin River was a quiet, decent town. There were people there he thought highly of—Mel and Jack being two. Preacher was an odd-ball, but good-hearted and helpful. Paul Haggerty was a stand-up boss. Of course, he'd had no expectation that they'd come to respect him, but to his amazement, they were perfectly friendly toward him. And the job with Haggerty—pure luck. If he'd been Haggerty, he'd never have hired himself. But it was working out great. There was plenty of overtime when he wanted it. Haggerty paid a fair wage and the benefits were good. The men he worked with were quality crews. Haggerty had high standards.

It didn't leave him much spare time, but what was he going to do with spare time? He'd always been a loner, some-thing that intensified when he was growing pot. It was a habit he was slowly trying to break—it made sense for him to come out of the darkness and have people in his life, like he used to. They might not trust him, but he trusted them. They were transparent, to the last one—not real compli-cated, living authentic lives, invested in their families and friends, protective of their own, their town. So he had begun to slowly enter their world. He picked up a packed lunch from the bar every morning at about 6:00 a.m.—Preacher made it the night before. Then a couple of nights a week he'd take dinner and a beer there and catch up on local gossip and national news on the bar's TV. The rest of the time he either worked or tinkered around the rental house.

His father taught him something real useful when it came to fixer-uppers—always do what shows the most first. So the first thing Dan did was replace the window glass in that one broken window and reinforce and repair the front porch. Took him a day and a half. Then he hired some of Haggerty's boys to scrape and paint the house while he painted the porch—he wasn't going up on those ladders.

Dan wasn't about to invest in a new roof if he didn't own the place, but he did have the existing roof repaired so he wouldn't drown in the next big rain.

Next, he pulled weeds, threw down some topsoil, tore out the cracked sidewalk with a crowbar and shovel and put down patio stones instead. He planted flowers along the front of the house. A little daily sprinkling and some spring sunshine and he had a green yard bordered by colorful flowers and a pretty little yellow house, trimmed in white.

Once he was inside, which was about three weeks into his tenancy, he could work evenings when he felt like it. He tackled the easiest and most visible stuff first. He washed the nicotine off the living-room and dining-room walls, patched and painted. He borrowed a big industrial floor sander from Paul and turned the living/dining area into a beautiful L-shaped room in about ten days with paint, stain, varnish and floor wax. He scrubbed up the stone fireplace and it was looking good. Then he scrubbed down and painted the bedroom—it took only a few evenings. The only furniture he had was a bed and a small table with two chairs that he left in the dining room while he tore apart the kitchen.

He'd been in Virgin River six weeks, in his little rental for just over four, and he was really pleased with what a minimal amount of money and some work could do. The kitchen was going to take more than a couple of weeks, and would be a lot more expensive than the work he'd done so far, but he was making good money and he'd take it slow. He scraped off the old, damaged linoleum floor and removed all the cupboards, since some were already missing doors and they were too old to be a standard size. He ripped out the counters, keeping just the sink and moving the appliances away from the walls.

He got rid of the old, peeling, yellowed wallpaper, textured the kitchen walls and was painting away a Sunday afternoon when there was a knock at the door. He went, roller in hand, and opened the door. "Well," he said, grinning. "My landlady. Funny, I wondered if I'd ever see you again."

"The house," she said. Her mouth hung open and her eyes were huge. "Good God!"

"Oh, is it okay?" he asked her.

She shook her head and he thought, for a second, she was going to say he'd gone too far and she hated it.

"I never even imagined it could look like this. It's incredible. When I pulled up, I thought I had the wrong house."

He grinned at her. "I should probably stop. If I do a good enough job, you're going to want it back and I'll be in the camper shell again."

"You don't have to worry about that," she said. "I'm never living here again."

"I'd given up on you. I asked Jack if he thought you'd be back and he said he didn't really know. He thought there was a chance you'd just let the house go. Can't imagine why you'd do that…."

"No, you probably couldn't. Chalk it up to some bad memories."

"Must have been horrific," he said, and she merely nodded.

The house wasn't the only thing that looked different. She was looking pretty good herself. The last time he'd seen her, she'd been hauling trash all day, but even after that, she had strong looks that held up. He put her at somewhere around thirty. Maybe five foot six or so. Slender but not skinny; long legs, good hips. She had an unfussy style—hair that curled under just above her shoulders, makeup he could see her freckles through.

"I'm owing you rent," he said, pulling out his wallet from his back pocket. But she just walked past him into the kitchen.

"Holy cow," she said. "Stripped bare."

"Uh, yeah. This is going to take a while because of the cost. Couple of months, at least, depending on things like overtime. It needs everything. I'm doing the floor and walls first, cupboards and counters next, and appliances one at a time. This is also going to be more expensive than some grass seed and paint. Lots more. I hope you're planning to let me stay here cheap for a while to make up for the investment."

"Sure. I don't want it."

"I don't even know where to start with that bathroom. Nice big room, but it's a nightmare the way that shower's put in. Plus, I'm going to have to give up the bathroom during the remodel, and after living in a camper shell for a while, that shower, ugly as it is, comes in real handy. Especially when you work construction all day, then again at home all night." She didn't say anything, just looked around in wonder. "That bathroom could use a tub and shower, and new toilet." Still, silence. "I'm not taking on that back room till I've been here a year or more. Fact is, it needs to be ripped off and rebuilt. Hey—we in the same solar system here?"

"Oh. Sorry. Gee… Um, what's your name again?"

He sighed. "Dan Brady."

"Sorry, Dan. I'm just blown away by how good the place

looks. And in a little over a month. You must have worked yourself to death."

"Nah. A little after work, a little on the weekends." He still held his wallet in his hand. "I owe you like a month and a half rent. Cash all right?"

"Sure. Yeah."

"Next time the rent's due, I can drop it off in Eureka when I'm over there, if you'll give me an address. I get around that way at least once a month, buying stuff like paint, caulk, repair stuff. Maybe we could grab a quick bite, talk more about what I'm thinking for the house, get to know each other a little, you know...."

She tilted her head. "You don't know about me, do you?"

"Ah—you lived here. Your mother died and your father is with a brother? That right? You work and live in Eureka, right?"

"I'm an alcoholic," she said, straightening almost proudly.

"Ah. Expensive date or enjoying sobriety?"

"Over seven months sober. I know the exact number of days. Hours."

"Good for you. So, if it doesn't freak you out for me to know where you live and if you'd like a free meal—"

"I don't get involved with men."

He looked stricken for a second. "Oh God, I'm sorry, Cheryl. I didn't mean to mislead you—I wasn't expecting to get involved. I just thought rent money, early dinner and someplace casual. Listen—"

She started to laugh to herself, softly, shaking her head. "Paranoid," she said quietly. "Goes with the territory. Listen, Dan—I wasn't an ordinary drunk. I was a very drunk drunk. Did a lot of regretful things. That's why I don't come back here, where it all started, where I was at my worst.

Ask anyone in town—they can all tell you about Cheryl, the town drunk. You don't want to have dinner with me."

He gave her a small smile. He stuck out his hand. "Cheryl, meet Dan—ex-con."

She didn't take the hand, but lifted her eyebrows slightly. "For…?"

"Growing weed."

"Aw, Jesus, you a druggie?"

He shook his head. "Never used dope, I just grew it for the money. I was in a tight spot, a family member needed help, I couldn't think of anything else and I'd met a guy way back who knew someone who knew someone who could set me up and I could make a bunch of money fast. And I got caught and did time." He grinned. "Ask anyone around here about Dan, the grower."

"What are you doing here? In Virgin River? Fixing up an old shit hole like this?"

"I'm getting my life back. What are you doing?"

"Okay, okay, touché." She reached into her shoulder bag and pulled out a scrap of paper and a pen. "Here's my phone number. Call a week ahead and clear a time with me. And I don't know about a meal—I'll have to think about that."

"Good," he said. "You think. I'll paint. And here's three hundred dollars to catch you up. Though now the place is looking better, you probably want a friggin' security deposit, huh?"

"Doesn't anything bother you?"

"Anymore? Not so much."

Cameron had put off calling his parents for as long as he could. Though he was thirty-six, it still mattered a great deal to him what they thought of him. So, after a light dinner with Abby at the cabin, he told her he was going to call his mother. She groaned and leaned against him. "It's going to be all right," he told her, giving her a kiss on the forehead. "But, Abby, I'm not going to lie to my parents and pretend I just got involved with some pregnant girl."

"I know," she said softly, nervously. "I'm going to the bedroom," she said.

She had no idea how happy it made him when she said that—*the* bedroom, not *my* bedroom. Because night after night they lay there together, kissing, touching, fondling, not having sex but having everything else. For Abby, as huge and uncomfortable as she was these days, sex was way down on her list of things she needed. She just took comfort in the touching, the affection, nearness. For Cameron, it was a little more than that. His emotions were definitely sexually charged. He found it crazy and beautiful that he wanted her just as much round with the babies as he had the night they'd conceived, when she was so small, so svelte. Of course he couldn't keep that a secret from Abby, nor did he try to. She even offered to help with that. "Let me, Cameron," she said, touching him intimately. "There's no reason you have to be frustrated." And he had said, "I'm waiting for you, and that's the way I want it. After these little ones are born and you're recovered, we're going to rock the walls of this cabin."

He couldn't remember a time he'd been happier. And it was in that frame of mind he placed the call to his parents.

"Mom?" he said. "How are you?"

"Great, Cam. How's the little town?"

"Perfect. Pour a glass of wine, Mom. I have something important to tell you."

"Really?" she said. "Go ahead...."

"Doctor's orders," he said. "Come on now, I have a surprise. A very nice one."

"Okay, okay," she laughed. "I hope you found yourself a wonderful woman in that little town…."

He paused, hoping she'd taken his advice about the wine. "Well, as a matter of fact…"

"Really? Who is she?"

"Actually, I found her last year. Last fall, in Grants Pass."

"You never said anything," she said.

"I didn't think there was much to say. I really fell for her, but she had complications in her life. When I met her, she'd been separated from her husband for almost a year and they were getting divorced. It wasn't too soon for her to think about another man, but it was too soon for her to get involved. At that time, at least. She had to get her legal affairs straightened out. So, as much as I hated it, we lost touch for a while. We connected again in January, her divorce final. Her name is Abby and, Mom, she's wonderful. Beautiful and sweet and perfect."

"Aw, Cam, I'm so happy for you. Why didn't you tell us?"

"Lots of reasons, one being that I wanted some time with her first. And of course, Abby having been married once, she wanted to take it slow. You understand."

"I suppose. Where does she live, Cam? When can I meet her?"

"She lives here now, Mom. With me. And it won't be long before you can meet her, but there's one more thing. During that short time we knew each other in Grants Pass, we had a little…ah, a little…blessing, that's what it was. We had a blessing. Well, actually a couple of blessings. On the way. Soon." Dead silence answered him. "It came as a shock to poor Abby at first, and I admit—I was pretty sur-

prised, but we're very happy about it. Happy and excited."
Silence. It stretched out. "Mom? Twins. We know one is a
boy, but the other one is hiding." Again, a vacuum.

Then he heard his mother shriek, "Edward! Come here!
Cameron got some girl pregnant!"

"Mom! Just have a little sip of that wine!"

"I think it's going to take something a little stronger!
Twins? You got some girl pregnant with *twins*?"

He couldn't help it—he laughed. "Mom," he said. "She's
not some girl—she's not a girl. Her name is Abby and she's
thirty-one."

"Cameron, how in the *world*—"

"Now, Mother, I'm not going to explain. You'll just have
to trust me, I've never been careless and neither has Abby.
So—here's the deal. She's probably going to go early, though
the babies are due the second of July. Anytime, Mom. Abby
wants to have her mother come as soon as they're delivered,
so I hope you can be a little patient. Twins is a pretty big—"

"Cameron! Are you *married*?"

"Not yet, Mom. Even though we're in this together, completely, we just haven't had time to get married. That will
come—we'll take care of the details. No point in rushing
it now. Besides, we're not going to be fooling anybody, including the great-grandmothers and great-aunt Jean, by
rushing into it right now. They're nearly here."

"Dear God in heaven," his mother said. And in the background he could hear his father, Ed, saying, "What? What?
What?"

"I'll call you the moment they're born. Tomorrow, when
I'm at the clinic, I'll get Mel to take a picture of me and
Abby and e-mail it to you. By then you will have calmed
down."

"But, Cameron," she said, "you haven't given me time to knit anything!"

He laughed again. "Well, get started. Abby's really ready to unload. She just has to make it a couple more weeks to be completely safe."

"Oh, dear God in heaven," she muttered. "You couldn't have told me any sooner?"

"There were details to work out, Mother. This is how it is and you're going to be gracious. Abby is understandably stressed."

"Of course I'll be gracious! Just answer me one question, and be honest with me, because I always know when you're lying. Do you love this wo—Abby?"

He smiled. "Mom, I loved her the second I saw her. And I love her more every day." He heard his answer in his mother's heavy, satisfied sigh. "There now, go take care of Dad before he goes crazy, and I'll e-mail a picture tomorrow sometime. Mom, congratulations. I love you."

He hung up and got himself a beer out of the refrigerator. He popped the top and went to the bedroom, leaning in the open doorway. Abby was sitting cross-legged, her iPod earphones plugged into her ears, deep breathing with her eyes closed. He just watched, smiling at the sight. She was a vision.

She opened her eyes, took the plugs out of her ears and looked at him expectantly.

"She was very surprised," he said. "And a little pissed off that I didn't give her more time to knit something."

"Oh my," she said, taking a breath. "Did you tell her it was an accident?"

"No. I told her it was a blessing. And the best thing that ever happened to me."

* * *

Dan Brady had not envisioned that in just a couple of months in Virgin River, he'd be able to walk into that little bar and be accepted as one of them. They didn't make a big fuss; it wasn't like *Cheers* with everyone shouting welcome. No, that wouldn't have been to his taste anyway. What was nice was to go during the busier times of day and sit up at the bar and chat with whoever was around, just as if he was one of the neighbors, which he was. In prior years, before he'd settled in this town, he would only go to the bar at midday when hardly anyone was around.

He sat up at the bar and found himself facing Preacher. "Hey there, brother," Preacher said. "Heineken?"

Dan smiled. He didn't let on how much it pleased him to be greeted that way. "Thanks" was all he said. "You doing bar duty tonight?"

"Just for a few. Jack's over at the clinic, loading up Mel and the kids so she can take 'em home. He'll be right back. Paige is minding the stove while Dana's in the high chair back there, and Chris," he said, tilting his head to the far end of the bar where the six-year-old sat, "is doing home-work."

Dan frowned. "Homework? In first grade?"

"Is that crazy or what? Thank Jesus I didn't go to that school. Man, I had nuns, and I thought I had it rough." Dan laughed. "It's not like it's trigonometry," he went on. "He's drawing pictures and making numbers and letters, but still…."

"Still," Dan agreed.

"Excuse me. I have to check if we're making progress." And he wandered down to his stepson.

A moment later Jack was holding the door open for Hope

McCrea. She stomped inside wearing her muddy running shoes and lavender sweatsuit with brown stains on the knees. He'd spent a good amount of time talking to Hope. Well, he'd been listening to Hope. It was gardening season for her. She tended a very large garden every spring and summer. Living alone as she did, she didn't have much use for all her produce, so she gave most of it away and the deer and rabbits drove her crazy, getting in her garden.

She sat up beside Dan while Jack went around the bar and without being asked, poured her a whiskey. Then she pulled out her Marlboros. After a brief hack to clear her throat and lungs, she lit up. "I have news," she said to Jack and anyone who would listen. "I bought the church."

"You did what?" Jack asked.

"The church. The Lutherans aren't sending another minister this way—we're just too small for their tastes. Or for anyone's, it appears. I've been making offers for six years, but they were set on selling the church to some other denomination. But finally they had to admit defeat—no one wants it. So I lowered my offer, crazy fools. Got it for a song." She cackled. "Got it for a hymn."

"Jesus, Hope—are you just richer than God?" Jack asked.

"I have a couple bucks and nothing to do but buy and sell things. So, I'm going to sell the church." She sipped her drink. Puffed on her cigarette.

"But, Hope—you said no one wants it," Jack pointed out.

"Well, none of those religions want it. I'm going to sell it on eBay."

It was silent for a second, then Jack, Dan and Preacher burst into laughter.

"Oh, go ahead and laugh," she said. "You'll see. Someone's going to want a church. That's a good church. Little roughed up at the moment, but it can be considered a fixer-upper."

Jack leaned on the bar. "Let me guess—you have some old pictures of that church, right? When it was beautiful, right? And you're going to float out those pictures and snag some poor rube, like you did Mel."

"Mel hasn't complained in years," Hope said, puffing.

"Mel?" Dan asked.

Jack gave the counter a wipe. "Mel took the job here based on a bunch of pictures Hope sent of a pretty little town and a cabin in the woods she could use for free for a year. Cabin looked like new; town looked thirty years younger. The cabin was probably in worse shape than that Creighton house you're working on, and the town…? Well, you've seen the town. Mel was furious."

"She's got a sharp tongue, that one," Hope said, making Jack laugh.

"So, Hope," Jack said, "what if satanists buy the church?"

"Good luck to them." She shrugged. "This would be a real bad town for someone who's no good to try to make a go of it. I'll post up old and recent pictures, so people know what they're getting into."

"Who'd want a church?" Dan asked.

"Someone who needs to preach, I'm thinking," Hope said. "Or satanists, who Jack and Preacher will run off and make sorry they ever got the idea." She sipped the last of her drink, put out her cigarette. "You're going to have a lot of venison come in the bar soon, Jack. I'm going to shoot the goddamn deer if they don't get out of my yard."

"I can't take illegal venison, Hope. You try this every spring. Why don't you put up a good fence?"

"I have up a good fence! They jump it! And the god-damn rabbits dig under. Bastards."

"Now, is that any way for the owner of a church to talk?"

"I just own it, Jack," she said, pushing up her glasses. "I'm not exactly the religious sort."

"Is that so?"

"This town could use a little religion, I think."

"And why is that?"

"Been a long time now, but that church used to be full all the time. Of course, it was full of poor mountain people and there wasn't any parsonage, so the pastor got himself relocated. Couldn't hardly feed himself on what poor mountain folk put in the plate. But things have gotten better around here since I was younger. Lotta farmers and ranchers and—" she leveled her gaze at Dan accusingly "—construction workers moved in. They can fill up the collection plate. It's time to try it again." She gave Dan a pat on the shoulder and left the bar, scuffling out the door.

Dan looked up at Jack. "That is one strange woman."

"Oh-ho, she's peculiar all right. But she's always thinking about the town. I'd love to get a look at her will. She's crafty, and I think she must have a ton of money. And no living relatives." He lifted an eyebrow. "Looking for a wife? Mature woman with big black glasses and mud on her knees?"

Dan laughed. "I don't think I could drink that one pretty, Jack. But gee, thanks for the tip."

"How's it going at the house?"

He sat back. "The landlady showed up today. Now, there's an interesting woman."

"She is that."

"She tells me she was the town drunk," he said.

"She was," Jack confirmed. "She got in treatment and seems to be doing great. She's a whole new person."

"What was the town drunk like?" Dan asked.

Jack looked upward, thinking. Then he brought his gaze down to Dan's. "Know what? I'm not going to talk about that. Cheryl is a good person who had a mighty big burden with her drinking. I'll tell you the truth, I never saw any hope. But I see her now and she's not the same woman. Honest to God, I would've thought that even sober, she'd be a little slow-witted, unmotivated. Damaged. But she seems to have beat the odds—she's just incredible. I want her to make it."

"She's making it," Dan said. "That's nice, that you won't talk about it. Must've been kind of bad."

"Buddy, we've all been through bad times we'd like to forget."

And like an introduction to bad times personified, the door opened and Rick came in, using just a cane for assistance. Dan noticed that Jack frowned before he smiled. "How you doing, son?" he asked.

"Better," he said, leaning on the cane. "I'm getting used to the cane. Haven't been on my ass all day." He sat up at the bar.

Dan turned toward him. "Dan Brady," he said. "We met once, a long time ago. You might not remember."

"That's right," Jack said suddenly. "The night Paige got snatched! You remember, Rick?"

"Yeah," Rick said, putting out a hand. "You're the one who knocked the bad guy out with the flashlight. I'd almost forgotten about that."

"Sorry about the leg," Dan said. "You starting to feel okay with the prosthesis yet?"

"Nah, it still hurts some."

"You watching for breakdown? That can slow you down...."

"You know about this stuff?" Rick asked.

"A little bit. So, you watching that?"

"Not only am I watching it, I go to PT three times a week where they're watching it. I'm covered. Right now, all I want is to walk without pain."

"Aw, you'll get that. Then what?" Dan asked.

"I dunno," he said. "Jack, what do you think? Think I earned a beer and some dinner?"

"Two conditions. I walk you home and we take something home to your gram."

"Done," Rick said, patting the bar.

He was a good nine months away from twenty-one, but he'd lived a lot more than most men his age. And he'd put in a rough week of three PT sessions and two counseling sessions.

"What are you doing around here?" Rick asked Dan.

"Working for Paul Haggerty. What are you going to do? You must have lots of options."

"I said, I don't know. Right now, I just have to get a leg. Walk in it. Then maybe I'll be able to think."

"There's always school," Jack said, putting down a beer and retrieving his coffee cup. "That GI Bill, that's a great opportunity."

Rick lifted the beer, took a sip and said, "I'm thinking about it."

Right away Dan knew, the kid was still depressed and screwed up about the war, the injury, the missing leg. "This little town you got here, Rick—nice little place. I come from down the coast. Sebastapol. Near Bodega Bay. Not exactly a real small town. You grow up here?"

He nodded.

"So, when did you join the Corps?"

Rick looked at Dan. "If it's okay with you, I don't feel real talkative right now."

"It's all right by me," Dan said. "Jack, whenever Preacher's ready with dinner, I'm ready."

"You got it," Jack said, scowling briefly at Rick.

While Rick nursed his beer and then picked at his dinner, a few people who came into the bar approached him, said hello and patted his back. Their brows were furrowed as if they were feeling sorry for him and Dan knew, not a great thing to do. Right now Rick probably felt as though that was what he needed, maybe enjoyed it a little, but this kid was tough and strong and pity wasn't going to help much.

Dan didn't even see the next group come in. A couple and a girl. They sat at a table near the window. It was when Rick turned and looked that Dan followed his gaze and saw the girl connect with him. Beautiful girl. So beautiful and so sad, Dan was almost jealous for a second. He couldn't see what Rick's eyes were doing, but their eyes must have been locked together. The girl's mouth hung open at first, then closed. She turned to the woman at her table, a small redhead in her fifties, whispered something and then fled the bar.

Rick pivoted back.

Dan gave it a minute before he said, "Now, that was interesting."

Rick took a slug of his beer. "She used to be my girl."

"Hmm. Before the leg?"

"Yeah."

"She can't deal with the leg?" Dan asked.

Rick swiveled his angry gaze to Dan. "This your business, buddy?"

"Dan. The name is Dan. Just curious. Seemed like she looked really sad, not put off. But maybe I imagined that."

"She's not put off, but it isn't going to work for us anymore. Will that do it for you? Can you leave it alone now?"

"Sure, kid. If that's what you want."

"That's what I want."

Whoa, Dan thought. This is one tough customer. He had enough mad in him to burn buildings.

It wasn't ten minutes later that the couple, minus the girl, approached Rick. The small redheaded woman put a hand on his shoulder and said, "How are you doing, Ricky? Getting along any better?"

"I'm doing pretty well, Connie. Thanks. You staying for dinner?"

"I think we're going to pass," she said. "Listen, just so you know, I think about you all the time, pray for you that you'll get adjusted and stuff."

"Thanks," Rick said meekly. "Um, Liz. She doing okay?"

"She's trying, Ricky. She's stronger than she looks. She's trying."

"Good," Rick said.

"Take care then," Connie said. And they left the bar.

And Dan thought, this guy is imploding.

Twelve

Walt Booth had dinner at his daughter's house at least twice a week. With Muriel away, Vanni was even more conscientious about making sure he was invited regularly. His daughter so enjoyed cooking, it was always a pleasure to have her do it for him. Then after dessert, if it was still early, he'd take his coffee to the great room and sometimes rock the baby for a while before Matt was settled in bed. Sometimes Paul would join him there, take in a little of the television news, but Paul was often occupied in the garage, working on built-ins for the interior of their house.

Vanni refilled Walt's coffee while he rocked little Matt on a typical evening. "You've been awfully quiet lately," she said to her father.

"Maybe I just said everything I have to say. Maybe there's nothing left."

"Ha-ha," she said, smiling. "Then tell me what you hear from Muriel." And Walt's chin immediately dropped. "Uh-oh. Have you and Muriel had some kind of trouble?"

Walt looked up. "I don't know if it's trouble or not, but she's not exactly pleased with me right now."

"And why is that?"

He shrugged. "She can't get away from that movie. She'd like me to farm out the dogs and get Shelby to feed the horses, and for me to go to Montana for at least a long weekend."

Vanni sat back on the sofa, holding her own coffee cup. "And the problem is?"

"I don't particularly want to go to Montana," he said.

"Well. That must make her feel completely special."

He grunted. "I don't belong there, where she's working."

"I can't imagine she'd ask you if she thought you'd be in the way. In fact, it might be good for you to see her at work. I know if she'd asked me, I'd be on the next plane. I'd love to visit a movie set."

"There you have it, Vanessa," he said. "I can't see myself on a movie set. It's completely out of my experience. I'd probably just embarrass her."

"What nonsense! It would be fun, Dad! You'd not only learn more about what she's doing, you'd have a little time together in the mornings and evenings."

"I'm not so sure it would be fun...."

"Dad...? What did you say to her?"

He made a face. "It's more what she said to me. I told her I didn't think it was such a good idea, me going to her movie set, and she drew a line in the sand." He shook his head. "Not really like Muriel, but that's what she did."

With some exasperation, Vanni said, "Do you think you can possibly make this explanation any more confusing? What's going on?"

"When I told her I didn't really want to come to her movie, that I'd feel out of place and strange because I don't know anything about movies, much less making them, she said..." He cleared his throat. "She said that was ridiculous, there wasn't anything special about this location set—it was just a lot of working people. Grips, carpenters, cooks, et cetera. I had to Google 'grips,' that's how little I know. And she expected me to make an effort or she was going to be left to assume she didn't matter enough for me to swallow down a little unease so we could have some time together."

Vanni grinned. "She told you."

"She hasn't called since. And my calls go to voice mail."

"How long has that been going on?"

"All week. We usually talk every day."

"Apparently, Dad, you haven't left the message she's been waiting for."

"Apparently."

Vanni just stared her father down for a long time, until he said, *"What?"* Then she got up, went to the mantel and pulled a framed five-by-seven picture from it. She handed it to her dad, who took it with his free hand while he held on to his sleeping grandson with the other.

"Remember that?" she asked as he looked at the picture.

It was one of Vanni's favorite pictures. Walt was wearing his mess dress, the military version of a tuxedo, and Peg was wearing a lovely, slim black gown and string of pearls that now belonged to Vanni. A smile found his lips. "Your mother was such a beautiful woman. I was never good enough for her. You look like her, you know."

"I know. Do you remember when that was taken?"

He shrugged. "We attended a lot of military functions. I saw your mother in that dress a hundred times."

She sat on the couch and leaned toward him, her elbows on her knees and her hands clasped. "You were on your way to dinner at the White House. Not one of those big gang dinners that the president and his wife pass through for five minutes, but the real deal. There were to be twelve couples—all high-ranking generals and their wives. Mom was going to meet the first lady, get a tour of the private living quarters, have dessert with the first lady. She was very nervous. I remember her saying she was going to feel out of place—she was a horsewoman, private pilot, gardener, skeet shooter, mother. But it was important to you, Dad. And she was proud of you, she would do anything to show how proud she was to be your chosen partner."

Walt's eyes glistened. It was easy for Vanni to do that to him. He stared at the picture of Peg, missing her still.

And missing Muriel so much.

"So," Vanni said. "I think you know what you should say in the next message you leave for Muriel. It had better have your flight-arrival times in it, or you might be kissing goodbye the best thing that's happened to you in at least five years. The way I see it, if you could expect my mother to step up and do things that made her uncomfortable because it meant something to you, you'd better do so for your current woman. If you don't, you're going to lose her. And that makes no sense."

Walt lifted his eyes from the picture.

"We'll get the horses fed and the dogs watched," she said, smiling.

Mel Sheridan had a wonderful time taking a few digital pictures of Abby and Cameron to e-mail their mothers. The totally unexpected part was that Abby and Cameron started to get into it, and Mel was delighted. She, naturally, loved pregnant bodies, pregnant couples. She loved preserving the images for posterity.

She took her camera out to the cabin and shot a few pictures on the porch—Abby leaning against the rail beside the red potted geraniums, Cam beside her. Then Cam behind her, his hands on her belly. Then Cam behind, hands on the belly, lips on her neck. Cam kissing the belly, while Abby's head was tilted back in a laugh. All the while, Cam was whispering things that made Abby smile, touch his face, kiss his head. And before they knew what was happening, Mel had coaxed them out of some of their clothes. It took hardly any doing, really. Soon they were topless, his hands strategically crossed or placed over naked breasts, the green of the forest and dappled patches of sunlight behind them. In one, buried behind them in the trees, a doe looked on.

They were a beautiful couple, magnificent photos, Cameron and Abby so obviously in love with each other and the babies that produced that unbelievable mound. Mel spent the morning loading the pictures into the computer and then onto a disk. Cameron and Abby selected a demure, fully clothed photo to send to the mothers, but Abby took the disk to Vanni's house to let her see them all.

"Wow," Vanni said. "These are incredible. Which one did you send to the mothers?"

"This one." She pointed. A front view, clothed. "The rest we're keeping for our private collection, but I wanted to show you."

Just viewing the pictures, so intimate, so trusting, so in love, started something of a chain reaction. Vanni said, "I want to throw you a shower," she said. "Just our friends, not the entire town. Right away. Saturday afternoon...."

"Oh, I don't know..."

"What in the world is it going to hurt?" Vanni asked. "Still pretending you're not pregnant?"

"Well, that ship has sailed...." Abby said.

"No kidding," Vanni laughed. "Give up, Abby. Hardly anyone has all the details, but there isn't a person around here who doesn't know you're having these babies together. You live together, for God's sake. You go to doctor's appointments together. We'll just have a nice buffet, invite couples who already know just about everything. Those people who don't already know Cam's the daddy are pretty clear he intends to be. You don't have to say anything about it. Just come and enjoy yourself."

"I have to check with Cameron, but—"

"Cameron?" Vanni laughed. "Would this be the Cameron who begged you to be his roommate so he could be at your beck and call? The same man who can't keep his hands off you in public? Oh, you're a riot. Pregnant women really are a little out of reality, huh?"

"I get your point...."

"And just for good measure, we'll invite your mothers...."

"Oh, now wait just a minute," Abby said, gripping her belly as if it would fly away.

"Don't worry," Vanni said. "They're both on deck to get down to Virgin River the second the babies come, right? They're not going to come now, for heaven's sake. Not on such short notice with the births imminent. It would be *crazy*."

Abby just kept shaking her head, but she picked up the phone and called Cameron at the clinic, running Vanni's plan by him.

"Sure, why not?" he said. "A shower would be fun for you. And Vanni's right—our mothers aren't going to descend on us now."

So, Abby called her mother, Cameron called his. And both sets of parents commenced packing at once.

"Oh God," Abby moaned, leaning back on Vanessa's couch, rubbing her belly.

"Don't wig out on me," Vanessa said. "They have to meet sometime. Not only am I sure everything will be fine, I'm sure they'll like each other very much."

Cameron held Abby in his arms, in their bed. "I don't want you to worry," he whispered. "We're going to have a nice weekend."

"So much for going low profile," she whispered. "We're having a party and introducing our parents to each other. Everyone is going to know."

He chuckled and ran his hands over her belly. "Nothing low profile about this," he said.

"I'm very close to my mother," she said. "She's like my best friend. But even though I'm over thirty, I never could let myself tell her exactly how this happened. Just that I met someone and because of the divorce, we didn't continue to see each other. She wasn't happy about the fact that I didn't contact you, but at the same time I think she was afraid for me to contact you…. In case, you know…"

"In case I was a real bastard, like the first guy," he supplied. "And what have you told her about us? Now?"

"That I met a wonderful man who cares about me and the babies…."

"But not that I'm the *same* man?"

"Not yet, no."

"You're going to have to tell her now," he said. "Or my mother will."

She swallowed. "Do you promise not to leave my side the entire weekend?"

"I promise to protect you from our mothers. My mother's very nice, in an extremely nosey, interfering sort of way."

She smiled. "And mine's very nice, in an extremely bossy, conniving sort of way."

"But both our fathers play golf," he said, smiling. "That will keep them busy all weekend, going over every course and every hole they've ever played."

"And our mothers? What do you suppose they'll be going over?"

He gave her a little kiss. "I promise not to leave your side all weekend," he said.

Brie called Abby on the Thursday before the shower. "I have an early baby gift for you. I was hoping this would come together in time. I received a very courteous phone call from none other than Ross Crawford himself. We spoke briefly. He wondered why you wouldn't be accepting any alimony, he wanted to know if you were married."

"And what did you tell him?" Abby asked.

"Simply, you needed the alimony to pay off his credit-card debt, as ordered by the court, and once that debt was cleared, you preferred to support yourself, as you always had. And that you weren't married. I did do one thing— I just couldn't help it. I said that, of *course,* you had no knowledge of the credit cards, never held them, hadn't signed for them, had never made a charge of any kind, were never issued copies of the statements, and that it was my opinion you shouldn't have been responsible in the first place. But what's done is done and you'd like to move on now—no hard feelings. And like the genius he is, he asked, what credit-card debt? I told him he'd have to check with his lawyer—it was part of the divorce settlement he signed. He said he'd do that and as far as he was concerned, everything was resolved and he sends his best."

"His *best*?" she laughed. "How nice of him."

"I asked him to follow up my letter and our phone conversation with a letter stating that he wouldn't seek any further compensation from you, signed by him and not his legal staff, saying the matter is successfully closed. He did so, Abby. He couriered it to me. I didn't want to call you until I had the document in hand. It's resolved. The prenup is in your past. I'll make a copy for your file and give you the original. You can safely assume he's not after you for any reason. How does that feel?" Brie asked.

"I wish I could say I felt ten pounds lighter," she answered, rubbing a hand over her round middle. "But I'm very relieved. Thank you so much."

"It must be wonderful to have it behind you."

"I feel a little foolish. I wish I'd talked to you about this situation the second I came to Virgin River. I had no idea it could just go away like that."

"Well, it didn't go away just like that. According to your settlement agreement, that bill had to be taken care of. But never panic, Abby. Just as Cameron said, things like this can usually be worked out. The only important thing now is that you and Cam can get on with your lives. Are you feeling well?"

"I feel enormous. I haven't seen my feet in so long, I'm not sure I still have feet. My back is killing me and I have a new mystery pain every day. And I don't know if word's gotten out, but our parents are coming down for the party this weekend. They'll meet each other. Ugh."

"Are you worried about that?"

"I'm worried about the questions—none of which I feel like answering. You know the ones—how did this happen and when are you getting married?"

Brie laughed. "Tell them your attorney advised you not to answer any questions right now. You have other things on your mind. Like making it through the shower without going into labor. What does Mel say about your progress?"

"You mean Mel and John and Cam, the delivery team? I see them every week. We just found out Cameron's dream has come true and baby number two is a girl—one of each. Just what he hoped for. It's a good thing, too—I doubt anyone's ever going to talk me into doing this again."

"Well, if you don't mind me saying so, it sounds like things are going very well for you and Cameron. You make a nice team."

She laughed. "I don't mind you saying so. I don't think we're fooling anyone. We're nuts for each other. Love at first sight. Instant family."

"Abby, that's just wonderful. I haven't known Cameron all that long, but I can't help thinking he's a great guy. And with this legal business behind you, your way is clear for a very happy family life."

"I have more immediate concerns. Brie, when you were this pregnant, did you have contractions all the time?"

"Abby," she said, "I've never been that pregnant. I just had one on the way, and when I got down to the last two months, I thought I was going into labor every day, but the contractions never got regular or obvious till D-day. And there was no mistaking it."

"I have a little dilemma. I have too many cooks in the kitchen. John and Cam both want to induce at thirty-seven weeks, if I make it that long. Mel wants to wing it—she likes Pitocin as a delivery tool when indicated, but she prefers her women to go into labor on their own. Everyone agrees, the babies are in position and ready to go. I think the docs want to control the environment while Mel wants to keep it as natural as possible. And I don't know which way to go."

"Where are you having the babies?"

"I'm going to the hospital. Given the facts of lower birth weight, we're erring on the side of caution. Mel's good with that—she delivered babies in a big-city hospital for years before coming out to the mountains. But the doctors want to monitor everything, and she wants me to have as pure an experience as possible...."

Brie laughed. "You'll figure it out. In fact, the decision could be taken away from you—you might beat them to the punch. You're not thirty-seven weeks yet."

"Close. I'm dilated a little bit."

"Well, cross your legs—I'm helping Vanessa cook for the shower!"

By dinnertime the Friday night before the party, the McCalls and Michaelses were in Virgin River. Cameron made arrangements for both couples to have cabins at the Riordans' little resort along the river. Abby and Cameron met them there, introduced everyone, and as Cameron predicted, they were completely polite to each other.

Susan McCall was a small, roundish woman with short blond hair who had raised an only child and worked in community service her entire married life, everything from PTA to library to charity work for the poor. Her volunteerism in Seattle was every bit a full-time job. Beth Michaels had raised three children, Cameron being the oldest, while working as a dental hygienist. She was Susan's physical opposite, tall and thin with dark hair that framed her face. They were both strong, willful, energetic women in their late fifties. Primed to be grandparents.

During their getting-acquainted dinner at Jack's, Beth Michaels said, "I was just wondering if you're ready to tell us how you met and—"

"We met by chance in Grants Pass," Cameron said. "Abby was attending a wedding and I was having dinner in the same place with my partners."

"And then?" Beth pushed.

"And then I fell right in love, and after a little coercing, Abby fell in love right back."

"Cameron," his mother admonished, "there were very few details in that account."

"Hmm," he said, sipping from a water glass. "How about that."

"And your plans for marriage?" Susan McCall asked.

"You'll be the first to know, Mom," Abby answered.

The mothers exchanged glances while Abby and Cameron clasped hands and smiled at each other. As a united front, they were holding their own very well.

Abby and Cam took them on a tour of the clinic and showed them the cabin where they were living. Before they could fuss about the size or rustic quality of the place, Cameron assured them they'd be looking for something larger after the babies were born and life had adjusted somewhat.

Vanessa, Brie and Paige planned a beautiful Saturday-afternoon party to take place at the general's house—Vanni's deck and yard were not yet as she wanted them to be for a party. Outside on the general's deck the men could enjoy their cigars while inside, the women would have good food, beverages, gifts and lots of space to get acquainted. Vanni invited the Sheridans, June and John from Grace Valley and their spouses, Nikki and Joe from Grants Pass, Shelby and Luke and Art.

Nikki and Joe arrived early to help with the food and decorating—the women hung pink and blue streamers around the dining-room table, along with balloons.

Unlike most of the other couples present, Cameron stayed close to Abby. He fetched her food from the buffet, refilled her water glass, cooed over the gifts as she opened them. There were wonderful little outfits, practical supplies, the special extras every young mother present had found to be essential.

Preacher and Jack had closed the bar for a few hours in the afternoon, but left their wives and little ones at the shower to get back in time for the dinner hour. Everyone had such a good time and the food and drink was so plentiful, the sun was setting before people started to drift off. Cameron loaded the gifts in his SUV to take back to the cabin and the crowd had thinned before Abby said, "Cam, where are our mothers?"

"I don't know," he said, looking around. "Ask your dad if he knows."

Ed Michaels had no idea. Chuck McCall couldn't say. It appeared the ladies had disappeared.

"You and I should talk without our kids or husbands," Beth Michaels had said to Susan McCall.

"Oh yes," Susan had replied. "But there's a party going on. Think we can slip down to the stable or something?"

"Forget it. Come with me."

"Should we tell someone we're leaving?" Susan asked.

"No, let's just drift away." She smiled. "They can search the whole town in five minutes. No worries. We're going to the *bar*."

Susan smiled back. "I like the way you think."

"Hmm. There's a reason our kids get along so well."

Ten minutes later they pulled up to Jack's and went in. Jack was behind the bar and the look of shock on his face caused Beth to laugh lightly and whisper, "We'd better be quick. Look at him. He's going to give us up."

"In a heartbeat," Susan agreed.

"This way." Beth found an isolated corner of the bar out of the range of dining patrons and they hopped up on stools. Jack was there immediately, slapping down a couple of napkins.

"Ladies?" he asked.

"Martinis, I think." Then she looked at Susan, who nodded in agreement. "Dry."

"Okay then," Jack said, turning away to fetch drinks.

"All right," Beth said. "I know nothing. Cameron said he fell hard for a woman, but she had divorce complications. I had no idea he had a woman in his life. But it's absolutely clear he adores her. He loves her completely. Do you know anything?"

"I didn't know how closely Cameron figured in this until a couple of days ago. Abby told me that this wonderful pediatrician she met in Virgin River was, in fact, the babies' father. First I heard of it. But you're right—they're dead in love. And more pregnant than I've ever been."

"Ditto," said Cameron's mother.

"I can tell you about the divorce, however. Nasty little piece of work. I was shocked Abby married him so quickly in the first place, and I think she was, too. We met him briefly—he seemed okay. But…"

"Do tell," Beth encouraged.

Jack put a couple of drinks down for them and stood there for a second. Then when it was clear they weren't going to talk in front of him, he moved away.

Susan told the story of Abby's terrible, short marriage to a rock star, and the prenup that bound her and sent her into hiding, and the bills he dumped on her as she was trying to get out of it all.

"She was only with him for a couple of months before he ran out on her?" Beth asked, aghast.

"That about sums it up. Somewhere in there, before she signed her divorce papers, or maybe shortly after, she met Cameron," Susan said. "I didn't know it was Cameron at the time. I didn't know who it was and frankly, all I cared about was that my daughter be safe and content. All she wanted to do was clear that debt and get on with her life, but then she met Cameron again, when she was clearly pregnant."

Beth sipped her drink and shook her head. "Dear God, what if they hadn't seen each other again! Cam wouldn't know about the babies! And I wouldn't know about Abby."

"And I wouldn't know about Cameron," Susan commiserated. "When she said she couldn't talk about how this all happened, I never imagined a wonderful man like Cameron being involved. Beth, our children are both a little crazy."

"Susan, they're not children. They're almost as old as we are."

Susan giggled. "That's a fact."

"Well, are things cleared up now? With the divorce and all?"

"The divorce is long done and the other stuff—who

cares?" Susan said. She lifted a hand to Jack for a couple more martinis. While he was mixing them, she said, "Chuck and I said we'd get rid of that debt for her so she wouldn't have to go to such lengths. But Abby's proud. And stubborn. When she was growing up, there were so many times kids teased her, called her spoiled, being an only child and all. She wanted to clean up her own mess. If the debt wasn't bad enough, she'd gone through everything she'd saved just to get through the divorce. That man—the ex-husband—he was ruthless. I only met him that once. Really, he seemed harmless. I was so wrong. I never expected all he put her through."

Jack put down two more martinis for the matrons who didn't look at all like matrons. He lifted an eyebrow and one corner of his mouth and went away. They were locked in some serious conspiracy.

"Well, then here we are," Beth said. "We've got a couple of kids with a couple of kids on the way, and they clearly love each other. What are we going to do?"

Susan took a sip of her martini. "I don't know about you, but I'm not going to rest until I see them married."

Beth threw back her head and laughed loudly, earning a glance from Jack. "I love an ambitious woman. So, I have a favor to ask."

"Sure."

"I know you'll be zipping down here the second the babies come and I know the mother's mother gets special privileges. Let me come soon, please. I promise not to crowd the cabin and I'll do all the shit work without getting in the way."

Susan looked up at the ceiling, thinking. Then she

glanced back at Beth. "Give us three days. And I'll split the snuggling and shit work with you."

Beth put a hand on her arm. "You are a good woman. I made my son-in-law's mother wait a week."

They both laughed loudly.

"Do you think we stand a chance of getting them married before the babies come?" Beth asked.

"I don't know. They seem to have made up their minds about certain things, not that they're sharing. And Abby's very stubborn when she's made up her mind."

"She seems to be perfect for him. Everyone's entitled to a mistake here and there. Not to mention they have babies coming. Any second…"

"Maybe if we put our heads together…."

The door to the bar opened and in came Ed Michaels, Chuck McCall, Abby and Cameron. They stood just inside the door and stared at Susan and Beth who had a couple of empty martini glasses apiece sitting at the bar.

"Just what are you two up to?" Cameron asked.

The women grinned largely and Beth said, "Just getting to know each other, Cameron."

Abby tugged on Cameron's sleeve to bring his ear down to her lips. "I never once thought it might be worse if they liked each other," she whispered. "They're going to be a pot of trouble."

He grinned and slipped a kiss on her lips. "Nothing we can't handle, baby. Stick with me."

Dan Brady didn't waste any time calling Cheryl. It wasn't that he thought he'd met the perfect woman. Nor that he'd met someone as screwed up as he was. It was purely that she was attractive, interesting and was at work on getting her head on straight—a trait they seemed to share. Finding kindred spirits was rare enough that this was worth digging into.

"It isn't time for rent money," she said.

"I know. I have to drive to Eureka to order flooring. I thought we could have coffee or something. Or lunch. Or early dinner. Maybe Denny's early-bird special."

"Didn't I tell you to take it easy—that I wasn't sure I was breaking bread with you?"

"You did," he said. "I thought I'd get on your dance card before you're booked."

"What is it you want?"

"Not so much," he said. "I'm thinking patty melt and fries. How about you?"

And she actually laughed. That wasn't a bad start. With a much nicer attitude, she asked, "What is it you think we can talk about?"

"You can talk about anything you want. I can probably tell you about home construction and remodeling in Virgin River, which is what I do. Or, if you're interested, I have a little experience in agriculture." Again she laughed. "You can always tell me about your work."

"Well, there's the thing. I wait tables in a diner. Which is why dinner at Denny's doesn't hold great appeal. You understand."

"I do get that," he said. "In fact, that's probably good. Why don't I get us a couple of big, messy sandwiches, a couple of bags of chips, a couple pickles, some iced tea, and we can meet in a park? Weather's damn nice right now."

"When?" she asked.

"I only have Saturday afternoons and Sundays off. Either one of those work for you?"

"Sunday," she said. "I start at 5:00 a.m. and finish up around two. I could shower off the grease and see you around three. There's a common in Old Town…"

"I know the place," he said. "I'll bring the lunch."

Dan hadn't had anything that even vaguely resembled a date in years. At least six, maybe more like eight. He'd had a conversation or two in a bar that went no place, because he didn't really want it to. So what was it about Cheryl? The crazy thing was, before he knew anything at all about her, she seemed so stable. Like she had lead in her shoes and wouldn't tip over during a big emotional wind. It made him laugh to himself. And then what does he learn from her? That she's struggling to get her life back and could be on shakier ground than he ever was. Well, that might be a stretch. Hardly anyone had been on shakier ground.

On Sunday he found her in the common in downtown Eureka. She got there ahead of him. She sat at a park bench, legs stretched out, face turned up to the sun, relaxing. Eyes closed. He stood in front of her until his shadow fell over her and she opened her eyes. And she didn't smile.

But he did. He put the sack of sandwiches and drinks on the bench between them. "Still pretty unsure if this is a good idea, I guess. Cold cuts okay with you?"

She accepted the tea first. "Sorry," she said. "Trusting is such an issue with me."

"Met a lot of people along the way you couldn't trust?"

"I'm not even sure if that's it," she said. "I'm not real relaxed about my program yet. I'm always on the lookout for something that can trip me up, make me decide to take a drink. Because if one thing made it through all the cement in my head, it's that if I have one drink, I'm probably going to die." Then she smiled a very contrite smile. "It was nice of you to do this. But I still can't figure out why, and that makes me tense."

"Cheryl, I've been divorced over six years. I've had my own rocky time. I grew pot and went to jail. I don't have a lot of friends. I'm just starting to make a few in town. And they're cautious, as they should be. I'm probably not the safest bet. I mean, I know I am—because I'm totally clean. But given my history… I'm not surprised that people…you know…"

"And did you think that I would be a good gamble, given I'm the town drunk?" She bit into her sandwich.

He grinned at her. "First of all, you're not anymore. Maybe you were, but you're not. Haven't been for a good long time. Second, I didn't know squat-diddly about you when I suggested we share a meal sometime. I just plain liked your looks. Not your beauty—although you really do have that. I liked that you looked sturdy. Solid and sensible. I know—you explained, you don't necessarily feel that way. But you look it. I thought I'd take a chance." He ate part of his sandwich, rinsed it down with tea. "When I was a younger man, before a bad marriage and other things, I had a lot of friends. I haven't for a long time. I'd like to get back to that. Have purpose. Friends."

"You have purpose now?" she asked.

"I do," he said, nodding. "I'm determined to take that old house from shit hole to quaint. I can do it, too."

"Is that enough of a purpose?" she wanted to know.

"For now, it is."

"Okay, let's cut right to it. What the hell were you doing growing weed? Just explain that."

"Oh hell, that's almost the end of the story…."

"I have a whole sandwich to eat," she said. "A big one,

by the way. You must have thought I looked hungry or scrawny."

"I thought you looked healthy," he said. "We have to go back a ways to get to all the whys. I'll try the condensed version. I worked construction for my dad south of here— tough old son of a bitch, but a damn fine builder. I went in the Marines, for a change of lifestyle and benefits and... I thought I'd like the life. I married a girl way younger— I was twenty-seven and she was eighteen. Anyone with a working brain would look out for the problems with that, but not me. 'Course, being doubly stupid, I got her pregnant right off. I was sent to Iraq, where I was wounded and medically retired. By the time I recovered, she was already moving on."

"Do you have a child?"

"Had. A son. He got sick when he was four. An unusual and fatal heart condition—he was on the transplant list. My wife had already remarried and divorced a second time and in a stupid and desperate move, I decided I'd grow pot for a fast-money turn and buy the kid a heart if I had to. I wasn't exactly rational. I didn't just grow a couple of rooms full of cannabis—I set up several grow sites with caretakers to watch 'em. I made a lot of money, just like I intended to, but it didn't do anything to help my boy. Cash," he laughed. "We named him Cash. What irony."

Cheryl was quiet for a moment. "I'm sorry."

"Thanks," he said, regaining his composure and eating more of his sandwich. "So, I got caught. And I cut a deal. For a couple of years I fed the local cops information about growers I knew. By the way, if you tell that part around here, it could get me some attention from bad people. It's entirely up to you, what you decide to say, but that's a fact."

"I might be able to keep a lid on that. Maybe."

"Thanks. So, I got them some serious arrests, but I knew all along I was eventually going to have to either run or do time. I actually tried to run at the last minute, but I waited too long. I wouldn't have been good on the run—that was never what I wanted. What I wanted was a real life. I'd had an eye on a real life for years—since I was eighteen or so. I wanted to bring home a paycheck, meet my buddies for a beer some Friday nights, throw the ball out front with my kid, have someone soft and cuddly next to me in bed and maybe even bring her home flowers for no reason once in a while. I was going to be a better builder than my dad, but what's more important, I was going to be a better husband and father. I mean, my old man thought it was real sharp to be strict and stern, but I got the idea early there might be a better way. I lost sight of that goal for a while. I was kind of screwed up and just practiced being a badass—way worse than anything my dad ever was."

He crumpled up his sandwich wrapper.

Cheryl was quiet for a while. She ate a little more, then folded what was left of her sandwich very neatly inside its wrapper. "Good story," she said. "I bet it took you months to make that up."

"You wanna try your story out on me?" he asked.

"I don't think so."

"You don't believe me? You think that whole thing's a line? Like I'm using my prison record to get in your pants or something?" he asked.

"Stranger things have happened," she said with a shrug.

"I highly doubt it," he said. He stood up. "I got arrested right here in Eureka. Call the sheriff's department and ask for Sergeant Delaney in Narcotics. Tell him you want to know how much of a liar I am before you ever talk to me again. You know where I live. I believe you have the number."

He turned and walked out of the common, got in his truck and drove out of Eureka without ordering flooring for the house.

Dan had been through enough in the past few years that he didn't ponder her reaction for too long. He knew from the start, from the second he got back from Iraq, that things weren't going to be simple for him. And after he'd crossed a bunch of lines, made himself a felon, he had very few expectations of people snuggling up to him. He didn't blame her one bit. He wasn't going to bother her again. He'd call her to drop off rent money if he was going to be out her way, but other than that, she had no need to worry he'd stalk her.

Tuesday night, while he worked in the kitchen of the old house, the phone rang. He stared at it for a second—there were three possibilities. Wrong number, someone who didn't know the Creightons weren't there anymore or Cheryl. "Hello?" he said.

"Okay, on Sunday I'll bring the sandwiches," she said.

He laughed into the phone. "Sergeant Delaney must have given me a very bad report card or I wouldn't be hearing from you."

"If I had instincts, I'd follow them. I think we might be two screwed-up people who aren't exactly good for each other. Maybe we should forget the whole idea."

"Whatever you want," he said.

"Argue with me a little, huh?"

"Nope," he laughed. "I know what I'm up to. You have to make your own decision. Your problems, such as they are, don't worry me much. Besides, they're yours. I've been working on mine for years now. I'm feeling pretty good. Sandwiches in the park or no sandwiches in the park." She was quiet. "Cheryl," he said seriously, "I don't have expectations. It's just time for me to move toward people again. That's all. There was no 12-step program for what I had to deal with. It's been a long, dark night."

She sighed deeply. "Okay. Three o'clock. Same bench."

"I'll be there."

Thirteen

Walt paid way too much money for his airfare to Montana, but there were only two options—book his travel two weeks out at a cheaper rate or get the hell up to Montana, where Muriel waited for him, at any cost. He'd called; he left the message: "I'm coming. I need to be with you." And after ignoring his calls for a week, she had called right back, "Oh God, I need you to be! Hurry!" So the Friday after the shower at his house, Walt was on his way.

Muriel gave him an address for the house she was staying in. He arrived in Missoula by three, rented a car and by four o'clock he was in a little town smack between Butte and Missoula. He bought groceries and arrived at her house by five. It looked to be a small two-story with a dormer in an old-fashioned neighborhood. Children were riding bikes up and down the street, an elderly woman was kneeling in her front-yard flower bed, digging away; an old man sat across the street on his porch and Walt automatically gave him a wave. He waved back as if they were old friends.

I'm a screwup, he thought. Muriel had told him the production had rented her a nice little house in an ordinary neighborhood, yet this was not at all what he expected. He shook his head. It was *exactly* as she had described, and yet he'd assumed it would be flashier. He'd wallowed in some weird self-pity because she'd gone off to make a movie, forgetting that he knew her. Knew every inch of her. He'd been disgracefully out of touch, not hearing her, not listening. When he complained he didn't know anything about movie people, he had no idea how correct he was.

The key was under the mat, just as she'd said. There were a couple of rockers on the porch and he was tempted to just sit there a while and take in the neighborhood. It wasn't unlike the little house he grew up in, except they hadn't had a porch. Muriel would need a porch; she loved the outdoors. Did the neighbors bother her? he wondered. If she brought her glass of wine out here, did the neighbor women all converge on her to ask questions about that movie taking place just out of town in the shadow of glorious mountains?

He carried his groceries inside first and he almost laughed. A small dining room was just inside the door and a little farther ahead was the living room—just big enough for a fireplace, sofa and two overstuffed chairs, a couple of side tables. The upholstery was old, faded floral. It was clean but old-fashioned and worn.

The kitchen cabinets were painted a faded pink, of all things. The sink was even pink, the appliances old and white. When he opened the refrigerator to put away his groceries, he found her celery, carrot sticks, cheese, sliced turkey breast and hummus. He smiled to himself as he unloaded salad makings, Chilean sea bass, rice, baby green beans, French baguette and butter, white wine and a bottle of Pinch.

Then he went for his suitcase and found the bedroom

she used. He left his suitcase at the foot of her double bed. That was okay, he thought. He didn't intend to let much space get between them at night. He poured himself a drink and went out to the porch to wait. He'd been in the country a long time; he'd missed the sounds of a neighborhood in early evening. Children laughing and yelling, women talking over the fence, a lawn mower somewhere down the block, the slap of the newspaper on the front walk as the paperboy flew by on his bike.

It wasn't long before she drove up to the house, turning a rented truck into the driveway that led to a detached garage out back. He filled his eyes with her—she looked exactly as she did when he drove up to her house back in Virgin River. Jeans, T-shirt covered by a denim shirt with the sleeves rolled up, boots, a cowboy hat. She walked toward him, he came down the porch steps and immediately put his arms around her. He gave her a nice little kiss and said, "I shopped for our dinner. I'll cook for you."

"That would be so wonderful. I could have showered out at the set, but I was in a hurry to see you. It's been long and sweaty and horsey. Let me shower off the grime, then I'll join you for a drink."

"Perfect. Try not to take all night."

"I'll be quick," she promised.

She went into the house, Walt following. She hung her hat on the antique rack just inside the door, sat to pull off her boots and headed for her room. He heard a door close and momentarily, the banging of old pipes as the shower turned on. He'd already checked out the bathroom across the hall from her bedroom—nothing in this house was remodeled. It had a claw-foot tub with a shower curtain.

He sat at the same old hat rack and pulled off his boots,

placing them next to hers. He studied the sight and liked it. Her boots should be by his all the time. He walked down the hall to her bedroom, pulled his shirt out of his pants and off, laying it over the only chair in the room. And then, despite the noise of the shower, he heard something odd. Soft sounds, as if maybe she was singing off-key in the bathroom.

He pulled off his socks and pants and decided to join her, whether she liked it or not. He gave a knock, then let himself into the bathroom. When he pulled back the shower curtain, she had the washcloth over her face. "Make room," he said. "I'll wash your back. Then I'll wash anything else you have in mind." And he stepped into the tub.

She turned away from him and he knew—something was wrong. He turned her back and pulled the cloth away from her face. It was hard to be certain with the water flowing over her, but he thought maybe she was crying. Muriel didn't cry. Not unless the director said, "Cry!"

He wiped a big thumb under her eye. "What's this?" he asked softly.

"Silly," she said, shaking her head. "I'm just tired."

"Muriel, honey, I've seen you knee-walking tired after working on that house of yours. You saying movie work is even harder than that?"

She looked up at him. She put her hand against his cheek. "I didn't think you'd come," she said quietly.

"But we talked. You knew I was coming."

"I mean ever," she said. "I thought that if I didn't come to you, if I didn't live across the meadow, you'd let days and weeks and months separate us if I wanted to work. I thought I was a convenience. I didn't think you'd meet me halfway."

He smiled down at her, slipped his arms around her

naked body and pulled her against him. He lifted her chin with a finger and kissed her tenderly. "I was foolish," he said. "I don't know what was the matter with me. I let that whole business of you being famous intimidate me. This won't happen to us again, Muriel. The next time we're in this situation, we're going to plan our weekends and days off together. I'm just so damn happy I got a second chance. I knew you were pissed." He gave a shrug. "Besides, you haven't been the least bit convenient. You're actually a lot of trouble."

"I missed you," she said. "I thought you wouldn't make the effort. Just for me."

"*Just* for you? For God's sake, I'm in love with you!"

"That's what I hoped. But then you grew so distant. I didn't know if you were in some kind of pout, or you were letting go of me."

"I'll be honest—I didn't want you to leave. It took you no time to spoil me, Muriel." He kissed her and ran a hand over her breast, the other sliding over her bottom and bringing her close. "It's a real spoiled man who just wants everything to stay the same." He chuckled. "And if there are going to be any changes to the routine, the man gets to bring it on."

"But you said I should fulfill all my ambitions, that you'd be rooting for me!"

"I knew that was the only decent thing to say, and I meant it. Until you left and I was missing you."

"You understand, it had to be something important for me to give up the contentment I found with you."

"I'm getting that, Muriel. By the way, this is the part where you tell me you're in love with me, too."

"I don't want to jinx us," she said. She gave a little hiccup of emotion. "Plus, I miss my animals."

He shook his head, then lowered his lips to her breast, kissing. He ran a tongue over her nipple and lifted his head and looked into her eyes. "I want to hear it."

"I swear to God, I didn't cry over my last three husbands."

"Do you always have to bring them up?" he asked.

She smiled at him as her hand wandered. "Maybe we should talk about the fact that even when I mention ex-husbands, you're hard as a baseball bat."

"Are you done with your shower?" he asked. "I might have the erection of a twenty-year-old right now, but if I try to do it in this tub, I could break my sixty-two-year-old back. And then I'll be no good to you."

"We can't have that," she laughed. "And really, to be completely honest, that's not the erection of a twenty-year-old. At least as I recall. Go with forty-year-old." She smiled and shrugged. "As I recall."

"Come on," he said. He put her hand on him. "That's solid steel, right there."

"Walt," she said. "I'm in love with you. It feels like the first time I've ever been in love. I don't want it to go away. I hate being here when you're there. I can handle little bits, but not long separations. I'm happiest with you."

"I'm not going to let this happen to us again, honey. I'm not giving you up. And if any of those hotshot movie stars flirts with you, I'm going to shoot him dead."

She laughed. "Walt, you just sweep me off my feet when you get all tender and talk murder like that."

"No more crying, honey. I love your smile. I love your smart-ass remarks, your laugh, the way you don't let me get away with anything. Now, come on, you dry me off and I'll dry you off and then we'll go at it like a couple of kids."

"You're on."

* * *

Walt had the weekend with Muriel. After dinner, they went back to bed. She put a DVD in her portable player and they watched half a movie before pausing it to make love again. In the night, she woke him for yet another. In the morning, sex was the first thing on his mind.

Muriel took him on a tour of the movie lot on Saturday, introduced him to a few people who were working, showed him her trailer. "You could as easily live here," he said, impressed. "This is a helluva RV."

"I know, and there are nights we work late and I just shower and sleep here. But it's good to get away from all this commotion to decompress. I like that little house."

"Do all the other actors live in little rented houses?" he asked.

She shook her head. "They all have different needs. A couple stay on the lot, some stay in hotels in Butte or Missoula. A lot of crew stays in the motor lodge at the end of town. And some crew brought families and their own RVs. There's something like a tent city on the other side of the lot."

"It's not fancy," he said. "I thought it would be fancy."

"Not usually. There's a lot of money wrapped up in this—people are working hard to get the job done, and on time. Every day we spend here costs tens of thousands of dollars."

They spent Saturday afternoon touring the local area from the car, stopping off in some antique stores because it was an addiction of Muriel's. They ate in a diner in a town no bigger than Virgin River, bought a few things to take home for dinner and Sunday-morning breakfast, sat on the front porch with their glasses of wine and people waved to them as they walked by.

They visited a local stable and took a couple of gentle horses out along a mountain trail, walked along a local river holding hands and had long, seamless, almost endless talks about everything and everybody.

And then Monday morning arrived, in spite of the fact that both of them wished it never would. Muriel had to report to the set and Walt would drive back to Missoula and fly home. She had to leave the house before he did, so he walked her out onto the front porch to say goodbye.

"That was a damn fast forty-eight hours," he said.

"I'll talk to you tonight, though it could be late. It was wonderful having you here, even if it was only for a little while." She smiled up at him. "I've never had so much sex in my life."

"Really?" he asked, lifting an eyebrow. "Even when you were younger?"

"Even then."

"I must be getting better with age," he said. "I'm coming back for another round."

"You are?"

"Yep. I'm going home and making airline reservations for a couple of weeks from now, so put it on your calendar. And I'm going to keep coming back often until this godforsaken movie shit is over."

"It might be bad luck on my Oscar for you to refer to it that way."

"I just hope your next movie isn't filmed in some Middle Eastern desert—I've seen enough of those in my life."

She lifted a brow. "My *next* movie?"

"If you decide to retire for real after this one, I can live with that," he said, grinning. He ran a knuckle along her cheek. "Did we talk about everything? Anything lingering out there we didn't cover?" She shook her head. "Well, there's that one thing that kind of goes with I'm in love with you," he continued. "If you want to get married, I'm game."

"I don't know..."

"And if you don't want to, it's okay. As long as I have your naked body up against mine on a very frequent basis, I'll get along. I'm leaving the whole issue completely up to you, Muriel."

"Why, Walt?"

He shrugged. "I don't have a problem with marriage. I liked it, it worked for me. No boogeymen or curses as far as I'm concerned. Whatever you decide you want to do, either way I'm claiming you. Don't try to wiggle out of it. It's a done deal."

"I don't want to get out of it. I like you."

"You *love* me," he corrected. "Passionately. Desperately. Insatiably."

"I do," she laughed.

"You make me feel twenty-one," he said. "Honest to God. And when the fabulous sex simmers down a little, you're the best friend I've had in a long time. Muriel, you're not a convenience. I'd walk across a mile of cut glass in my bare feet to hold your hand and talk to you for one hour. You're everything to me."

She sighed deeply and her eyes glistened a little. "I'd better go before I give up the only Oscar of my lifetime by playing house with you."

"Tell me I'm everything to you, too," he said.

"Damned if you aren't," she said. "Now kiss me in a way that will hold me for a couple of weeks."

"Kind of took you by surprise, didn't I?" he teased. "Admit it, you didn't think this would turn out to be so much, did you?"

"Walt, the second I saw you blush when you asked if I was married, I knew. And I wanted you. Right then. Right there. Sweaty and naked on the trail."

That made his smile huge. "You didn't let on."

"I hadn't wanted something like that in a long, long time," she said, smiling. Then she rose on her toes and planted a big sloppy one on his lips, holding him close. "I *adore* you," she whispered against his lips. "I'll count the seconds until you're back."

Cheryl brought sandwiches to the park the next Sunday afternoon and Dan brought them the Sunday after that. It didn't take them long to fully share their unfortunate pasts. When Cheryl began telling him about when she started drinking heavily as a teenager, he said, "You don't have to tell me all this, you know. It doesn't make any difference to me. I like having a picnic with you because of who you are now."

"Are you opposed to hearing it?" she asked.

"It's not that. But you don't have to run it by me to see if I'm going to stick or run scared."

"Dan, I've told the story so many times, I can do it in my sleep. That's what we do at AA—tell our stories. It's kind of amazing how we can still find new things in the old story after months. After years."

So he listened. It started in high school and just got worse and worse until by the time she was in her mid-twenties, she was drunk most of the time. Then she told about Mel Sheridan coming for her one morning, carting her off to a treatment program right in Eureka and now she couldn't let herself get very far away.

"I think that's a good woman there," Dan said of Mel. "That man of hers, now, there's a piece of work."

"Jack?" Cheryl asked. She laughed. "Oh, I had a bad thing for Jack, back when I was drinking. Bad. I'd have followed him *anywhere!*"

Dan picked up her hand and held it. "You over that now?"

She got a strange look on her face. "Listen, I can't handle anything more complicated than friendship...."

He gave the hand a squeeze and smiled. "Try not to get ahead of me, Cheryl. I don't have anything complicated in mind. This is all I'm looking for—Sunday picnics with a nice woman, maybe a little handholding sometimes. Maybe we'll get closer down the line, maybe we'll just be friends who have a sandwich and tea. This is okay, don't you think?"

"I guess," she said doubtfully. "It's just that I haven't had a regular, normal, healthy relationship that I can remember."

"Me neither," he said. "It's kind of scary wonderful, isn't it?"

Dan wasn't making any fast moves, and it was extremely deliberate and well thought out. He didn't call during the week except to be sure they were on for Sunday. It wasn't just because she was so skittish—it was also him, cautious. After a wife leaving him and a son dying was followed by a stint in jail, he wasn't at all interested in a relationship that was going to suck the life out of him. All of a sudden, after all the healing he'd had to do, he was real reluctant to threaten what turned out to be peace of mind.

His recovery had been a long, arduous one. He came home from Iraq wounded and with some emotional issues, a lot like young Rick now. In fact, from the time he left for Iraq until he was released from prison, it had been one excruciating journey. Well, he was barely coming out of a long, dark tunnel. He wasn't going to throw it away by moving too fast with a woman who had her own recovery to worry about.

But he liked her. She was cool and didn't know it. When she could let go of that whole town-drunk thing, they talked about when they were real young kids and what they thought they'd grow up to be. Dan had always liked to build, but he thought he'd be building race cars. Cheryl loved animals, but never had a pet growing up. She had wanted to be a veterinarian, but in fact had barely finished high school. Their jobs right now were real mundane, construction and waiting tables on the early shift in a diner, yet just filling in the blanks for each other could soak up at least a couple of hours. They talked about the people they dealt with on the job and friends of theirs. Cheryl had a whole network of friends through AA who'd become her lifeline and Dan claimed some of his newer acquaintances from Virgin River.

He filled her in on Rick—Cheryl had known Rick since he was about two. "He's really struggling with all his stuff—the war, the amputation, the girlfriend, the body image—you name it. He has a smorgasbord of crap to deal with. I keep looking for an in to tell him we could talk about some of that stuff. I've been there, man. But he's got me at arm's length. He's not letting anyone close. I think it's killing Jack slowly."

They didn't have to get much beyond that second Sunday lunch before laughter was as natural for them to share as the stories of their hard times, their daily lives, their gossip.

Really, he didn't care if it was only Sundays for a long time. He found himself looking forward to them. And he kept it his secret that he was growing more attracted to her. She was so vulnerable, he decided right away that he'd give her any opportunity to move closer, but he wouldn't rush her at all. There was no question, she'd run for her life.

There was something about a Friday-night dinner at the bar that called to Dan, even though he was on the job bright and early every Saturday morning. Paul had deadlines and Dan was giving his best effort to helping meet them.

Maybe it was memories of his younger years when he'd either meet with the crews he worked construction with or maybe the Marines he'd served with, but he rarely missed a Friday night at Jack's. He'd have a cold one before dinner, often with Jack and Paul at the bar. Hope almost always made an appearance, looking pretty ratty and cranky. After a whole five days of physical therapy and counseling, Rick Sudder had a real need for that Friday-night wind-down. And Jack let him have a beer. One.

And there was another development in the bar.

Every Friday night since the unfortunate fleeing incident, Liz would come in by herself, right around five o'clock. She'd ask Jack for a giant cola to go. Dan had learned that Liz came to Virgin River every Friday after school, stayed the weekend to help her aunt out in the store and went home to Eureka Sunday evening.

And Rick was always there. It wasn't like Liz wouldn't know that.

Liz always stared straight ahead while she waited for her cola; Rick glanced at her without saying hello, without acknowledging her. She never looked at him either, but when her cola was delivered, she flashed that beautiful smile of hers right at Jack, put her money down and left the bar, ignoring Rick.

Dan didn't have to wonder long if that was eating at Rick. He was sitting two stools down from the kid. Paul stood at the bar beside Dan and they were talking about one of the houses under construction. Dan saw the whole routine go down. And he knew that just that smile alone, let alone that face that could stop traffic, must have been driving Rick crazy. He had to be one messed-up dude to let her go. To her back as she was leaving, Rick said, "Can't you even say hello?"

She slowly turned, regarded him coldly and said, "To you? Not till you grow up." And then she left.

Dead silence hung over the bar as Rick returned to his beer. He stared into it for a while, then he pushed it back and stood up. He used a cane, but didn't really need it. He had a very slight limp, but it was getting better.

"I'll walk you home," Jack said.

"Jack—I got it! I'm fine!" Rick barked.

Jack stopped. He stayed behind the bar. "Great," he said to Rick's back.

It was a long moment before Dan said, "That's a powder keg."

"Tell me about it."

"You see any improvement in his attitude? He getting along any better at all?"

"Not one drop," Jack said. "He's got the good prosthesis now—no more preparatory limb. He could be doing a lot better than he is. Attitude is holding him up. He's just plain pissed off."

"Obviously," Dan said. "And the girl—"

"He decided she could do better and broke it off with her. For a while there I was more worried about her. I thought it would half kill her. But now what we got is a different situation. She's obviously done taking his shit. He dumped her when, not only does he need her, she needs him. And now what we have are two pissed-off, hurting kids who have been through way too much."

"You know, I've been looking for just the right moment," Dan began. "I could maybe talk to him. I took a bad load of shrapnel in the leg and got medically retired from the Corps. I went through a lot of painful PT and can't ever trust the leg again."

Jack frowned. "I thought maybe I saw a limp some-times...."

"Now and then," Dan said. "And I don't do rooftops or ladders, as I informed the boss here," he said, lifting an eyebrow to Paul. "One minute I'm upright, the next I can be on my ass. You learn to live with it. But I remember having a very bad time getting there."

"What do you think turned you around? If you don't mind my asking," Jack said.

"I don't know, man. I had about twenty things that were no good going on all at once," he replied, shaking his head. "I had a young wife. She left me while I was in country. There was illness in the family. I was screwed up on so many levels. And it didn't help that my leg hurt all the time. I think after a while I got tired of being on a constant downward spiral."

"I got a question. It's real personal, but there's a reason I have to know the answer."

"Go."

"Were you suicidal?"

"As far as I can tell you, no. I whimpered for a long time, then I got fighting mad. But then, I didn't exactly take the most law-abiding route to fighting back. Not a good choice for me, but there you have it. You worried he's suicidal?"

"I don't even know when to worry about something like that," Jack said. "He hasn't said anything to me that makes me think that. But Jesus, he hasn't said much of anything at all. The kid's just tough as hell to read."

"You can always ask him," Dan said.

"How do you ask that question?"

"You say, 'Hey, Rick, I can't help but notice you're in terrible shape. Are you having any suicidal thoughts? I have to know.' About half the time if you ask the straight question, you get the straight answer."

Jack pondered this for a long moment. "You know, Brady, you ended up surprising me. I gotta say, I never thought I'd be having a conversation like this with you. All touchy-feely and honest."

Dan grinned. "I love you, too, Jack," he said.

Rick wouldn't even admit to himself that the counseling appointments being crammed down his throat had a payoff. There wasn't any sane reason for it, either. First of all, Jerry Powell was certifiable. Second, Rick didn't feel like talking about his issues. Third, he dreaded every one and he left exhausted—wrung dry and shaky.

But, these hour-long sessions seemed to have a bizarre calming effect about two hours after they were over. Once he started opening up about his feelings a little bit, it came easier. Every time he walked in Jerry Powell's door he'd say to himself, "I'm not telling him anything personal today." And then that whack job would ask exactly the right question.

"How are you sleeping?" Jerry asked.

"I don't know. Not so good."

"What's disturbing your sleep?" he asked.

"Lots of things," Rick said. "Iraq. Leg pain. Stuff."

"Okay, let's start at the beginning. We've talked about Iraq—want to go over some of that for me again? As it pertains to sleep?"

"How do you mean?" Rick asked.

"Are you having nightmares? PTSD stuff—pictures in your head you can't turn off? How's it affecting you?"

"Sometimes I have nightmares, yeah. I guess I'm going to have them forever."

"Tell me about the nightmares."

"What if I don't want to?"

"Well, that's your prerogative, but here's how counseling usually works. If you can bring it out in the light of day, take a good look at it, sometimes your mind helps you deal with it on a conscious, rational level as opposed to subconscious level, and the nightmares fade. So, my specific question is—what nightmares are you having? Iraq in general? A specific incident? Your injury?"

Rick shook his head to try to shake the question away, but it didn't work. When he looked at Powell, the therapist was waiting. Expectant. "There was a thing that happened that I can't get rid of. The squad in front of us blew up. Eleven of them died with one survivor. Sometimes I dream I'm the survivor. I'd rather blow up than be the survivor. You know?"

"You saw them die?"

"They were blown apart everywhere, right in front of us. It was a wide-awake nightmare."

Rick saw Jerry wince and it gave him perverse pleasure. *Yeah, it was about the ugliest sight a guy could witness.*

"Is that what you see in your nightmares?" Jerry asked.

"Sometimes."

"Other things?"

"Sometimes. I killed a guy in Iraq, and I saw his face. It was really too far away for this to be possible, but I swear I saw the expression on his face. It was like he saw me shoot him. Sometimes I dream about that."

"Is that something you worry about? Regret or lose sleep over? How does it work on your head?"

Rick thought for a minute. "I don't worry," he said. "I'm not sorry. But I wonder how it wasn't me who was shot. Killed. We were aiming at each other and I was the lucky one. We didn't find his body—there's a chance he lived through it. But I don't see how."

"How about the incident in which you were wounded?"

"I can't remember that."

"Maybe that's lucky," Jerry said. "Unless you're kept awake by it, haunted by it, like it's trying to surface…."

"Nothing like that. It's a blank. One minute I was walking down a street, the next minute I was waking up in Germany."

"How about the pain? Shouldn't you be ahead of the pain now? It's been a while. And you have medication."

"Yeah. I'm getting there."

"Okay, let's jump right ahead to 'stuff.'"

"Huh?"

"You said, Iraq, pain, stuff."

Rick smiled. "For someone who doesn't take notes, you have a dangerous memory."

"What kind of stuff?" he asked again without missing a beat.

"Okay. I think about my old girlfriend a lot."

"Think about her how?"

"It's complicated...."

"I'm pretty smart, actually. I can probably get through this," Jerry said.

"She's giving me a hard time."

"Oh?"

"She hates me."

Jerry waited patiently, irritating Rick.

"I knew it was going to be hard on her, telling her we couldn't be a couple anymore. I figured there'd be tears and stuff. But then she'd get over it. I knew it would take a while, but then some guy would ask her out or something. Eventually she's going to be all right."

"What about this is keeping you awake at night?" Jerry asked.

"You know, this isn't easy on me, either," Rick snapped. "Staying away from her isn't exactly simple. But it's better this way."

Jerry leaned forward. "Listen, I think you're going to have to try to be more specific. I'm not sure I'm following. We've talked about the girlfriend before and as I understand it, you explained to her that you couldn't be her boyfriend anymore and that upset her. Correct?"

"Correct," he answered tightly.

"And now she's angry?"

"Whew," Rick said, shaking his head. "I go to Jack's every Friday afternoon for about an hour or so. After a week of PT and *you,* I'm wrecked, so Jack lets me have a beer and some dinner. She comes to the bar every week, knowing I'm going to be there, and she won't look at me. I mean, she won't even *accidentally* see me. Won't speak to me. Smiles pretty at everyone else and it's like I'm not there."

Jerry tilted his head. "You don't want to be her boyfriend anymore," he pointed out.

"Well, I *can't* be. It's no good that way. For her. Believe me."

"Okay, let me get this right," Jerry said. "You told her you're through—you two cannot be together. Sounds like maybe she believes you. Did you expect her to be a little more gracious about it?"

Rick glared through narrowed eyes. "You're a smartass, you know that?"

"Sorry, that's not my intention at all. I'm really trying to understand what about this is off. What about this is costing you sleep?"

"She could say hello," he barked.

"Is it possible she's angry with your decision to break it off with her?"

"Well, no shit! She even told me to grow up, like I'm being a real baby about having my leg blown off!"

"Did she say that?" Jerry asked.

"No, but that's what she meant!"

"Are you certain?"

"Of course I'm *certain!*"

"Did she tell you exactly why she thought you should grow up?" Jerry asked.

"Listen to me! She didn't *have* to!"

"I see, I think. So, her apparent anger with you is costing you sleep?"

He hung his head. "It's hard," he said softly, temporarily defeated. "It's like she doesn't get that it hurts me, too. It's hard to stay away from her, hard not to be with her. For a long time, like four years, Liz was my whole life. I mean, everything. I was totally faithful to her while I was away from her. And she was faithful to me. She was a virgin before we…you know? She liked to tell me all the time that even though it worked out to be so hard, with the baby and everything, she was still glad that I was the first and she wanted me to be the only one. For a long time I wanted that, too." He lifted his head. "I miss her a lot, you know. I miss everything."

"Everything?" Jerry probed.

"That whole life I used to have—everything. Jack and Preacher, good times, hunting and fishing, laughing at every stupid thing. It was great watching Jack get in trouble with his wife and she'd dress him down good. And he'd back-pedal like mad." Rick laughed in spite of himself. "We'd go fish and if I hooked something, he couldn't stay out of it—he'd be all over me, telling me what to do, like I've never been fishing before. Once he got into it with Preach—he got right in Preacher's business and told him not to get involved with this woman…." Rick laughed and shook his head. "Preacher took Jack *out!* I didn't think anyone could get a punch off on Jack—Jack's a fast guy, and powerful. Preacher knocked him *flat*. I saw Jack's shiner—it was awesome. And Preacher married that woman—Paige."

It was silent in the office for a while.

"I used to be part of everything that went on there. Now I'm not."

Jerry asked, "Do you feel abandoned by your friends?"

He shook his head. "I cut 'em off. Really, I'm a god-damn curse."

"Did someone tell you that?" Jerry asked.

He shook his head again. "They tell me that's not true, but it kind of looks like it is, don't you think?"

"How's that?"

Rick sighed. "We've been over all this," he said impatiently. "About a hundred times. Bad things happen to people I get close to. I laid it out for you."

"I recall," Jerry said. "Why don't you tell me about your anger."

Rick leaned back in his chair and huffed at Jerry like he was just plain ridiculous. "Gimme a fucking break here, Powell."

"Oh—you don't feel like talking about that?"

"I'm totally pissed off. Like this is news?"

"Believe me, I'm all too aware. I'm wondering, if you talked about it a little more, if it might become apparent that these decisions you're making to cut the important people out of your life, are driven by that anger. Rather than by sound reason. I wonder if the anger over what your war experience and injury have cost you is clouding some of your judgment in these issues. Maybe you're just so goddamn angry, you want to hurt yourself even more."

"You think I shouldn't be angry?" he asked, tears sparkling in his eyes. Tears that Jerry knew Rick would not let fall.

"Oh, heavens, Rick. Anyone would be angry. But it's up to you whether you drive the anger or the anger drives you."

"What the *fuck* does that mean?"

"It means, you have a right to your anger. Every right. So what we should look at is—what is the object of your anger? Jack? Your old girlfriend?"

He shook his head. "I'm not mad at them, man. Well, if

I'm mad it's only because they want everything to be all right, and it's not."

"I see. How much of your anger do you direct at yourself?"

"Why would I do that?"

Jerry shrugged. "Why would you? Good question."

"Well, I'm not mad at myself. I'm doing what has to be done, that's all."

"Ah. And that is?"

"Listen, asshole, I have to cut Liz loose, before she wastes her whole life on me. And she would, she's that kind of girl. She hasn't gotten much good from me so far."

"Rick, do you have any respect for anyone?"

He stiffened. "What do you mean?"

"Do you respect Liz, for example?"

"Of course. If I didn't respect her I wouldn't—"

"If you *did* respect her, you'd probably assume she could make her own choices. I've suggested this before, I think."

"Don't you listen to anything?" Rick demanded.

"Raptly," Jerry answered. "You are doing what you think has to be done."

"Exactly!"

"Except, wh: ʼ you're just plain angry about the way things went in Iraq? What if the actions you're taking are a greater punishment on you than anyone else?"

"What bullshit," Rick said, wiping impatiently at his eyes.

"That life you miss, Rick? It's right where you left it. But you're too angry and afraid of disappointment to let yourself return to it."

"That would be stupid," Rick said. "I'm not stupid, and I'm not just afraid of a little disappointment."

"I didn't say little," Jerry pointed out. "In your case, weighing in combat, disability, death, I'd say the disappointment is substantial. Life altering."

Rick ground his teeth. Okay, so what if that was true—he was afraid that if he assumed he could slip back into his old life, he'd not only let everyone else down, but it would kill him to see any of them hurt any further? "You are the most annoying jerk I've ever known," he said to Jerry.

"It's a dirty job," Jerry said with a shrug. "Since our time is nearly up, I'd like you to think about that for next time—that you're angry and afraid, which is reasonable, and also potentially destructive. If we can explore where that anger is directed, for next time, maybe we can—"

"I know where the fucking anger is directed!" Rick nearly shouted. "At everything that happened for the last twenty years! My parents, my girl, my baby, my war!"

Jerry gave him a second. Then he said, "Yourself."

"No!" Rick insisted. "No!"

Jerry did not look at his watch or break eye contact to look at the clock. Finally, in a low voice he asked, "Did you let them all down, Rick? By getting wounded and disabled?" Rick looked at four or five different points around the room, looking high, like the answer would be in the ceiling of Jerry's little office. "If this hadn't happened to you," Jerry went on, "would you be able to pick up where you left off, carry on, with your best friends and your girl?"

"You are totally nuts," Rick said, but the tears that always gathered in his eyes began to roll down his cheeks and he swiped at them.

"Does the anger drive you or do you drive the anger?" Jerry repeated. "Are you mad at yourself because you got hurt?"

"That's just stupid," Rick said, but he said it more softly. Then he put his face in his hands and his shoulders shook a little. It was a full minute before he lifted his head and turned glassy eyes at Jerry. "Face it. If it hadn't happened, things would be all different. It was like the straw that broke the camel's back. I might have never seen that it's all on me, that I'm the one—" And then he put his face in his hands again.

Jerry let him simmer for a while, pretending not to cry when he was actually coming apart. He knew Rick wouldn't reach for a tissue, that would be too telling. His shoulders trembled, but Jerry could hear the desperate mewling sounds of a man trying not to give in. When things calmed down just a little, he spoke. "Rick, there are some facts that have nothing to do with you that eventually you have to accept. One—a drunk driver caused your parents' deaths. One hot little sperm and one determined little egg made your baby on the first strike. Most of the stillbirths recorded have no known cause—a very tragic statistic. And—someone threw the grenade that took you out. Everything could have been different, but there was nothing you could have done to make it so."

"What are you saying?" he asked, lifting his head.

"You're not going to get much satisfaction from blaming yourself. You'll keep going in circles because you're faultless. You've had some rough deals, but you've also had some extremely lucky events."

"Yeah? Like?"

Jerry kept his gaze level. "Oh, let's see. A grandmother, by your account a very good woman, who devoted her life to you. A couple of outstanding mentors who stepped in to father you, support you, teach you. A girlfriend... Not many men find a girl, at such an early age, with the kind of commitment you described to me. And then a few traumatic things happened that—"

"I didn't think I'd let them down like this...."

"Say what, Rick?"

"I thought the Marines would work for me...."

"Maybe they don't feel let down. Maybe you got things from the Marines that are valuable, just muddy right now because of the trauma."

"You don't get it," Rick said, sounding weaker. "That stuff can't happen. We're trained, alert. It's not just one pair of eyes, it's a unit. That's how we got to be the strongest force in the free world."

"Unexpected things happen..."

"It wasn't an accident," Rick said. "It was hostile, and our job is to evade hostile attack. I finished every training gig first in my group. First..."

Jerry paused. "The stuff that happened wasn't your fault. Some bad, unfortunate things do happen to people without their participation. Like a wheel falling off a car, even though all the lugs were tight. Like—"

"Jerry," Rick said, glassy-eyed, stopping him. "*All* the wheels fell off this car."

Jerry leaned forward. "Rick, focus for just a second. Listen to me. I'm a crisis counselor—do you know what that means?" Rick stared blankly at him, but he went on anyway, knowing he might have to repeat this more than once. "It means that when a crisis occurs in the life of a perfectly normal person, I have the training to take that person by the hand and lead them through the fire and out the other side, where once again they'll feel like a perfectly normal person who has dealt with trauma. That's what we're doing here, Rick. You and me. We're going to get through this."

Rick was quiet for a long time. Then he said, "I don't buy it."

Jerry sat back, relaxed. "You will."

Fourteen

Brie Valenzuela wasn't expecting clients, nor was she planning to go to the prosecutor's office where she did consulting work. There was no court today, so she was dressed in jeans and a sweatshirt. It was a good day to catch up on paperwork. She sat at her desk in the office attached to her home, little Ness asleep in her swing beside the desk, when there was a knock at the office door.

She knew at once this was probably a business call as opposed to a friend dropping by. There was a front door to her house as well as an external office door, beside which a sign was mounted that read, *Brie Valenzuela, Esquire*. That door was always kept locked when she was alone and not expecting anyone. She went to the door and looked out the peephole. There was a man there, mid-thirties or so. The fact that he wasn't scary looking didn't influence the way Brie handled things. "Just a minute," she said.

She moved Ness, swing and all, through the door that led from her office into the kitchen, without waking her. Then she closed the door adjoining her office to the house. Having been both a criminal prosecutor and the victim of a violent crime, Brie never relaxed her standards, not even in Virgin River. She tucked her Glock into the rear waistband of her jeans and opened the door. "Yes?"

"Are you Brie Valenzuela?"

"I am," she said.

He put out his hand. "Ross Crawford. How do you do?"

"Well, this is unexpected," she said, accepting the hand. "How can I help you?" she asked without inviting him farther into her office.

"I'm trying to find Abby," he said. "She sold her town house, and her parents refuse to tell me where she is or deliver a message to her. The airline would only tell me she took an extended leave."

"I'd be happy to forward a message. Would that help?" Brie asked.

"Yes, absolutely," he said. "I really need to talk to her."

Brie took a breath. "Mr. Crawford," she said patiently, not at all oblivious to the fact that he didn't look like a rock star. "I'm sure you realize that from this point on, your attorneys should do the talking. Your divorce has been final for some time and the settlement is satisfied."

"Oh, it's not about that exactly," he said. He wore expensive jeans, no rips or tears or chains, a flawless white button-down rolled up at the sleeves, Italian boots. His hair was a bit on the shaggy side, attractively so and curling at his collar, and he was clean shaven. "It's personal stuff."

"All the same, Mr. Crawford."

"Just call me Ross. Listen, I understand if you don't want to tell me where she is—she wouldn't want anything to do with me now. But if you could please contact her and tell her I'd like just a few minutes of her time—"

"Of course," Brie said. "And where should I deliver her answer? That business manager's address in Los Angeles?"

"No, no," he said, shaking his head. "Could you call her now, please? I'm sure you have the phone number. I'll wait."

"Mr.…Ross, I don't think you should be too optimistic. Honestly, my advice to her will be that she decline. As I said, the conversation should be between—"

"Attorneys, I know. What do you think got us into this mess? This doesn't have to do with divorce or settlements or— Well, it has a little to do with it. It's my amends, Ms. Valenzuela. I have to make amends. It's one of my steps. I'm trying to graduate from a treatment program."

Brie folded her arms over her chest. She wasn't about to be reeled in by a smooth-talking addict. "Another one?" she asked.

"Third time," he said, lifting his chin and straightening. "I'm a real hard sell. If you'll please call her and ask her if she'll give me fifteen minutes of her time, I'll never bother her again. Believe me, I know I'm asking a lot. The rule is, make amends where it won't make the life of the person you're apologizing to more difficult. And the list is long. So long. I'll meet her somewhere neutral if she'd like. You can be there—it wouldn't change what I have to say. Please?"

Brie took a breath. "Do you mind waiting in your car? I should have some privacy for the call."

"Sure. Listen, please tell her I don't want to upset her life in any way. I swear I'll leave her alone after this. And really, tell her, I'm an idiot, a fool, an addict and imbecile, but I've always been nice when I'm clean. I'm fair. She'll remember that. Hand to God."

"Mr. Crawford," Brie said sternly. "Be prepared. The answer could be no. In which case you'll have to complete your steps without her assistance."

"Well," he said, hanging his head, "I hope she'll see me. If only for a few minutes. I'd like both of us to be able to get this behind us so we can move on."

"I'll be sure to tell her you said that," Brie promised. "Excuse me now."

Brie sent him back down the walk to his car. She took a deep breath, checked on the baby first and when Ness was found sleeping contentedly, she called Abby at the cabin. She explained everything Ross had said. "I don't know what's included in his amends, Abby, and I don't want you unnecessarily upset. I'm not sure I recommend this, even though I'm all for working through domestic disputes and laying them to rest, if there's a mediator present. I can serve in that capacity, unofficially. Or, it's perfectly all right to decline this request. In fact, I could tell him that you'll reconsider in a few months—that right now is not a good time."

"Do you know he never once took my calls when I wanted to know what was going on with him? When I wanted to discuss the terms his lawyers set forth? I wish I wasn't curious. The fact is, I'd like to know what he has to say about it now."

"You're very pregnant. I don't want you back in court because of some egregious prenup."

"We have this letter saying it's over. Right? I'll see him," she said. "But only if you'll be present."

"It's just me and the baby here," Brie said. "I can't reach Mike. Would you be comfortable bringing Cam? If not, I'll call Jack. He'd come out. Just to hedge against any kind of reaction that you and I and little Ness can't handle."

"Oh, I don't think Cameron would miss this for anything," Abby said. "But if he's tied up with patients, I'll stop by the bar and grab either Jack or Preacher."

* * *

Brie took a couple of minutes to brew coffee, change the baby, fix up a bottle that would keep her quiet and then, after a good fifteen minutes had passed, with the Glock stowed away again and Ness on her hip, she opened the door to signal Ross from his car. "She's coming," she told him when he came up the walk.

"Ah. She *is* here, then."

Brie tilted her head. "With all your resources, you probably could have learned that on your own, without coming to me."

"There's been too much of that sort of thing," he said. "Can I just sit over there and wait?" he asked, indicating the sofa and chair in the corner of the room.

"Sure. What do you mean, there's been too much of that?"

"Aw, my manager hired people to keep my back. It was supposed to be for the crazies, you know? I get 'em sometimes. Abby's not crazy. She's just a nice girl who got hooked up with a wrong guy."

Brie shook her head sadly. "Turns out we agree on some things," she said, going back to her desk. She sat in her chair and gave the baby a bottle while Ross opened a thick spiral notebook, pulled out a pen, flipped it open and began writing. After a few minutes he looked toward Brie and Ness and said, "How old is she?"

"Six months."

"And you manage a baby and lawyering?" he asked.

"It's a small town," she said. "I'm seldom overworked. Which is how I like it."

"How'd you meet Abby?" he asked.

"She was referred."

"I thought she had a lawyer."

"Did she?" Brie asked, although she knew. Brie was of the opinion her former attorney hadn't helped her much. Or maybe he was just up against too much of Ross's money. "Are you documenting this meeting?" Brie asked him.

"This?" he asked, tapping the notebook. "Oh," he laughed. "No. This is my compilation of sins and crimes. It's not easy to remember every one of them, since I was high and plastered most of the time." He went back to writing.

Brie heard the car door outside and lifted Ness into her swing, getting it started. She went to the door before they could enter and opened it for Abby and Cameron. Ross put down his notebook and stood expectantly. "Hi, folks," Brie said, holding open the door.

And then she came inside, Cameron close on her heels.

"Whoa! *Abby!*" Ross nearly shouted. He hit himself in the chest and wobbled a little on his feet, his eyes wide and shocked. "God!" Then he shot a look at Brie. "Why didn't you tell me she was pregnant? I mean, *pregnant!*"

"It wasn't my place to tell you. It's certainly not pertinent to your business."

He walked toward her and reached for her. "Good God, come over and sit down."

She pulled away from him. Cameron was at her back, his hands on her upper arms. "You'd better leave Abby to me," Cameron said calmly, firmly.

"Oh man," Ross said, running a nervous hand over the top of his head. "Sorry, man." Then he stuck out a hand, careful not to get too close. "Ross Crawford," he said.

Cameron gave a curt nod over Abby's shoulder rather than shaking hands. "Dr. Michaels," he said.

"You're her doctor?" Ross asked.

"My fiancé," Abby said.

"Whoa," Ross laughed. "Okay, this is just a surprise, that's all. If you don't mind me saying so, you could use a little more than a fiancé there, Abby."

"I mind," she said. "Now, what's so important, Ross?"

"Gimme a second," he said, looking at her. "I'm sorry, but you're awful pregnant, Abby. Kind of distracted me."

"Well, get a hold of yourself and get down to business. This is pretty inconvenient."

"Yeah, I guess it is. Sorry. Um, can we sit?" he asked, swinging a hand toward the sofa and chair. He stepped out of the way. "Go ahead, you two. Gee."

Once they were all seated, Ross just stared at Abby. Cameron put an arm around her shoulders and said, "Can we please move along? I might have patients waiting back at the clinic."

"Huh? Oh, sorry, Doc. Abby, I didn't know what was happening to you with that whole divorce thing. I was high."

"Weren't they your lawyers, Mr. Crawford?" Cameron asked tensely.

"Yeah, sort of. Listen, I'm here to make amends, but it's dicey. I have to do this without making excuses, so I'll try. I went back on the road after we got married and after only about a week I started using. I met a woman at a party of some kind and gave her a job as an assistant band manager. The other guys said she was trouble and wouldn't have anything to do with her, but I had started sleeping with her, so I ignored them and let her take care of some of my stuff. She got herself some credit cards. I didn't even remember about them until your lawyer told me. They were supposed to be for business expenses, but I didn't pay any attention. She played go-between with my lawyer and I signed anything she put in front of me. Hell, I think she was the one who contacted the lawyer, I was too toasted to do that. I've been either high or in treatment for the last year and a half. My last incarceration was for six months in Mexico. It wasn't until I talked to your lawyer here that I found out you got soaked for all her charges. I never saw those cards either."

"Weren't you sober long enough to look at the paperwork you signed?" Abby asked.

He shook his head. "Nah, I was messed up. Sometimes I was in worse shape in treatment than when I was using and playing guitar. But—I'd been out of the last treatment center a couple of months when the letter came from Ms. Valenzuela saying you'd paid off the credit-card debt and didn't want any more alimony. My brain was working pretty well by then, so I called your lawyer here. I was finally cleaned up enough to look into it. Abby, I'm sorry—I would never have asked you to pay any of my bills. I wouldn't have stuck you with *her* bills, for sure. Your lawyer shouldn't have allowed it."

She scooted forward as much as she could. "Ross, I had one lawyer, the best one I could afford after I took all the equity money out of my town house and cashed in my 401k, but you had *four* lawyers. Four, Ross. By the end of it, I felt lucky to get out of the whole mess as cheaply as I did."

"Aw, Abby, those were just back-up thugs from his office—I didn't hire 'em. Man, you must hate me so much."

"Yeah, that's the bottom line," she said, folding her hands over her belly.

He grinned at her. "I'm sorry—this is not funny. But you look so cute. Really big. You ready to give birth or something?"

"You have no idea," she said. "Are we done here?"

"Almost. Okay, so the woman, the assistant manager, her name was Autumn, she got fired a long time ago. The boys picked out a new treatment center and said that was it—if I committed for six months of treatment and stayed clean for a year, they'd *consider* giving me another chance in the band. Otherwise, that was it for me. They told Autumn to hit the road, and I went into treatment for the third time." He shook his head. "I wish I could find someone to blame for the drugs, but the truth is, it was all me. I thought I was such hot shit when the band picked me up and the first time I saw that white powder, I plowed into it so fast.... And man, I loved the stuff. I've been mostly high for over ten years. I hate what it did to my life, but I did love the stuff. Made me feel invincible.... Until it didn't anymore.... I'm learning to like being level and not so destructive. But sometimes it's powerful hard."

Abby struggled a little bit to get to a standing position, Cam at her side giving assist. "Well, I hope you make it this time, Ross. When you're straight, you're not a bad guy. Too bad it's so scary to count on you staying straight."

Ross stood. "Abby, you never asked for anything in the settlement, you should have gotten out of the whole thing without a problem, without it costing you a cent. You shouldn't have needed a lawyer at all. And, you were supposed to be getting some support while we were separated. Close as we can figure, that went in Autumn's purse, too. Staying crocked all the time is real expensive all around."

"Can we just close the door on it now?" Abby asked. "I really need to get on with my life."

"You sure do," he said with a smile.

She winced and leaned over her stomach slightly.

"You all right, babe?" Cameron asked softly, bracing her from behind.

"Oh, you know," she said. "I just can't grow anymore."

"We have to be going, Mr. Crawford," Cameron said. "Abby needs her rest. She's uncomfortable."

"Sure, I'll hurry this up," he said. "I fired the lawyer. I'm using Greg's firm now. The lead singer—remember him? He's straight as an arrow and has some good people on retainer. I gave them the job of figuring out what my shyster set you back and I want to make restitution...."

"Forget it," Abby said. "The credit-card bills were paid off with your alimony and I don't want your money. I want it over, once and for all."

"Oh, you'll get that. I promise, I'll never bother you again after—"

"Haven't you spent enough money on drugs, treatment, lawyers and bad managers who robbed you blind?"

"Yeah, I lost a ton of money on stupidity. There's a little left. It feels kind of good to spend some responsibly for a change. Let's see, there was forty-seven thousand in Autumn's credit-card bills, your 401k wasn't that big—just twenty-two. Six years in that town house only earned you about thirty in equity—should've been more, but—"

"Ross! Forget it! I defied your prenup!" Her hand covered her mouth suddenly and her eyes darted between Brie to her left and Cameron behind to her right. "Shit," she said.

But Ross grinned. "Really? You mean while I was sleeping with Autumn—as she robbed me blind—you were having a relationship with this doctor dude?"

"Not until the weekend before I signed the papers. So keep your money and just let me go."

Ross shook his head almost sadly. "You were alone for

nine months? Aw, Abby, I agreed to that prenup safeguard when it was suggested, but I never would've held you to it when I was stepping out on you at the same time. I mean, I'm a lot of things, but I'm not pure evil." He shrugged. "I guess it could happen that a woman you've been married to a few months takes you for millions," he said. "I thought I should guard against that, but hey, I've made more than one mistake, obviously. I'm just happy that you found a good person and you're having a family, like you always wanted. And I'm jealous—I wish I could have that life. It's going to be a long time before I'm sane enough for a relationship with anyone besides a sponsor." He pulled an envelope from his back pocket. It was folded in half.

"Ross, I mean it—your money is just going to mess me up. Cameron and I, together, we've cleared all this up so we have a fresh start, and—"

"It's not really for you," he said, handing her the envelope. "It's for me. It's very important to me that at the end of the day I made it right with one of the nicest people I know. After about ten years of screwing up people's lives, you gave me a chance, Abby. You believed in me when you shouldn't have, and all the thanks you got was getting screwed because I cared more about drugs than I did about you, or me, for that matter. If you don't want it, donate it to charity. Start a college fund for the kid there. Do whatever you want. It's real important to me—it's helping me get well."

She took the envelope gingerly. She peeked inside and screamed. "Eyyyyyyeeee!" She scrunched the envelope in her fist.

"Don't hurt it, Abby," Ross said, taking a nervous step toward her.

"Ross, you've lost your mind! It's for a hundred and twenty-five thousand dollars!"

"I know. It's a little short. It should be bigger, figuring for nine months of support you never got before the divorce was final. I swear I told her to send you money. I'm sorry I didn't know about all this sooner. Right about the time our divorce was final, I entered treatment for six months. I was out of pocket, just got out a couple of months ago."

"Ross, I can't. I can't."

"Like I said, do something good with it. Feed the hungry. Educate poor children. But, Abby, it's a cashier's check and it's money you were swindled out of. If you burn it, it's like burning cash, so don't go nuts. Doc? Maybe you could talk some sense into her. I mean, I appreciate how honorable she is, but it's her money. It's not a donation—it's just what it cost her to get screwed around by my business manager and lawyer. And me. I guess first off it was me. Abby was robbed."

"We'll talk about it," Cameron said, taking the squashed envelope out of her hands. "It won't be burned."

"Works for me, but hell—try to use it on yourselves. It was her retirement and condo, for God's sake. She worked hard for that. Abby, I'm glad you're happy. I really am." Then he smiled sadly.

Abby turned around to face Cameron. She had tears in her eyes. "Are we done now?" she asked Cam.

"I think so, honey. You okay?"

"No. I'm in labor."

"Aw, Jesus, why didn't you say so?"

"I wasn't sure. Now? I'm sure."

"Okay, sit back down here," he said, tossing the envelope on the side table and easing her down onto the couch.

"Let's take a minute to see what we've got before we activate Mel and John."

"We've got one right after another," she said. "Hard. Long. Getting stronger. Pretty soon I'm going to have to start deep breathing."

Brie got right over there. "Any idea how far apart?"

"No," she said, shaking her head. "I was listening to Ross. But close and getting closer. This has been going on since you called, but I saw a chance to have this over with him before the babies came and I— Cameron?" she asked, turning her frightened face to his. "I'm nervous. Is it okay? It's over thirty-six weeks, right? We'll be okay, right?"

"We're going to be fine, baby. And they'll be fine."

"Will they come too fast?"

"We'll have Mel pick us up in the Hummer just in case. Brie? Call Mel?"

"Sure," she said, heading for the phone. When she turned to pick it up, she saw Ross backing toward the door, his eyes on Cameron and Abby.

Abby had her hands on Cam's face. "I love you so much," she said. "I wish we'd just gotten married when you first suggested it. I want them to have a father."

"They have a father, baby. We'll get it done as soon as you're recovered a little."

"We'll put your name on the birth certificates."

"We'll do anything you want. Right now it looks like we're going to deliver." He smiled and gave her a kiss. "You didn't want to wait for the Pitocin, I guess."

"I made it long enough for them to be healthy," she said, leaning against him. "Didn't I? Please tell me I—"

"They're going to be perfect, Ab. Trust me, honey."

Brie watched Ross. He had a melancholy look on his face

as he lifted a hand to her to wave goodbye. For a second she was frozen, then she lifted her hand in return. No time for farewells between Abby and Ross, which was probably for the best. She made a mental note to retrieve and protect the check that lay on the table.

She dialed as the door closed behind Ross. How must it feel, she wondered, to know that you've squandered your life? To see all you lost?

"Mel? Hey, Cam and Abby are here and she's in labor. Contractions very close together and she says they're strong and long. Cameron asked if you'd bring the Hummer to take her to the hospital, just to be safe. Very good—I'll tell them." She disconnected and said, "As soon as she can leave the kids with Jack, she's on her way." Brie grinned. "So—what an exciting day this turned out to be. So much for boring paperwork!"

When Mel arrived at Brie's office, she took a couple of minutes to talk with Abby about her contractions. "Get in back with her, Cam, and I'll drive. Her water hasn't broken and I think we have time. Tell me if I have to pull over and trade places with you."

While Mel drove, she listened to Cameron trying to coach Abby through her breathing, trying to soothe her, rubbing her back. But when they arrived at Valley Hospital forty-five minutes later, she heard Abby snap, "Of *course* I'm doing fine. Can you stop *touching* me so much?"

Mel smiled to herself, but then she hurried. She put the Hummer in park at the hospital's emergency entrance, ran around to the back and lifted the hatch. "I want you to stay on the gurney, Abby," she said. "Cam, give me a hand here."

"I can probably still walk," Abby began to argue.

"No, do as I say," Mel instructed. When she and Cameron had rolled her into the hospital and up the elevator to labor and delivery, they were expected. Mel asked a nurse, "Is Dr. Stone here yet?"

"Not yet, but he said he was coming right over."

"If you can still reach him, tell him to put a wiggle in it—I think I'm going to find she's in transition."

"Will do," the L&D nurse assured her.

In the birthing room there were two plexiglass bassinets, two warmers stocked with diapers so tiny they could fit in the palm of her hand, monitors and IV stands. Cameron and Mel cautiously transferred Abby to the bed. Mel pulled off Abby's shoes. "I'm going to ask Cameron to help you get into a gown, Abby, while I change into scrubs. When we're both changed, I'll check you. How's that?"

"Fine," she said, rolling carefully into a sitting position on the bed. "Oh!"

"What, honey?" Cam asked her.

"My water! Oh God, I'm totally sitting in a puddle."

"Then let's change quickly, shall we?" Mel said, throwing her purse and bag in a corner out of the way and heading out of the room for a quick change. On her way toward the nurses' lounge and locker room she said to one of the nurses, "We're gonna roll in there. Get me the pediatric nurse and I'll need some help until Dr. Stone arrives."

"I've arrived," she heard a voice say.

She turned and smiled at John Stone. "Great timing. Our patient is moving up on the docket, water just broke, and I haven't even checked her yet."

"But what do you think?"

"Nine or ten," Mel said with a shrug. "She had a nice little personality shift just as we were arriving."

"I'll check her." Then he smiled at the L&D nurse. "She's got great instincts. Get your delivery team in there."

The room became busy even before Cameron had helped Abby all the way into her gown. John Stone was waiting for her to ease back on the bed, snapping on a pair of gloves. People started filling the room—two pediatric nurses, a couple of labor-and-delivery nurses, the pediatrician arrived, and Mel was back by the time Abby's knees were raised and John Stone was examining her. One of the nurses was monitoring fetal heartbeats. "What are you feeling, Abby?" John asked her.

"Pressure," she said. "Low pressure. I think maybe I have to use the bathroom."

John pulled out his hand, stripped off the glove and said, "Not anymore, Abby. Let's break down this bed," he said to one of the nurses. "Abby, there's only a tiny strip of cervix left—you ready to push?"

"I could try," she said.

"In a second or two, you're not going to have to try." No sooner said than she was lifting off the bed on pure instinct, bearing down. "There you go," he said, grinning. "Mel, take the first one."

"My pleasure," she said.

The L&D nurses removed the bottom half of the birthing bed, rolled forward a table on which the delivery instruments and equipment lay under a sterile drape, and Mel and John shared the space at the end of the bed. Mel pulled a stool up to the front-row seat where she was rhythmically and systematically stretching Abby's vagina around a growing crown of hair. She was telling Abby to push push push push push and, "Go ahead and rest for a minute."

"I missed the epidural," Abby said breathlessly.

"I know the feeling," Mel laughed. "Ready to go again, Abby?"

Abby lifted slightly, Cameron assisting at her shoulders, and before even fifteen minutes had passed, Mel said, "Here we go, just one more," and a baby came into her hands. While holding the baby in her lap, she deftly clamped and cut. "Ah. Ladies first." And within moments she had moved out of the way for John Stone to take over, bringing the newborn up onto Abby's chest. "Nice, very nice. Take a moment to rest and meet your daughter, then we have to do that again. Let's dry her off, Cam," she said, rubbing a soft towel over the baby's tiny body.

"Is she big enough? Is she, Cam?" Abby asked. "She looks so tiny."

"I'm guessing five pounds," Cameron said. "What do you think, Mel?"

"I think she liked it in there. Look at those arms flail, listen to that voice. Oh, you two are going to be busy. Abby, have a quick look, sweetheart, then let's get her warmed up and bring out her brother. Hmm?"

"I don't want to let go of her," Abby said.

"You're going to get her right back. She just needs to be cleaned off, warmed up, diapered and swaddled. By that time, you'll be counting fingers and toes on her brother."

"Oh God, look at her, Cameron. How can I be in charge of something this tiny?"

He laughed. "You should get help from a pediatrician. How about that?"

"Why didn't I just marry you when I had the chance?"

He leaned down and put a kiss on her lips and on the baby's head. "I'm not going anywhere, honey."

Abby and Cameron had less than two minutes to examine and fawn over their daughter, when a low groan came from Abby. That sound alone brought the pediatric nurse to the bedside, scooping up the baby to get her cleaned, weighed, measured and checked over by the doctor. As soon as the baby was cleared from her, John Stone said, "Go ahead and push when you're ready, Abby. We're going to bring this fella down and into the world."

Just a couple of minutes later, Abby had another baby in her arms. Mel and Cameron were drying him off while Abby was cooing over him, touching him, kissing him. She didn't even notice that the nurse was washing her up, that the field of birth was being cleaned and cleared away, the bed reassembled. It was only another fifteen minutes before Abby held their daughter while Cameron held their son.

"Your daughter is five pounds, two ounces and your son a strapping five-seven. Both of them eighteen inches. Nice work, Abby. You grew them into going-home-from-the-hospital weight. They're beautiful," Mel said.

Abby, holding her daughter close, looked up into Cameron's eyes. She smiled. "We're a family now."

"Yeah, honey." He leaned down to give her a kiss. "Thank you."

Fifteen

There was a lot of commotion at the bar when Hope came in and announced to Jack, Paul and Dan that her third attempted eBay auction on the old church was under way and the bidding started high enough for her to actually sell the property.

"You are kidding me," Jack said, astonished. "Do you know who to?"

"I've had a couple of contacts, asking for details. One is a minister who's been teaching for the past few years and wants to get back in the pulpit and another is an artist who wants to live in the church and use it as a shop to make everything from stained-glass pieces to decorative candles. There's one other—I have no idea who. It's going to go by midnight next Wednesday."

"I think Preacher's watching it," Jack said. "But I haven't figured out that whole eBay thing yet."

"Jack, it's eBay-dot-com," Dan said. "You can do this. If you need me to, I can come over to the house and show you."

"I'm not so sure I want you to know where I live," Jack said, wiping the counter.

Dan grinned. He liked that—some grief from Jack. Buddies ribbed each other, and if a guy liked you a lot, he hit below the belt now and then. "Maybe your wife could get you checked out on eBay. You could put in a bid, raise the stakes for Hope here."

"Yeah, and end up with a church. Just what I need."

Paul lifted his beer. "I hope whoever gets it needs a good builder for a remodel."

"If you don't get a contract on that church, it'll take the new guy a year to put it right," Jack said.

Rick listened to all this with half an ear. He didn't really participate in the discussions at the bar. Each week he sat farther to the end of the bar so he wouldn't be expected to say anything. The joke was on him, he thought. No one was in the mood to cajole him into being sociable anymore. Jack let him have his beer and before he was half through it, put a plate of food in front of him.

He'd trained this old town of his pretty well—he gave them an hour or so of glum silence once a week and now they didn't pester him, asking him how he was getting along, et cetera.

Then it happened, as it always did. She came in. He could set his watch by her—five o'clock Friday night. He couldn't really say whether she came to the bar other times, because he didn't. Of course, he could change his schedule and avoid her. But no, he couldn't make himself do that.

She looked so damn beautiful. All of eighteen. How could she look so pure and innocent when he knew she'd been having sex since she was fourteen? With him!

"Hey, Lizzie," Jack called out. "Wait till you hear this! Hope's got bidders on eBay for that old church!"

"No way," she said, her smile beaming. She walked right

up to the bar and stood between Dan and Hope, elbows on the bar.

"Way," Hope said, pushing her glasses up on her nose. "I don't think I'll make a killing, but I might get it opened up again."

Rick secretly admitted he'd started sitting at the end of the bar so he wouldn't have to turn his head to look at her when she came in. Or when she left. He wanted to be absolutely sure she wasn't even glancing around, checking to see where he was, and still manage not to even see him. She wasn't. It was as if he was invisible.

"But will you get a minister to open it up?" Liz asked.

"With a little luck. But if you think about it, the most important thing is that it not look like a boarded-up old church anymore. Goddamn thing's an eyesore."

"Nice talk for the owner of a church," Jack said.

"Ach, I'm just a broker. How was your high-school graduation, Lizzie?" she asked.

"Awesome," she answered. "I wasn't exactly valedictorian or anything, but I graduated on the honor roll. A miracle." She beamed proudly.

"And you partied?" Paul asked.

"Sort of," she said with a shrug. "There was a big open house at the school. Then there were some other open houses around town—I went to a few. Some girls and I had a sleepover."

"Some *girls*?" Dan asked. "Shoot, what's happened to this world? When I graduated high school, a long time ago by the way, there was an all-night party for boys and girls. And a lot of funny business."

She giggled. "There was an all-night party, but I just passed on that. I hung out with my girlfriends."

"Congratulations," Jack said. He pulled a big envelope

out from under the till and handed it to her. "Mel and I are very proud of you."

"Oh, Jack! What's this? You shouldn't do this!"

"Lizzie, sweetheart, you showed 'em. You worked your tail off. That deserves a reward. You're…what do they say now? You're bad?"

She laughed at him. "I think that one's over. You're the bomb is still around—for people your age."

Jack just shook his head. "Hard to keep up. I bet you're glad the long haul is behind you."

"For now. I'm working full-time all summer, then I start at College of the Redwoods in September."

"Where are you working?"

"I'm checking groceries at Albertson's Sunday through Thursday—all p.m.'s of course, since I'm new. And at Connie's on Friday and Saturday."

"That's more than full-time, that's two jobs," Paul said. "When are you going to play?"

"Mornings, I guess," she said with a smile. She ripped open her card to read it to herself and when it opened, a hundred-dollar bill fell out. "Aw, Jack," she said softly. "After all you and Mel have done for me, you sure shouldn't have done this." He just shrugged and Liz put the card down, stuffed the bill in the pocket of her jeans and reached out for him, circling his neck with her arms so she could give him a kiss on the cheek. "Thank you, Jack. That's so sweet. I'll thank Mel myself later."

Rick was dying as he watched. Of course, he hadn't bothered going to her graduation, nor had he given her a card or even congratulated her. And he wanted those arms around *him,* those lips on *his* cheek. Not that he'd done one thing to deserve it.

Jack fixed up her giant Coke to go and put it on the counter. "On the house, Liz. We're all proud of you."

"Hear, hear," Paul said, lifting his beer. Hope raised her Jack Daniel's, Dan lifted his bottle of Heineken, Jack toasted with his coffee cup.

"Thanks, that means a lot," she said softly, maybe emotionally. "I'd better get over to Connie's."

"See you later, honey," Jack said.

Rick felt his eyes burn and his head start to pound as he watched her leave. His eyes dropped to her perfect butt, her long legs, that beautiful sheath of soft hair, and remembered how every inch of her felt under his hands. He could smell her, taste her. This was the love of his life, his childhood sweetheart, the girl he was going to marry, until life threw them a curve. He turned on his stool, grabbed his cane and followed her. Because he was slower getting around, she was nearly to the corner store by the time he was at the porch steps. "Hey!"

She turned toward him, frowning.

He slowly and clumsily descended the porch steps, walking toward her, his limp suddenly much more pronounced.

Dan saw Rick leave and followed, standing just outside the bar door on the porch, his arms crossed over his chest. Watching. Listening.

"You do that on purpose?" Rick yelled at Liz. "Just to punish me?"

She shook her head. "What are you talking about?"

He got a little closer. "Acting like I don't exist like that. You won't even look at me. Is that how bad I gross you out?"

"Shut up, Rick. You're acting like an ass again."

"*I'm* an ass? For asking why you won't even *look* at me?"

"I thought that's what you wanted! You want everything we were to just go away! Right?"

"It's not exactly like that," he said.

"Bullshit, it *is* like that! You said we can't even be friends! So back off—you got just what you wanted!"

Jack had heard the shouting, knew who it was and stepped out of the bar. He was about to go after Rick, shut him up before it got worse, but Dan put an arm across his chest. "Let it happen," Dan said.

"I care about Liz. If Rick's going to be a jackass, she doesn't deserve—"

"Let it happen," Dan said. "She's fighting back."

"I don't know," Jack said, shaking his head.

"It's their bone, Jack. Don't chew on it."

And Jack stayed, joined by Paul a moment later.

"You know it's not what I want! It's how it has to be!" Rick was yelling at her.

"Why? You never did say!"

"You know why—I did too say! Because you can do better, that's why!"

She laughed meanly. "Ain't that the truth! But why? Is it about the leg or the fact that you're such an asshole and you treat your best friends like crap?"

"Sorry if I'm not a happy-go-lucky idiot, Liz!" he shouted, leaning heavily on his cane. "I might have one or two things on my mind, y'know?"

"Oh, I know. You. Your mind is all filled up with yourself and how much you pity yourself. Because you're the only one ever hurting, right?"

"Look around," he yelled, and it was at that point that he saw the three men on the porch. He didn't care. "How many other one-legged dudes you see hanging out here. Huh?" He stepped closer and so did she. Even though they got closer, their voices got louder. "Maybe you could just cut me some slack, Liz."

"I've cut you plenty of slack, Rick, but I'm done. I can't do anything to please you. You want me to go away quietly, then you want me to fuss over you like you're some old friend of mine? Or maybe I'm supposed to feel sorry for you because you're a cripple! You're out of your *fucking* mind!"

"Don't say that word," he yelled at her. "Don't say words like that!"

"What? Words like *mind*? Which you're fucking *out of*? Go to hell!"

"Don't swear like that! You're not like that!"

"Guess what, asshole—I don't belong to you anymore, so you don't tell me how you'd like me to talk!"

When she turned to go, Rick grabbed her wrist and whirled her back toward him, which caused her to drop her Coke and graduation card in the street.

Again Jack stepped forward to intercede. This time it was both Dan and Paul who pulled him back. "Don't get in this, Jack," Dan said. "He has things to work out. So does she."

"He wasn't raised like that," Jack said.

"He wasn't raised to go to war and get wounded either. Let him go."

"What do you *want* from me?" Liz asked Rick, twisting her wrist out of his grasp. "Maybe you like to see me look at you all sad and hurt so you can feel like big stuff. Or maybe you were expecting me to beg. Is that what you want?"

"I want you to look at me! I want you to say hello to me! I want you to treat me like a human being!"

"Yeah? I wanted that from you, too! But you don't think anyone besides yourself deserves to be treated with kindness or respect. You have to give as good as you get, Rick, that's all there is to it."

"Sorry if I'm not unselfish enough for you, Lizzie! It gets tough, trying to figure out how to take a goddamn shower much less how to get the rest of your life back!"

"You think you're the only one who wants their life back? Maybe you think you're the only one who needs understanding, is that it? You hurting, Rick?"

"Yeah, Liz! Yeah! I'd trade anything to just be what I was before!"

"And so would I!" she screamed at him. "I'd give both my legs if you could have yours! You think I wouldn't have given my arms *and* my legs just to see you holding a *living* son in your arms? You think I wouldn't give my eyes so you wouldn't have a limp?"

"Stop it! Don't say that!"

"It's true! It's the truth! And not for me—for *you!* Hell, I don't care if you limp. I don't care if you wheel yourself around—it's not your stupid goddamn leg I care about. I prayed all the way to Germany! I told God if you were dead when I got there, I wish I could go with you! But when I got there, you weren't dead! You just told me to go away! Like I was dead. Sometimes I wish I was!"

"Shut up! Don't say that!"

"I'd give my *life* if you could be happy again! I swear to God, I'd give my—"

"Stop saying that!" he screamed, and he shoved her. She was pushed backward a few stumbling feet.

Jack took a giant step forward and Dan pivoted quickly, putting himself in front of him. "Gotta let 'em do it, Jack. It's their battle right now. We'll get a piece of it later."

"I should stop it before it gets—"

Dan looked over his shoulder in time to see Liz turn and run toward the corner store, but instead of going inside, she got in her car. She pulled away from the store and drove out of town. Dan looked back at Jack. "You. Stay put. You're way too close to this."

Dan went down the porch steps and moved toward Rick. Because he was moving kind of fast, he had a little hitch in his step. When he stood in front of Rick, he put his hands on his hips. "Did you actually *push* that female?" he asked.

"How about you mind your own business," Rick said hotly.

"That's not gonna happen, boy. Where I come from, we don't stand around and watch a man get physical with a woman and mind our own business. You looking for a fight, is that it?"

"Out of my way," Rick said, leaning on his cane and trying to get around Dan.

Dan kicked the cane, sweeping it out of Rick's hand and sailing a few feet down the street. Then he gave Rick a shove, just like he'd given Liz, and in just one second, Rick was flat on his ass.

"Hey! What the hell?"

"How about you fight with someone who isn't afraid to hit back? How about that?"

"Funny," Rick said from his place on the ground, "I think you might have a little advantage there, friend."

Dan grinned. "That right?"

Dan bent at the waist, leaned over and began unlacing his boot. He pulled it off, leaving a thick white sock. He straightened, unfastened his belt and dropped his jeans to mid-thigh and there it was, the silicon sleeve of a prosthetic limb right shy of his boxer shorts.

Dan lowered himself to the ground slowly, carefully, then pushed the pin to release the suction on the sleeve to free his stump. Since the ankle of his prosthesis didn't bend, he had to work the artificial limb up through his pants' leg and lay it on the ground. With the help of his hands, he pushed himself up on one leg, balancing with some difficulty. Once standing on one leg, he pulled his jeans up again, zipping and belting them. He pulled the empty pants' leg up and tucked the end in the front pocket of his jeans. And with all the grace of a ballet dancer, he was solid on one leg. Totally solid.

On the porch, Jack muttered, "Holy Jesus."

"I wondered about that," Paul said. "That unsteady knee of his isn't his. Well, I mean, I'm sure he owns it and all..."

Dan balanced nicely. Years of practice had left him quite proficient. "You think the playing field is level yet?" he asked Rick. "Because I can't take off the other one."

"Holy shit," Rick said, raised up on his elbows.

"Tell you what, you keep yours and we'll go a few rounds. I'm no little girl. And I'm just like you. How's that?"

"I am not fighting with you, man," Rick said.

"You ought to be ashamed, treating that girl so bad," Dan said calmly. "I don't know what's got into you. If yelling at her isn't bad enough, you put your hands on her. And not in a sweet way."

"It's not your business," Rick said, but some of the hostility was gone.

"Thought I explained about that," Dan replied. "I don't stand around and watch a man get tough with a woman and look the other way. You have to answer for it. For being one mean, weak dick. You want to answer to me or to her?"

Rick just stared up at him. "How you stay upright like that, man?"

"Practice."

"How much practice?" Rick asked. "How long have you had it?"

"Been a few years now. I got mine in Iraq, too. And I was just as screwed up as you. Time we got this all straight, boy. You've whined and whimpered about long enough now."

Rick shook his head. "You don't even wobble around."

"One of the neat little tricks I wish I'd never had to learn." Dan reached in his pants' pocket. "Do you know where to find Liz?"

Rick nodded.

Dan threw his keys at him, hit him in the chest with them. "Go find her. Beg her to forgive your sorry ass. That, or go a few rounds with me."

"Hey! I can't drive!"

"Why not? You gonna get rides the rest of your life? It's the Ford truck with the camper shell."

"It's my *right* leg!"

"Then accelerate and brake with the *left!* Jesus, have you been in a coma all this time? Aren't you even thinking about how to get on with your life?" Dan put out his hand and with the help of that and his own hand pushing himself up, Rick got off the ground. "And for God's sake, be careful. It's the only truck I have. When you find her, don't be too surprised if she breaks your other leg. If I were her, I would."

Standing, and in considerable awe of the one-legged man he faced, Rick said, "Listen, I know you mean to help, to teach me a lesson, but I'm not screwed up on purpose...."

"I know that, son. But you can get better on purpose.

You ever want to talk about it with someone who's been there, I can do that. But not right now. Right now, take care of that girl."

"What am I supposed to tell her? Because we both know I'm not good enough for her."

"Then I suggest, right after you beg her to forgive you, you thank her. Because she's just crazy enough to think you are. Now, my beer's getting warm. We about done with this circus?"

Rick tossed the keys in his hand. Then he turned and went to fetch his cane, carefully bending to get it off the ground.

Dan stood in the street until Rick had backed the truck out of its parking spot, accelerating too fast, breaking too hard, almost taking out the vehicle it was parked beside. Dan winced. It wasn't as though that old truck didn't have plenty of scrapes, but if the kid drove it right off the mountainside, he'd be real sorry he staged this whole production.

He bent to lift his prosthesis and boot. He started hopping back toward the bar. Before he got far, Jack was down in the street, draping Dan's arm across his shoulders.

"Fancy," Jack said. "You should be an acrobat. You have some serious skills."

"Half the time I am an acrobat."

"Where'd you send Rick in your truck?" Jack asked.

"I told him to go find Liz and beg her forgiveness."

"And if they just duke it out again?"

"Aw, don't worry. She can probably take him. Now, I need a bathroom or someplace private to drop my drawers and reassemble. I don't want to show Hope my shorts."

Rick had lied when he'd said he knew where to find Liz—he could think of a hundred places. One of those places was her house in Eureka. As he drove out of town, his first thought was that he wasn't ready to drive on freeways. He wasn't even ready for these country mountain roads he'd grown up on. He was going real slow, breaking cautiously around the curves. He'd almost forgotten about looking for Liz. He was busy learning to drive again.

But driving turned out to be okay. He was a little clumsy on the gas and brake for about ten minutes, so he headed for Valley High, though he knew she wouldn't be there. He just wanted to practice, to be sure he wouldn't end up in a ditch.

Twenty minutes into his driving experiment, he decided to go looking for her, and it was not because Dan told him to. The second she ran away from him, he knew. He wasn't getting out of this business the way he'd planned. He felt two choices staring him in the face. Either he had to make peace with his leg and his life or he had to go away somewhere he could be alone forever. Where no one would ever remind him of all his bad experiences, all his losses. When he thought of making things right, he felt the sting of tears in his eyes, but when he thought of being alone forever, his throat closed so tight he couldn't breathe. He had both reactions, to facing those two alternatives, within a matter of less than sixty seconds.

He drove out to a place in the woods where they used to park—no one was there. He drove through some vineyards in the valley, passed a couple of big trucks on a two-lane road, a daring move for a one-legged driver. The sun was starting to sink behind the mountains to the west; he'd have to get the truck back before long. The crazy fool, giving him a truck! Wasn't he worried that Rick would just take off and never come back?

He drove aimlessly for a while, wondering how that guy was an amputee and nobody had even known it. Or maybe some people had known, but not Rick, because he was in his own head all the time. It was the act of driving, the freedom of driving, that made him wonder about some things. Like, *had* he expected Jack to drive him everywhere for the rest of his life? One of the first things they taught him in PT was to have a bar installed in the bathroom, something to hang on to, steady himself. It was definitely time to do that now. He'd fallen twice and took a lot of baths sitting on the edge of the tub. He hated baths.

He didn't expect to find Liz. He'd go to the store later tonight or tomorrow and find her, talk to her. Or, failing that, he'd either get Jack to drive him to Eureka or borrow Jack's truck. He had no idea what he'd say, but...

But would he work? Go to school? Hunt? Fish?

She'd killed him with what she'd said. She wished she was *dead*?

He thought back, way back, to when she was lying in that bed at Doc's, writhing in pain as she tried to give birth. He'd held her small, sweating body close to his chest, promising her he'd never let her go. They knew the baby was dead, but there were times during that nightmare that he remembered thinking that if he lost her as well, his life would never mean anything again. And back then he'd still been a little confused about whether he loved her enough to make a life with her, and yet he knew losing her would kill him. It was the same right now—he'd told her they couldn't be together, but the thought of her dying ripped his heart out.

What had he done to her? And why was he kidding himself? He'd never stop loving her.

He found himself headed for the river and once there, he saw her car. He shook his head—he should've known. It was the last place they'd been together. He parked, swallowed his fear and got out. He used his cane, careful of rocks and holes, and made his way to the river's edge. She was leaning back against a big boulder, half sitting, half standing. "Liz," he said to her back.

She looked over her shoulder at him. "Go away," she said.

He walked toward her. "Liz, I'm sorry."

She looked back at the river. "Just go away. I refuse to fight with you. And I can outrun you."

He laughed softly in spite of himself. "No kidding." He went to stand in front of her. "I'm sorry, Liz. I am out of my mind."

"So I noticed," she said with a sniff. She turned away from him to swipe at her damp cheeks.

"I don't want it to be this way," he said. "Between us, I mean."

She looked back at him. "Well, Rick, I have to admit, I don't have a clue how you want it to be. You told me to go away and I tried. You made it real clear you didn't love me anymore.... All those phone calls... I thought maybe..."

He gave her a second. "You thought what, Liz?"

She looked down and took a breath. "I thought after a while you'd start to think like your old self again and you'd appreciate it—that I never gave up on you. That I loved you no matter what."

"I did, Liz. Appreciate it. I just thought you'd be wasting your life on someone like me."

She stiffened slightly. "Because of your leg? Your stupid leg?"

"It went past the leg," he said. "I thought that I brought bad luck. That a life with me would be full of bad experiences. I mean, you and me, we've had our share. You know?"

A huff of laughter escaped through her tears.

"What?" he asked.

"I thought it was me. I thought if it wasn't for me, everything in your life would be all right."

"Liz…"

"Well, didn't I get pregnant right away? I had just barely gotten my period back then. And then I let our baby die. And then because that hurt you so bad, you went to the Marines…."

"Holy Jesus," he said. He reached for her, his arms going around her waist, pulling her hard against him. "How could you think that? You didn't make any of those things happen!"

She held on to him, putting her head against his shoulder. He felt her shrug. "As much as you did."

"Holy God," he muttered, "we are so screwed up." He felt her arms tighten around him, holding him as she sobbed against his shoulder. He ran his hand down that wonderful silky hair. "Hey, hey," he said softly. And it all came back to him, how it felt when he held her, comforted her. "Come on, baby, I'm sorry. I'm so sorry," he said. In the back of his mind he wondered why he wasn't able to do this three months ago. It was so natural, so right.

"You don't know how long I've waited for you to hold me," she said.

"I've held you before. Right here, in fact," he reminded her.

She shook her head against his shoulder. "There wasn't an ounce of love in that," she said.

He pulled away from her a bit, lifting her chin with his thumb and finger. "Nothing like that's ever going to happen between us again, Liz. I promise."

"What *is* going to happen between us?" she asked softly. "Are you just trying to make me not mad at you, but then go back to that business that we can't be together anymore?"

He smiled at her and kissed her cheeks one at a time, softly, gently. "We have to be together. If we just bring each other a ton of bad luck, we'll need someone to hang on to through it."

"God," she said, laying her head against him again, crying. "I didn't want you to ever see me cry again," she sobbed. "I hate being a wimpy girl."

"You're not. I wish I was as strong as you. I don't know why I couldn't get it together. Jesus, I just couldn't get any of it, you know? You better understand something, Liz— I'm never going to be like I was. I'm never going to be that kid that just grins through every ugly thing. That part of my life got blown up."

She leaned away from him. "Really? And you think I didn't get blown up, too?" She shook her head. "Jack said, when a soldier gets wounded, everyone who loves him gets wounded."

"Jack," he said, as if he just thought of him. "Aw, Jesus, Jack."

"What, Rick?"

"Oh man. Did he ever say anything to you about me?"

"Like what?" she asked.

"Like he was counting the minutes till he could put me down like a sick dog?"

"Jack? Of course not. He's been worried, I know that…."

"If you think I treated you bad, I treated Jack worse. God, I don't know how to fix that up."

"You better fix this up first," she said with an assertiveness he was unaccustomed to in her.

"Huh? Didn't I?"

She shook her head. "I don't want to go back and forth on this, and just because you feel guilty about yelling at me doesn't mean we're okay. We have problems, you and me. Like you said, we're so screwed up. I want to get out of this mess and be as much like regular people as we can. When the baby died, the school counselor got me a therapist who helped me with that and after a while, I could talk about it without being angry, without crying. That's what I want for us, Rick. I don't want to always be scared that you're going to leave me any second."

"We'll work at that," he said. "We'll do a lot of talking. But I gotta—"

"I have the same therapist now, getting me through this thing with you. I want you to go with me."

He shrugged. What was one more counselor? "Sure, if that's what you want."

"He's nice. He's helped me so much. He's kind of goofy, but you might like him. Never mind what you think of him—just go along. The work is going to be you and me, getting on track."

"Did he tell you that? That if we got back together, we should have counseling?"

"He did," she said with a nod. "And I think he's right. No way I could have gotten through the past few months without him. If it hadn't worked for me before, I probably wouldn't insist on this, but I'm a believer now."

"Sure. Okay."

"And promise you won't make fun of him. Just put out of your mind that he's strange and listen and talk. Okay?"

"Okay," Rick agreed. "What's so strange about him?"

Rick asked, thinking about adding another weirdo into the mix. But what the hell, his weirdo had worked out.

"Well, he's funny looking. Tall and skinny with big ears and a long, hooked nose. And he thinks he was abducted by aliens."

Rick pulled back, holding Liz's upper arms. His face was frozen in shock for a moment, then a huge laugh erupted from him. "You are fucking kidding me!"

"Oh, I see how it is—you can use the F word whenever you want…"

"Jerry Powell? Liz, that's who I've been seeing!"

"Come on," she said, shaking her head.

"Yeah," he said, grinning. "That's the nutcase that got me this far. Honest to God, sometimes I hate that psycho—but I have to admit, it's helped, though I sure couldn't tell you how." He laughed again. "Yeah, I'll see Mr. Spaceman with you. Can we merge our appointments so I don't have to put up with him three or four times a week?"

"I can't believe he didn't tell me," she said, shaking her head.

"Liz, it's the rules. He doesn't talk about patients." He couldn't stop laughing and it felt both strange and familiar at the same time. He used to be a laughing fool. Lately he'd found it hard to find humor in anything. "What a kick. Come on, Liz, I gotta get the truck back."

"The truck?" she asked.

"Yeah. Guy at the bar—Dan—he loaned me his truck."

"You *drove*?"

"How did you think I got here?" he asked.

"I figured Jack was waiting on the road."

"Nah. Old Dan, he picked a fight with me. He didn't like how I was treating you and he was right. Also, he took off his leg. I had no idea he was an amputee. That showed me." He shook his head. "People have been talking to me for months, and they weren't all able-bodied like our whack job Powell or Jack—I was in group therapy with amputees who made it all look easy. But something about today changed everything. I'm going to figure out what after I try to apologize to Jack and return the truck."

But he knew what. Several factors collided. Jerry got through to him, made him see that he was unsuccessful in escaping his old life. Then Liz fought back, giving him every punch he deserved. Then Dan took off his leg and balanced perfectly on one. *Perfectly,* like he didn't even need the prosthesis. Then he held Liz the way she was meant to be held, with tenderness and love. It was all coming together. Took too damn long, but it was coming together.

Rick followed Liz back to town, gave her one more kiss and made a date to meet her on his grandma's front porch later. Then he took a deep breath and made his way into the bar. He recognized Dan's back at the bar. His leg was all put back together. Friday night, the place was pretty busy, but there was an empty stool on Dan's left.

Rick maneuvered himself onto the stool and put the keys down next to Dan's coffee cup. "Sorry. Took me a while."

Dan turned and peered at him.

"You didn't have to wait. I'd have gotten the truck back to you somehow."

"I didn't wait," Dan said. "I had dinner and I can walk home from here."

"You have this whole business down pretty good now, huh?" Rick said.

"It's like missing a couple of teeth. You learn to chew on the other side."

Rick laughed in spite of himself. "Teeth?"

"It wasn't easy," Dan said. "I took the hard way. You don't have to. Lotta help around here."

"Um, speaking of help…" Jack was on his way down the bar. "Uh-oh."

Jack grabbed a towel and a glass. Then he was in front of him, glaring down at him, wiping the spots out of the glass to keep from choking him. "Liz all right?"

"Yeah. I found her out at the river and we had a talk. Nice and calm. I told her I was sorry for that whole business. For everything."

"I ever see anything like that again, I don't know if I can keep from beating the shit outta you. I know I taught you better than that."

"I'm sorry, Jack. That was horrible and I know it."

"It was all I could do to keep from dragging you behind the shed."

A smile came to Rick's lips. Jack was in everything, meddling, and it often got him in trouble. "I'll bet," Rick said.

"I think we step up the counseling appointments. If you can't adjust, maybe you can learn restraint." He lifted a brow. "That's never been your long suit, as I recall."

"As it turns out, that's going to happen. Liz won't get back with me unless we go to the counselor together."

Dan's head swiveled sharply toward Rick. "You sure she's just eighteen?"

"She had to grow up fast," Rick said. "Jack, I know I owe you a ton of apologies. I'll walk down after breakfast tomorrow. We can talk about it. How's that?"

"You saying you turned a corner here?" Jack couldn't stop himself from asking.

"Sort of. It was kind of like a bomb went off in my head." Then he winced. "I wish I hadn't said it like that."

With the towel in one hand and the glass in the other, Jack leaned his big, meaty hands on the bar. "You telling me that this lunatic taking off his leg was all you needed?"

Again Rick laughed. "Yes and no. It was probably more about seeing how I'd treated Liz. I love that girl—but I've been treating her like crap for months. I hurt her so bad, just because I have shit to deal with. And her saying she'd give up both her legs if I could have mine? Give up her life if I lost mine? God." He shook his head. "I think I've been getting to this. That nutcase you send me to twice a week said sometimes people have to hit bottom before they start to build up their strength again. The way I treated the girl I love, after the way I was brought up, first by my gram and then by you—shit, man. We don't treat our women that way and I know it. I saw the bottom, saw what kind of man I could turn into if I don't get a handle on this. He also said I was more mad at myself than anyone else. I think I was getting close to sanity anyway. Then this crazy loon took off his leg. I've never seen anyone stay upright on one leg like that." Rick grinned and elbowed Dan. "That is truly awesome. I don't know how you did that. It's like you studied under a karate master or something. I'm *so* going to learn that. But first I'm installing a bar in the shower."

"You do that, kid," Dan said, sipping his coffee.

"Can I have a Coke, Jack?"

Jack was speechless. Stunned. "I...ah...need some glasses. 'Right back...."

Jack escaped into the kitchen. He wasn't stupid enough

to think that all Rick's adjustments had suddenly fallen into place, but in four months this was the first glimpse he'd had of his boy, the boy he loved like a son, the boy he'd gone all the way to Germany for, even though there'd been a chance he'd have to bring him home in a box.

He leaned on Preacher's worktable for a second, staring down, his breath coming hard and shallow. He felt the tears in his eyes and his heart pounded. For a while he didn't think it would ever happen. He'd been afraid Rick was going to be mean and angry for the rest of his life when there was no young man Jack had ever known who used to be more filled with light and joy. Not in all his years. Rick was the finest example of a young man Jack could name.

"Jack?" Preacher asked. Jack looked up. "Aw, did you do it again? Did you wash the bar sink with that disinfectant and then touch your eyes? Christ, you are the slowest learner I know. Come on, come on over here and we'll rinse 'em. Flush 'em out."

"They're rinsed," Jack said quietly. "It'll be fine."

"You gotta watch that, man! You're gonna go blind, for God's sake."

"I got it. I need a rack of glasses," Jack said, sniffing.

"I just put a rack out there not five minutes ago," Preacher said.

Jack ground his teeth. Inside he felt as if he'd just been born. But he said, "Gimme a rack of goddamn glasses, all right?"

"Sure," Preacher said. "If you drink a little of that disinfectant, might kill the bug up your ass."

Sixteen

By the end of June, Rick and Liz had met with Jerry "the Spaceman" Powell several times. It had been a hectic month for both of them. Rick was still going to physical therapy twice a week, but now he was driving himself. He'd found himself a Toyota truck with an extended cab that would keep him in wheels for a few years; his monthly disability check covered the payments. And Liz was working two jobs, leaving only her mornings and Friday and Saturday nights free. They didn't have a lot of time together, but the time they did have was sweet.

There was something to be said for growing up with your mate, learning from each other as experimental kids, taking that knowledge to the next level. That guy from rehab in San Diego was right—the prosthesis leaned right up against the wall while Rick and Liz made love. Tender, wonderful, sometimes a little wild, always satisfying love. The missing leg didn't seem to matter at all.

"You sure this is enough for you, Liz?" Rick asked her. "A guy with one leg?"

"Rick, we have a lot of years ahead. There are going to be times I'll come up short, I just know it. I expect you to love me the same even in those times. Is that too much to expect out of you?"

"Nah. You're more than I can deserve in a million years."

"To answer your question, I never even notice that the leg is gone. Really. The only time I notice is when you complain about the stump hurting. The truth is, I find you stronger. Braver. Smarter. I'd say I love you even more, but that's just impossible."

After Liz and Rick had their Friday-afternoon appointment with Jerry, Rick would follow her back to Virgin River. They'd go to the bar together where Liz would get her large cola to go on her way to work at her aunt's store and Rick would stay on for a while, visit with the neighbors, have dinner and meet Liz on his gram's front porch after the corner store closed.

So much had changed for both of them in just a few weeks. Rick was no longer the quiet and morose young man who kept his friends and neighbors at bay with unfriendliness. He looked forward to having that one beer a week with the guys, and even turned up at the bar more often, just to visit. And far from being embarrassed by his amputee status, he wore long shorts and laced boots, his prosthesis visible. And while his gait might be a little slow and at times unsteady, he no longer used a cane.

On just such a typical Friday afternoon, Rick and Liz walked into Jack's, holding hands. They jumped up on bar stools and met with his grin. "Hey, kids, what's up?"

"Large cola to go," Liz said.

"You got it, sweetheart. Rick?"

He laughed. "Oh, you know what I want. Cold draft, please."

"Coming up." Jack put it in front of him and asked Rick, "You starting to work out a little bit?"

Rick took a sip and draped his arm around Liz's shoulders. "Some light weights. But I've gained about ten pounds since I've been home." He gave Liz a squeeze.

"I'm going over to Connie's," she said, giving Rick a kiss on the cheek. "I'll see you later."

"Later, baby," he said.

When she was gone, Jack lifted an eyebrow. "Looks like things are going better for you and Liz these days."

"Better and better. I have some plans for the rest of the summer, starting with, I'm going to help Paul part-time. I talked it over with him—neither one of us knows how much help I'll be, but I'm sure I can stay upright and hold a paintbrush. He said he might put Dan in charge of me."

"Brady," Jack laughed, shaking his head. "Who would have guessed he'd work out?"

"I'm still trying to figure out how he got up that hill so fast back when we were looking for Paige. I didn't see him do it, but remember? Before we knew it, he was up the hill and bonked that guy on the head, knocked him cold." Rick took a drink of his beer. "He said when I get a little more confident, he'll show me some one-legged tricks." Jack laughed.

"I signed up for Redwoods—I'm going to school in the fall. I'll go with Liz."

Jack took a breath. "Kid, you don't know how good it makes me feel that you're making plans."

"I don't think I'm going to be at Redwoods long," Rick said. "I think I'm going to be forced to leave the area."

"That so?"

"Not like I won't be around," Rick said. "You're here. Gram's here. And who knows, I might be getting ahead of myself here, but I'm interested in architecture. And there's no bachelor's program around here. Humboldt U doesn't have one in that major."

"Architecture? That's the first time I've heard that," Jack said.

"Yeah, I know. Me and Liz went over to Redwoods and Humboldt U, looking through all the catalogs. I met with a counselor, talked to some people. I'm good at math and I like drawing and building. I talked to Paul a little bit. My main interests and abilities seem to lean toward architecture or engineering. I'm thinking way ahead now, but it looks like I might aim for the University of Oregon in Eugene."

Jack looked down and wiped the counter.

"You gonna get all funky about that?" Rick asked. "About me going away?"

Jack looked up. "Rick, if I can send you off to the Marines and stay standing, I guess I can handle sending you off to college. I put a little something aside for that, you know. We talked about it. I'd like to help."

"Jack, you don't have to do that…"

"It's not a lot, Rick. When I said a little something, *little* was the operative word. You'll have the GI Bill, but you also have living expenses."

"I'm sticking around through summer," Rick said. "To work, see what I can learn from Paul and Dan, to stick with Jerry the Spaceman for a while." He laughed. "That nutcase has some ideas that just fit in the slots, you know? One look at him and you'd never guess it—he's really such a dork. Toward the end of summer, before school starts, me and Liz are going to find a place of our own in Eureka. She's got a really good job at that Albertson's grocery. She thinks she can keep it while she goes to school. She might have to go to part-time if school is hard for her, but you know what?

She's finding out she's way smarter than she thought she was." He grinned proudly.

"Settling down?" Jack asked doubtfully.

"This will be it," Rick said. "We're moving ahead. We'll live together now, that's how it has to be. Living apart isn't working for us anymore. You have to give us some credit— we waited. We're not teenagers anymore."

"Well," Jack said cautiously, "she is."

Rick grinned. "She has till the end of August to change her mind."

"Ricky, buddy, did Liz talk you into this? I know she's always wanted to—"

"This was my idea, Jack. It's just better with her. But we're trying not to move too fast. First we live together and do a year of Redwoods college and next summer we get married."

"Whoa."

"We need each other, Jack. I don't think there's anyone I counted on more than I did Liz. You, maybe, but you're just not as soft and cuddly." He grinned boyishly. Then more seriously, he added, "There's no point in just finding things to keep me busy while we get older. Besides," he said, lifting his beer and taking a sip, "when you think about it, we're not all that young. Maybe in years, but not in experience. Me and Liz, we had to grow up kinda fast. And the only thing that hasn't worked against us—we never lost interest. We've always loved each other. That's been put to the test a bunch of times."

Jack was quiet for a minute. Then very solemnly he said, "There's just one thing that worries me, Rick. You two, you've gotten real good at holding each other up during the hard times. How about when there aren't any hard times?

How will you hold up then? Will you take each other for granted? Get bored?"

Rick cracked a big smile and let go a laugh. "Oh man! Please—throw me in that briar patch, huh?"

Jack turned away and pounded on the wall, bringing Preacher out of the kitchen with a pretty confused and interrupted look on his face. "What?" he scowled.

Jack was already drawing a couple of beers. "Rick's got some plans, Preach. Go ahead, Rick. Lay it on him."

Rick gave Preacher the condensed version. Unlike Jack, who was known to borrow trouble, especially where relationships were concerned, Preacher just stuck out a big hand. "Good for you, Rick. Congratulations. I think you kids are due a few good breaks." Jack handed him a beer. "Here's to you. You and Liz. I'm real happy for you."

The three of them raised their glasses in a toast.

"Thanks, guys," Rick said. "I'd never have made it through anything without you."

"We wouldn't have made it without you either, buddy," Jack said. "I'm real happy for you. And I'm real damn proud of you, son."

Dan Brady had been meeting Cheryl in the park in Old Town Eureka every Sunday for a couple of months and looked forward to every one. Those afternoons became one of the highlights of his week. He took great pride in filling her in on all the Virgin River happenings, and while their lunch together had covered an hour in the early weeks, by the end of June it had stretched to almost three.

They had covered pasts that were difficult to overcome, for both of them. Some of that had to be talked about and put away if they were going to accept each other as friends.

But once that was dispensed with, their picnics became an easy three hours, filled with storytelling and laughter and ending with an affectionate peck on the cheek. The kind casual friends gave each other. When he told her about the day he dropped his pants and took off his prosthetic limb to make a point for Rick, left hopping one-legged in the street, she laughed so hard she had tears running down her cheeks, and people in the park were staring.

Dan was no longer unsure of how he felt about her. Cheryl was no longer suspicious of Dan's motives.

He draped an arm along the back of the park bench while he talked to her. "So, Rick started working for Paul Haggerty, and Haggerty told me to keep him with me, to train him, keep an eye on him, make sure he didn't take on too much. Boy, if Rick knew Paul was looking out for him that way, it might piss him off. He's a lot better, but he's still got that edge of pride, you know?"

"How's he doing on the job?" Cheryl asked.

"It's only been a few days and he's holding up pretty good. If he didn't have a new prosthesis, I'd have him hauling trash. But I'm teaching him drywall and texturing. I figure anyone can paint."

"Anyone but me," she laughed. "There must be a trick to it. I tried to paint my bedroom where I'm staying. It looks like I went after the walls with a scouring pad and dirty white paint."

"Really? How'd you like me to fix that up for you?" he asked.

"No, thanks. But I wouldn't mind if you told me the secret."

"No secret, kiddo. Good brushes, good paint on a clean wall and a primer if the wall isn't going to hold the paint— like if you stripped off wallpaper and there was some backing left. People run into trouble when they buy the cheap stuff or don't prime a wall that needs it. I can show you how to use masking tape and caulk to make a straight line." He ran a knuckle along her cheek. "Why don't we fix it up together. I'll give you some tips so you never need me for painting again."

"You're trying to tempt me into letting you get closer into my life," she said with a laugh. "Tempting me with paint."

He grinned at her. "No. I'm looking for an invitation to your bedroom."

"There are five women living in that house. If you're ever in that bedroom, it'll be for painting."

"Would you be embarrassed?" he asked her, lifting his eyebrows.

"You might be attacked. Only one of the five has had a man in her life in the last millennium. And it wasn't me."

"Cheryl, I don't want to scare you, but I think maybe you have a man in your life now. You just haven't had sex. That I know of," he added with a shrug.

She laughed at him. "What have I done, getting mixed up with you?"

"Come on, it's been nice. Admit it," he said, leaning toward her and brushing his lips against hers. "Nice. Come on."

"Nice," she said. "But you know I don't want to get into anything complicated."

"Oh, Jesus, Cheryl, I'm sorry—I didn't mean to mislead you. I didn't have anything complicated in mind…". Then he smiled.

"You've used that line on me before." She put a hand against his cheek, then she grew briefly serious. "We're pretty screwed-up people, you and me. We have some heavy past issues. What if we get together, then go back to being those screwed-up miserable people and take each other down into the hole?"

He thought about this for a moment, looking deeply into her eyes. "Honey, I've been there, down in that hole. I'm not going back that way. You can't make me. And I, for God's sake, have no interest in ruining you. How about that?"

"What are you looking for?" she asked him.

"Today? I'm thinking a real kiss, arms around each other, pressed close, wet and sloppy and longer than half a second. And then, I think I'll call you Wednesday night after work, just to see how your day was."

"I have an AA meeting Wednesday night...."

"You could tell me what time is good to call. I'm very flexible."

"And then?"

"One of these days I'd like to take you out to a nice dinner. Nothing scary or fancy, just nice. Quiet, good food, a place to talk while we eat where there's no risk of bird shit. I don't expect you to miss a meeting, I could pick you up afterward. Get you home early enough to get some rest before the early shift at the diner."

"I have a couple of days off a week," she said. "I could hit an early meeting and we could actually have dinner at dinnertime." Then she smiled.

"You're not fighting me on the idea," he observed.

"So far you haven't suggested anything that I ought to beware of."

"Honey, I have no interest in scaring you." He rubbed that knuckle along the smooth skin of her jaw. "You're pretty and smart and being with you is good. If it's good for you, too, we'll keep going. The second it stops being what you want, all you have to do is say so."

She shook her head and smiled. "If I'd run into someone like you years ago— Aw, forget it, that had nothing to do with it."

"What?" he asked.

"It's just this trap alcoholics sometimes get tempted by. Like if my life had been better, I wouldn't have been a drunk. The truth is, my life wasn't better because I'm an alcoholic. It had to do with addiction, not luck or intelligence or the right man."

He grinned at her. "I sensed a suggestion that you might almost think I'm the right man."

She patted his cheek. "You seem to be working out so far."

"I'm going to put in appliances in a couple of weeks. That old place of yours is starting to shape up nice. Any interest in seeing it?"

She looked down. "I'm sorry, Dan. I know you've worked hard and spent good money. I don't mean to downplay that. It's just that house, you know? I hate who I was when I was there. Just stepping in the door, even when it's all fixed up, takes me back. I hate it. I don't care if I ever see it again. And I'm so sorry because that must hurt your feelings."

"Nah," he said, pressing her hand against his cheek again. "Not a problem. In fact, why don't I just finish the job fast as it can get done and you can put it up for sale, get it out of your life. I'll tell you what—I'll snap a few pictures for you. That way you can get an idea what I've done and not have to walk through the door."

"But if I sell it, where will you live?"

He shrugged. "I'll find something." Then he smiled. "Maybe something a little closer to you, if you don't think that's too pushy."

She shook her head. "I don't know why you're doing this…"

"Aw, honey, you're one of the most special women I've known. I'm real sorry you lived so many years without knowing that, but if that's what it took to get you to this place in your life, good for you. I'm proud of you. Plus, I'm just plain attracted to you. Sorry, it's the God's truth, but don't get worried. I can deal with the fact that you turn me on." He grinned. Then he became serious. "Cheryl, you're sweet. Good to the bone, kind-hearted, strong, beautiful, so easy to talk to…" Tears started to run down her cheeks. "Baby, don't do that," he said, wiping away a tear with his thumb. "I'm sorry, I'm pushing on you—I didn't mean to."

She shook her head and sniffed. "No one's ever talked to me like that before. No one's ever said those things about me before." She sniffed again. "I think that's the nicest thing anyone's ever said to me." Then she got a scowl on her tear-stained face. "Dan Brady, if you're playing me to get in my pants, I'm going to shoot you dead."

He burst into laughter and pulled her against him. "Okay, Cheryl. If it turns out I'm one of those no-account losers just looking to get laid, you go ahead and kill me. But if you're smart, you'll wait till I get that god-awful bathroom remodeled. Jesus, that's going to be a nightmare."

She snuggled in his embrace. "Don't make me shoot you dead," she whispered.

"Okay, darlin'," he whispered. "How about a phone call on Wednesday night and you see if you can wrangle a night for dinner. That work for you?"

"Hmm. That's gonna work."

"Come a little closer. Press up against me here, right on this bench. Kiss me like a girlfriend, I want to see if

I should go to the trouble of calling Wednesday night." She scooted closer. He threaded his fingers into her soft hair, cradling the back of her head in his palm. He pulled her mouth against his and let his eyes lower as he moved over her mouth slowly, deliberately, deliciously. Their heads tilted for a better fit; their lips parted and they both moaned softly. They didn't hurry. When the kiss broke, he smiled very sweetly. "Might not call Wednesday," he said. "Might have to call Tuesday. And Thursday. Unless I'm crazy, you're ready for that."

"That's about all I'm ready for...."

"Good," he said with a grin. "I like the job of talking you into things."

"Just out of curiosity, do you make love with the fake leg?"

"No, baby," he said. "I make love with lips, fingers, words and essential body parts. It's been a really long time, but I think once I get in the stream of things, I'll remember how it's done." He gave her forehead a kiss. "You worried about it?"

She shook her head. "You're going to give me plenty of time, right?"

He smiled and brushed her hair over her ear. "I'm going to give you anything you need."

Walt Booth leaned against his truck in the small parking lot at the Garberville airport, the runway on the other side of a fence. Muriel had called him from the jet shortly after takeoff to tell him when she'd arrive. The studio Lear was dropping her in northern California and then proceeding to L.A. with the director and another actor. It wasn't long before the aircraft was in sight. He watched a perfect landing, then the Lear taxied to the boarding area. Airstairs popped out and Muriel was the only one to deplane.

She returned as she had left, wearing jeans, boots, a light suede jacket even though it was almost July, and the cowboy hat. She was followed down the stairs by the uniformed cabin steward who handed her a small carry-on bag. But unlike at her departure, she now had more luggage and a very large suitcase had to be retrieved from the baggage compartment. She shook the steward's hand and pulled her bag behind her on its own wheels.

Walt had told her exactly where he'd be waiting. He pushed his hat back on his head, crossed one long leg over another, his thumbs hooked into the front pockets of his jeans, and waited for her to come through the small building that served as passenger check-in, dispatch, offices. He enjoyed the sight as she walked toward him, admiring her long, slim legs. She stopped a few feet away from him and smiled. "How are you?" he asked.

"Just about done," she said, smiling.

"Just about?"

"I'll have to travel some when it's out, do some promo. And there will be events—Cannes, the Oscars, Golden Globes, that sort of thing." She grinned. "I'll have to get manicures and pedicures and special gowns. And you'll have to let me dress you up for that stuff."

"Aw, I don't know…"

"You really wouldn't argue about this, would you? I want you with me for things like that. I want you right beside me, and we're leaving the pitchfork at home."

"That would be kind of coming out to the world, wouldn't it?"

"It would," she affirmed.

"Spoil your chances of getting it on with your personal trainer, you know."

"My personal trainer is named Helga, and most of the time I hate her!" He laughed at her, tilting his head back. "At least you don't have to fly to Montana every couple of weeks. You should be thankful."

"I might miss Montana," he said. "Good things happened with us in Montana. Full weekends of good things."

It was her turn to laugh. "I can make sure you don't miss Montana too much."

He grew serious. "I'm so damn glad you're back. I can see you every day."

She stepped toward him, leaving her suitcase behind. She put her hands on his shoulders and he put his on her waist.

"I need to fatten you up a little," he teased. "You've lost weight."

"Weight I could stand to lose, too. Just being with you seems to plump me up."

"Are you worn out, honey?" he asked.

"I'm tired," she admitted. "I'm so looking forward to lying in your arms tonight for a good long sleep. Do we have obligations?"

He shook his head. "I told Vanni you were coming home this afternoon and that I would be indisposed for at least twenty-four hours. We'll catch up with all of them on the weekend."

He pulled her closer and swept the hat off her head, pressing his lips to her forehead. Just as he did that, there was a *click-whir click-whir click*. They both turned their heads toward the sound, startled. "Are you kidding me?" he said.

"Jesus, that makes no sense," she said, spying a photographer with a powerful camera sneaking up on them from behind a parked car. "Me? Why would anyone want a shot of me?"

"Maybe it's who you're spending time with that's the news," Walt said with a shrug. He pulled her closer against him. "Let's make sure there isn't any doubt about that." And he swept over her mouth with powerful intentions and, just as he had secretly hoped, the clicking went on and on and on. When he let the kiss run its course, he pulled back just a little and laughed. "That ought to do it."

"That was very unlike you," she said. "You don't normally like that sort of thing."

"Muriel, honey, I'm dead in love with you and it suits me just fine for the whole world to know it."

She lifted an eyebrow. "So, you'll let me dress you up for the production events?"

"I might."

"I'm dead in love with you, too, darling. And so damn glad to be home. Where I hope to stay for a good long time. And, you're going to wear whatever I say."

"I will," he said. "It's my aim to make you happy."

She patted his cheek and smiled. "We're going to do just fine, you and I. Let's get out of here and be alone a while. I need some peace and quiet."

"In Virgin River?" he said with a hearty laugh. "Girl, this little town can fill up with more drama than your movie set."

* * * * *